# MARCH TO NICAEA

# BOOKS BY TOM VETTER

## Historical Fiction:
*The Siege Master Series: The Recollections of Lord Godric MacEuan on the First Crusade:*

*CALL TO CRUSADE*—Volume One
*THE SIEGE MASTER'S SONG*—Volume Two
*MARCH TO NICAEA*—Volume Three
*BONE-CRUSHER: A Godric MacEuan Novella*

## Undersea Adventure Memoir-Anthology:
[Writing as LCDR Tom Vetter, USN (Ret.)]

*30,000 LEAGUES UNDERSEA: True Tales of a Submariner and Deep Submergence Pilot*

## Travel Adventure Memoirs:
*Travels With Gabriela: A Lover's Tribute*

*GUIDO'S BUS OF DEATH and Other Misadventures*
*HELLO AGAIN, EUROPE! [...Now, Where Can I Pee?]*

## Flash Fiction Anthologies:
*BE CAREFUL WHAT YOU WISH FOR*

Find them on Amazon, B&N, Apple, Google, Hoopla, CreateSpace, Lulu and at **www.tomvetterbooks.com**.

# MARCH TO NICAEA

## The Recollections of Lord Godric MacEuan on the First Crusade: Volume Three

✠ ✠ ✠

# Tom Vetter

*An Imprint of*
**Tom Vetter Books, LLC**
*Publishers*
*www.tomvetterbooks.com*
**Dumfries, VA**

First Edition

Book design by Thomas Vetter
Copyediting by The Book Scrubber

ISBN-10: 1941160263.
ISBN-13: 978-1-941160-26-8.

"Verbera mos persevero insquequo spiriti amplio"
[The beatings will continue until morale improves]
— The Vetter Family Motto

# Dedication

To Nick, Nate, Gabe, John Matthew, and Harrison:
Don't tell Mom:
When I have a trebuchet, you will be its crew.

# TABLE OF CONTENTS

# TABLE OF ILLUSTRATIONS

✠✠✠

A treasure I discovered between the writing and the publishing of this novel was the availability in the public domain of the many wonderful engravings by Gustave Doré and others. I couldn't afford to commission the original works, if that were possible, but I am proud to give them new life as illustrations here. I hope you enjoy them as much as I do. Credits for each can be found at the back of the book.

✠✠✠

"Deus lo vult! God wills it!" Pope Urban calls for the First Crusade.

# PREFACE: THE MANUSCRIPT

✠✠✠

Forty years ago, working a summer job to pay for college, I was paid to clear junk from the house of a professor of medieval history, a deceased bachelor who left all to his school. The contents of the house had already been auctioned and the executor wanted the place cleaned for sale. In a dark corner of the attic, I found an overlooked trunk filled with his old papers. The executor told me to trash it, but when I asked for it to haul my stuff to and from college, she demanded ten bucks. I stuffed the receipt in my pocket and the trunk in my old station wagon.

The weekend I finished that job, I dragged out the trunk and went through the contents. Under heavily edited drafts of papers on the First Crusade, I found a manuscript on old parchment, the text in Latin written by a shaky hand. This was the work of someone else, drafted long ago. And thanks to an executor's greed, I owned it.

I could not understand much of it then, except to discern that it was a memoir of some kind, written by one Godric MacEuan, Baron of Cenachedne, wherever that was. I had no time to go through it, so I put it in the trunk and packed books and clothes on top. It stayed in the trunk, and after college it went into the cellar, still in that trunk.

Only recently, after my folks passed away and I was clearing out their house, did I come across it again. Now the trunk was a box of nostalgia with a mystery at the bottom. I thought it might be

1

interesting to learn what Godric had been so determined to tell.

It took me two years. Thanks to Latin translation software, I could glean the gist of his narration, and then wrestle out the nuances. In the end, I was able to relate Godric's memoir in colloquial English. This book, and its successors, is the result.

It is a remarkable tale. In summary, it is this: Godric MacEuan was a master of siege warfare, who built the nuclear weapons of his age and used them during the First Crusade to recover Holy Jerusalem.

In Volume One, **Call To Crusade**, Godric told us of his privileged childhood in the court of King Malcolm III, his enslavement, freedom re-won, barony, squiredom with Count Robert of Flanders, pilgrimage to Jerusalem, battles for and favors won in service to the Byzantine Emperor. We also learned of his return to Scotland, his knighting, and his defeat of the evil MacanFhirMhóir.

In Volume Two, **The Siege Master's Song** Godric writes of his service as sheriff-at-large to King Malcolm; of the conflict between King Malcolm III of Scotland and King William Rufus of England; of the tragedies that resulted; of the sieges he undertook at Loch Goyll, Alnwick, Argences, Le Houlme, and Bamburgh; and finally of his call to join the First Crusade.

In this volume Godric continues to relate his adventures: The start of the First Crusade, the long march across Europe, the Crusaders' conflicts with Byzantine Emperor Alexios I, the siege of Nicaea, the battles outside its gates, and its conquest at last. Subsequent volumes will continue his story, describing the tribulations to gain Antioch, and finally, the great siege to recover Jerusalem.

Godric MacEuan was a remarkable man. This is his story.

✠✠✠

For the Defense of Christ and Christendom.

# ONE

✠✠✠

Father Time has overtaken me, and I cannot outrun him any longer. As things are, I can barely stay out of his grasp. Soon he will reach a bit farther, or I will stumble, and he will have me in his icy grip. So I must relate this tale now, for I have little more time to set it down.

I am Godric MacEuan of Jerusalem. I am called so, not because I was born or lived there, but because I journeyed there, twice now. My first journey was on pilgrimage, as squire to Baron Jean de Bethencourt, a brave knight among many in the retinue of Count Robert I of Flanders, Peer of France and a true knight in all ways. In peace came we to the "City of Peace," for *Jerusalem* means this; and Count Robert's company departed the same way. Sir Jean and I left somewhat earlier, on lathered horses at midnight, with arrows in hot pursuit.

A decade later, I returned to Jerusalem in a large army, leading my own retinue amid the army of Count Robert's son, Robert II. This time I came to reclaim that city for Our Lord by force of arms. In that I succeeded. I did not do it alone, but I swear it could not have been done without me. And for doing so I earned the name Godric Hierosolimitanus — "Godric of Jerusalem."

But I must tell this tale in a proper way and that must await its time.

Through the years, I have been a page, a squire, a knight, a baron and sheriff-at-large of Alba with authority throughout that realm. I have also been a slave and a blacksmith — events I have related.

But most often have I been a siege master, a man who engineers the downfall of great fortresses and conquers them. By the time the Great Commission to Recover Holy Jerusalem from the Islamites began, I had already defeated castles at Dunnottar, Loch Goyll, Alnwick, Argences and Le Houlme, escaped a siege at Edinburgh, and forced the capitulation of Bamburgh.

But mighty as these were among the strongholds of Europe, they were nothing compared to what yet lay ahead: Great fortress-cities built of stone, ringed with ditches, high walls, numerous towers, and triple gates. they were impervious to all we had — except the siege engines I built.

So my greatest challenges still lay ahead in this, my tale, and greatly did they test us. But our war cry was "Deus lo vult!" — "God wills it!" And for Him and with Him, we fought until we prevailed at last.

✠✠✠

One day in the Spring of 1096, when I was buried in parchment, trying to deal with the clerical side of preparing for war, a slender young lad of about fifteen came, another of many such, to entreat me to take him along on pilgrimage. Frankly, I was disinclined, for he looked pale and weak, as if he had grown up in a monastery's scriptorium, locked away from both sunlight and hard work. But he seemed familiar, with an appeal I could not identify. So I questioned him — hard, but not harshly — about what he could do that would make him of value. "From where do you come, lad, and what are you called?"

"Sire, I am Ed...Edward," he stuttered in a high-to-low voice not yet fully descended with manhood. "I am the natural son of a priest from Durham. He sent me into a monastery in my youth, where I was educated. But I do not wish to take vows, and I want to see the Holy City, so I fled to Dunfermline where they could not retake me. There I heard of your enterprise, and walked all night to ask if I might join."

Thus, part of my instinct was proved right. Edward could indeed read and write — in Anglo-Saxon, Norman French, Latin, and Greek. He could read and quote Scripture and knew much history. He could do sums and keep books. He could make lists, read invoices, and write receipts.

My steward, Derrick, was already burdened — as always — with the affairs of the manor and the barony, and he would remain behind to attend to these. I had no other cleric or clerk to do this work and hated doing it myself, yet would greatly need such skills throughout this endeavor.

Edward said, "Lord Godric, I know of your greatness, and I want ever so much to be part of your retinue. I have no means, but in return for my expenses I will work at whatever you set me in order to go with you." He looked at the mess of parchment around me and said, "If you need a clerk, sire, I would be proud to be of service." He clamped his mouth into a determined line, but his eyes still held a plea I could not ignore.

So I said, "I will need to think about taking you, Edward, but a man needs to eat, so go find Derrick the Steward and get a good meal." Then I picked up the scads of parchment before me, waved them in frustration, and said, "If you truly want to go, come back and help me with all these damned lists. Prove yourself useful and I will consider taking you with me as clerk."

In less than a quarter-hour, he was back at my elbow, discreetly burping mutton and barley stew. By the end of the day, he had all my correspondence in hand, and after that, I never even considered leaving him behind.

At my direction, Derrick furnished Edward with new clothes and other necessities from our stores, for he came with nothing but tunic, breeks, and worn-out shoes. After that, he was always to be found close by my elbow, clutching parchment, ink, and quills. I became so used to barking, "Edward, make a note of that" that I am afraid I came to think him part of the camp furniture. Like my shadow and footprints, he was not an actual part of me, but he followed wherever I went just as they did, and I confess I gave him just as much thought.

✠✠✠

As thousands of knights did elsewhere all over Europe, I let it be spread widely that I would answer the call of Holy Father Pope Urban II, and lead a contingent of volunteers to rescue the Christian East and retake Jerusalem from the Islamite Army of Satan for Our Savior. I would take with me no one who did not wish to go, for I had made this journey once already, and knew we had a difficult and dangerous quest ahead of us, one from which many would never return. There was nothing to gain by taking with me anyone unwilling to go.

To his credit, Sir Cedric was more than willing to go, even keen on the whole endeavor, which was well for the both of us, as I would greatly need his help. I soon heard as well from Sir Hamish and Sir Cormac: both wished to go. Hamish was hale and more than welcome, but I had misgivings about Cormac, for he was nearly fifty, and I felt sure the undertaking would kill him. I urged him to become a coregent in support of Lady Aleine instead and live among his friends in my manor, where he would better serve God by caring for our people. He protested much, but knew the truth when he saw it, and acquiesced before long. Carrick told me he was privately relieved. "All those years in hard saddles has given old Cormac much trouble in his nether regions," he said knowingly. I was not sure what he meant, and hoped I would never find out.

Soon I began to hear from other nobles and knights in Scotland, and commoners came as well. I was certain we would need to lay siege to the mighty fortress cities I had surveyed for Count Robert's father during the pilgrimage, so I accepted those craftsmen with strong skills in shaping wood and iron, and underwrote their expenses. We would require great siege engines to conquer, and I needed their skills to help me build them.

I bought tools to work wood and shape iron, and bellows to take along. My own machines were too cumbersome to take all that long way, but timber we could gather there, and iron and charcoal we could buy. Good tools we needed to bring. I also bought sinew and rope in great amounts, for these powered the engines of war, and kegs of good Danish tar — once I used it to burn down Andrew's castle; now I would use it to burn infidel castles.

I put my smiths to work making spikes, ratchets, pins, and the great iron brackets and fittings like those on the great siege machines I had measured and sketched in Constantinople. We packed sets of them in sturdy wooden chests — one chest for one machine. Once there we would cut and shape timber and use these fittings to assemble siege engines on the spot as needed.

Now all the time spent with Vegetius's *De Re Militari*, all the effort scouting eastern fortresses, places with timber, forage and water, and all the data on siege machines I had put in my codex would now be put to good use. I vowed to be ready.

✠✠✠

Some history is needed here for a wider perspective on the grand venture I was about to undertake. First, this fight against Islamic invasion was not new; indeed, it had been going on in many lands for five hundred years. At the decree of their prophet, Islamic invaders had spread their religion at the point of the sword, trying to put the whole world under the rule of the "Faithful," men who demanded that all worship their god Allah, obey their declarations about his will, and submit to their rule. The only alternatives they offered were continual extortion, slavery, or death.

As Emperor Alexios himself had told me, Islamites had seized the Christian lands that had stretched across all of northern Africa; indeed, all the land south of the Middle Sea. They had taken all the lands around Jerusalem and north of it, practically to the gates of Constantinople itself. They had seized Sicily and the islands in the Middle Sea, conquered almost all of Spain and invaded Italy. They had raided deep into France[1], reaching the city of Tours until Charles Martel finally stopped them and drove them back out of France.

All inhabitants in the lands they conquered were forcibly converted or forced to pay regular tribute just to live a half-life of subjugation. And all who resisted those two choices were enslaved or murdered.

What was new was that *finally*, after five hundred years of relentless onslaught, all Christendom was actually uniting, fighting back with a counter-offensive aimed at the heart of the invasion, the very city all Christians cherished most. The spiritual head of the Roman

---

[1] Yes, I know. All of these nations are modern constructs that did not exist at the time of the First Crusade. I use them here, rather than the plethora of little kingdoms and feudal states that did exist then, to help readers comprehend the extent of Islamic conquest at the start of the First Crusade.

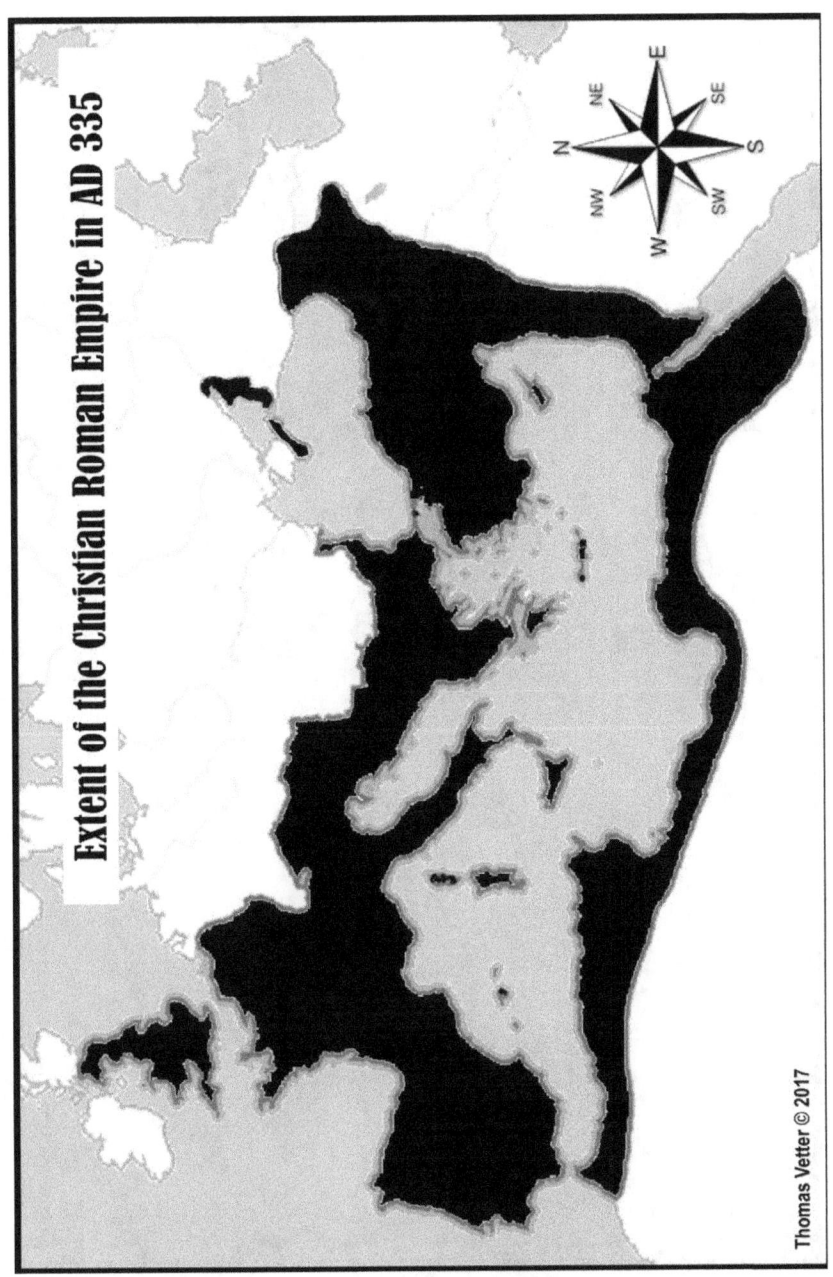

Extent of the Christian Roman Empire in AD 335.

Remains of the Byzantine Roman Empire in AD 1096.

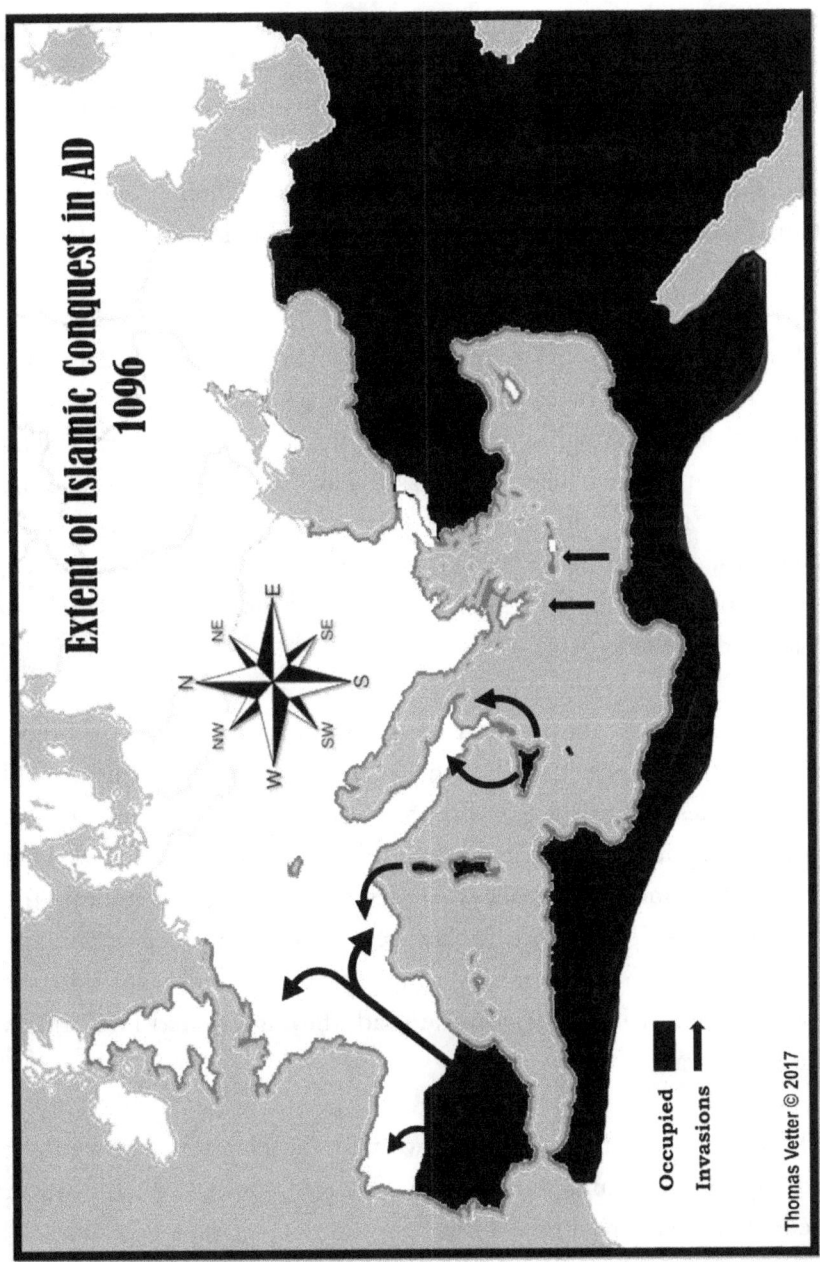

**Extent of Islamic Conquest in AD 1096.**

Christian Church and Christ's successor on Earth, Pope Urban II, had cried, "Enough, no more!" He called upon the second sons of nobles and knights, the landless ones, to wage war upon brother Christians no more. Instead, he urged they to rise up, put their faith and skill with arms to holy use, end this unrelenting assault upon Christ's faithful, and save both Christians and Christendom itself by pushing faithless Moors and Islamic wolves out of Christian lands.

This time Urban's call to crusade was widely heard and quickly accepted.[2] Throughout Western Europe in the first half of 1096 AD, nobles and knights began raising money and followers willing to make an "armed pilgrimage," as it was then called, to rescue the Eastern Empire and free the City of God from the unholy Islamites. In Flanders, Normandy, France, Provence, Toulouse, Lotharingia, Swabia, and elsewhere, men — and women as well — made a decision to go.

Knights, squires and men-at-arms, priests and monks, grooms, blacksmiths, wagoners, all made preparations. The wealthy sold land, castles, crops, and goods to raise money for arms, armor, horses, wagons, foodstuffs and supplies. The poor gathered what they could and sometimes fled debt and servitude, joining the retinue of a knight or lord for the benefit of his protection and any plunder he might share. Many simply picked up and went on their own, banding with others on the road, they aggregated into armies along the way.

The Holy Father forbade taking women and children, but some of both disregarded him, and women willing to cook, wash, and warm beds found ways to go.

---

[2] In 1074, after the Byzantines were defeated by the Seljuq Turks at Manzikert, Pope Urban's predecessor, Pope Gregory VII, had issued a call for *milites Christi* (soldiers of Christ") to march to Byzantium's defense. Unlike Urban's, Gregory's call went unheard or ignored.

**The War Cry of the Crusaders.**

All of these common folk had ample reason to want to leave. Aside from the enormous spiritual benefit of remission of all sins and an immediate entry into Heaven should Death find them along the way, they had much to flee and little to fear. Drought, plague, famine, and poisoning by blighted grain had afflicted them at home for decades; an adventure like this seemed better than continued hardship. Life on Crusade seemed only marginally harder than life as it was, and the promised rewards were infinitely better.

The end of the millennium was at hand. In that very year — 1095 — there were signs and portents in the skies: a lunar eclipse, a meteor shower, aurorae, and a comet. Great things, foretold by God, were happening.

It had been a thousand years since the Savior came, and the very skies showed us great signs that He was about to return as He had promised. When He did, He would establish His Kingdom in that very city we would liberate from the spawn of Hell that infested it. And when He did, they would be there to greet Him. They would live with Him forever and hunger, thirst, weep, and die no more.

✠✠✠

In Cenachedne, a number of knights and squires came to find me, and lads hoping to become squires as well. I made it clear to each to disregard all they had heard about becoming rich or gaining lands of their own in foreign places — it would not likely happen. I had been there and had already seen what they hoped to see. What they would certainly see was desolation, hunger, thirst, great struggle, suffering, pain, disease, and death—lots of death, too much death. It was likely that they, too, would find death, far more likely than anything else.

Some turned away at that, dismayed and discouraged; just as well, for they lacked the fortitude and resolve to do what would be needed. In so doing they saved their lives and reputations, if not their souls.

Those that persisted in their desire to go were of two kinds: first were the dreamers, who did not heed my warnings, preferring their own illusions to my truth. They would soon learn by experience how right I was, and most would fall away when they did. Often the wisdom would come too late to save them from their folly.

And then there were those who, well warned, still wanted the journey, the struggle, and the battle. They would be my true companions, the real "Soldiers of Christ." Too many of them would die, but it would be for the right reasons: for their faith and for each other.

I insisted that all these volunteers equip and arm themselves to the best degree that they could. I told them of Turks and Pechenegs and what their arrows would do. There was no point going into battle if the first arrow they met struck them down. Any who thought their protection good enough was given the opportunity to reconsider after I had it hung, uninhabited, on an archery target, and then shot it with a Pecheneg arrow from my Pecheneg bow. If it stood up, they could wear it and go. Soon I had a pile of discarded gambesons, and Carrick's shear found constant use as I set my craftsmen to work, mounting iron plates into each of these to armor it.

I required each knight to bring a warhorse and a travel horse for himself and his squire, four packhorses for the two of them, and two horses for each retainer he brought, one to ride, and one for baggage and sustenance. We would not walk to war, though many others did and sometimes we would be forced to. To cover seven leagues every day, as we had during the pilgrimage of 1085-88, we would need the strength and endurance of horses. And once battle was joined, we needed horses to replace those killed.

I did not know how long this armed pilgrimage would take, but I knew how long the peaceful version had: three years. I added another year and told each knight he had to raise the monies to sustain himself and his entire retinue for four years. If he did, he could go with me; if not, then I would not take them, for they would starve in a distant land when their means ran out. That thinned my potential ranks quite a bit, but those who came with me fared much better in the actual event.

✠✠✠

Having no arrangements or dispositions to make, many thousands of common folk gathered quickly and were keen to be away. On 12 April 1096, an enormous group of many thousands left Cologne under the command — if it could be called that — of a knight named Walter Sans-Avoir; that is, Walter "the Penniless." Eight days later, many more thousand — some say 40,000 — started out from Amiens, led by a priest named Peter the Hermit.

Other groups left from the Germanic lands. From Saxony came a band led by a priest named Folkmar. Gottschalk the monk headed another from the Rhineland and Lorraine. These worthies decided Pope Urban's call included cleansing the Christian world of all the supposed enemies of Christ, and although most bishops and priests decried it, they set about purging the cities through which they passed of Jews. After all, Jews had wealth for the taking, and who deserved it more than "the poor soldiers of Christ," as they styled themselves?

The first instance came in late April 1096, when a large band came to the town of Speyer, which had a sizeable Jewish population. They seized all the Jews they could catch and massacred them. The Jews who could escaped to the king's palace and to the cathedral, where both king and the bishop protected them, and sent their soldiers to hunt down and execute the perpetrators.

**The People's Crusade in Hungary.**

A month later, there was a similar occurrence in Cologne; locals there planning to join the great commission slaughtered the Jewish residents here and spread their wealth among themselves.

Had I been sheriff there, I would have herded those "poor soldiers" into a church, wedged shut the doors, and burned it to the ground.

✠✠✠

As I learned later, Count Robert did in Flanders much as I did in Scotland. He let it be widely proclaimed in Flanders and its surrounds that he would join the "armed pilgrimage" and lead a contingent of proper knights and men-at-arms to Jerusalem. As part of his preparations, he named his beloved wife Clementia his regent in Flanders during his absence. Knights flocked to his banner, for he was known to be a great warrior deeply devoted to God and unquestionably blessed with courage and wisdom of counsel, despite his youth.

In the next six months, he drew together a force of about eight hundred knights and three thousand men-at-arms; hundreds of servants, craftsmen, and priests to support the army; and pilgrims seeking the protection of a formidable force as they traveled through now-dangerous lands.

That spring of 1096, Baron Sir Jean de Bethencourt was also making his preparations in Hainaut. His beloved Isabeau needed to remain behind in Hainaut, for they now had a small army of young children that she was rearing — the time she been prisoner in a Turkish harem had a positive aspect, it seemed — and his barony would need a regent to govern in his absence.

✠✠✠

By the time we departed for Flanders, I commanded a squadron of twenty knights, an equal number of mounted men-at-arms — mostly their squires— and one hundred-twenty footsoldiers. These last were the servants and craftsmen, whom we dressed, armed, and trained to fight as soldiers when there was need. The craftsmen were in my pay and equipped by me, for their special skills would be crucial to our success.

To train and lead them I named Sir Hamish second in command, for I trusted no one more. Father Thomas used to say, "Satan soon finds employ for idle men" and we needed no such trouble. So Hamish and I devised a plan of exercise and training that kept all those fighting men busy most of the day and too tired for mischief by night. Many of the older knights had not been so engaged since their days as squires, and there was grumbling about its necessity, not to mention an endless complaint of pains, sprains, and bruises.

But they only complained among themselves after I gave them this answer: "Christ suffered much more for you. If you find this too hard to endure, go home, for what lies ahead is far worse. His victory does not need your help." Some resented the implication or the reminder, but I did not care. In the event, few left and all who remained trained harder afterward.

As for tactics, I knew what we could expect of the Turks. Sir Jean and I had learned and practiced tactics that would counter and defeat what the Turks would throw at us. I taught Hamish and Cedric, and they taught the others, Hamish the knights, and Cedric the squires. My reputation for having already fought and defeated both Turk and Pecheneg provided enough reason to pay heed. And it even helped some of them to live to see Jerusalem.

There were a number of personal preparations I needed to make before we departed. I named Aleine regent, knowing that Sir Cormac and her father Carrick would support her with aid, advice, and backing for her decisions.

Then there was my warhorse. CiùinLùth was still strong and handsome, but the horse was a decade older than he had been during my first pilgrimage. I was about to ride two thousand leagues and fight God knew how many battles. CiùinLùth had already done that once and that was enough. I felt that, like Cormac, he ought to spend his last years in peace at Cenachedne instead. So I bought a splendid black destrier of about six years as my new warhorse, and named him LaochDubh, meaning *black warrior*. And CiùinLùth? He continued his favorite career, siring great colts and fillies from the dams of southeastern Alba.

My squire, Colin MacDuib was a cheerful, strapping lad from Saint Andrews in Fife who had previously served King Malcolm and Queen Margaret as page, and had been sent to me as a squire by Earl Causantín of Fife, no less. He had come in the summer of the previous year, and was shaping up well — not that I told him that, of course. Again, I wanted no man who did not come voluntarily, and my high regard for Colin demanded I give him the same choice. So I summoned him and laid the decision to stay or go at his feet.

"Colin! What am I to do with you? Shall you stay or shall you go? I give you the option to return to the Earl with my favorable report of your progress and conduct, and a good chance to earn in safety your knighthood with another lord here. And out of regard for you, I advise you to do that."

The young dolt just grinned at me, awaiting what was coming.

I scowled. "Or, if you are a daring young fool, you can remain my squire, join the great commission to recover Jerusalem with me, and probably die a horrible death in a distant land, as I expect to do. I give you this, the one chance, to stay or go as you choose."

"I've been packed for weeks, sire." was all he said. And with that, it was settled.

✠✠✠

But the most important preparation of all was the time I spent with

Aleine. Once I decided to go, the decision seemed to give me a new sense of purpose in life. As my preparations proceeded, some of the old me returned, and with it a deepened bond with Aleine. But I also felt conflict and guilt in preparing to leave her again. My duties of the past seven years enforcing the law for the king had kept me coming and going. But this was different. I was not leaving for a week or a month, I would be gone three years or more; and there was a good chance I might not return.

So I made a concerted effort to spend time with Aleine, for this was what she longed for and enjoyed most. She too knew there was always the possibility that I might not return, or that she might not be here when I did. We did not speak of it, but we began again to cherish the time we had with each other and I to dread our parting.

✠✠✠

As the time for my departure grew close, Aleine and I spent more and more time together, and clung to each other more closely at night. And in the afterglow of lovemaking one morn we cuddled, and she asked me again why I thought I must go.

"*Why* must it be you, Godric? Are there not enough knights elsewhere to do this? You have been gone so much in the past few years, and I miss you so when you are away. Why must you go?"

Why must I go? It was a fair question, and I gave her the best answer I could.

"My love," I said, "The Holy Father has called upon Christendom's men-at-arms to rescue the Christians in the Holy Land, and save Alexio's empire from the unholy Islamites. For five hundred years, nothing has stopped them. Every year they take more and more. If we do not stop them there, drive them back, they will come here too. Wherever they go, they bring murder, rape, torture, coercion, oppression, slavery and death. No Christians are safe anywhere. And the Christians they conquer are better off dead.

"I have been among them, and I have seen what they do. Jean and I saved Lady Isabeau from them. I would not have you, nor any good woman, subjected to such cruelty. I am a knight and a sheriff, a defender of justice and law. In good conscience, I cannot remain here and let others do what I am sworn to do.

"And though I have had my fill of blood and death, I feel guilt for all the innocent people I failed to save from evil men I had to kill to stop them from murdering yet others. All these haunt my dreams. But the Islamites are far crueler, more rapacious and remorseless, so they must be stopped also. The Holy Father promises salvation and reparation from sin by saving God's people. Should I not do so?

"And there is this: I have seen the fortresses our knights will face, and know they are beyond anything Christian knights have ever seen. I have learned how to attack them, and I have built siege machines that might --- I say, *might* --- be able to take them. But I fear I may be the only man in all Christendom who can. I don't say this to boast, but because it is true. I have knowledge, insights, skills and experience few men have. And I fear that if I do *not* go, they may fail to win Jerusalem. So I believe God drives me to do this. Unless I go, His will may not be achieved.

"Some say the world will end with this century; and that a few years hence, Our Lord will return to Jerusalem to judge all men and reign forever. But His city is held by men unworthy of Him, unbelievers who commit unspeakable sins on behalf of a false god they claim is He. Should I not go to recover His city and His throne? Should I not welcome His reign, help Him displace all the miserable pretend king like Rufus and Donalbane? And when He does rule again, should I not offer myself to any service He might assign me?"

She was silent for a time, but hugged me the tighter. Then she said, "I cannot say I want you to go. But yes, I think you must." Tears filled her eyes, and then she buried her face against my chest. All I could do then was hold her as she quietly wept, and feel dismay and self-loathing for making her do it.

A bit later, she wiped her tears, sniffed deeply, and said, "Go then, if you must. But I want something from you, a gift in parting. Fill me with your babies. For it may be all I have of you. And if God must take you from me yet again to serve His purposes, mayhap He will give me a bit of you to cherish in your children, until we are reunited — and together always, to part no more."

How could I refuse her that? I could not. So I did just as she asked.

✠✠✠

**The Departure.**

# TWO

✠✠✠

In early summer of 1096 — the end of June, I think it was — we were at last ready. I bid farewell to Aleine, Carrick, Alice, and Cormac, and led my retinue to Levan to board a small squadron of ships—we needed several just to transport all our horses. The voyage to Calais was for once uneventful, with good weather and favorable winds speeding our way. Again ashore at Calais, we reassembled and rode beneath a large banner depicting Christ's cross, so that those we met would know that despite our arms, we were peaceful, enroute to join Pope Urban's great armed pilgrimage.

In mid-July, we reached Tournai, where Anselm's letter had said Count Robert II would gather his retinue. On pastureland on the outskirts of the city, we found other lords and their retinues encamped. While Hamish and I organized our encampment on well-drained land near them, I sent Sir Cedric, who volunteered to serve as my aide, to find Count Robert. He returned in a short time and we rode together to Count Robert's headquarters tents amidst his growing army.

"Godric!" cried Robert, with a huge smile, and clasped my hand in a hard grip. "How good to see you again! It has been too long." And indeed it had. When we had last seen each other a decade before, I was a new squire, he newly knighted and just named Regent of Flanders as his father prepared to lead our pilgrimage to Jerusalem.

"Thank you, sire. It is wonderful to see you again as well. I am most impressed with the army you raise here."

"Yes, it grows daily, thanks to men like you. You will find many of your old friends here in our midst. Father Anselm! Look who has come! This is your doing, I believe, the fruits of your eloquent pen."

Anselm was indeed there, hale and ebullient despite ten more years. He would truly be an asset in many ways. We hugged, as old friends do.

"Father, you have much to answer for," I began, "My millers have learned to use your al-ambik, and produce some astonishing drink."

"We must share recipes, Lord Godric. God knows we will need as many as we can find to cope with the drought we face." Anselm had made the pilgrimage I had, and knew as I did the horrid dearth of drink in a land filled with teetotal heathens. "Do you remember these two miscreant scamps? Now they are knights and aides to the Count — God help us! Nicolas! Theodoric!"

Grinning, the two appeared to clasp hands and pound shoulders. Nicolas and Theodoric were the very same pair of Greek lads who accompanied Sir Jean and me as our squires from Constantinople on our return to Flanders. They had completed their squiredom the previous summer, and now served the count as knights and aides.

Also in the count's retinue I found Sir Lethold de Tournai and his brother, Sir Engilbert de Tournai. Lethold had been a squire with me during that pilgrimage, and had helped Jean and me free a nun — now Jean's wife, Lady Isabeau — who had been held captive in Governor Artuq's harem, creating a diversion that allowed us to escape the city. Now he, too, was a knight, keen to free Jerusalem from Artuq's grip.

And then powerful arms grabbed me from behind.

"Ahh! My-jumped up squire has joined us! I hoped you would turn up!" With that, my assailant spun me around and wrapped me in a fierce bear-hug. Baron Jean de Bethencourt, the knight I served as a squire throughout that pilgrimage, and my brother in more than one desperate fight, was apparently glad to see me. Jean had brought his own entourage of knights, men-at-arms, and servants.

I was glad to see him, too. Indeed, he was a big reason I was here.

I grinned. "Anselm said you couldn't possibly manage without me. What was I to do? Isabeau would never forgive me if I let you blunder off to Jerusalem and get yourself killed. I'm just here to ride along and watch your back."

"I hope you brought your toys with you! Those palisaded campgrounds you took in Normandy are nothing compared to what we face in Anatolia. Nicaea? Antioch? Jerusalem? Do you remember? Solid stone bitches, every one of them!"

"I remember," I said, digging out my codex. "Anselm wrote all down for me back then, and I've been studying it again of late. And this time I have a true nutcracker, one like nothing you have ever seen."

✠✠✠

At thirty-one years old — just five years older than me — Count Robert was young compared to many of the other leaders of this pilgrimage we later met — the so-called princes who led what has since been called the First Crusade: Robert's cousin, Count Stephen of Blois, was twenty years his senior; and his first cousin, Duke Robert of Normandy, ten. Raymond de Saint-Gilles, the Count of

Toulouse, was twenty-four yours older; Duke Bohemond, seven years. Only Tancred, Bohemond's nephew, was younger than Robert at twenty. Yet Robert's wisdom more than made up for his relative youth, and his counsel often held sway when his intemperate elders bickered with each other.

**Count Robert II of Flanders, a prince of the First Crusade.**

The count chose to do what his father had done by inviting each of the barons in his entourage into his military council. This assembly enabled us to coordinate our plans, duties, and movements. More importantly, it created a unity of common purpose that grew from each baron's sense of ownership in the great commission upon which we all had voluntarily embarked.

From my earlier pilgrimage, I knew how important this was, for although each lord commanded his knights and followers, we needed a military council to govern the whole army, with one true leader to inspire and guide the council. And Count Robert was that very man.

Soon after my arrival, the count invited Baron Jean and I to dine with him. Robert and Jean had been squires together and were well-acquainted, as anecdotes they recounted of the mischief they got up to did attest.

Both had heard brief accounts, rumors really, of my destruction of MacanFhirMhóir's castle and OdinsØye's great stone tower, and they were eager to hear in detail how I had accomplished it. As it was most germane to what we would face soon enough, I recounted those events, then told them of my tree-bucket[3], *Bone-Crusher,* and my preparations to build us similar machines to use against the fortress cities we would encounter in the Holy Land.

And it was soon clear that the count knew of our work as scouts for his father, Robert the Frisian, during the pilgrimage of 1086-1088, for he asked us to perform that role and lead the scouts for his army. Once again he loaned us the services of Father Anselm in a reprise of his earlier role. Given the knowledge we had collectively gathered and amassed in the little codex I still carried, it seemed fitting enough that we should now use it for this holy commission. I

---

[3] As explained in **Bone-Crusher**, Godric wanted to call his first trebuchet a *'helepolis,'* as the Byzantines did their *'capital'* (most powerful) siege engines. But his father-in-law Carrick couldn't pronounce that, calling it by its main components: a big throwing arm (tree) and a counterweight (bucket). Godric bridled, but eventually acquiesced to call it a "'tree-bucket'," forerunner to its English name "'trebucket'," which the French later mangled into *'trebuchet'*. ☺

hoped it would still be accurate and of value a decade later.

✠✠✠

By day, the training grounds set up beside the growing encampment rang with the clashing of blunted training swords on blades, shields, and mail as knights and squires practiced. Horses were exercised and mock charges thundered through the day on pastureland along the river. Sergeants drilled groups of servants armed with spear and shield into footsoldiers. Those with skills using bow or crossbow practiced at archery butts set up at the base of a hill that stopped all the overshot arrows. On the generally downwind side of the great encampment, bladesmiths, armorers, and farriers worked at forges and fires. Sudden wind shifts occasionally added their smoke to that of the cookfires, the vile clouds blanketing the camp, leaving all of us coughing and choking for breath.

A market fair quickly sprang up alongside camp, as tradesmen and merchants flooded in from Tournai and the surrounding towns, setting up booths and selling everything from arrows to sacred relics, ale to mail. Foodstuffs of all kinds were offered, and business was brisk. Taverns set up in tents offered ale and other diversions, and despite the earnest efforts of our chaplains and constables, business in those was brisk, too. Fortunately, these activities were generally peaceful, after stern notice went out that all freeborn miscreants would be driven from camp, and masters fined for the transgressions of their servants.

By night, the entire encampment was lit by the glow of fires as men clustered to eat, drink, and recline in usually cordial camaraderie. Every knight there was present through personal choice and at personal expense, and certainly every squire and servant had been given opportunity to remain at home. Doubtless later many would regret they had not done so; but as yet, no one had a good reason or enough tribulation to wish it.

✠✠✠

We remained encamped there a full month, training and preparing for the long march ahead. The Holy Father, Pope Urban, had set the 15th of August as the designated date of departure of the holy 'armed pilgrimage' for recapture of Jerusalem and the Holy Land. Retinues of various counts and barons from Flanders, Normandy, Hainaut, and France were still coming in to join us. The pope had forbidden taking women and children with us, and, with one notable exception of which I will relate in due course, we did not.

But other parties had already departed earlier on — unsanctioned pilgrimages of common folk, with women and children among them, in defiance of the Holy Father's decree. And they set out without making any of the preparations we made for sustenance and self-defense. Later, we learned that all of these contingents either caused trouble or soon found it along the routes they took, and none lasted long in Turkic lands, much less reached Jerusalem. But a large number of women and children — survivors from those rash and ill-prepared bands — joined our ranks along the way, and well before we reached Jerusalem. Our rescue of helpless refugees from these groups is the reason why you now hear of women and children in the army of Christ. We did not bring them with us, but in good conscience we also could not leave them behind.

✠✠✠

But sleep was hard to come by. Since the trial by combat of Arkil Morel months earlier, I was again haunted at night by troubled dreams, in which I relived painful events of the past dozen years again and again. Some nights, Andrew and OdinsØye stood on my arms, pinning me helpless, as Morel stood over me with his sword poised high, and Rolf struggled with Aleine to cut her open and steal her child. Other nights I was tied to an archery target as laughing Pechenegs or Turks took turns shooting me full of arrows. On yet other nights, with my arrow still through his head, King Solomon set fire to my manor as a choir of all the good folk trapped inside sadly sang, like monks:

> *Why did you leave us . . . for far-off Jerusalem?*
> *Why did you go . . . and leave us to die?*
> *Why did you travel . . . to far-off Jerusalem?*
> *If you had not gone . . . we'd still be alive.*

I began to dread lying down to sleep altogether.

It was as if part of me could not—would not—forgive or forget acts my mind told me I had. I am afraid it was my conscience.

In many ways I felt grief for the fact that I could not keep death away from the people I loved. Had I hanged Andrew myself, my people would yet live. Had I slain OdinsØye after I fought Bjorn, three houses of religious folk would not have been massacred and robbed. Had I been there to defend my king and stop the murders of Malcolm and Edward, Margaret would not have died of shock.

But despite my best efforts, many I loved had been crushed by tragedy or death, and I could not help but feel responsible—that it was either my doing, or my failure to do, that had brought about all those tragic outcomes.

It was my conscience that haunted me, I knew, for bringing cruel death to some and failing to save others from it. I began to dread sleep, and worked all the harder so that when I did, I was weary enough that I slept without dreaming at all. Far too often, I awoke soaked in sweat, the only way to escape the terror of my dreams. I sat up then or paced about, sometimes all night. Drink helped bring me dreamless sleep, but it left me moody and truculent by day, so that all avoided me rather than risk my wrath.

Something had to change or guilt-fueled rage would consume me.

✠✠✠

In the middle of August 1096 we set out south, our assembled force now called variously the "Army of Flanders" and "Count Robert's Army." By means of couriers, Count Robert had arranged to meet his cousins, Duke Robert of Normandy and Count Stephen of Blois, at specified locations along the route south. We departed in time to join them at Vézelay on the route south in mid-September. Then, joined into one larger force, we intended to march through Lucca and obtain the blessings of Pope Urban as we embarked on this sacred campaign.

Just before we marched, Count Robert gathered all of us in a nearby hollow where a platform had been erected. With the nobles and knights in close, the squires and men encircling them, the count addressed his army in this way:

"Noble knights and men of Christendom: we have banded together by common accord to serve a great commission, one to which we were each called by His Holiness, Pope Urban, one which serves the will of God Himself. On the morrow, we march. We begin a great quest, a holy quest, to wrest Jerusalem, the Chosen City of God, from the clutches of unbelievers and infidels. We do this to deliver it direct into the hands of our Savior, Jesus Christ, so that with his triumphant return to earth He may dwell with us to rule as King of Kings forever.

**The Soldiers of Christ make the Vow of the Cross.**

"Nothing must stop us. No one will stop us. We march in hope of eternal salvation and the absolution of our sins as proof of God's favor on our penitence. No penance can be more worthy, no sacrifice more worthwhile than the dedication of our lives and fortunes to achieve this triumph for our Savior. All here are sinners, but our commitment to this cause will prove to God and Man our repentance from sin and our love of God in Christ.

"Brothers in arms, I salute you now for your commitment to this endeavor. And I call each man here to confess his sins, make his vow and receive his pilgrim's cross . . ." As he said this, an aide raised a banner of white emblazoned with a plain cross of scarlet. " . . . Let each man sew it on his garb, each knight and man-at-arms paint it on his shield. Yesterday we were individuals. Today we serve just one cause and we bear only this standard.

"Today we are soldiers of Christ! After today, our only battle cry is: *Deus lo vult* — God wills it!"

As this, every man there echoed that cry, and seven thousand men shouted with one voice, "*Deus lo vult!*" over and over.

Then the several scores of chaplains and priests who had joined our ranks to minister to our spiritual needs spread out through the vast throng, taking confessions, granting absolution, obtaining vows, and then giving each man a strip of scarlet cloth from which to fashion his cross. Many among us wept openly, first with shame for their sins, then with gratitude from the grace of absolution, and finally of sheer joy to be part of this blessed undertaking. I confess myself to have been one of them

✠✠✠

The year 1096 was a bountiful one everywhere, which helped us enormously. Our departure was timed to ensure we could find fresh provisions and fodder for our animals as we marched, for we had no way to preserve and haul all the foodstuffs we would need to sustain us. Treasure and monies we could and did haul in great quantities, but food we had to buy or forage for along the way, and water we obtained from rivers, streams, and lakes. Our livestock alone easily drank entire wells dry.

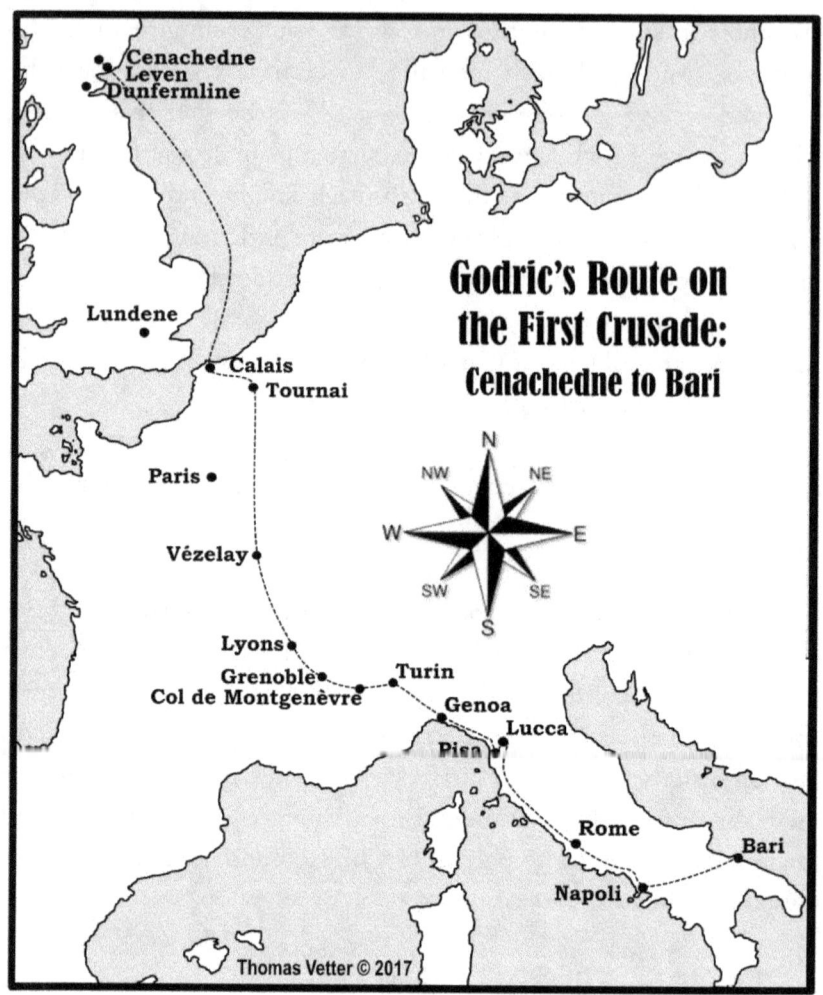

**Godric's route on the First Crusade: Cenachedne to Bari.**

Like the pilgrimage of 1086-1088, we marched south, but we did not follow the same route. I say *marched* because although the nobles, knights, squires, and mounted men-at-arms rode, we did so amid a considerable number of wagons and carts loaded with tents, armor, weapons, camp furniture, provisions, and chests of monies pulled by draft animals, and of course a vast force of footsoldiers, craftsmen, and servants. Strings of mounts, together with herds of cattle and flocks of sheep, were driven along the route with us, these latter gradually becoming food. And so we moved at speed of animals and wagons, not at the speed of horsemen, about five leagues daily.

In the van rode our scouts and envoys, who marked the route for the main body and negotiated our passage with landowners, magistrates, and merchants. After all, these were Christian lands and we could not merely pillage our way through them. Instead, we requested and paid for the use of pasturelands for encampment and grazing as we passed. Given our holy commission, most of the time the fee was forgiven or purely nominal, a landowner's gift to God's soldiers on their way to serve the Lord.

Our immediate destination was the city of Vézelay, a hill town and the site of a Benedictine abbey famously housing the bones of Saint Mary Magdalene. It was here on the first of September we were to meet the other armed contingents led by Count Robert's cousins. Duke Robert's army was coming from Normandy to the northwest, while Count Stephen brought his from Blois to the west. Our journey there was the longest at fifty leagues, but we arrived a few days early to find Count Stephen in waiting, encamped in fields along the river east of the abbey on its hilltop. We camped there as well.

And then we waited.

A week passed before Duke Robert's army arrived. Always and famously short of money thanks to his over-fondness of drink, gaming and wenches, the duke was said to often have to stay in bed because he was so poor — or spendthrift — that he had no clothes. From personal acquaintance I knew it had happened, but also that it was more gossip than truth.

**Duke Robert of Normandy, a prince of the First Crusade.**

In the event, he had been delayed while trying to secure sufficient funds for his campaign. Finally, he had mortgaged his dukedom to his brother, King William Rufus of England, in return for 10,000 marks of gold,[4] but the money had been slow to arrive and he wasn't about to march without it.

Whatever his love of vice and lack of wealth said about him, Duke Robert had another reputation, one of great courage and tactical genius on a battlefield. From my time serving him in Normandy, I found it to be accurate. And I was most glad of it, for what I knew we faced in the Holy Land would demand al of his skill and still greatly test his martial reputation.

---

[4] All true!

✠✠✠

I went to visit with Father Anselm, and within the sanctuary of confession, told him of my dreams and the night terrors I felt, and confessed that I believed it due to all the deaths I had caused or inflicted. Anselm listened silently, and when I ran out of words, he said this:

"My son, it is true you feel guilt, and right that you do, for to you, God's commandments are clear, especially the fifth: Thou shall not kill. But you are not right in your understanding. You killed men — Máel Snechtai, Morel, Solomon, the Turks, and the Pechenegs in battle, where you fought in defense of yourself and others. Given your vocation as a knight — aye, that is a vocation, no less than mine as priest — there was no sin in that, for it was not murder you did, but battle to defend the lives of others, or to enforce the laws of the king.

"You slew MacanFhirMhóir and OdinsØye because naught else would keep them from hurting others. They earned violent death by inflicting it on innocents. You were but the tool that brought it.

"As for the innocents who died before you were able to prevent it or despite your best efforts — your manor-folk, the monks and nuns slain by OdinsØye, your mother, king, queen and prince — you should not take guilt from their deaths. That was God's will, however cruel it seems. He wanted them with Him. You could not and should not have prevented it. Their suffering was part of the mystery of their redemption and they have found true happiness now in His presence.

"So I will do this: I will give you an absolution you do not require, and a remedy you do. And in God's good time, He will heal your heart and your mind. Until then, put all your heart and energy into doing God's will with this pilgrimage. And wait on Him to heal you."

Then he said the words of absolution, gave me a flagon of his best *spirit*, and bade me to visit whenever I had need of him. I left him with new hope and a lighter heart.

Afterward, the dreams were less grim. Unfortunately, the dreams did continue.

✠✠✠

The Crusaders march through Rome.

# THREE

✠✠✠

The three armies now combined — Normandy, Flanders, and Blois — had swelled our number to something like three thousand knights and twenty-four thousand soldiers and camp followers. Moving so great a force demanded we march in smaller bodies, so we continued our march in our original contingents, but coordinated our movements by mounted couriers.

From Vézelay we marched south for Lyons, and reached it in mid-September. From there our route took us south and then east as we made our way into the Alpine mountains, passing as we did from the kingdom of Burgundy into Lombardy. Through Grenoble we marched, and then over the mountain pass called, in Latin, *In Alpes Cottia*,[5] used by Roman armies even long before the Savior's birth a thousand years ago, according to Anselm.

On this journey, my duties of command were demanding, and I could not as often ride in the van as I wished. Overseeing the scouts and evaluating their reports was only part of my duty. We barons supervised the setup and takedown of our camps, dealt with the lords and landowners along the route, and ensured the good care of the livestock — our most critical asset. We also maintained good order along the road, dealt with transgressors, and kept close watch on the baggage train and its guard, for our wagons carried vast fortunes in monies, armor, weapons, and provisions — a most

---

[5] Today named the *Col de Montgenèvre*.

tempting target for sneak thieves and robber barons. The count could not be everywhere, after all, and we were his deputies.

**The First Crusade on the march.**

In turn, Cedric became my proxy with the scouts. He needed the opportunity to learn the art of scouting as I had, and riding with the scouts was hard work, but fun. I could hardly deny him that.

When I could, I rode with the count or Baron Jean, and the time in the saddle together gave us the opportunity to catch up on the events in each other's lives during the years we had been apart. I much preferred hearing of their lives, but did, when pressed, recount the highlights of my years as sheriff-at-large, and my vengeance for the deaths of Malcolm, Edward, and Margaret upon de Mowbray and Morel.

"And what of King Rufus?" Jean asked. "Surely he was author of all."

I scowled. "How do you punish a king? You cannot. But you can take vengeance, and I have vowed to do so someday. His time will come, and he will suffer for it, God willing — by my hand or another's. But first I must help win final victory for the King of kings."

"Amen!" said the count.

✠✠✠

A curious incident occurred one day in Lombardy as I was riding between van and baggage train. I was alone and riding slowly for once, for the road was clogged with bands of men, animals and wagons going the other way.

But the road was momentarily empty when an arrow shot from the underbrush ten yards off to my right and struck me — hard — beside the right breast. I reacted as ever I do in battle — instantly and without conscious thought, as long training had instilled — by drawing my Damascene sword, wheeling LaochDubh, and spurring him hard. Indeed, the horse screamed with outrage as the spurs raked his loins. Then he shot like a bolt along the path of that arrow.

In an instant, we burst through the screen brush. Before I could prevent it, LaochDubh ran down the archer even as the man struggled to nock another arrow in time.

The man screamed as he went down, the cry cut short as we passed over him. Quick as I could, I reined hard and wheeled back to confront him, but there was no further need. My attacker lay without moving, and it was clear never would he again.

I swore as I dismounted and went to the body. In running over the archer, LaochDubh had stepped squarely on him twice — two hoofprints of soft earth marked the spots — and a half-ton of horse had crushed both breath and life from his chest.

I swore again bitterly, then. Not for my assailant — no, I felt no pity for him. But I had hoped to hear from his lips why his arrow was still lodged in my side, and who had given him a reason to put it there. Now there was no way to learn it on this side of eternity. The only clue as to who he was or where from was a distinctive color and pattern to his aketon, which I took a piece from and kept.

The attack was unprovoked, in a place I had no enemies I knew of. Was it an attack to commit robbery? I had no great sum on me, though once dead and stripped, my armor, horse, and weapons alone would have bought him a large farm or a small manor. It seemed strange, but I had no other logical explanation for it then.

And the arrow? As I disentangled it from surcoat and mail, I realized it should have killed me, for although I wore chainmail of the best quality — and as both a warrior and blacksmith I knew there was no better — its bodkin point had punched right through. Only Martun's Damascene iron plates, sewn into my jack[6] beneath the mail, had stopped it, flattening the point with the force of impact.

As it was, I had a bruise the size of an apple where it struck. And ever after, that spot has been tender to the touch, paining again when pressure was applied to it, as if a new reminder from God of both my mortality and His grace.

✠✠✠

We passed through the city of Turin in the first week of October,

---

[6] A jack of plates is a padded vest of layered leather or canvas and wool felt, with iron plates sewn between the layers, creating a medieval version of ballistic vest.

and by the third week, reached the Middle Sea at Genoa to follow the coast road south. As we approached the city of Pisa, we turned inland a dozen miles to reach the town of Lucca where dwelt his Holiness, Pope Urban II (for anti-pope Clement III, the hand-picked prelate puppet of Germanic Emperor Henry IV, then occupied Rome). Here we encamped and waited to allow all three of our contingents to arrive and form the entire army. This took more than a week.

Then with great ceremony, our envoys and a guard of honor escorted Pope Urban into our midst.

"Brave knights and men of Christendom! We are most gratified that you have heeded our Call, and have come, united as one body, to serve Our Lord and save His people from the hordes of Darkness. Kneel now that I may absolve and bless you in your Holy Mission."

Then to our great joy he blessed all of us, and called upon God Almighty to preserve us, grant us victory over all our foes, and take directly into Heaven all who fell from every cause on our campaign.

The blessing had a profound effect upon every man, thrilling us all to the core, and inspiring us to risk all, for Christ's Vicar on Earth had given us God's assurance that He would make saints of us all.

At once, *"DEUS LO VULT!"* erupted from every throat, many thousands of them, repeated over and over, until it resounded from the very mountainsides as unseen angels around us took up our cry.

The following day we resumed our march, traveling once again southeast along the coast. It was not nearly as cold for the month here as it was at home, but it was certainly not summer here either.

✠✠✠

In mid-November, we reached Rome. We kept the bulk of the army encamped outside the city, but I accompanied a delegation of nobles inside, to the great church of Saint Peter — built more than seven centuries earlier by Emperor Constantine, said our ever-informed Father Anselm — to leave gifts of thanksgiving to God upon its great altar.

And it was in that great church that the ardent supporters of Wibert, that false pope who called himself Clement III, came forth with naked swords and stole all the gifts we had just laid upon the altar. From the rafters inside, and the rooftop outside, they threw stones down at us as we lay prostrate before the altar in prayer. We might have fought them, but to do so in that church was a great sacrilege and gained us nothing, for our attackers had damned themselves already. So instead we withdrew to resume our march.

✠✠✠

From Rome we continued southeast to a point just north of the city called Napoli, where we turned to the east. Skirting to the north of the great smoking mountain they call Vesuvius — the very chimney of Hell, said Anselm — we marched across the duchy of Apulia for the seaport of Bari. Apulia was then ruled by the Norman descendants of Robert Guiscard, the present duke being Guiscard's son, Duke Mark of Taranto, known more commonly by his father's nickname for him, "Bohemond" ("The Huge One").

It was on the 1st of December that we reached Bari. There we learned that Duke Bohemond and his nephew, Tancred, were also raising armies for the march on Jerusalem. The news was welcome, for it meant that we might expect to have two or three times our number of fighting men when we departed Constantinople.

In Bari, we also learned that Count Hugh of Vermandois, brother of King Philip of France, had passed through Bari with his contingent of armed pilgrims just a month or so earlier, the first group to do so. But many among them had promptly been lost at sea when a storm sank some of their ships near the destination port of Dyrrachium.[7]

The news of that disaster caused consternation in our combined military council, for it split opinions about how to proceed. Here is how I recall it:

Count Stephen was much alarmed. "This proves the winter weather is already upon us, and with it comes increased risk of storms and shipwrecks. If we attempt to cross now, we risk drowning our forces en-masse, long before ever we reach the Holy Land."

Count Robert said, "While I agree that there is that chance, at any time of the year the weather is both good and bad. We know not which we will have — today, tomorrow, or on any given day. Only God knows what weather He will send us."

Duke Robert was dispassionate, after crossing the English Channel many times and at all times of the year. But he was in many ways entangled with Stephen, who was not phlegmatic at all.

Stephen refused to budge. "I will not cross! I will wait for spring."

So Duke Robert said, "If Stephen will not cross, perhaps we should all delay until the weather improves with spring."

Robert turned to Jean and me. "My lords, you made this journey before. What do you think?"

---

[7] Now the city of Durres, Albania.

I said, "Sire, this sets back our entire timetable. We need to leave Constantinople before the hot weather makes crossing Anatolia unbearable with the summer heat and drought. We will kill far more among us that way than we might drown."

And Jean added, "Delaying the winter only squanders the substance and funds of the least among us. Who will reimburse their loss?"

Stephen said, "God will, from the wealth of the cities we take next summer. We should camp nearby in Calabria and wait for spring!"

Count Robert frowned. "We are the Army of God! Surely He will hear our prayers and grant us good weather whenever we cross!"

"He didn't do that for Hugh!" cried Stephen.

The disagreement grew hot and at times came close to blows, for some thought their courage or commitment demeaned, while others felt equally ridiculed as impetuous fools. And in the end, we could only separate along the two lines of the argument and agree to meet again in Constantinople.

And so it was that those with Count Robert embarked immediately to cross to Dyrrachium, while the retinues of Count Stephen and Duke Robert marched to off Calabria and wintered there. And in the event, we did not see them again until May of 1097 when they finally again rejoined us outside Nicaea, even as we lay siege to that city.

✠✠✠

**The Crusaders cross the Adriatic from Bari to Dyrrachium.**

The lure of gold is powerful, and despite the winter season, an army of men with gold seeking crossing drew vessels to Bari from all along the coast, each master eager to fill his hold with men, horses, and cargo in return for as much gold as he could get. And it was just as well, for we collectively needed many such ships to carry our army across. Each leader in Count Robert's army needed to arrange for his contingent. I judged I needed three large ships to transport mine.

I was no mariner, but I knew iron and wood, and I knew men. I had myself rowed out to each of several of the sturdiest. After touring each ship with the master and judging for myself the strength of joints and the soundness of planks, I negotiated our fees of passage. In consequence, I might have paid more than I needed to, but the safety of my men mattered above all, and my gold would do no good at the bottom of the sea.

The fifty-league voyage took a day and a night. As it happened, the weather held, and we all crossed safely. Having made several sea voyages, I knew what to expect, and did not suffer the landsman's malady, but Colin, Edward, and many others were pale and wan from vomiting by the time we disembarked. Once ashore, I bought casks of good small beer from the locals in Dyrrachium and had the sufferers well dosed with it. With its nourishment, all recovered quickly enough.

It took more than a week for all of us to cross, as the ships shuttled east one day and west the next, ferrying men and horses from one coast to the next. In the meanwhile, we encamped a league east of the castle that protected the harbor and city of Dyrrachium on the plains beside a small lake. With each day, ships brought across more of Robert's army, and our numbers grew on this shore even as they dwindled back at Bari. Finally, with God's blessings, we were all reassembled, having lost no one to the hazards of the sea. And with Father Anselm officiating, we celebrated Mass in thanksgiving.

✠✠✠

As we awaited the arrival of all our army, there arrived a party of envoys from Basileus[8] Alexios, accompanied by an armed escort. Count Robert summoned his military council and, since Jean and I were known to have experience with the Byzantines, called upon us to translate and advise him as needed. The envoys were clearly cold and wary. After all, the two armies they had already met — Hugh's and Bohemond's — had been more like invaders than allies.

---

[8] Basileus is the Greek title for the emperor of the Eastern Roman/Byzantine Empire.

To our surprise, the commander of the escort was one of the Oikeioi knights Jean and I had trained nearly a decade earlier as we awaited the arrival of Count Robert's father, Robert the Frisian, on his return from Jerusalem. You will recall that Jean and I had left quite some time ahead of him, with a rescued nun beside us and arrows whistling past. And as we waited in Constantinople the emperor had put us to work trying to make proper Frankish knights of his household guard, the Oikeioi.

The escort commander, whose name I believe was Giorgio, recognized us immediately, greeted us warmly, and in Greek announced his happy discovery to the head of the envoys, along with a short summary of our renown as the heroes of the Battle of Demotika. That changed the atmosphere considerably, as the envoys realized that ours was the army the emperor had specifically begged Count Robert's father to send.

In consequence, things changed quickly. The envoys happily ordered up a market fair so that we could resupply our people as we waited for the rest. They supplied us with guides and letters of passage that would gain the cooperation and support of the towns through which we would pass. And most valuable of all, they gave us news that mattered much in the days ahead.

First and foremost, we learned that the Pechenegs that had caused no little trouble a decade earlier had been mightily defeated and obliterated as a military force in a battle at Levounion in 1091 — a victory won in no little part by five hundred Flemish knights sent to Alexios by Count Robert the Frisian. And the victory was so overwhelming that most of the eighty thousand Pechenegs who fought there still rotted on that spot.

Little wonder, then, that our welcome was so warm. But it also meant that we faced no such threat this side of Constantinople.

That meant we could march as quickly as walking men and animal-drawn wagons could.

The second important item we learned was that Duke Bohemond had crossed ahead of us and landed at Avlona in early November. And although he had carefully proclaimed his newfound friendship to the basileus and peaceful intentions toward his empire, the envoys were decidedly skeptical.

The head envoy frowned. "Bohemond, and his father before him, brought army after army of invasion to our shores, seeking to make theirs this empire, or all the parts of it they could seize, anyway. They are hungry men, greedy in the same way as their rapacious Norman forebears, who believe they have a God-given right to take whatever they can, and keep it if they are strong enough to hold it. We have every right to worry. This is just the latest of their armies and we fear that this declared campaign to aid us is just another ruse to seize our territory. The duke professes himself already a prince or king — all he lacks is a kingdom to rule."

This news greatly disturbed Count Robert, but it bothered Jean and I no less. For we had each come to drive back the Islamite threat, not to help other avaricious men steal kingdoms from their rightful ruler. And that night, Count Robert said much the same to the two of us:

"Barons, I need to make an urgent and important request of you. If you are willing, I need you to march to Constantinople with all speed and reach it before Bohemond does. I want no entanglement with any schemes he has, nor those of any other prince headed for the Holy Land. Do either of you harbor ambitions for a kingdom of your own, or for any kingdom other than Our Savior's?"

I have to admit, the thought of carving out a kingdom for myself had not even occurred to me. Serving as a knight of Christ and winning back His Kingdom was the sole goal and full extent of my aspirations. If I was ever to rule a kingdom, it would be by God's decree. I knew Jean felt the same — I did not even have to ask.

"No, sire!" we said, confirming our unity in thought as well as purpose.

Robert said, "Good! I am of the same resolve, and I need Alexios to know it directly. Both of you are known to and respected by him. I could have no better emissaries than the pair of you to make my case. Are you willing to go?"

Jean looked at me and said, "We are, sire."

Robert nodded. "Thank you. Both of you have already been through these lands, and your forces are mounted to move at a speed that our army cannot. If you wish to leave some of your men and heaviest wagons with me, I will safeguard them as my own, and bring them with our force. I would go myself, but, alas, I cannot proceed quickly enough to overtake Bohemond's month-long lead. Do you think you can?"

I knew I could. With a glance at Jean I said, "Sire, we can, and will."

Robert nodded again and handed Jean a sealed letter. "Take this then, and go. Your contingents are already crossed. Take of them as you wish and go — tomorrow if you can. Outpace Bohemond and reach Constantinople before him. It may be I misjudge his future intentions, but I am determined to remain untangled from any petty ambitions. Convey to Emperor Alexios my father's love, my sacred oath of peace and friendship, and this, my written pledge that I will lift no hand against him, support any scheme to take territory from him, nor aid creation of any state he does not authorize. In turn, I will make all speed and will give him my oath of friendship and fealty when I reach him. If you are willing, do you the same."

Jean said, "Sire, we will march tomorrow morn, as quickly as we are supplied and have our people in readiness." I nodded to signal my agreement, and we quickly took our leave, for we had much to do.

✠✠✠

Back in my camp, I summoned my council and explained the nature and urgency of our mission. After a short discussion, we decided I should go fast and light. I took a well-mounted force of fifty: ten knights, ten squires, and thirty mounted yeomen, and only the monies and stores we needed for three months. Count Robert expected to reach Constantinople by April, and we would reunite our two contingents then. Jean did much the same, and so we fielded a force of about one hundred men. For each man we took two horses — one to ride and the second for provisions and baggage — alternating the horse ridden each day to spare the beasts and so speed our passage.

I made assignments and then gave orders for breakfast at first light, and departure at dawn. Hamish would remain behind to command the bulk of our contingent to bring them and our heavy wagons of siege stores in company with Count Robert. Cedric would serve as his lieutenant. It was a big responsibility. In the bottom of each chest, buried under the iron brackets and fittings for siege engines and a false bottom, was hidden a thick layer of coins in sacking, monies we would need to feed and equip ourselves through all the years this adventure might yet demand. I hated to do it, but I knew from long acquaintance that Hamish would see our men, equipment and treasure safely through, or die in the attempt — and I knew well that he was damned hard to kill.

While Hamish and Cedric saw to the organizational details, I focused on the route of our march to Constantinople. I sent Colin off to the Byzantine emissaries with the letter Edward quickly wrote to explain our mission and request of them a good guide. Within an hour, Colin was back, in his company an impressive squire named Mixali — the Greek name for *Michael.* Colin told me Mixali was the escort commander's own squire, so I knew I could rely on him. Just as importantly, Squire Mixali knew that he could rely on us.

I sent word to Jean, and together we conferred with Mixali.

The squire brought fresh news. "Bohemond's sea crossing took weeks to accomplish. We are not sure when he left Avlona, but his army marches on foot over a southerly route for Thessaloniki, their pace about a league or two a day. We do not think they will reach that city before January."

We then carefully considered the routes Mixali knew, and I compared each with those in the old Roman *Itinerary* Anselm had copied into my codex a decade earlier. We decided on a route that used many of the old Roman roads, which we knew would allow us to move as quickly as possible. We decided on a route from Dyrrachium through Ohrid, Vitolia, and Vodena to reach Thessaloniki, the second largest city in the Byzantine Empire after Constantinople.

Mixali judged the distance at two hundred seventy miles — about ninety leagues. The route was sinuous, following river valleys through rugged mountainous terrain much of the way, and that would slow our pace. But we judged that if we could travel four to five leagues a day, we could reach it by Christmastide and ahead of Bohemond.

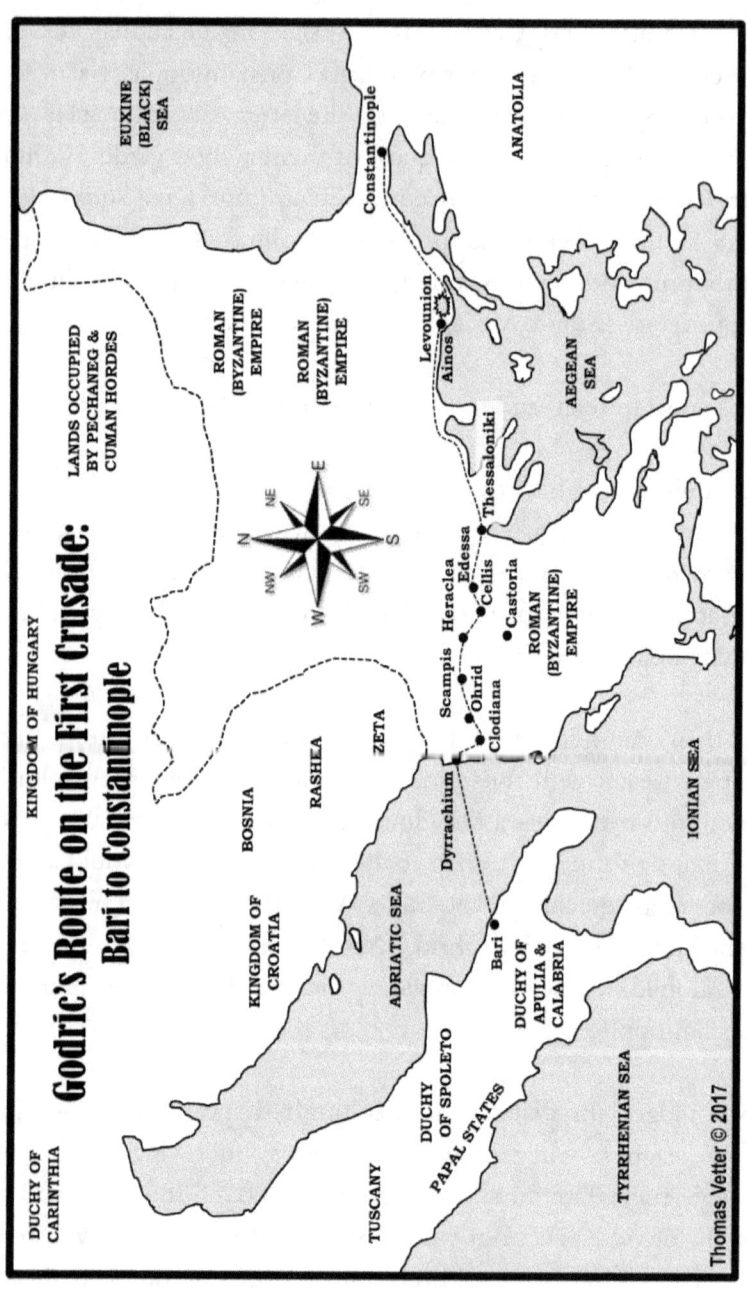

Godric's route on the First Crusade: Bari to Constantinople.

I had Edward write down our planned route from the codex — the names of stopping points and intervening distances — and sent it to Count Robert, for it offered him the fastest route as well. We would mark our route by signs we left, and leave warnings if we found any portion would not support the needs of the army — although, with the men he had at his disposal, the count could fell trees, remove obstacles, and repair bridges if he so needed. Later, we would do this when necessity demanded on our march toward the Holy Land.

✠✠✠

The rising sun was still just a glow behind eastern mountains when we mounted and left Robert's army the following morn, which was the eighth of December. We rode with it on our left as we followed the old Roman road south along the sea through the morning, turning southeast and then east along the northern bank of a river watering a fertile plain flanked by mountains in the afternoon, covering five leagues to reach the remains of Bohemond's encampment at Clodiana before sunset.[9] The next day we followed the river east through narrowing valleys seven leagues to Scampis,[10] once a sizeable Roman town, according to Mixali, but now nothing but a small village for the folk who farmed the surrounding valley.

Day after day we pressed on, to the northeast and southeast as we wound through the mountains, and then around the northern shore of a sizeable lake. Three days and eighteen leagues brought us to Ohrid, a city important to the empire on the northeastern shore of that lake. I noted that people there reacted with alarm as we rode, and Mixali told Jean and I that Bohemond had captured it a dozen years earlier, leaving a lasting wariness in the inhabitants to knights dressed as we were. But the banner given us by the envoys told folk

---

[9] Peqin, Albania today.
[10] Elbasan, Albania nowadays.

we had the emperor's favor, and as they saw it, their alarm quickly subsided.

Two days later we reached Heraclea, called Bitola by the Bulgar locals. The town sits in a mountain basin, and we were on guard while there, for the folk who lived there were antithetical to the emperor, preferring Bulgar rule — twice they had revolted, and they seemed ready to try once again. But our business was elsewhere and we did not tarry, continuing again southeast and east for Edessa. We departed the usual Roman road for a shorter, less-used route Mixali knew reached Edessa by way of Cellis[11] and which we reached five days later.

Edessa was a sizeable town, where our banner again served us well, for Bohemond had also taken Edessa in 1083. But Alexios had driven him out and the town prospered again under Byzantine rule.

✠✠✠

Christmas was drawing close, so we hurried on. Five more days and twenty-five leagues brought us to our immediate goal — Thessaloniki, which we reached on Christmas Day. Here we could rest a few days, renew our provisions and gather news of the emperor, of Bohemond, and of the route before us.

Thessaloniki was then the second largest city in the empire, surpassed only by Constantinople itself, and Mixali told us that more than one hundred thousand people lived there. It was an astonishing number; no city in all of the western kingdoms we knew of had that many people. At home, Dunfermline could not boast of even a tenth that many.

---

[11] Kélla, Greece.

The city was built at the head of a gulf on the great Middle Sea, but it stretched along the shore and inland several miles. We encamped in pastureland just outside the boundary and Mixali went into the city to gather news and spread word that we wanted a market. Within hours, merchants and tradesfolk came to us with provisions, for not even Christmas will deter men from seeking good profit.

Mixali soon returned and brought fresh news. Bohemond and his army, it seemed, were encamped in Castoria,[12] some thirty leagues west of us, where they intended to celebrate the Nativity of Our Lord. By being well-mounted and riding hard, we had passed them by. There was little chance that we would not reach Constantinople long before they did.

Mixali told us something else, something I thought important. Bohemond's past had caught up to him. A decade before, he had come with his father as a conqueror, only to be beaten back by Alexios. Now, the towns he had raided, looted or conquered then still remembered him well and refused to sell to him, fearing that his request of markets was but a ruse to get them and their goods out of the safety of city walls. Nor were their fears unjustified, for when the tradesfolk and farmers refused to sell, Bohemond reverted to his past form and stole what his army needed — cattle, horses, asses, provisions — whatever they could. The word spread ahead of him, increasing the alarm at his approach and making the next market all the less likely. As a result, his force was slowed more than he may have wished, for they were foraging as much as they were marching. Beating him to Thessaloniki was no great feat, then, in the event.

We rested there three days, and with both men and horses refreshed we rode on, again following the old Roman road. Thanks to their

---

[12] Kastoria, Greece.

engineering and the less rugged terrain we made a good distance each day, generally close to seven leagues.

✠✠✠

Two weeks and ninety leagues after leaving Thessaloniki, we reached the River Evros close to where it joined the great Middle Sea. We were encamped there on the plain alongside the road when a messenger from the Byzantine envoys we'd met at Dyrrachium came by, as he too rode from Thessaloniki to Constantinople. When he stopped to water his horse, Mixali recognized him and, at my suggestion, invited him to join us for a meal. I hoped we might come by news thereby, and I was not disappointed.

From him we learned that Count Robert and our army were on the march. They had left a week after we did, and he had encountered them on a plain west of Edessa. They were making about three leagues a day, but had been slowed by the narrow mountain roads between Cellis and Edessa.

He told us that Bohemond was still many days west of Thessaloniki. After spending days celebrating Christmas at Castoria, he resumed the march to Constantinople. But he had encountered a fortified city of heretics, so-called because they did not adhere to his sense of our Christian faith. I knew from my earlier pilgrimage that the entire Church in Alexio's Empire might have been considered such, for their patriarchs, as they call the bishops there, were at odds with Pope Urban over points of Christian dogma, and had been for generations. But Bohemond decided the offense given God by these worshippers was too grievous to leave to His judgment; so he decided to avenge the insult on God's behalf, and had the city surrounded and besieged. Unready as it was for an attack from a supposed ally of the emperor in time of peace, they could not resist long, and yielded. Flush with victory, Bohemond had the town first sacked for whatever it could provide his army. And then he had it, and all its inhabitants, burned to ashes.

That news infuriated me. To my mind, having once been a sheriff enforcing the laws of my king, Bohemond had no authority or right to slaughter an entire city of people in another man's kingdom for any affront he perceived, no matter how egregious their disbelief. And I could not help but remember that my evil half-brother Andrew had done the same to my friends, the manor-folk of Cenachedne. So when, as we supped, some of the knights in our entourage chose the mirthful topic of dispatching heretics in different ways as a source of humor — "roast heretic for the Epiphany feast," I think their joke went — my fury boiled over.

Before I even realized it, I found myself on my feet. "Listen, all of you! If any of you came with me hoping to slaughter men, women, or children of whom you disapprove over matters of faith, you need to join another company, for you are not welcome in mine. If you think murder of disarmed men a joking matter, go join Bohemond! And if you think it right to burn women and children because they believe differently than you do, consider this. I allowed you to come with me so you could atone for *your* sins, not so you could entangle me in your outrageous new ones. Go elsewhere! You do not belong here!"

"Sire!" said one, but I cut him off. "Hear me! I do not go to Jerusalem to kill Turks because they do not worship Christ. I am going there to *stop* them because they use such violence to force Christians to abandon Christ for Mohammad. The Turks follow their prophet Mohammad because he said he is the voice of God on earth and that Christ was only a prophet, not the Son of God. But Mohammad and Christ cannot both be telling the truth. Whom do you believe? God Himself named Jesus as His Only Son, and since Christ is the Son of God, what need was there for

Mohammed? Only Mohammad says otherwise — a man who never performed a miracle, and died just as all of us do. But even he said he saw Christ in Heaven. Who says they saw Mohammad there?"

I shook my head to clear it and so dampen my fury. "The men we go to fight do just as Bohemond has done —murder those they consider infidel, apostate, or heretic. They enslave the innocent. They extort, rape, and torture those who do not accept their faith and their iron-fisted rule. They choose Mohammad because he allows what Christ forbids, and in so doing, gain power over their believers to do as they like, self-proclaiming that they do the will of their god. In truth, it is power they worship, not God. I will have naught to do with men like that, and any Christian who behaves like them is my enemy as much as an Islamite infesting the Holy Land."

"But Duke Bohemond took the cross. . ." said one, who withered into silence as I turned my outrage on him.

"Let me finish; then draw your blade if you disagree. Bohemond took the cross for power and gain, not salvation, or he would do as we do. We cannot do as Bohemond has done and expect Christ to give us victory. We must be better men than that to deserve it. The people Bohemond burned were Christian, and no one but Christ knew whether they were truly heretic. I can say for certain that the Duke of Apulia is not Heaven's Judge; nor are you or I. Christ Himself is, and only He. If you behave as Bohemond does, you will never live to see Jerusalem, for you will not deserve it. And I predict that Heaven will not give Jerusalem to Bohemond for this very act. We shall all see if I am wrong."

I glared around the fire at the circle of astonished men who sat dumbstruck at my rant. I did not care. Bohemond had done a monstrous thing, they all needed to know it, and I would not tolerate men like that in my company.

At that, Jean pulled me down, and thrust a tankard into my hands. "Drink!" he ordered. "You have made your point. They are ashamed of themselves and you don't need to rub their noses in *la merde* for them to know it."

I subsided, then, and after an embarrassed silence, new topics arose among the men around the fires, and cheerful conversation returned. But I slept badly that night, haunted in tortured dreams by the fiery deaths my people had suffered. And once again, they sang their sad song from the flames.

✠✠✠

The following day on the eastern flank of the river Evros we rode through the village of Ainos.[13] On the flat plains north of the village, I saw a vast field of scattered black mounds and countless gleaming white objects. As I looked at Mixali for explanation, all he said was, "Levounion, sire."

Spurring my horse into a canter, I rode that way, Jean and many of the others following. As I rode among them I realized what I saw.

The blackened objects were charred timbers, burnt remains of thousands of wagons like those I knew the Pechenegs used. The myriad shining white objects on and around the pyres' residue were bones — mostly skulls, spines and pelvises of both people and horses — now picked clean by carrion birds and insects, and bleached white by the bright sun. Broken weapons rusted and cloth and harness rotted everywhere.

In Dyrrachium, we had been told that Emperor Alexios had won a great victory here six years before, long enough before our arrival to

---

[13] Today called Enez, Turkey.

explain why all the bones were picked clean. But until I saw how vast was the field of remains I could not comprehend how many men — and women and children, too, for the Pechenegs brought their families with them in those horse-drawn wagons — had fought and died here. Truly, the number was huge.

Here lay most of the eighty thousand Pechenegs — for we had been told that they were nearly wiped from the face of the earth that day — with many thousands of their horses. And scattered throughout among them were the bones of the basileus's Greek troops, Cuman allies, and horses, which had never been recovered for burial elsewhere.

The battlefield covered perhaps four square miles, and from the spread of the bones I could see what had happened here. The Greeks had come from the north and east, their approach hidden by a line of hills right up to the time the attack began. They caught the Pechenegs completely by surprise, hemmed in by the river to the west and the sea to the south. Unable to flee south, the Pechenegs had fallen back to the river, hoping and mostly failing to escape across it. And most of them had died there, for there the bones were thickest, the blackened timber still arranged in the wagon circles Jean and I knew from our battle against the selfsame Pechenegs at Demoticho a decade earlier. Indeed, it might have been the same battle — for the tactics we had used then were identical. But the results this time were dramatically more impressive.

From my elbow, Mixali spoke. "It was the knights of Flanders that most made this victory possible, sire. Five hundred of them made a thundering charge from the north and east. They made a splendid sight, and when the Pechenegs saw them they were truly terrified. The knights rode straight through the disorganized front line the Pechenegs threw together, slaughtering all before them and driving the bulk of the horde into a wild flight westward. I saw it — I was a messenger for the commanders then, stationed with them on that hill." He pointed at the closest to the northeast.

"Once their lines broke, they never recovered. Most were forced to retreat into the wagon circles, where they defended themselves with arrows. But the knights' armor was impervious, so the Pechenegs shot at their horses instead. But it was not enough, for we took each wagon circle in turn, the mounted Cumans riding in and out to pour in arrows, followed by phalanxes of well-armored infantry who entered each circle and butchered every adult inside. The children and relatively few adults who surrendered were captured. Now all the remaining Pecheneg men serve the emperor as his mercenaries."

His description caused my memories of the Battle of Demoticho to come flooding back: the great growing stink of blood, piss, and shit; the constant screams of dying men and horses; the arrows hissing by or striking with a whack that bruised despite tough mail and gambeson; the fields of corpses and vast smears of blood on grass that marked the paths of the phalanxes; my arrow through the eye-hole of ex-King Solomon's helmet; waking in a wagon filled with wounded men, my head banging on the side, and the foul taste of horse-piss in my mouth.

I shook my head and shoved the memories back into the dark pit in my mind where they lurk always, ready to pounce as I sleep. But not right then, for I had things to do.

✠✠✠

We rode on then and had no further misadventures; without incident we traveled the remaining fifty-four leagues in just ten days, finally reaching Constantinople on the twenty-fifth of January 1097.

✠✠✠

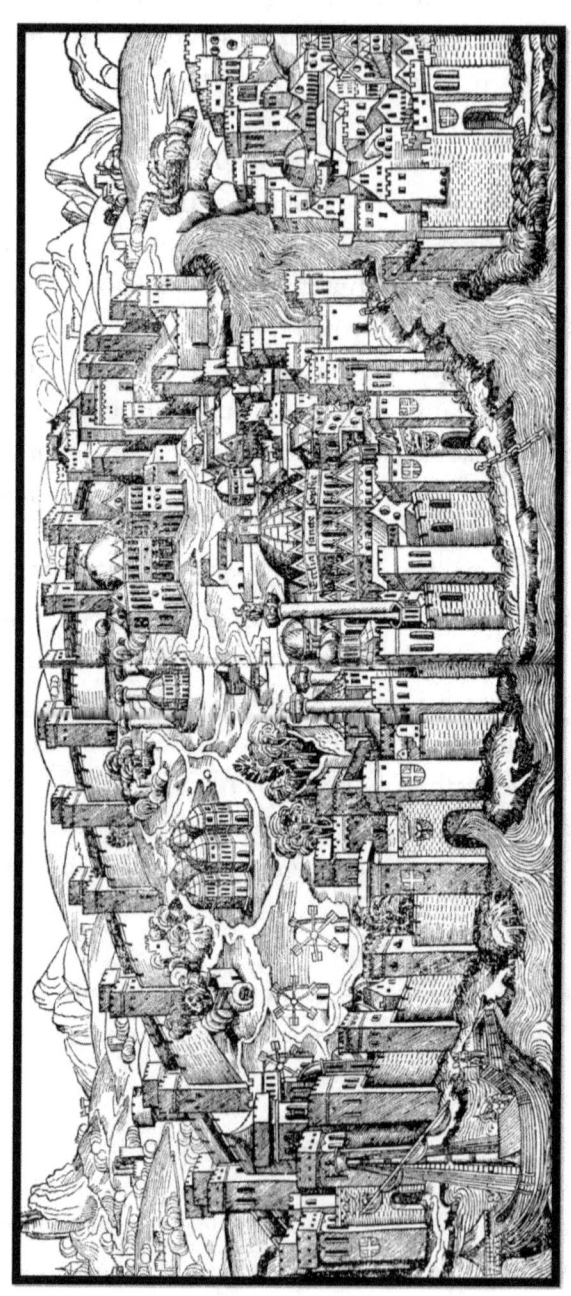

**Medieval depiction of Constantinople.**

# FOUR

✠✠✠

As always when it came into view, the great city of Constantinople was an awesome sight. The double line of stone walls (and in some sections triple!) interspersed with regularly-spaced towers never failed to impress me — even as it set me to think about how to breach them, for that was my chosen profession.

When we reached Constantinople, we were met just outside the Golden Gate by envoys of Emperor Alexios. As at Dyrrachium, they were initially stiff, formal, and not at all friendly, for they thought us the emissaries of Bohemond. Mixali quickly informed them otherwise, and told them that Jean and I were the emperor's cherished friends, the heroes of Demoticho, who came now as emissaries of Count Robert, son of the very man the emperor had begged for military aid, and of which we were the vanguard. That made a substantial difference, for their attitude towards us changed instantly, and we were truly welcomed, their smiles revealing a relief all too evident.

Nevertheless, they — most apologetically — asked us to encamp wherever we chose, but outside the walls of the great city. "We humbly beg you to understand that many western knights and armed men come to us now, not all of whom are as well-meaning as we know you are. The emperor thanks you for responding to our most urgent need. But he also asks that all without exception make camp outside our walls, for the city has no space to accommodate so many foreign troops and he would see that neither you nor his subjects have any trouble, the one from the other. We will see to it that within a day you have a market fair at your encampment to supply all your party might require."

The knights with us grumbled, for they thought it an affront to their honor, but Jean and I understood. Well-armed men by the tens of thousands were converging on Constantinople from all directions, men with very different notions of hospitality and mores from those of Constantinople, and Alexios had good reason to be cautious. Among these men would be Bohemond, who had always wanted an opportunity to bring an army inside Constantinople's formidable defenses — and then stay on as its newest emperor.

So we told the envoys we would be happy to camp outside the walls, and that they would find us between the Gate of St. Romanus and the River Lycus. In turn, we requested an audience with the emperor at his earliest pleasure, for we brought news and assurances from his new ally, Count Robert II of Flanders. To this the grateful envoys quickly agreed, saying they were sure the emperor would want to see such faithful old friends. I asked that they convey word of our arrival to our old friends, Domesticus Tatikios and Megas Anticensor Demetrius, with our wish to pay our respects. To that they also agreed, and then they took leave of us.

As we pledged, we rode another mile north outside the great walls, and camped on the shallow slope between the Gate of St. Romanus and the River Lycus. The gate offered a direct route to the emperor's palace, and a short walk for merchants willing to sell to us, while the river afforded us water and forage for our many horses and a pleasant place to camp. There we pitched our tents and hobbled our horses to graze, rest, and roll on the grass between the camp and the river.

True to their word, enterprising merchants came to us that same afternoon, and by the following day a small market flourished beside our camp. We rested, refreshed ourselves, made camp as comfortable as we could, and began our wait for Count Robert.

✠✠✠

The day after we arrived, an Oikeioi squire brought us news and an invitation. The lad was about sixteen, scrawny as all Greek troops seemed to be, but earnest and impeccably mannered, a credit to his calling.

With a bow, he began a carefully rehearsed message. "The Basileus Alexios does most certainly wish to see his old friends, the Heroes of Demoticho, a week hence at midday. You and your companion knights and squires are here given passes to freely enter and enjoy the city as you wish. The basileus wishes that you remain encamped here, for your comfort, and ready access to water and forage for your horses, for sufficient of these cannot be had within the walls." And then he handed us a sheaf of papers that proved to be passes allowing our free passage into the city.

He took a breath, thought a moment, and went on. "Domesticus Tatikios and Megas Anticensor Demetrius have both been notified of your arrival. Both express pleasure to hear it and hope you will call at their homes when you wish. I am to convey your message to each in reply."

Jean and I thanked him and asked him to inform both that we would call on Lord Tatikios on the morrow and Lord Demetrius the day following. With a repeat-back of our message to ensure he had it right, he bowed again and departed.

We then summoned our knights, informed them of our collective right to enjoy the city, and enjoined them to exercise good judgment and better conduct so that we might keep it for the duration of our stay. With this, morale soared. Quickly we dressed, our white surcoats, with red crosses of pilgrimage sewn on front and back, worn outermost over our mail. Then it was off to see the sights of the great city, with a only small duty detail left to guard the camp and maintain good order there.

As for our men, they were content where they were. The market fair beside the camp gladly provided all they wished most for, which predictably meant ale, food, music, and women. With all that, what need had they elsewhere?

✠✠✠

That same evening, a loquacious wine merchant from the city told us that ours was not the first force to arrive, for the Duke of Lorraine, Godfrey of Bouillon — traveling overland much as I had in 1086 — had reached Constantinople a month earlier on the twenty-third of December, leading a great army. And as we enjoyed free samples of his wares at the evening fire he told us what ensued.

"Almost immediately, though neither one sought it, Basileus Alexios and Duke Godfrey stumbled into conflict. The duke initially camped his army right here, where you are now. But the huge number of men and beasts encamped upstream of the city on our water supply risked inflicting us with sickness, so the emperor asked them to relocate and camp on unbuilt ground inside the walls instead. The duke complied, but the new site offered no water or forage for the animals. So then his squires and servants had to forage around the area daily to feed and water their animals.

"When some of the duke's men began seizing forage from citizens and watering animals in the public drinking fountains, it caused great outrage among our people. The emperor had his Turcopole and Pecheneg mercenaries patrol the troubled areas to stop the abuses, but Godfrey's men believed the emperor's invitation into the city entitled them to whatever they needed. Arguments between the two sides led first to skirmishes and then open brawls. And when some squires and men of Lord Baldwin, the duke's brother, were killed, Baldwin took out a force of fighters and ambushed a Turcopole patrol, capturing sixty men. Survivors of the earlier fights identified among the prisoners some of men who had killed his men, so Baldwin had them killed in turn. Then he brought the other prisoners to his brother."

The merchant paused to pass his wineskin around our circle again, and then resumed his tale.

"Naturally, this did not sit well with the emperor, who demanded the duke punish his brother for the executions and make reparations. Instead, Duke Godfrey roused his army, marched out of the city, and re-camped here as he had first done.

"Furious, the basileus sent out his own troops to drive off Godfrey, but Godfrey expected a possible attack and was ready for it. His army drove the Byzantine forces back into the city, killing seven Greeks in the process.

"A stalemate ensued, lasting five days before Alexios and Godfrey met face-to-face under a flag of truce. Neither leader gave ground or apologized, exactly. But both men were wise enough to realize that continued rancor between them worked against their mutual interest, so they struck a bargain. The emperor told the duke that forage and water for his enormous number of animals was freely available and in plenty across the strait in Anatolia, and then offered to have his navy ferry them across. The duke agreed to take his army there if, in turn, the basileus provided a market there that sold all the duke's men needed, just as the city had, and to provide alms to the duke's poorer men so that they might be able to buy enough to live. The basileus agreed, and an accord was struck. And the duke and his men are encamped there right now."

After we heard all that, our knights and men were much mollified, understanding finally why we were camped outside the city and that Alexios had granted us a great privilege by allowing us to do what he had denied Godfrey. To be fair, we were a tiny body of men and animals compared to Godfrey's — our hundred men and two hundred horses were dwarfed by his many thousands of men and animals — and we posed no great risk to the city's water. But it was the fact that the relationship Jean and I had with the emperor was still so strong that we had been trusted outright when the duke had not — that is what truly impressed our followers.

I bought the wine then, for the story was well worth what the wine was not, given the headaches that mediocre vintage gave all of us.

✠✠✠

The following afternoon Jean and I made our way through the city to the great house of Domesticus — that is, General — Tatikios, who was expecting us. The reunion was bittersweet, for it was built on an odd relationship. Ever since I saved his life in battle against the Pechenegs a decade before, I was ceremonially the general's "father." The title, "Roman Crown of the Preserver," that he had awarded me for saving him, meant that Tatikios would always honor his obligation by treating me as if I was his own father. Yet, despite that, we never really developed a strong affection between us. Indeed, I think we were too much alike to love the other very much. We got along well enough, though, and Tatikios was always gracious.

We found that the general was at his most cordial, hale and finely dressed in embroidered silk robes. A splendid new gold nose, which replaced the one he was born with but had lost in battle many years earlier, gleamed in strong contrast to his swarthy skin.

He had had a fine supper ready for us. In turn, I brought him a gift: a finely crafted Norman-style sword with a Damascene blade that Carrick had made with some of the Wootz steel I brought home with me from my earlier pilgrimage. It was just as magnificent as the one I carried, and well worth the quarter-pound of gold that Carrick earned from them.

Over a leisurely supper, we took turns relating tales of events over the intervening decade. Tatikios told us of the destruction of the Pechenegs at Levounion, and the Cumans at Adrianople in 1094. Jean told us of his rapidly burgeoning family and the splendid estate he was creating at home in France. I told them of my destruction of MacanFhirMhóir and OdinsØye, the treacherous deaths of King Malcolm, Prince Edward, and Queen Margaret, and how I punished their murderers.

Then the conversation turned to the great venture upon which we were about to embark. Over dessert and wine, Tatikios told us what had just happened to the army of commoner pilgrims, the Peoples' Army, as it was now called, who had answered Pope Urban's call in 1095. Their adventure, begun in hope and excitement early in 1096, had ended in a series of disasters just three months earlier. I relate now his version of events, as best as I can recall them:

"A great host of common folk from all over France and the Holy Roman Empire who heard the pope's appeal and decided to take up the cross assembled in April of 1096, into a great *Peoples' Army*, led by the monk called Peter the Hermit and Frankish knight Walter, called "The Penniless" from Sans-Avoir, his true surname.

"After great trials and a very long walk, this unruly mob of peasants reached Constantinople in July of 1096. The emperor hardly knew what to do with them. When they set out, they were already destitute and hungry, too poor to make any provision for their own subsistence. They had already eaten everything they brought with them along the way, and then they foraged off the land and stole from the inhabitants of the lands through which they passed. Here at Constantinople, they stole everything they could lay their hands on, thieving from homes, shops, public buildings, even the palaces. They even climbed up to steal and resell lead ripped from the roofs of our churches."

"What did the emperor do about that?" Jean asked.

Tatikios frowned. "Alexios had the mercenary Pechenegs round them up and drive them out of the city. But he couldn't force them to go home, and he couldn't let them continue pillaging the people of the surrounding area. So on the sixth of August of 1096, he gave them provisions, and had our navy ferry them — the many tens of thousands of them — across the Propontis[14] to a vacant old army encampment at Helenopolis[15] in Anatolia.

"Helenopolis is just two days' march — fifteen leagues —— from Nicaea, the new capital of the Seljuq invader, Kilij Arslan I, who now calls himself the Sultan of Rhum, and the home of his army. Knowing what could befall them, we advised Peter and Walter to use the encampment as a safe haven to house the women, children, and sick while the men campaigned, and that they should wait until experienced knights like you — whom we had heard were coming — arrived to help mount a true military campaign. But they ignored our advice completely, saying "God Himself will fight for us, so what need have we of knights?" Instead, they simply armed the men

---

[14] Sea of Marmara.
[15] Civetot/Civetote.

among the rabble, with whatever weapons they could, to make them into footsoldiers after a fashion.

"Then, small companies of adventurous rogues in their army — in reality, just bands of armed robbers — began pillaging farms and villages around Helenopolis for anything they might provide. It did not matter that their victims were Christian — all local farmers and shepherds already oppressed by their new Islamic overlords under their tenet of 'Koran, tribute, or the sword.' The Turks only managed to take these lands from us a few years ago. Since then the Seljuqs, who have neither the ability nor wish to farm any of the land they conquer, had no choice but to let these Christian farmers live so long as they paid tribute, a heavy tax of cash and crops the Turks extort under pain of death. In truth, these Seljuqs are vicious bloodsuckers, parasites dependent for subsistence on the 'People of the Book' on whom they prey."

I shook my head, knowing by instinct what was coming. Over the past decade, I had far too much experience with men like these: Pecheneg marauders, MacanFhirMhóir's rogues, OdinsØye's raiders, and Rufus's land-thieves. And I had learned to hate them. They invariably thought the way to wealth was by force of arms, robbing, stealing and looting others; when the just way to prosperity was to create, invent, grow, build, or make things others needed and sell them for a fair profit. But men like them could never be taught. For them the truth had to be hammered through their thick skulls.

But Tatikios's story continued. "At the end of August, the Peoples' Army was as ready as they could be, and a cohort of thousands of armed Frankish peasants marched south, seizing all the newly-harvested crops and animals as they went, and massacring every farmer who protested. They managed to travel the fifteen leagues to Nicaea undiscovered, and surprised the city and its young sultan, Dawud Kilij Arslan ibn Suleiman ibn Qutulmish, called Kilij Arslan,

First Sultan of Rum, who was otherwise preoccupied with his war against his rivals, the Turkic rulers who killed his father. The sultan disdained the armed mob outside Nicaea, and sent out a small cavalry force to drive them off. But the Franks were too numerous, managed to encircle the horsemen and then cut them to pieces. Only a few Turks managed to escape back into Nicaea.

"The Frankish mob had no means to take the city itself. As you saw on your earlier pilgrimage, it is encircled by double walls of stone, defended by strong towers spaced an arrow's-flight apart all the way around. But they did succeed in sacking the homes and buildings built outside the walls, and killed many more unfortunate Christians in their misguided zeal.

"Buoyed by their perceived success, they returned to Helenopolis boasting of victory and displaying the foodstuffs and loot they had taken. That convinced the multitude in the camp that God had blessed their efforts and emboldened other to greater rashness."

"I'm guessing that this didn't bode well," said Jean, shaking his head. His instincts were as keen as mine, it seemed.

Tatikios nodded. "The eighteen-year-old sultan, Kilij Arslan, was outraged at being both surprised and defeated, believing that these events cost him prestige in the eyes of his army and his people, so he wanted revenge. And an opportunity for revenge occurred almost immediately, for in mid-September another raiding party of six thousand Swabians marched south, led by a knight named Reinald. They bypassed Nicaea as too formidable a target, but they found an empty Turkish fort just four miles away at Xerigordon. They decided it would provide an ideal base from which to pillage the surrounding region and promptly occupied it on September 18.

"Word of the fort's seizure reached Nicaea almost immediately. Kilij

Arslan sent out his general, Elchanes, with a force of fifteen thousand to wrest it back. On the twenty-first, Elchanes arrived and laid siege to the fort, trapping Reinald and his men inside. Too late did they realize that the fort had no source or stores of water inside, and no chance to bring in any. The stream the fort depended on flowed nearby but it was out of reach outside the walls. So their thirst became Elchanes' greatest weapon."

I nodded. Six thousand men need a lot of water. Elchanes had done just as I had at Argences, and I knew before Tatikios said it that they were doomed.

"The Swabians resisted fiercely, repulsing every attack. But when the little water there ran out, the defenders weakened quickly and their wounded began dying. Some were driven to acts of desperation: drawing blood from their animals and drinking it, some drinking the piss as others passed it, and many covering themselves with moist earth in the hope it would relieve their suffering. But to no avail.

"After eight days they could take no more, so they surrendered the fort on the twenty-ninth. In so doing Reinald sought terms to save himself, even offering to join the Turks and fight other Christians. The Turks agreed to spare any man who renounced Christianity for Islam. Reinald and about two hundred others agreed, so Elchanes let them live; but he then promptly made slaves of them. The others refused to renounce their Christian faith, so Elchanes slaughtered them without mercy.

"And while these Swabians died to hold their ill-chosen citadel, the bulk of the People's Army sat in Helenopolis. Their leader, Peter the Hermit, had gone to Constantinople seeking more supplies, arms, and military support from the emperor, and the experienced military men among their leadership thought they should wait until he returned. But one among them, Geoffrey Burel, had no such doubts. He was popular among the masses, and believing in the divine support for their mission and in his own destiny, he urged all of them to march, first on Nicaea and then on Jerusalem.

"Then news came in, brought by a pair of treacherous Turks who were, in fact, spies of Kilij Arslan. Instead of reporting the slaughter of the Swabians, they told all a lie of success: that the Swabians had not only had held the fort at Xerigordon, but they had captured Nicaea as well, with tremendous loot, plenty for all.

"So Burel seized upon this report, and had his associates spread it throughout the multitudes: Nicaea was theirs, with loot for all who got there quickly. The excitement among those who had never known plenty grew like a fever, and swept all wise counsel aside. Burel announced that he was taking command, and that only cowards would want to stay in Helenopolis with women, children, the old and the sick when he led the army to Nicaea."

Jean and I listened, then, silently and with dread, for we could guess what was coming.

Tatikios shook his head. "And so on October 21, Geoffrey Burel led an army of twenty thousand men south, with many idiots among them bringing their women and children along as they marched out of Helenopolis. They got only a league. And then, as they marched through a narrow wooded valley near the village of Dracon, the army of Seljuq Turks lying in wait on both hillsides sprang their ambush, blocking not only the way forward, but also the way back, surrounding the terrified masses and raining arrows into them. The carnage was terrific, and a rout ensued — the panicked masses vainly trying to flee back to Helenopolis, and the brave fighting men among them futilely trying to defend them with a counterattack.

"Few who started out made it back. Most of the men-at-arms were slaughtered in the fight or afterward, for only the children, the more comely women, and those willing to convert to Islam were allowed to live on by becoming Islamite slaves. The rest were put to the sword. Some say as many as sixty thousand pilgrims died there.

"But stout-hearted Burel abandoned them early and escaped the trap. He and a few others who had horses made it back to Helenopolis, where three thousand people — mostly women and children left behind — took shelter in an old castle on the site, and held off the Turks until our navy returned to rescue them. You see, the basileus had kept a patrol vessel there to keep an eye on the pilgrims, and it brought us word of the two disasters.

"So the emperor immediately dispatched Constantine Katakalon, the best naval commander he has, and a strong naval force by ship to Helenopolis. The Turks withdrew with their captives as the Greeks arrived, and Burel and his band of survivors were saved. Katakalon gathered all still at Helenopolis and brought them back to safety in Constantinople."

"With that, the Peoples' pilgrimage ended — a lesson in abject failure. Peter the Hermit remains here in Constantinople hoping to go on to Jerusalem. The other survivors have gone back to where they came from, or joined the city beggars. Burel swaggers about, waiting, no doubt, for a new opportunity to promote himself. Someone should send him on into eternity before he gets the chance to kill thousands more through his arrogance and stupidity."

Tatikios was right, of course. But no one would do it, for killing the criminally stupid is still murder, both a crime and sin. But for Burel, it might be only nominally so, and in my view, possibly well worth spending an extra century or two in Purgatory.

✠✠✠

Despite its horrible outcome, the People's Army disaster provided one benefit, of which I took full advantage, first with my own retinue and later with Count Robert's army. I related these tales several times to different gatherings and used them to make several crucial points, which were:

✠ Our Seljuq enemies do not practice Christian warfare — that is, a just war between warriors that spares the women, children, the wounded, helpless, and sick. The Seljuqs war upon all, and relish cruel treatment of the helpless. Do not expect mercy of them, and bestow it with caution, for you will not receive it in return — expect nothing but treachery should it prove possible.

✠ Our enemies are implacable, ruthless, and treacherous — they have no sense of personal honor or mercy such as we know it. They only spare Christians their lives at the cost of their souls — eternal damnation for converting to that false religion — or for profit, for they spare women, children, and craven cowards only so they can sell them into cruel slavery under other Islamites. All others they kill without mercy and usually with great cruelty. It is much better to kill them first.

✠ Water is critical in the lands we are entering, and the sources both scarce and often dry. But critical as water is, it is only slightly more important than forage and food, for all are often unavailable — first, because the region is desolate, and second, because our enemies will lay waste to or poison the sources to prevent us from using them. We will only be secure when we have these in abundance, so we must ascertain these are actually present beforehand, and then secure them for our use on an ongoing basis. Scout them out, secure them, and hold them to the last, for dearth of them means certain death sooner or later.

✠ To march blindly into the lands ahead is a stupidity bordering on willful suicide, for to do so means you will walk into a trap, as that dolt Geoffrey Burel did. We do not know these lands as the Turks do, so we must always scout — ahead, to both sides, and behind! Without having scout patrols out, moving as we move, and sentry posts to give warning when we stop, we are blind and easy prey for this wily and ruthless foe. It is always better to lose a few men in order to spare the bulk of the army by obtaining their warning in time.

✠ And finally, remember that the inhabitants of the Anatolian and Syrian lands are largely still Christian. The Seljuq Turks are recent invaders, who conquered these lands — or, at least, the cities in them — only in the last decade. Nicaea, Antioch, Edessa, and other towns are still inhabited mostly by Christians, now cruelly oppressed under their new Seljuq masters. Therefore, do not harm or loot them as Seljuqs would — without thought or mercy — for when this is done to fellow believers, it is both sin and crime. Rather, pick out the Seljuqs and do unto them what they do to helpless Christians. In that, we only impose God's just vengeance on them for their crimes against His true people.

I considered these lessons so important that I am afraid I became a troublesome bore trying to impart them. Some knights and squires — thinking themselves beyond such lessons — would roll their eyes and subtly mock my too-earnest efforts to pass them along. But I knew to do so would save lives, and I stubbornly continued to tell the stories and preach the lessons they taught.

And the men who mocked rather than learn? Those that I caught at it I assigned to scouting duties on the march through Anatolia until they learned their lessons the hard way, and began teaching others.

And what did I learn? Those lessons, certainly. But more than that, I realized there were now three men I wanted most earnestly to meet: Geffrey Burel, the self-sure idiot who had stupidly led thousands of trusting Christian pilgrims to martyrdom. And Sultan Kilij Arslan and his man Elchanes, who claimed to have won great victory for Islam by murdering thousands of helpless prisoners and scores of thousands of untrained men, defenseless women, and children. Men as brave as them would certainly not fear engaging a Christian knight in personal combat. They might even relish it.

I certainly hoped so. Indeed, I began praying for it.

✠✠✠

The following day Jean and I went to the home of our good friend, Megas Anticensor Demetrius, the emperor's chief military engineer, siege master, and chief of scouts and spies. We had first met him during our pilgrimage to Jerusalem in 1086. Indeed, Demetrius and I had ridden together daily between Constantinople and Jerusalem — in both directions. Demetrius was then disguised as a simple scout — profane, dirty, and reeking of garlic — under orders from the basileus to spy on us to assess our value as fighting allies.

Despite his mission, mutual friendship grew among us. And on our return to Constantinople, Demetrius gave to Alexios such a glowing report that Alexios then entreated Count Robert the Frisian to send him five hundred such knights from Flanders to help him defeat his enemies. The Frisian did this in 1089, and those knights drove back the Seljuqs in 1090 and won Alexios his great victory at Levounion in 1091. This so impressed Alexios that he then sent an appeal to the Frisian and Pope Urban that had led so many more to take up the cross and our arms for Christ with Urban's call to crusade.

A decade had since passed since we old friends last met, and we were all surprised by what time had wrought. Demetrius and his still-lovely bride, Anna, were older, of course, but both wore their years well. Their six children had thrived and grown into tall — well, taller — healthy adolescents and young adults. Most of the children were gone now, married and living lives of their own, but the youngest two — babes when we last saw them — were still at home to vex and entertain their parents.

It was Anna who greeted us first. "Baron Jean! Baron Godric! How well you look, and how splendid! Can it be that you are even taller than you were? Certainly more muscled! How do they grow men so large in Flanders? Never mind. Come here and give me a hug!"

Behind her, Demetrius was amused, again evaluating and measuring us. Indeed, he had always done this. Before we knew what he was really up to, we thought this a kind of self-amusement, like enjoying the antics of a toddler or clever pet. But in the decade since, I had gained a much greater experience of men and could now read them too, just as he did. And I read approval in what he saw.

We adjourned to a most pleasant courtyard, completely walled about, and surrounded by a covered paved walkway, doors to other rooms opening at intervals along the way. Beds of flowers and fragrant plants paralleled the central side of the walk, punctuated by paved paths that led to a central fountain beneath a large trellis upon which grew grapevines, as yet denuded by the winter season. But both the sun and the day were warmer than typical, and it was pleasant there.

So we all sat around a table there in the sun, drank wine, and talked both of old times and events since. Jean spoke of Isabeau, happy at home with a manor house full of children, and I of my bride, Aleine, and tiny daughter Margaret Alice, now in my splendid new manor with her parents. I avoided all the tales of battle at home —

they could be told to Demetrius at some other time — but I told a shortened summary of my career as King Malcolm's sheriff-at-large, and of course, my experiments building and using my siege engines. When I made mention of my tree-bucket, *Bone-Crusher*, Demetrius could not hide his surprise and keen interest, and I knew I would be spending another day in his company, discussing our technical advances in the engines we built.

A wonderful dinner followed, and we ate together again as we had in older times when Jean, Isabeau, and I lived in the house Demetrius rented us, and had visited each other regularly. Those had been carefree days. But now the dark shadow Islam had cast over their land found us even here, and the talk turned to what lay ahead.

In the past decade, the Seljuqs had seized more and more of Anatolia, so that now only the peninsula across the Bosporus and the islands off the coast remained in Byzantine hands. The empire had never been smaller. But in the last few years, the Pechenegs, Cumans, and Normans had each been defeated, bringing peace and stability to the Thracian — that is, western — half of the shrunken empire. And Demetrius told us the emperor had great hopes we would help him retake the cities to the east, restoring all that had been recently lost.

At Demetrius's suggestion, I returned alone the following day, and we spent our time in martial discussions. In the intervening years, he and I had each built large versions of the small model I had left in his hands in 1088. In my case, I had built seven successive prototypes, culminating with *Bone-Crusher*, the counterweight tree-bucket I had used to destroy OdinsØye's stone tower five years earlier. It, and my other engines, were all too cumbersome to haul across all Europe. But I had brought in my baggage train chests that held all the iron brackets and fittings needed to rebuild my siege machines with locally-harvested timbers when the need arose.

For his part, Demetrius had done as I suggested, and showed my little model to the emperor. Alexios was always a general at heart, and he found it as intriguing as had Demetrius and I. So Alexios provided the funds and Demetrius, too, built a succession of machines. And he too found, as I had, that they were completely capable of destroying themselves as quickly as any target, because unless strongly built and heavily reinforced, the machines in action were more powerful — or violent — than their joints and members could withstand.

But Demetrius had also prevailed. And although our machines looked very different, they functioned in essentially the same way: the long throwing arm was hauled down by traction and held by a release mechanism while the sling was loaded. And when the release was tripped, the huge counterweight whipped the arm and its sling back, up, and over, hurling a projectile a long distance with great force. And now, just as I had predicted, her name was *helepolis*, or "City-taker."

✠✠✠

At the appointed date and time, wearing our finest armor and attire, and accompanied by well-scrubbed squires, Jean and I presented ourselves at the antechamber to Emperor Alexios's throne room. We were expected; and after but a brief delay, shown straight in.

The emperor looked much as I remembered him from a decade earlier — resplendent in heavily embroidered silk of gold and black, his high gold crown gleaming. But the hair it encircled was more gray than black now, and the face more deeply furrowed, with lines that indicated worry and responsibility were ever-present. Alexios was much more worn than I would have thought.

**Alexios Komnenos I, Emperor of the Byzantine Roman Empire.**

Still, when his eyes fell upon us, the smile that appeared on his countenance was as bright as ever. I had the distinct feeling we had brought a rare ray of heart-felt joy to the man. Truly I hoped so, for he had treated us most generously for the deeds we had done.

"Ahh, at last — the Heroes of Demoticho grace my court once again!" he exclaimed as we bowed deeply at the foot of his dais. "Once again I thrill, just as I did when you brought me victory over the Pechenegs. And I see the noble ladies of Flanders care well for the men they love. I trust Baroness Isabeau is well. And is there a Baroness MacEuan also?"

"Isabeau is most well, thank you. And Baron Godric managed at last to ensnare his beloved Aleine in matrimony, sire," said Jean, with a wink at me.

"And yet they have consented to allow their lords to return to our realm to help us fight off the accursed Seljuqs?" His black eyes were just as penetrating as before, and I had the feeling he could read my soul as easily as he could a manuscript.

I said, "They know us too well, my lord. They would rather have our love from a distance than our constant fretting under the same roof."

"Hmm. I can see their point of view — two men such as you would be hard to live with if great things were happening without your help. And you, my lords? You know what lies ahead, yet return willingly, even eagerly?"

Jean said, "The Holy Father has called us, Great Basileus, to aid not only you, but Our Savior Himself. We have come not only to help wrest back your lands from these damnable infidels, but to help our Lord establish His Kingdom of Heaven in Jerusalem. And when he returns as He has promised, we intend to hand Him the city's keys."

Alexios smiled and said, "I truly hope you succeed, and that I can join you when He does, with Constantinople's keys to offer as well." He paused. "Then I understand that I can count on your help in the battles to come? I could not have two better warriors at my side."

With a look at Jean, who nodded, I said, "Sire, we are here to pledge our own fealty to your cause, and more importantly, to pledge that of the son of your old friend, Count Robert the Frisian, who has been taken from us by Heaven. But his son, the second Count Robert of Flanders, now leads an army of thousands here, one that includes our own men, and which will arrive here before month's end. The count wished us to pledge his support and fealty directly to you, and convey his determination to avoid entanglement in any plans or ambitions of the other princes and commanders also on their way here. When he arrives, he will directly renew the pledge we make now on his behalf."

The emperor nodded his understanding. "I accept your pledge of fealty and his. By doing this, I know that I can trust him and you to honor the promises you make. But I wonder why you thought this necessary?"

I said, "Sire, Duke Bohemond follows us, and we know that he has invaded your realm previously. We hear he has taken the cross as we did, but if he still retains or now hides ambitions that may bring him into conflict with you, we wish you to know that we will not take any part in his plans. Count Robert had this same concern, and sent us ahead to assure you of his friendship and to make this same pledge."

Alexios frowned and said, "The duke and I have battled before, and it cost me many good men and much treasure to drive him back whence he came. I do share a concern that he sees this expedition more as an opportunity to gain a land to rule — at my expense — than as a mission in service to the Son of God. Bohemond has never willingly served anyone, and Christ Himself will find he is a most reluctant and difficult vassal." The basileus smiled then, but it was a knowing and rueful smile.

Then he looked at us again, most directly. "When I commended and rewarded you two so long ago, I knew then I was repaying you for giving me something more valuable than gold. I was not wrong. That gold was far less precious than your loyalty. I thank you for it, and I want to repay you yet again." He paused and then said, "We are old friends, and I would cherish the opportunity to hear of your lives in the past decade. Please return to dine with me here tonight at sunset."

Of course, a request such as that could not be refused, nor had we any inclination to do so, for it is a rare honor. I knew the emperor had once extended it to Count Robert the Frisian, and so it must mean the emperor wanted to discuss with us something most important to him. So with a glance at each other, we assented. "Until later, then," Alexios said, and with a bow we took our leave.

✠✠✠

As we exited the throne room, we encountered a beautiful young lady of about fourteen years of age. I confess I did not recognize her, nor even pay much attention beyond noting her beauty. But she stopped dead as she saw me and said, "Godric?"

In that instant I realized who she was, and turning, I bowed and said, "The only person in Constantinople who ever called me 'Godric' is Sebastokratorissa Anna. How are you, my princess?"

She smiled at that, and said, "And Godric was the only man in this city that ever addressed me as 'Princess.' It *is* you!"

"In the flesh, Princess. I have returned to aid your father the basileus, only to find that you are no longer a pretty little girl, for you have grown into a most beautiful woman!"

She blushed and smiled at that, well-pleased with the compliment, for although acquainted with courtly speech from infancy, compliments paid so directly were clearly still a novelty.

"Thank you, Lord Godric. It is clear to me now that I was right to think you a mighty warrior, but wrong in thinking you a barbarian. I humbly apologize for ever doing so."

"Princess, you need never apologize. Deep inside me lives as wild a barbarian as ever was. But he's sealed in a bottle until summoned. I pray you never meet him."

She smiled at that, and said, "I think I have already met him, and liked him very much." And she was still smiling when, with an exchange of bows, we went our separate ways.

Jean grinned and said, "You, a bottled barbarian? Anselm has a lot to answer for, doesn't he?"

"Shut up!" I growled — and then grinned back. "Yes, he does!"

✠✠✠

We did dine with the emperor that evening, an excellent meal in a small dining room off the throne room. It was a quiet meal, just the three of us present. I say emperor, for that is what he was. But Alexios was always a soldier first and a general at heart, so we ate that night as military men. But of course, since he was also an emperor, we let him choose the conversation and spoke only in response to his questions, never enquiring except with respect to the topics he chose.

Of Jean, he enquired after life with Isabeau, whom he had met a decade before, even to the point of arranging their marriage, and of their flock of children. And when he learned I had served my king as sheriff, he pressed me about those duties, and asked me to tell the stories of defeating MacanFhirMhóir and OdinsØye.

"You know, Lord Godric, that Demetrius had showed me the little model of the siege engine you made when last here, and it seemed so ingenious that I had him build a succession of them. It took a number of tries to get all the members and joints sufficiently strong. But when we did, we found the machine to be tremendously more effective than any previous weapon in our arsenal. You have just told a similar tale of experimentation, test, trial and error that led to the engine that destroyed OdinsØye's stone tower. And it, too, was of a design based on your little model?"

I could see that he was intrigued, and perhaps inwardly a little concerned, to know that I had done the same as he and Demetrius had done. I am sure he wished to make sure I harbored no plan to use my counterweight tree-bucket against Constantinople. So I gave him every assurance I would not. After I did, he proposed sending Demetrius and some of his engines with us to aid in the recapture of Nicaea, Antioch and other fortified cities that the Seljuqs and Fatamids had wrested from him.

Alexios frowned. "There is just one major problem with doing that. If I allow men like Bohemond to enter Anatolia with a vast army *and* my capital siege weapons, I have nothing to constrain whatever ambitions they harbor but the pledges of fealty and self-restraint they make on their personal honor, assuming they have any."

Jean said, "Sire, you have one other. The other leaders, having made the same pledges, will be obligated to oppose plans that entangle them in personal schemes that would force them to violate their own pledges. And that is a powerful deterrent." I nodded my agreement.

Alexios nodded thoughtfully. After that insight, he enquired into the characters, virtues, and foibles of Count Robert of Flanders, Duke Robert of Normandy, and Count Stephen of Blois. I am sure he was seeking insights to better judge and deal with the many military leaders now enroute to his capital as they arrived.

Jean and I both gave glowing praise to Count Robert's character and honor, for we knew him well and regarded him highly. We were more reserved in our answers with regard to Normandy and Blois. We told him that Robert of Normandy was widely regarded as resourceful, and brave to the point of personal recklessness in battle, a great tactician. I related meeting Normandy four years earlier under a flag of truce between Kings Malcolm and Rufus as Duke Robert and Edward Ætheling tried to stop a war between their monarchs. During those discussions, Robert and I developed a mutual liking, which began when we discovered that we mutually hated his oh-so-repellent brother, King Rufus. And I related how I had served the Duke of Normandy for most of 1094 in his campaigns against his brother, King William Rufus of England to save his lands in Normandy. Of Stephen of Blois, whom we only knew since marching from Flanders, we were able to report that he was very affluent, and brought his great resources to the venture.

Unfortunately, about the others we could offer no more information, for we were among the first to reach Constantinople, and had not met any of them earlier elsewhere. And I have to say that once we did, we came to understand the basileus's misgivings.

✠✠✠

Much as planned and hoped, Count Robert reached Constantinople a month behind us, on February 25, 1097. It was good to rejoin our retinues, who had made the journey in our footsteps — thanks to the itinerary we had left them, and the route markers we erected — without mishap. Despite the difficult route and the winter weather, they had little illness and no serious injuries in the company. At my request, Father Anselm celebrated a Mass of thanksgiving for our safe and successful passage.

Upon the count's arrival, we sent word of it to the basileus, who invited Count Robert, as the son of his old friend the Frisian, to visit his court at the count's earliest convenience. And thanks to our advance mission of diplomacy, both sides knew what to expect and welcomed the meeting. After a day to recuperate and prepare for the meeting, Robert was ready. He asked us to accompany him, which we gladly did.

Alexios welcomed Robert warmly. "My dear friend, Count Robert, welcome! Welcome to our empire and our fair city. Your friends here, the barons . . ." he indicated Jean and me, " . . . have praised your martial skills, knightly virtues, and wise counsel. All of these bring to my mind your father, a truly great man, whose friendship meant so much to me. And the five hundred Flemish knights he recruited for me have been my most valuable shock troops, winning critical battle after battle. I was deeply saddened to learn of his passing, and that the Count Robert I had heard was coming here was not he. But I am delighted to meet the son he thought so much and spoke so well of, and I trust we will be just as great friends."

I noted that Alexios was wise enough not to ask for an oath of fealty, and that Count Robert was wise enough to volunteer it, saying, "My Lord Basileus, I thank you for your warm welcome, and report that it is my great honor to bear Father's warmest greetings to you, for you were among the men he loved most, and were in his final thoughts. He always hoped that we would meet on the same good terms he had with you. Now that has happened. I come today to offer you my oath of fealty and friendship."

From my foreknowledge of and familiarity with both Robert and Alexios, I could see the two men take measure of the other, and come to like what they saw. That mutual respect was the key to all that followed.

At the time, Robert's oath, and those of the other leaders that followed him, seemed just a formality; but they were not. They were the only remedy at Alexios's command that could constrain the ambitions of men leading great armies through his realm, armies he had come to realize were ten times larger and so much more formidable than his own. Never had the Pecheneg, Cuman, Seljuq, or Norman invaders posed as great a threat to his empire. And unless these men could be made to pledge fealty and friendship that respected his realm and his rule, he could never prevent them from overwhelming his army and dethroning him.

But now Count Robert had set an important precedent, and with his oath, had gone from being a threat to Alexios's crown to an ally in the recruitment of the oaths of the others. Alexios hoped to gather these oaths one by one, from each prince in turn, before they and their separate armies assembled, and the leaders realized the power they had over him. For it was only by leveraging their fealty to him and encouraging rivalry among them that Alexios might hope to control them somewhat, so as to regain his lost lands in Anatolia without losing the whole empire to one of these "saviors."

It was a dangerous game, but it was a game of necessity. And Alexios was far more skilled and experienced in Byzantine diplomacy and politics than any of his predecessors, or any of the Frankish princes. Indeed, he had to be, for now his kingdom and his very life depended solely upon these skills.

✠✠✠

Because of the special relationship we now had with the emperor, he allowed Count Robert's army to encamp with us along the length of the western wall. By doing so, I realized Alexios was protecting his capital with our men — placing an army of pledged allegiance on the only ground by which the city could be besieged. His recent conflict with Godfrey had showed Alexios how close he had come to conflict with and besiegement by the Lorraine army. But I knew Alexios always learned such lessons well, and took pains to never make the same mistake twice.

It was early March of 1097 now, and we still had two months to wait; Pope Urban's chosen representative, Papal Legate Ademar, had set the First of May as the date on which all the armies were to be assembled at Constantinople so as to enter Anatolia as a united force. No one but God Himself knew how many we would be by then. But we knew that since God Himself had ordained our mission, there were certain to be enough of us.

In the meanwhile, we put our men to work training with arms on open grounds west of our encampment. Hamish and I drilled them in different ways: in individual combat, as small units, and in large maneuvers. Jean and I had our knights and mounted men-at-arms armor up and battle each other, using first blunted and then sharp weapons. I put up silver pennies for archery prizes and gave a fair number of them to men who could put an arrow through a ring the size of a helmet's eye. Most of us wore Norman nasal helms, but a few knights we encountered wore helmets that completely enclosed the head, as Solomon's had a decade ago at Demoticho. I tried one, but found its visibility much restricted and the hammer of echoing battle noise inside it far too confusing. Besides, Seljuq archers could shoot as well as we did, so I concluded that a helm like that offered too little protection to counter the disadvantages it imposed on my vision and hearing in battle.

I also arranged to use Demetrius's siege engines, and I took my siege men to the practice grounds. I brought Sir Cedric and Hamish with me, as both had operated siege engines when we battled OdinsØye. Together, we created teams to operate the various machines, and as they did we assessed the skills of each. Demetrius came out on several occasions to judge our performance and helped us adjust the manning and skills on each team until we were getting an optimal performance by his experienced standards.

I particularly wanted to try his tree-bucket, and he graciously allowed us to do so. I had no difficulty hurling huge projectiles with accuracy, having already built and used an engine of my own, and I saw with some satisfaction that he was taking note of some of my innovations, such as sorting, weighing, and painting the projectiles in different colors that denoted their weight.

"Why do you do all that?" he asked.

"In my early experiments, I found that by recording the weights of my stones and the distances I threw each, I could choose a given weight for a specific distance or force of impact. And after I weighed and painted them, I could simply call for a stone of a given color. And once we found we could hit a chosen spot with a given color, the team can hit it again and again simply by reloading the same color. Even better, the color system works the same way for each machine, though each color may work differently from engine to engine — my tree-bucket can throw a red hundredweight three hundred yards, but my onager will only throw that same red stone

one hundred."

"Godric, that's ingenious!"

"I found that in battle, we don't have time to do otherwise. It saves lives to do all this in advance, and once we know what works, these teams will hit targets repeatedly with little direct supervision, letting me command several engines with a system of pennant signals."

Demetrius nodded his approval and appreciation.

I also wanted to see again and operate his full-scale siege tower. Again he allowed us to operate it under my direct leadership. The tower rose to a height of about fifty feet, able to overtop the highest walls in the empire, the curtain walls of Antioch, he told me. Inside it had five levels, connected by stout fixed ladders that allowed several men to ascend at once. On the lowest level, a capstan allowed eight to twelve men to propel the wheels on which the tower was mounted to drive the whole tower ahead over level ground. The front side had archers' slits on all levels. The second level had two winches, which lowered drawbridges at the third and fourth levels, allowing men to reach the top of a wall at either level. The fifth level was a fighting top, from which archers and crossbowmen could clear defenders from the top of the wall they were trying to capture.

I had already measured and sketched the details of a tower like this a decade earlier, when Demetrius first taught me the secrets and details of siege warfare. But this is the first time I had the chance to actually operate a tower, and I had a distinct feeling we would need plenty of them to recapture the fortified cities of the Holy Land.

So, for the next two months, I had my siege men study the operation of these machines, and formed several teams assigned to learn to operate each one. And since I had hired skilled carpenters and blacksmiths to become my siege men, I also had them study the construction details of each machine, to ensure that we could readily build our own versions. We would not get another chance like this, and the success of our entire campaign, if not our very lives, would depend on getting each of them built right.

We erected targets of sailcloth held up by poles, each painted with a picture of an enemy onager —these would pose the greatest threat to our own engines and towers — or a fortress gate. We battered them with our projectiles, then re-erected them and attacked them again. We similarly built a mock section of curtain wall with poles and sailcloth and attacked it again and again with the siege tower, until each tower team could successfully manage the task.

Demetrius told us we needed to be able to fill the enemy's moats and trenches, and clear obstacles from the path of the siege tower, ere we would ever be able to reach his walls. So we dug trenches and strew boulders in the tower's path, and then filled and cleared them again while under attack by archers, borrowed from Count Robert to shoot with blunted arrows every sapper who foolishly gave them a target as he worked. After the sappers complained of their many painful bruises, we formed two-man teams, one man protecting the both of them with a mantlet as his mate dug, and switching when the digger began to flag.

Demetrius was a frequent visitor, appearing to see how we got on and offer advice where we needed it. Count Robert and his barons also came out of curiosity, drawn by the strange reports they got from the archer captains. Soon we had a regular crowd of noble onlookers — interested knights and squires, mostly — and our school expanded as Count Robert sent other units of men to learn from us. Competitions quickly sprang up among the rival teams and the training became more like war itself, until we had to remind them that we would soon face a real enemy to destroy rather than each other. Still, the training was a useful foretaste of the conflict to come, and undoubtedly saved the lives of some.

It was during this time that I began hearing the various weapons crews singing snatches of Cedric's musical nightmare while they worked — the tune he called *The Siege Master's Song*. Damnation! I thought we had left it behind in Normandy; but here it was again. I could only shake my head ruefully. I knew it would now follow us all the long hard way to Jerusalem.

✠✠✠

It was mid-March when to our camp came a Benedictine monk searching for me, bearing a most unusual gift — a letter from my beloved wife, Aleine. She had written it six months earlier and consigned it to the Benedictines for delivery. The order did so, passing letters from monastery to monastery in the direction of the recipient, along with monastic documents, in return for donations to support their charitable works of mercy. The young monk was finally fulfilling their pledge to deliver it to me.

In it, along with many declarations of love and the news that all at home — Sir Cormac, Carrick, Alice, and Aleine herself — were (as of then) in good health, she had one important piece of startling news: she was pregnant again. Moreover, the very midwife who had delivered her, now an old woman but a wise one who had delivered many children, said she believed that Aleine was carrying twins!

Nine months had passed since I left home. And as I realized that, I was at once both overjoyed and deeply concerned for her, for here was I, a thousand leagues away, and she was due to deliver a child or two at any time — indeed, she might have already done so! Did she and her — our — children survive that ordeal? Were they well?

There was no way to know until another letter found me. All I could do was wonder, worry, and pray — especially pray.

Jean consoled me. "Godric, I know you are so worried because you deeply love your Aleine. But you need to remember that her parents are there to aid her, she has an experienced midwife, and you already provided them a fine home and the wherewithal for the best possible care. What you can do now is to pray for the wellbeing of Aleine and your children. Oh, and you might send her a letter of love in return."

So I went to Father Anselm, poured out my fears, and asked for his prayers. Always understanding, he pledged to include them in his daily Mass until we knew for certain. And then I sat down and arduously wrote Aleine a letter. For once, I could not bring myself to dictate to Edward the contents of my heart.

✠✠✠

Gainfully employed as we were in the art and business of war, time flew by. Winter weather gave way to that of spring, and soon summer was finally nigh.

Unfortunately, I was unaware of these things for much of that time, for soon after Aleine's letter I was struck down one night after supper by such intense pain in my stomach and muscles that, had I been able, I would have ended the misery by my own hand. But fortunately, I was too enfeebled to do it, and so could only endure the intense suffering that followed.

It was Father Anselm who saved my life that night, and despite all the fun Jean and I had during our first pilgrimage ridiculing the good priest's efforts to learn all the secrets of medicinal alchemy from the unbelieving wise men of Jerusalem, it was that very wisdom he called upon to save me.

Confronted by my sudden and desperate illness, Anselm concluded that, as no other who ate with me had become ill, and my symptoms were unlike any illness in our company, I must have been poisoned. By whom and how would have to wait — for the time being, it was only with what that mattered. My symptoms confused him; but he remembered that several kinds of toadstool[16] — plentiful around us and most dangerous if added uncooked to food — would account for them, so he treated me accordingly.

I will not go through all of his efforts, for truly I do not know all he did. I do vaguely recall bleedings to rebalance my humors, and being forced to swallow several disgusting concoctions, much worse than his infamous wine-and-horse-piss remedy for blood loss, most of them tasting like gruel of charcoal. I do remember that he muttered, "Mock my medicinal studies, would you? Swallow this!" — and then incurring endless vomiting. I recall that I was struck too with chills ever so much worse than those of fording mountain streams of melt-water during my first pilgrimage.

Anselm said later it was a close thing. Had I eaten more of whatever had poisoned me, or been of less robust constitution, I would never have survived; but by God's will I lived, if only because I would be needed to accomplish His great commission to reclaim Jerusalem.

---

[16] Amanita muscaria, commonly called fly agaric or fly amanita, is a hallucinogenic mushroom that induces shaking chills without also causing fever. Food poisoning from several bacteria like salmonella will do the same. The false morel Gyromitra esculenta contains gyromitrin, a toxin metabolized into toxic monomethylhydrazine, which acts on the central nervous system. Poisoning by G. esculenta produces nausea, stomach cramps, and diarrhea, and when severe, can cause convulsions, jaundice, coma or death.

My memories of the next several weeks are poor, for I slept much of them as my wracked body recovered. I know I was tormented by strange visions and horrible dreams, some so odd that I am sure I toured Hell while I slept and sometimes even while awake.

My assailant and his poison went undiscovered, but Emperor Alexios soon came to hear of it, and sent his personal physicians to attend to me. They found Anselm had already done all that was both wise and needful, and that they could not improve on his treatments.

I do have one vivid memory from the night that illness struck me down. I remember awakening in the middle of that night, in bed in my dimly lit tent. I was freezing, shaking violently with chills, and shivering from a cold deeper than even Death itself could bring. And I was not alone.

In my bed there was another person — like me, completely naked, and clinging to me, trying to warm me and ease my shivering. In the dim light I could see that it was my clerk, Edward. Upsetting as that was, the real shock came a moment later when I realized that Edward was, in fact, a woman.

✠✠✠

The triple walls of Constantinople.

# FIVE

✠✠✠

A kind of horror and confusion swept through me then, for although I was completely helpless, my mind still worked well enough to feel a strong sense of revulsion in finding myself in intimate contact with another man, only to be completely confused a moment later by the very distinct realization that his body lacked all the masculine parts but had all the feminine ones.

I must have gasped and reacted, then, and in doing so, I awakened him/her, who said, "You live! Thank God! We feared we would lose you."

Through chattering teeth, I said, "*Who* are you? *What* are you? Why are you in my bed?"

"Do you not recognize your clerk, Edward? I see I must confess, for as you have just realized, I am not really he, I am she, and my name is not Edward — it is Edith. As for why I am in your bed, it is to repay an old debt. Long ago you saved my life twice. Tonight, I am trying to save yours in return."

Confusion wracked my mind. I knew no woman named Edith, nor had I ever saved any woman by that name. Well, I had — long ago, when a squire. But that was a little girl, Princess Edith, eldest daughter of good King Malcolm. And with that thought, I suddenly realized why Edward had always seemed so familiar, yet different.

I tried again to regain some understanding. "Edith . . . Princess Edith, my little companion on the ride to Romsey? Is it you?"

"It is — in the flesh — literally," she said with a little giggle.

That little girl had grown to womanhood in the past decade, only to mascarade for months at my elbow as a young man and my clerk. I felt completely confused and, suddenly, very stupid.

"Why are you here?"

"Anselm says you needed bodily warmth. And as I was the only one here both willing and suited to perform that service, here I am."

"Does Anselm know you're a — a — woman?"

"He does. But in this circumstance, he reluctantly agreed I was a more suitable source of warmth than Colin — after I insisted."

As the thought sunk in, I had to agree. "Remind me to thank him. But why are you *here*, in a camp full of soldiers headed to recapture Jerusalem, instead of being at home where you belong?"

"And where *do* I belong, Baron? A dispossessed princess, orphaned by her enemies, even as they try to control or seize our homeland by manipulating conflicts over the crown, setting my brothers the one against another? Should I truly be there?"

I was silent as she went on, all the while clinging to me tightly and rubbing life into my frozen limbs.

Through all this, I still shivered uncontrollably, totally helpless and incapable of movement. Edith rubbed my chest and limbs, her form tightly pressed against me. I should have enjoyed it, but I confess I could feel little but the icy grave.

"What I first told you as Edward was all true — well, with the one undisclosed exception. I was raised in a convent and there educated, as you know. I was pressed to take vows, but had no wish to do so. And I do want to see Holy Jerusalem. I did flee to Dunfermline in disguise so that they would not retake me. And when I heard of your enterprise, I did walk all night to ask if I might join. I knew you would refuse a woman — especially after you discovered she was a Scottish princess. But you thought me suitable to come with you as Edward, and I have earned my way — have I not?"

I frowned. "Yes, Edward has served me well. But I cannot allow my king's daughter to be subjected to the dangers that lie ahead . . ." I wanted to continue the argument, but I was so confused, disoriented, and completely exhausted that instead I just faded then, back into the blackness of my icy grave.

✠✠✠

In the days that followed, I wandered back and forth between two worlds — one a realm of the strangest dreams, and the other, more familiar one, in which Anselm, Edward . . . errr . . . Edith, or my squire Colin often hovered over me.

A week later, I was much recovered and able to leave my bed, though I could not go far, weakened as I was. Anselm had me eating little more than gruel and small beer. But I refused to remain an invalid, and began to walk about my camp, as far each day as I could. By the end of three weeks, my insides were better and my diet back to camp food. I began to train again, to rebuild my lost strength. By early April I was back to my old self, more or less.

In the meantime, I learned that Colin and Anselm had discovered

Edith's secret months earlier, Colin first — I know not how, being unwilling to ask. Edith, using charm and guile to prey on Colin's sense of chivalry, had managed to convince him to keep her secret. And when Anselm began to suspect, Edith disclosed her secret to him in the confidentiality of the confessional, which bound Anselm to keep it as well. Thereafter, the two had acted to protect her from harm by others and, most especially, from discovery by me. But when I fell deathly ill, Edith was determined to see me saved, and she did most of my nursing under Anselm's medical direction.

Now, her secret was known, but still only to the four of us. And for her continued safety, I became a member of her conspiracy. Later, Jean and his squire, Henri, joined us as well.

I was under no illusions that concealing her womanhood would lessen the risks to her — she was, after all, not the only woman in the army, for in the past several weeks many of the female survivors of the People's Army had attached themselves to ours, performing sundry services as their means of survival. No, it was because she was a royal princess of Alba, and were her true status known, she would be at great risk of kidnap for ransom.

There was no safe way to send her back a thousand leagues now, and no way she could be left here in Constantinople without disclosing her identity. Moreover, headstrong as she had proven herself to be, she might just attach herself to another contingent headed for Jerusalem. At least I could and would do all I could to keep her safe, and damnation, she already knew that. So it was best, I concluded, to have her continue in male disguise as my clerk than risk exposing her identity. If need be, I could explain her disguise and presence with the reluctant untruth that she was my mistress. But I could never protect her once it became known that she was in truth an adventuring princess.

And so this is how Princess Edith vanished from the face of the earth for four entire years — 1096 to 1100 AD. There is no record of her being anywhere in those years, and this is why no one knows anything of where she was all that long time[17]. Only a few ever knew that she came with me to recapture Jerusalem, and of the few who did know, only I still live who can reveal it.

✠✠✠

It was in early April that the vanguard of a great army approached the city of Constantinople, causing much alarm inside and outside the city until its many banners, each bearing a red cross on a white tableau to denote that it was borne by an army of pilgrims like ours, were visible.

The knight who was captain of the vanguard, Robert of Anse, came among us to gather news from us to convey to his lord. And from him we learned that Duke Bohemond, the Prince of Taranto, had finally reached Constantinople, and now sought to pay homage to the Basileus Alexios.

He told us that with Lord Bohemond came his nephew, Tancred, son of Marchisus, and many other Normans of Italy. When we asked if they had, as rumored, destroyed a city of heretics, Sir Robert affirmed that it was true.

"And in consequence, as we were crossing the River Vardar a few days prior to reaching Thessaloniki, the forces marching at the rear of our column, men of the Count of Roscignolo and his brothers, were attacked by the emperor's Pecheneg and Turcopole

---

[17] True! Edith disappeared from history following her parents' deaths, and did not reappear until 1100 AD when, with her marriage to King Henry I, youngest brother of Duke Robert and King William Rufus, she became Queen Matilda of England. Did she go on Crusade to Jerusalem? Perhaps—no one knows!

mercenaries in retaliation before they could cross. But Tancred, the Duke's nephew, led two thousand men-at-arms back across the river to mount a successful counterattack. After a furious assault they broke up the attack and rescued the count's men.

Shaking his head, he went on. "By agreeing to set the mercenary prisoners they captured free, Lord Bohemond finally obtained in return the services of two of the emperor's corpalatii,[18] who, together with our envoys, acted to intercede ahead of us to prevent further attacks and obtain markets from the locals so that we could feed our army without having to plunder our way the balance of the journey here. When Tancred's men did so anyway at one town, Bohemond was enraged, and forced them to return all the animals they stole. So we've finally managed to reach this city without further bloodshed on either side, as a result." And just in time, as it were, for the Feast of Easter, which in the year 1097 was on April 5, was upon us.

By then, I was on my feet again and largely recovered, although my meals were not, for my insides were still far too sensitive to the pallid collection of gruel and barley stews I ingested. But my strength had returned and I spent my days on the training grounds, pushing myself back to health by running, lifting, and in one-on-one and one-against-two sword drills with Jean and Colin.

I was keen to discover who had poisoned me, for now a second mysterious attempt had been made on my life, and my present assailant was still at large and undiscovered, free to try again and unlikely to fail a second time. But questioning all who had been involving in my near-fatal meal revealed nothing, for our meals were routinely cooked in a common area with servants and squires

---

[18] The best translation I could find for *corpalatii* was *heart of the palace*, meaning, I think, the emperor's close confidants, acting here as sureties, able to act for the emperor to guarantee Bohemond's further safe passage.

coming and going, so it would have been easy for someone to pour a poison into my food or drink once they knew which trencher or cup was mine. So those were the first things we changed: cooking for ourselves, away from the camp kitchen, keeping careful watch over our food stores, and noting who came and went in our area.

And I wore armor always from then on, my best chainmail over my jack of plate, despite the weight and discomfort, although I had done so much of the time for a decade, and so was used to it. And soon the demands of war would require continual wear anyway.

A few days after Robert of Anse visited us, Count Robert summoned all the barons and other lords leading contingents in his army to a council, at which we met Duke Bohemond and his nephew, Tancred. Having heard much about these two, I admit that I was most curious, and that having done so, my earlier prejudices were substantiated.

Bohemond was taller than any man I had ever met or seen. At six feet, I am taller than most, but he was at least a half-foot taller than me. His chest and shoulders were a bit bigger than mine, his hips and loins nearly as narrow. He was lean, with much muscle, little fat, and no belly. Like many of the Danes at home in Alba, his eyes were bright blue, his hair flaxen yellow, and his skin white, except that his face was tanned by exposure to a reddish hue. Unlike most knights, his hair was cropped to the ears and he wore no beard, but shaved his face clean of all hair but eyebrows. His armor was of the best manufacture, his clothes finely made, and his weapons set with gold wire chasing and jewels.

When he spoke, it was clear to all that he was intelligent, educated and cunning; and he had a fascinating air of charm, for the man was quite charismatic. But he also had about him an aura of malice and menace, one that made it clear that while God may have made him to become a king, he would likely be a ruler more brutal than beloved.

**Duke Bohemond of Apulia, prince of the First Crusade.**

His nephew, Tancred, was much like him in many ways, yet very different in others. He looked like his uncle in shape and coloring, but he was not so large — a bit smaller than me. He was younger, too, for Bohemond was twice Tancred's twenty years. The nephew was as handsome, intelligent, bold, courageous, and driven as his uncle, but he lacked Bohemond's airs of charm and command, yet radiated even more sinister cunning, malice, and menace. Tancred was a man you wanted beside you in battle, but he was certainly not a man you would entrust with your wife or your throne.

Count Robert introduced all of us lesser counts and barons to the duke, and he introduced his nobles in turn. They were in general a fine body of warriors, and I sensed that the Seljuqs stood no chance in battle against such men. When it was our turn, Count Robert informed all that Baron Jean and I had traveled and scouted the lands ahead of us, had won fame and success in great battles here, had encountered our imminent enemies before, and had seen the very fortresses that lay ahead of us. Robert also declared that I had unique experience and special skills with the siege machines we would need to conquer the Holy Land, and that drew Bohemond's interest to me as a rabbit draws a falcon's.

Bohemond's gaze was direct and steady on me as he said, "Baron, I will want to talk more with you about what lies ahead, both from your experience as a scout and a siege master, for I will clearly need both in order to win the campaign ahead. And you can teach us much."

I, not we. Bohemond had already decided he would lead our combined armies, regardless of what we thought about it, and had not even bothered to consult Count Robert about it. The count was as surprised by that as we were. Only Tancred was not.

And with that, something else became clear: Bohemond may have taken the cross as we had, but he was not like the rest of us. Even as he met the nobles commanding elements of Count Robert's army, the duke's eyes pierced yours while he decided whether you were going to be his asset or his enemy, and then they swept on, ever restless to discover his next asset or threat. And throughout that meeting, his eyes never stopped roaming; they were always searching for something he lacked. I knew then that someday and somewhere, Bohemond would become a king. But I also knew that there would never be enough for him, and that I wouldn't want to be his subject.

As for Tancred, his gaze locked on to me, and rarely left. I put it down to curiosity at first, but there was nothing particularly friendly in them, and when his gaze became annoying, I met his look and did not break the eye contact, even by blinking, staring sternly back at him. His look registered slight surprise at that, followed by puzzlement, and then cunning menace, before he finally broke the gaze as his uncle addressed him. And I realized that somehow I had made an enemy, for after that day he would never directly look at me again. I, in turn, never turned my back on him.

✠✠✠

As I recovered and we prepared for our campaign, news of other events came to us. Following his success with Count Robert, the Emperor Alexios was keen to obtain oaths of fealty from the other princes. Duke Bohemond was just as keen to take the oath, and did so on Easter Day. But before he did so, he asked Alexios for two concessions in return: first, that the emperor recognize him as the commander of the assembled armies, and second, when we won back the major cities of the eastern empires, that he become king, under the emperor of course, of Antioch and its surrounding lands.

We heard of these demands through Tatikios, who had heard of the attempt on my life and came to see how I was getting on. According to him, the emperor demurred on both, allowing that he had no objection to either, but that the other princes probably would and that they deserved to air their views before either decision was made. But Bohemond later held that only the basileus's answer mattered, and that Alexios had granted him both requests.

These events then prompted consternation and fury among the other princes, in particular Duke Godfrey, who thought such presumption and self-promotion demeaned the entire pilgrimage, turning it from military service for the Son of God into a mercenary campaign of conquest to crown Bohemond instead. Godfrey himself had given his oath three days earlier on the second day of April, Holy Thursday, without request for either concession or compensation. As for me, it only cemented my opinion that Bohemond took the cross in order to gain a kingdom he could win by no other means.

We heard that Tancred would brook no word against his uncle, and offered to meet in single combat any who opposed Bohemond's leadership. And while his courage was never in doubt, most knights thought there was an aspect to Tancred that was deranged, that his lust for power and blood violated his sworn vows as a knight. Fortunately we could just ignore him, and we did, which bothered Tancred even more.

✠✠✠

Because we were friends of emperor's envoys and their messengers, they often stopped in our camp for a meal or for some of Anselm's latest remedy, which had gained wide reputation and general favor under its nickname, "Anselm's holy water." Over the next few weeks they told us that Duke Robert of Normandy and his cousin, Count Stephen of Blois, had finally crossed the Tyrrhenian Sea beginning on April 5, Easter Sunday, hoping it would bring them good fortune. But one of the largest ships in their fleet broke up just off Bari while setting sail, in the view of all onshore. Four hundred men were lost, along with their horses, supplies, and treasure. Many still onshore waiting to cross promptly abandoned the pilgrimage and headed for home. But the rest crossed without incident or further loss of life.

Once they were all finally ashore, Duke Robert and Count Stephen immediately marched to join us. Meanwhile, another army from southern France, led by Count Raymond d'Aguiliers of Toulouse, but more commonly called Raymond of St-Gilles, had departed France in December and by marching an entirely overland route had reached Roussa on April 12.

✠✠✠

Eager to recover my former health, I put all my energies in building up my physical strength and in preparing my siege-men for the ordeals I knew we faced just ahead. I set about buying timber for engines and withes for mantlets because we would need much of both. I found I could get it transported by ship to Helenopolis and collect it there easier than hauling it overland to the same point. So I sent word to all the harbors of Constantinople that I had a cargo for Thanasi Lamphros, on whose ship Jean and I had escaped Jerusalem a decade earlier. I trusted the chandlers and tavern keepers would so advise him on his next port call.

Meanwhile, as the armies gathered more military councils were held, and I attended all I could. Alas, we had no grand strategy to follow, nor did we create one. Each great prince commanding an army seemed to have his own notions of what we should do and generally refused to defer to any other, so only the plans that offered the victors promise of a rich sacking met with widespread favor. Nicaea, Antioch, and Jerusalem were certainly on this list.

Edessa, Tripoli, Tyre, and others were discussed with split opinions.

Damascus they largely dismissed — too much effort for any worthwhile reward. Too bad, really, for as we learned much later to our great dismay, had we taken Damascus when we had the chance, we could have kept the damned Islamites divided and destroyed them piecemeal, as thoroughly as were the Pechenegs. Our Savior's kingdom on earth would have then been safe from them forever.

✠✠✠

Riding into our camp about this time on a tired old donkey came Peter of Amiens, better known to all as Peter the Hermit, the old soldier-turned-preacher who had led his Peoples' Army across all Europe to destruction outside Helenopolis. He was elderly, lugubrious, and short — or bent by age to appear so. He was also very lean, for they said he ate only fish and wine, no bread, fruit, or meat. He was browned by sun and dirt, for he refused to wash himself or his clothes, always wearing the same sackcloth robe and filthy cloak. I found from experience that when he preached, it was best to be upwind of him, for a swirl of the breeze, if you were close, would make your eyes water and insides gag.

"Brave brothers, warriors of Christ! I salute you! Thank you for answering both my prayers and this, my call to crusade. And let us all thank God that when I preached this our holy mission, His Holiness, Pope Urban, heeded my words and picked them up, spreading them wide and far, so that all of you would hear and so bravely answer my call, marching to war with me upon the unholy disbelievers who infest Holy Jerusalem and spread their murderous disbelief ever farther. Now I bid you welcome to my new army, an Army of God, an army truly blessed by Him to free our sacred sites and cleanse them of their idols and evil. Welcome! Come forward, each and every one, that I might bless you as well!" And waving a rustic cross of lashed sticks, Peter set about blessing all he saw.

**Peter the Hermit preaching the Crusade.**

I, who had known truly holy men like my mentor, Father Thomas, and the fine Benedictines of the abbey in Dunfermline, thought this man at the time a shabby mascarade, a dirty opportunist who chased self-importance guised as a holy hermit, indeed, some kind of holy warrior-monk. And my opinion of him never rose. But others among us — most of our common folk, and many of the nobles — accepted him as a truly holy man who had led the pope to discover the truth, and launch the call to crusade. Later, I am told Abbott Guibert of Nogent said that Peter was "semi-divine both in actions and words." Emperor Alexios himself was anxious to meet him, and received him, dirty as he was, in his splendid court. And Peter was with and among us ever after, exhorting us onward, and taking credit for every victory and miracle, even as we cut our wide and blood-drenched path into the very Sepulcher of Our Lord.

✠✠✠

The next army to join us, that of the Count of Toulouse, Raymond of St-Gilles, finally reached the great capital on April 26. With their arrival, we lost no more time. Count Robert's forces, with Jean's and mine among them, were still camped outside the western walls at the emperor's request, protecting it from a surprise siege by any army pretending to come to crusade in order to take the city and throne by guile. But the fair weather to campaign was already nigh — indeed, as one who had already known the heat we were to feel in the months ahead, I thought we had waited too long, setting our season for campaigning on weather in France rather than that of Anatolia — but the great princes would hardly listen to each other, much less to me. So the march to Nicaea would begin on the First of May, no matter what transpired.

Raymond did not tarry. After one day of rest, he ordered his army to cross the Bosporus beginning on April 28. Indeed, Raymond had already heard of the oaths the basileus was requiring, and for his own reasons, sought ways to avoid doing so. When the emperor sent him a summons to attend him at court, Raymond made an effort to instead cross the strait, which greatly angered the emperor, who threatened in turn to cut off all supplies to all the armies.

Knowing that would lead to disaster for us all, the other princes who had taken the requested oaths turned to Count Robert, the only man who knew Raymond at all well, to go to St-Gilles and implore him to change his mind.

Robert asked Jean and I to go along, for he thought our experience, both with the country ahead and in dealing with the basileus, might help him change Raymond's mind.

At fifty-six years of age, the Count of Toulouse ought to have been much too old for this campaign, but he possessed a strong physique and a stronger character, one much hardened by a life filled with strife and conflict. Even more developed was his aura of authority, for he was long accustomed to complete command. And although he was vastly wealthy in land and coin, a man who carried with him an enormous treasury, he was rather plainly garbed, his marks of wealth worn to identify him as a commander rather than to impress onlookers.

St-Gilles received us cordially, although I am certain he suspected our reason for coming as he did so. "Welcome, my lords! What brings you to my humble encampment when there is still so much to do?"

Now both Alexios and Robert knew that Bohemond and St-Gilles had battled each other previously in word and deed, that there was no love between them, and that this enmity potentially made Raymond and Alexios need each other as allies. So Count Robert wasted no time.

**Raymond St-Gilles, Count of Toulouse, prince of the First Crusade.**

"My lord, these barons . . ." he indicated Jean and me, ". . . are long acquainted with the basileus, and so know his mind and heart. They tell me Alexios fears that your mutual enemy, Duke Bohemond, would like to use the present circumstances and the proximity of his army to Constantinople in order to seize the throne. He has devised his demand for all the leaders of armies to swear an oath of fealty to him, in return for supplies of food as we campaign and any military support we might need, as a way of binding Bohemond in chains of honor. But for this to succeed, he needs all the great princes to take that oath. Now all have done so but you. Will you do so also?"

Raymond compressed his lips to a white line and gave a hard frown. "I am a Peer of France, a virtual king in my own land. The King of France himself is but my equal, one to whom I owe only lip service, not true fealty. I have no wish to be subordinate to any man, least of all to a monarch who now threatens denying food and support to the military mission he begged us to send him. I cannot see giving fealty to such a man."

I am sure Count Robert understood; I certainly could. It might have ended there, but then Robert said, "My lord, you may not have heard, but Duke Bohemond asked for supreme command over our armies, and for the kingdom of Antioch in return for his oath. If you do not take it, he will gain advantage over you in all councils, even though you command the largest army."

At that, Raymond swore. "That jumped-up Norman bastard did that? What incredible gall! I certainly did not bring all these men, all this treasure, across all Europe just to advance his personal ambitions! This campaign is about rescuing Christendom from unholy mongrels and taking back our holy shrines, not building monuments of empire for greedy men!"

He paced around his headquarters tent then, idly pounding one fist into the other as he thought, then with a sudden decision he said, "I will not give my fealty to a monarch who does not rule my country. But here is what I will do: I will give Alexios my oath of alliance that I will not attack him or his cities, nor seize any portion of his realm, and I will ally with him against any that do, particularly Bohemond, if they should. And this oath will be freely given and everlasting with one condition: that if the emperor should then withdraw the supplies and support he has promised us, the oath is broken and I owe him naught more." And he gave the three of us a hard look, the look a man gives when he has made a hated concession he knows he must. "Will that do?"

The count looked at us, and after conferring among us for a moment, we replied with a nod. "That will do!"

And with that Count Robert brought peace and conciliation between Alexios and St-Gilles, two stubborn men, both born to be generals and rulers, who came to respect and like each other well. Indeed, Alexios invited St-Gilles to stay in the palace with him, an invitation to which Raymond gladly assented. And he then spent a fortnight there, as the bond grew between two friends, until the demands of his army at the gates of Nicaea wrenched him away.

And so it was that Alexios managed, by strategy and guile, to bind us all with chains of honor, to do his will and win back his empire, using charm and treasure to achieve what he could not do by force.

✠✠✠

Among the first to Constantinople, we were ironically now among the last to cross the Bosporus and enter Anatolia before the May 1 marching date. As we broke camp and readied our contingents, one of the emperor's messengers stopped to tell us that the army of Duke Robert and Count Stephen had just reached Thessaloniki days before, on April 26.

Shaking his head, Jean said to Count Robert, "They should have had the courage to cross with you. Now I wonder if they will ever join us. I'll wager we will be in Jerusalem a full month before they catch us!"

The count smiled and said, "That's the trouble — wagers! It was always hard to get Robert out of bed. Too often, in his cups of an evening, he'll bet all of his clothes on a stupid wager, lose, and then have nothing to wear in the morning, unless his squire had managed to hide some."

But Jean was half-right. We were in Anatolia for two weeks, besieging Nicaea — to small effect, for lack of their men — before Duke Robert and Count Stephen finally brought up their army to complete a full encirclement of city by land, and cut off resupply and reinforcement by that route.

✠✠✠

On the twenty-ninth, the day before I was to cross the strait with my men, I was in great consternation trying to find another ship to transport my cargo of timber and other siege stores to Helenopolis when Master Thanasi Lamphros finally sent word — he had at last received my message and was waiting at the quay I had named to load it. I said a prayer of thanks to St. Peter for his assistance and rode to meet him.

Like me, he was a decade older, but he still looked as I remembered, unchanged by the years — skin and hair still bronzed by strong sun, new wrinkles at the corners of his eyes from squinting at coastlines hidden in haze. He was a good captain, one I had trusted once already with my life, so I knew I would find no better one now. His fee was fair, so we agreed on it, and I summoned my men to help his crew load our cargo, under guard nearby.

By day's end, the timber and other stores were aboard, quickly loaded by our combined crews. We agreed to meet at Helenopolis on May 6, the date I expected to reach that town marching overland. He would await us at anchor if we were delayed.

The following day we crossed the strait without incident. Other than Duke Robert's army, still marching eastward but far to the west, our vast army, one beyond actual counting but numbering then perhaps one-third million souls — was across. Europe and Christendom lay behind us. Anatolia, Syria, and the Holy Land — and the pride of unbelieving Islam — stood before us. But not much longer, I prayed.

At long last, our great commission — that which some now call the First, or Great, Crusade — had begun. It would be three years and more before ever I returned. Some of those who came with me stayed behind, holding on to what much blood and ten times as much sweat had finally won. Many more remain there as well, buried where they fell, until Our Savior Himself raises them up from the hot, dry sand.

✠✠✠

**Four princes of the First Crusade.**

# SIX

✠✠✠

It was the first day of May, 1097, when we began our march, leaving the Strait of Bosporus and heading into the unknown of Anatolia. I say *unknown*, not because I did not know these lands — for I had ridden this way a decade before — but because, this time, unknown dangers lay in wait for us.

We were headed for Nicaea, the fortified city that controlled the north-south route between the empire's frontier and the cities of the Holy Land. Alexios was most anxious to recover this city, which had been wrested away by the Turks just sixteen years earlier, and which had long been used as the closest fortified base from which to threaten Constantinople. The princes cared little about this, but concluded that it would be necessary to hold the city to keep our lines of communication and supply safe as we proceeded south.

Once again, Jean and I rode in the van, traveling the old Roman road along the coast to Nicomedia. Jean commanded a small army of scouts and spies who reconnoitered the route ahead for any signs of the accursed Seljuqs. I led a force of three thousand men who would serve the army as woodsmen and road builders. It was our task, where the road was too narrow or rough to accommodate thousands of wagons, tens of thousands of horses, and hundreds of thousands of men, to cut back trees and widen the road, clear obstacles, fill the washouts, improve crossings over or around ravines, and mark the route with signs for the many who would follow.

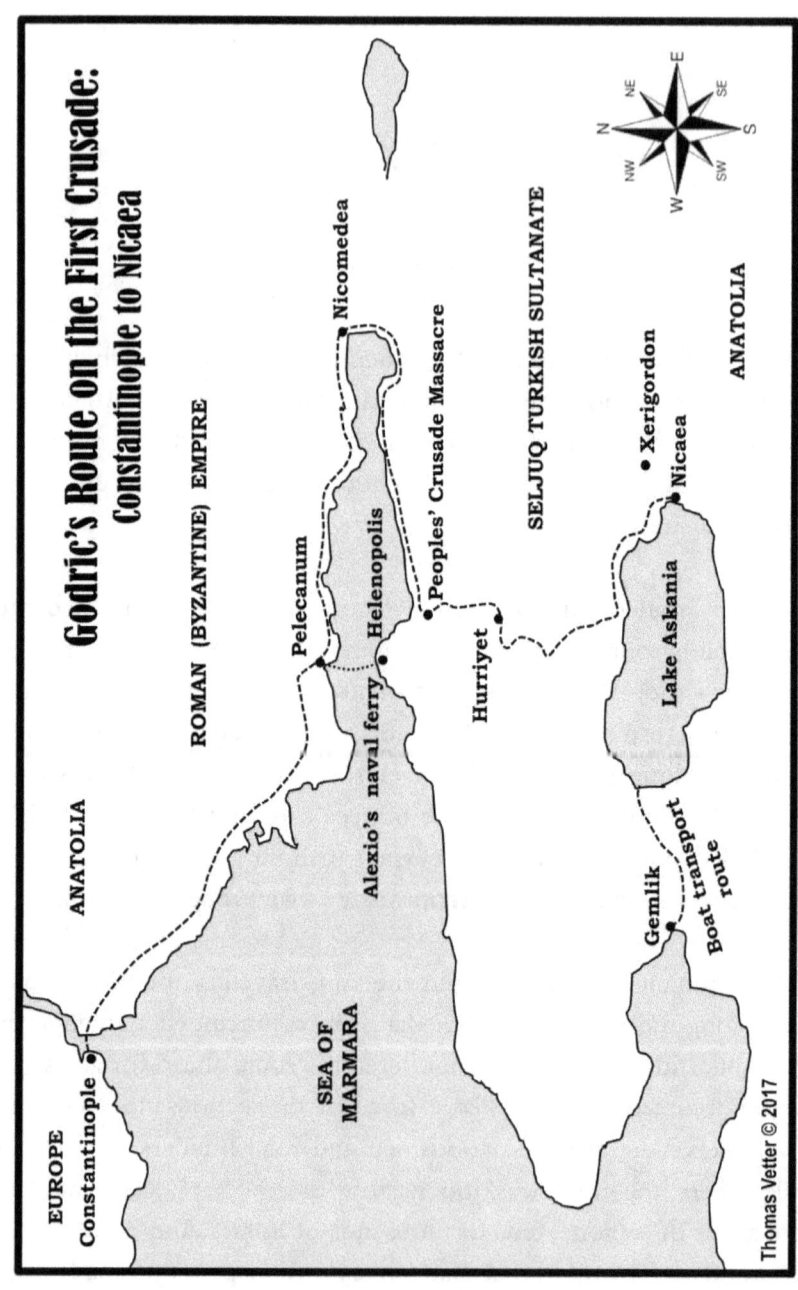

Godric's route on the First Crusade: Constantinople to Nicaea.

It was not by accident that we were chosen to lead these units. The council of princes who had led the armies — Godfrey, Bohemond, Raymond, Robert of Flanders, their lieutenants, and the lesser nobles like Jean and me — had met to confer before we marched, to discover who had experience with scouting and engineering matters, and to choose men to lead our march. After Count Robert named us and described our experience, no other names were offered, so our appointments were unanimous.

Not that either of us had any objections. I wanted to make sure I could get my wagons to Nicaea, and what better way was there than to command the men who would fix the roads we must travel?

But initially there was little to do. The coastal region was held by the emperor as far as Nicomedia, so we encountered no Seljuqs. And the Roman road was wide and sound still, a thousand years since it had been first built. So we made a good six leagues each day, reaching Nicomedia on the third.

But from there on we found the road too narrow to accommodate the army that followed us, so our real work began. I call them roads, but they were hardly that. In reality, they were little more than rough paths through woodlands and mountain valleys just big enough for perhaps two horses to walk abreast. Romans had built roads here too, but they had not been maintained by the Turks, and time and nature had wrecked much of their work.

So, as the scouts reported that the way ahead clear of Turks, I assigned men to clear a lane sufficient for five mounted men riding abreast, or two heavily laden wagons to pass side-by-side. To do this we cut trees, rolled aside logs and boulders, and filled holes and ditches that could break a wheel with logs, brush, and earth. We did all this because we could spare little time to free wagons stuck in the road, and even less to repair broken wagons. Just one such incident would bottleneck the march and open a gap in the column that our enemy could exploit.

As we went, we erected or carved into trees cross-shaped markers to indicate the route, arrows at forks to point out the route to take, and mile markers to denote the distance along the route. According to the emperor's scouts with us, it was forty miles between Helenopolis and Nicaea, so as we went, we marked out the miles from each end.

You might think all this road-building slowed our march, and to a small degree it did. But I used rolling assignments, setting a pair of men to clear a single tree; when they finished, they returned to the fore to take on another. With three thousand men working in front, trees fell aside continuously, almost as fast as men could march. The foremost men cut the trees. Behind them, men levered the stumps out of the roadway as others behind *them* filled the holes with earth and brush, and all moved ahead.

And as my little unit went forward, they left no impediments behind that would slow the bulk of the army. Horses walked and men marched without struggle, packing down the soil as they did so that the wagons behind them rolled readily. And at a steady pace behind us came a quarter-million men at least, perhaps even a third-million or yet more — all following our footsteps and our markers.

✠✠✠

One incident occurred then that I remember well. As I was stopped to direct my men in the filling of a small ravine we had to cross, Tancred rode up and said, "I've been enquiring about you, MacEuan, and I've just learned that you have slain relatives of mine. I think I'll kill you now."

**Tancred of Hauteville, Prince of Galilee.**

When he had tried to stare me down at our first meeting, I had had a feeling it might come to this. Perhaps he was hoping to cow me into some act of obeisance; if so, he failed. If sincere, he certainly wasn't beginning well, for his sword was in its sheath, and I stood on the left side of his horse.

*You'll not do it this way!* I thought.

Instead, I smiled at the boy. Despite his twenty years and a knighthood, he was still a spoiled child, not yet grown into the man he would be.

I asked, "Who were these family men of yours you allege I killed? Mind you, those I dispatched deserved it and much more. Know you that?"

Tancred sneered, "You murdered Jarl OdinsØye, my mother's third cousin. And you slew King Máel Snechtai of Moray, another of my cousins descended from my father's grandfather. I denounce you as a murderer, one who doubtless fears to face me in single combat."

There was no sense in letting this go, for it would only get worse. Tancred would not be ignored, and having been raised as his uncle's pet, he had never yet been thwarted or chastised, so he had grown up to think himself invulnerable. And his boyish self-doubt and fear of failure, unconquered and pent-up so long, had now festered into petulant arrogance and a disdain of others. So now, Tancred's pride needed pricking, like a boil, to drain off all that poison and let him finally heal.

So I smiled even wider at that, and said, "Both of those men died in the course of combat that they started. But lay on if you must. Know you that my squire is more fearsome than you, and my clerk tougher. I could kill you without even drawing my sword. But I pray you forget this nonsense and ride on, boy. Bother me no more."

My words bit hard, as I knew they would, and having started this in front of others, he could not back down now. So as he reached to draw his sword, I stepped back along his horse's left flank. I drew my damascene short-sword, ducked out of his reach, and slipped the blade between horse and girth as his sword slid free. I was in the only position where a right-handed mounted knight cannot truly reach his opponent, so he could only wheel his horse left, and flail his sword ineffectually at me.

But I turned with them. And my damascene blade, so sharp it actually could cut falling silk, effortlessly cut through the leathern girth. Then I shoved both saddle and rider up and off the right side of the horse.

As man and saddle fell in a heap, the startled horse ran off. Tancred, still tangled in his stirrups, lay stunned by the sudden fall. I pulled free his sword, kicked him in the head, and stepped on his throat to press his head to the ground. Then I slid his blade down, between his jaw and mail cowl, put a foot on the hilt, and drove the sword down, through the mail and deep into the soil, pinning him on his back.

As I did this, he recovered his wits, but now he was helpless. Nearby, his squire, unsure what to do, pulled his sword. I glared at the lad and said, "Try if you must, boy, but you will die trying, and then so will he. Look at what I have just done with him."

The squire blinked as the truth sank in. I said, "Let him lie here half an hour to think on his sins. Then free him. You will do him better service to show wisdom now than to kill him with stupidity born of haste."

Then I turned back to Tancred, who was struggling and cursing me, and said, "Tancred, I did you no wrong, yet you pulled a sword on me. We might have been friends. We might yet still be. But right now you are an arrogant idiot, and you deserved this, just as did those evil men you call cousins. Lie still now and consider this . . ." I put the tip of my short-sword into his mouth, and noted that he was suddenly very quiet, very still. ". . . Just as I said, I could kill you now without drawing my sword. A push on this blade and you leave this life for the next. Are you ready now for Final Judgment? I think not. Think on your sins, especially pride, and leave me alone."

With that I got up, sheathed my short-sword and went back to work, paying him no mind. For his part, he endured his humiliation and profited from it, for he never openly confronted me again.

The others who witnessed the incident passed on what they saw and heard, and soon Jean said, "I hear Tancred confronted you and came off the worse."

I shrugged and said, "I taught him only what you taught me my first week as your squire. He must be a very slow learner."

✠✠✠

As I recall it, the route from the Bosporus to Nicaea along the coastal roads is about thirty-five leagues, one hundred miles. Behind us came Duke Godfrey and his men. As the first army to reach Constantinople and cross into Anatolia, they earned the right and honor to lead the army's march. Behind them came Duke Bohemond and Tancred, Raymond of Toulouse, and Count Robert of Flanders, with Hamish and my siege supplies in Robert's baggage train.

A week later, on May 6, our van reached the vicinity of Nicaea. And it was that day I rode onto a promontory overlooking Nicaea, a half-mile away to the southwest, from hundreds of feet higher. I could see the entire city below on its vast plain, the great Lake Askania behind it to the west, and the whole encircled by hills and low mountains.

The walls of Nicaea are shaped much like the outline of an axe-blade: The curved cutting edge follows the shore of the lake, with the point at the top of the blade to the north, straight walls along the northeast and southeast sides, and a stub of a handle extending from the southern wall. Six gates penetrate these walls: one at the northern point; one in the middle of the long northeastern wall; one at the eastern corner; two in the southern wall; and one in the southwest niche. From these, roads extend to connect the Seljuq capital with the rest of the sultanate.

Seeing the great fortified city again brought back to mind all the notes I had made a decade before, when Jean, Anselm, and I had created a codex — a little book — of information about the fortresses of the Holy Land, and how one might conquer them. That seems most prescient now, but even then God knew He would bring me back to take this city, so He had made sure then that I would gain the means to do it. I gave Him thanks then, and dug that little book from my saddlebag to review what we had recorded.

"Encircling Nicaea, except at the lakeshore, is not one, but two concentric ditches, while the lake forms a vast moat close against the base of the western walls. Inside those ditches are two walls, built like those around Constantinople, both twenty feet thick. At thirty-five feet high, the inner wall is twice as tall as the outer. Circular defensive towers stand between the two walls at regular intervals of fifty yards on the south, and sixty and seventy-five yards on the north. There are about two hundred circular towers around the city, each higher than the inner wall. These walls and towers are built in layers of thickly cemented tiles and stone blocks, not of wood. The walls can be undermined, but it will take a good deal of time. Nothing I know of can batter a way through them."

I had to smile at that. We had written that before Demetrius had shown me the secrets of the basileus's siege armory, and before I had built, used, and improved them. Since then, I had discovered machines that could defeat these walls, given time, men, and the will to win. And I was about to prove my ability to do just that.

"The gate doors are of wood reinforced with metal, and there are three gates in succession. The road through them is completely enclosed by walls and towers, pierced with archer slits and murder holes. Upon breaching one gate one enters a killing field. The gates can be burned, but only with great difficulty and high cost in attackers' lives."

Reading this, I recalled that Demetrius had once proposed use of a fire-proofed "tortoise" — a steep-roofed siege-shed mounted on wheels and bearing a battering ram — as means to approach the gates to batter and burn them. We would need to consider building these if it appeared they could survive whatever defense the Seljuqs might put up.

"Given these difficulties, starving the city into submission would seem the best option. But the western wall stands at the lakeshore, and this poses a great problem with besieging the city, for vessels can come and go across the lake, connecting the city to sources of food and reinforcements that we cannot control without ships. The western walls are built with channels and gates so that boats can enter harbor basins. To starve Nicaea into surrendering, attackers must control the entire lake or build ships that can prevent other vessels from reaching the city by water. A defender can take pride in a fortress like this, but to an attacker it will be a nightmare."

Nicaea was not an easy city to take, then, by any means. Clearly, both the Byzantines and the Seljuq Turks had done it, but when I had asked him how, Demetrius shrugged and said, "To take Nicaea, you need either a traitor or a deal with the defenders."

I would come to learn how right he was.

✠✠✠

As the army of Duke Godfrey arrived, he called a war council to which Jean and I were summoned, for Count Robert had previously acquainted Godfrey with our expertise and knowledge of the city and region. To preserve any surprise we might still have, we urged the duke to immediately position companies of men to blockade all the gates with archers, crossbowmen, caltrops, and barricades of chevaux-de-frise. This would do no more than allow us to capture unwary messengers and prevent the city from contact with the rest of the Seljuq kingdom, for our outposts had not the strength to oppose any attack in force. But in isolating Nicaea, we prevented it from warning the rest of the kingdom and calling other Seljuq armies to its rescue. That was our purpose, and in that we succeeded, just long enough.

✠✠✠

The first evening we camped outside the great walls of Nicaea, we gathered to sup. As was our custom, together sat Jean and his squire, Henri; Sir Hamish; Father Anselm; Edward — in reality, the disguised Princess Edith; my squire Colin; and me. During a lull in the conversation as we ate, Colin called my attention to four yeomen clustered at a nearby fire to eat.

Scowling at them, he said to me. "Why you ever let those four join your retinue, sire, I'll never understand. They have no military skill, no discipline, and a nose for trouble. And I think they take an undue interest in us . . ." and in an undertone, he added, ". . . or in Edward."

Thus warned, I casually studied them. I had seen them, of course, and often, but never given them thought. So I said, "They are none of mine. I know all in my company. They belong to Jean's."

But Jean looked them, then at me. "No, they're none of mine, either. I thought them some of your craftsmen."

Now we all looked at them, because suddenly the four had become much more interesting.

To Colin I said, "Bid them join us, and we will find out who they say they are." Colin nodded and rose, walked to them and said, "The Barons MacEuan and de Bethencourt request the pleasure of your company." Pointing, he indicated us.

The four exchanged uneasy looks, but arose and walked the short distance to stand in the opening we made. They doffed caps and made awkward bows, then nudged forward one of their number, a tough little man with a squinty eye, thanks to the scar that ran across it from hairline to cheekbone, as their spokesman. He stepped a half-step forward and bowed again stiffly, as if it pained him to do it.

I smiled and spoke first. "Welcome, men! I trust our hospitality is agreeable. I have often seen you among us in the past few months. I thought I knew all in my company, as the good Baron de Bethencourt here . . ." I indicated him at my right, ". . . does his. But we do not know you. Who are you, and whence came you among us?"

Squint-eye gave us a greasy smile, which did not blend well with the unease in his manner, and the anxious twisting of his cap.

"Milords, we's four good English lads of London." He half-turned to indicate them with a sweep of the tortured headgear, as they in turn smiled and bobbed in acknowledgment. "We joined the company of good Duke Robert there. An' we came to France with 'im, and marched south with 'im and you. But when we got to Bari, there was all that ruckus 'bout whether we was to go on or stay. An' God 'elp us, we got swept along with' the wrong group, an afore we knew it, we was herded onta a ship an' over the sea. And when we got off, we couldn't find none of our mates, and then learned they was all back in Bari. But it was too late and we couldn't go back to 'em, so we jest sorta stayed with the ones we crossed with, which was your men and yours, yer lordships, beggin' yer pardon. And here we are, waitin' for Curthose — beggin' yer pardon, I mean Duke Robert, milords — an' eager to help you any way we can. Ain't we, lads?"

The last pronouncement sounded more an order than a question; and the other three duly smiled and bobbed again in assent.

I confess I did not believe the half of it — oh, they may have come to France with Duke Robert, but they did not join us by accident; of that I was sure. Still, I had no proof they had done any wrong, and Duke Robert would join us soon enough. So I said, "Have you names?"

"Aye, milord! This is 'Arry, an' Robert — we calls 'im Rob, sire — and Davy-a-Wessex. An' they calls me Big Tom." The last contained a tone of defiant pride, for he was the shortest of the four.

"Ah well, welcome to our company, Big Tom, men," I said. "We appreciate your enthusiasm, and will find useful ways for you to earn your way among us until Robert comes up. Sorry to have disturbed your supper. Will a pitcher of ale will make amends?"

They nodded thanks and eagerly returned to their fire to share their prize, drinking from it and passing it on from man to man.

To my companions, I said, "Henceforth, let us all pay careful heed to the whereabouts and doings of Big Tom and his lads, shall we?" And the way they nodded told me none of them had believed Tom either.

✠✠✠

The following dawn, the seventh, Hamish put our men to work, for we had much to do — unpacking siege gear and cutting trees and brush in nearby woods for materials to fortify our camp with chevaux-de-frise and mantlets against any counterattack by Turkish horsemen. I had Hamish keep Big Tom and his men busy with the cutting. Their awkwardness soon made clear their unfamiliarity with real work.

I had my skilled craftsmen begin building onagers and ballistae from the trees the others cut, as yet others began weaving gabion baskets and building mantlets from the branches and vines brought in. The former would be needed to protect our engine crews from arrows and stones, and the latter to attack towers and gates. It would take time to build enough of these and we would soon be too busy to build more, so we had no time to waste. The camp fortifications we built were portable, so that when we moved from this, our temporary camp, to one behind our place in line encircling the city, we could take them with us.

And as ever, the damned *Siege Master's Song* serenaded us all as they worked. Cedric had infected them all.

Meanwhile, I took a body of men and rode back to Helenopolis, where I found Master Thanasi and the good ship *St. George* anchored awaiting me. His crew brought the vessel to the quay with sweeps, and by a combined effort of his crew and my men, we offloaded the great timbers I had bought in Constantinople in order to build my siege engines. I told Thanasi I would seek him out again whenever I needed a trustworthy ship and master, and paid him well for his faithful service.

Then I used a tactic that Carrick had earlier devised, lashing wheeled axles I had had made under the largest timbers to make improvised wagons of them. In this way we were able to pull those heavy loads behind teams of horses the remaining distance to Nicaea.

✠✠✠

It was on the ride back from Helenopolis that Colin reined hard and pointed, "Look there!"

Great squadrons of scavenger birds circled a spot not far off our track. So I gave warning to the wagon train that they should be on guard while we went to scout it, and then we rode to investigate.

Slinking wolves and wild dogs slid away from us as we rode through the woods, and the horses grew skittish. Cautiously we entered a narrow valley, where my nose told what drew them: the great stink that always followed a great battle.

**The remains of the People's Crusade.**

And then we were among them — the bodies of tens of thousands of Christian pilgrims — men, women, some horses, and even children, lay everywhere. This was the slaughtering ground where the Seljuqs had fallen upon and butchered the People's Crusade.

Colin leaned from his saddle and vomited, adding a bit to the stench.

That massacre had occurred six months earlier, late the previous year. But the onset of winter had much deterred the rotting and the scavenging until spring. So now, only a month or two since the weather warmed, there were still ever so many rotting bodies to feed the multitudes swirling overhead and slipping in through the woods.

It was a horrific sight and an overwhelming stink, even to me, who had fought great battles and seen their carnage, both immediately and months or years later. Colin emptied his stomach more than once at the sight, and the gorge rose in me, too, though I managed to master mine, more by an act of will than anything else.

Almost all the bodies were defenseless commoners, found scattered about, singly or in pairs, where they fell from grievous wounds to heads and backs — cut down not in combat, but in headlong flight. After all, most of them came as an act of faith, not for conquest, and so they were completely unprepared to fight the ruthless foes they faced. Those who were armed fell in clusters, cut down back-to-back, as they fought an overwhelming number of attackers.

Men fell protecting women, mothers protecting children. We found no Turks among them, for few Christian men were able to mount any sort of effective defense that might kill an attacker, and the Seljuqs took all their casualties from the field.

The worst part of it was that the Turks had decapitated many, and piled up the heads of men apart from their bodies. These piles were of the greatest interest to the scavengers, for they held a vast treasure of meat, and the vultures and ravens covered them, hopping, jostling, flapping, tearing gobbets from the heads, and raising a horrid ruckus of noise.

I could not begin to guess how many of these heads there were — pile after pile, far too many to count.

More than anything else, these piles told me something. This wasn't the result of battle. In combat the dead lie where they fall, the severed head beside its body. No, this was done after the battle was over. Here the headless torsos lay all around the piled heads.

This was murder These were the men who surrendered, or were grievously wounded, and therefore of no value as slaves. So as the women and children were roped together and led off as slaves, the men were herded together here and ruthlessly beheaded.

And the men who did it? They were the very devils of Hell, able to implacably slay the defenseless by hacking the heads off the living, even as they wept and begged for a mercy nowhere to be found.

Colin realized it as well. Still a tender-hearted lad, he openly wept.

Not me. That sight hit me hard, and started in me a burning fury of hatred toward the men who had done this, imprinting an image of that scene so indelible that even now I can see it again just by closing my eyes.

I vowed then and there to avenge these poor men. I would hurl every Turkish head I could get back into their God-damned city.

✠✠✠

Our entire military force was so large that we could not possibly all depart at once, and so had to march in column, contingents leaving in succession, one after another, starting May 1, with the last on the eighth. On the march, our army stretched the entire thirty-five leagues. It took a week for the rearmost contingents to reach us at Nicaea, Count Robert's army, with my contingent and Jean's among them, finally arriving the fourteenth.

But as we reached our objective, a huge problem arose. With vast numbers of men to feed, our food supplies were rapidly shrinking. Not mine, per se, for I had bought much for my retinue, and those supplies came up in our baggage train. But the rest of the army might soon grow hungry.

The emperor had promised to send us vast supplies of food as one of his contributions to our campaign, but as yet none of his shipments had reached us, probably because we so clogged the roads with our numbers that they could only follow us. And now here at Nicaea, there were, of course, no markets or storehouses upon which we could draw. Over the winter the locals had already consumed most of their own stores, while it was too early in the season for any food crops we might buy or confiscate from the surrounding area.

Most contingents went on half-rations then, with much complaint and grumbling among the men. But Duke Bohemond, our self-appointed leader, seized the opportunity to act as such, and quickly sent word to the emperor to speed the promised food shipments. And true to his word, Alexios did so, rerouting the provisions by having them ferried across the Gulf of Nicomedia; for while it was fifty miles to Nicomedia and back to Helenopolis around this gulf by land, it was but two miles across by sea.

So as the emperor's ships ferried over our provisions, Bohemond sent trusted men and wagons sent to fetch them from Helenopolis. And by forcing units on the march to clear the road so they could pass, he sped the provisions on to our camps, where a great market was soon organized to sell food to all. With this improved arrangement, we did not again lack provisions during the ensuing siege of Nicaea.

How I wish now that had proved true later on.

✠✠✠

On the seventh, the military council of princes conferred, decided on siege positions, and began assigning postings to encircle the city. As each army arrived, it was posted to cover a portion of the city walls and block each gate in strength. We were not ready to begin the siege yet, so each army encamped at their post, but at a distance behind what would become their front line, well out of arrowshot from the walls.

The postings were these: Tancred had the northwestern wall from the lakeshore east to the northern point. Beside him to the east was Duke Bohemond, covering the northern gate and the northeast wall. Next to them, Duke Godfrey and his brother Baldwin had the northeast wall and the eastern gate. Then Count Robert, along the southeastern wall. Beside Count Robert were Count Raymond and Bishop Ademar of Le Puy, who was Pope Urban's legate, and as such, the official head of our crusade. Together Raymond and Ademar had the largest army, so they were assigned opposite the long southern wall with both its gates.

Somewhere in this long chain of warriors came Peter the Hermit, accompanied by his small band of stalwart survivors, all determined to yet see Jerusalem. I do not recall that they took any place in the line, nor contributed in any military way to our campaign. But they were present somewhere — probably where food was most plenty.

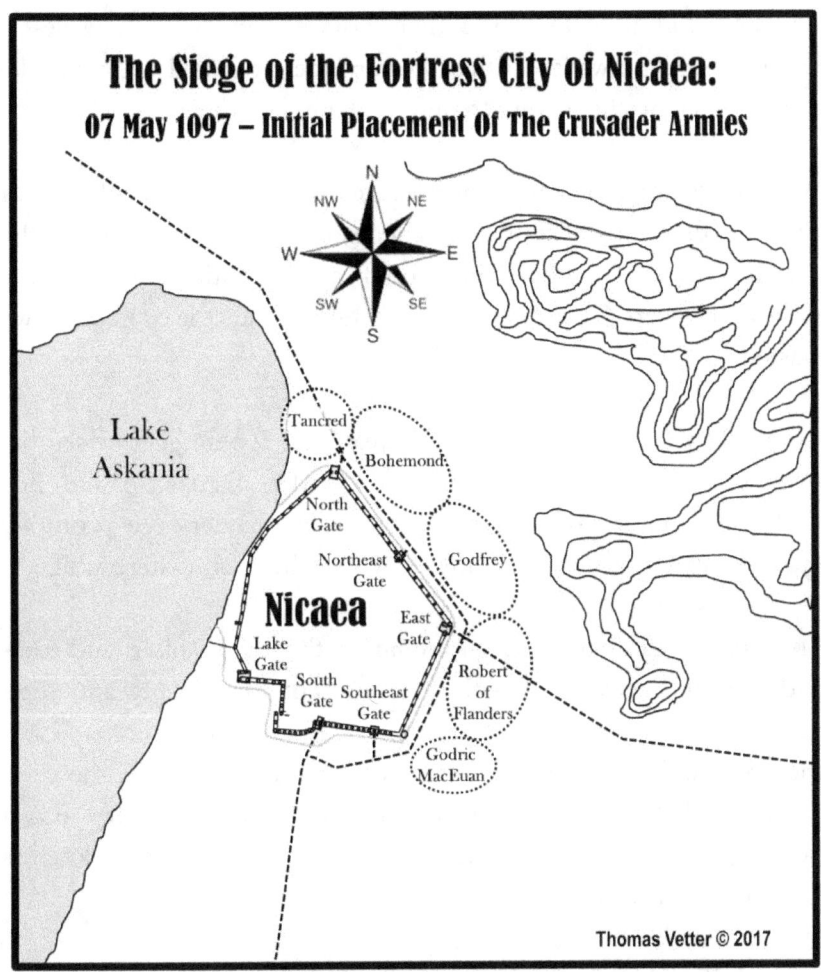

**07 May 1097: Initial placement of the Crusader armies.**

It had been earlier planned that as the last contingents arrived on the fourteenth, we would all send our men forward to create a siege line. And as we did, there promptly ensued a desultory exchange of arrows from both sides, more in experiment than anger. These were actually helpful, allowing us to determine where we ought to place the line. The Seljuqs favor a short recurved bow, which they use from horseback. It is powerful at short range, but lacks power at long distance. Nicaea was the garrison for units of these mounted bowmen, but now they and their horses were trapped uselessly within the stone walls, so their commanders ordered them to take their bows atop the towers to defend the walls instead.

We use longer D-shaped bows of yew, tall as a man, which can shoot farther and hit harder, enabling us to send arrows from the extreme range at which a Seljuq could reach, yet still kill men on the walls and towers. That gave us an advantage but, at least initially, we wasted it.

Count Robert arrived as expected. Jean and I were glad to see the rest of our retinues arrive in good order, thanks to the fine leadership of Sir Hamish, my deputy commander. We promptly made camp and moved men into place on the southeastern wall.

My place should have been in the line with Count Robert and Jean, and indeed I encamped with them. I sent my knights and their men-at-arms to join those of Jean and fight under his command, for their role and mine were different. They would fight in all the ways knights did. But it is a siege master's task to force entry into a heavily defended fortress, and in doing that, conventional knights have but a small role until a breach is finally made.

Instead, the place in battle for me and my engineers was wherever the breaching could best be done, and thus it was that my engineers and I went to work in many places. We were not alone at this, for each prince had brought siege men, and they all set out to do as I did. We all suffered some success and failure, and I witnessed both genius and idiocy at work all about the city. But more of that at its proper time in this tale of mine.

I will say that before we finished I saw more of Nicaea, more of the intense fighting, and more breach attempts, than any other man who was there. Indeed, still today, I have the scars to prove it.

But behind Robert, the expected army of Count Raymond and Bishop Ademar were nowhere to be seen.

Alexios had just established a military ferry between Pelecanum and Helenopolis, saving a fifty-mile ride by horse with a two–mile boat trip between the two towns across the gulf. And using this, messengers began to ride routinely between the princes and the emperor to share news and confer, the one with the other. By means of this, we learned then, for the first time, what had happened.

The evening of the fourteenth the princes called the nobles into military council, gathered in the big headquarters tent of Duke Godfrey. A messenger from the emperor had brought news: Raymond had not marched as planned because the emperor had invited the count to stay on in the palace with him, and apparently Raymond was so taken with Alexio's hospitality that he forgot — or decided to delay — ordering his army to march. Instead, Raymond's army sat in camp at the Bosporus a full fortnight, awaiting his order to march. And it was not until the emperor elected to bring a small army of his own to Pelecanum, on the northern coast opposite Helenopolis, that Raymond finally marched with him, departing on the fourteenth.

But Raymond's huge army could not use the ferry, and had instead to make the long march around the gulf. Starting as they did on the fourteenth, Raymond and Ademar would be on the march and unable to take up their position for another week. And all that week, the two southern gates would remain unopposed, with Count Robert's position forming our left flank, exposed on three sides to a potential Seljuq cavalry attack.

We also learned then that Duke Robert of Normandy and Count Stephen had finally reached Constantinople on the thirteenth, and after a week to rest, repair and replenish, would again — finally — set out to join us.

The entire council grumbled at that, for Robert and Stephen had made no particular effort to speed their way across the empire, and this meant they would now would not arrive until the start of June.

We all knew that the success of the siege demanded a complete encirclement, and we needed the many men of Raymond, Ademar, Robert, and Stephen to do that. But now we would not have them for another fortnight. And we could not simply wait for them, for at any point a Seljuq army might arrive to rescue the city.

Instead, we had to start immediately and do our best without them. And at the council that night, we began at last in earnest to take the city . . . and immediately began to do it badly.

I do not recall now who first put forth the idea, although I should But someone proposed a pre-dawn attack by men with ladders crossing the open ground and scaling the walls under the protection of our archers. It was a bold plan, and might work, and it drew great interest, for it offered early victory, a rich sacking, and negligible damage to the city's defenses.

It was also potentially stupidly fatal. And when the opportunity was given, I said so. "My lords, this plan is bold and most appealing for that reason. But we have not reconnoitered the ground between the wall and ourselves. There are two ditches before the walls. What traps lie in them? We know not! There are two walls: what lies between them? Again, we know not! To get over the first to be trapped by the second is no victory. What strength are their archers? We know not! Do they have siege engines inside the walls or ballistae on their towers? We know not! And because we know not, this plan will kill many good knights and men from ignorance.

Let us instead spend another day in careful reconnaissance and then plan our attack from knowledge."

I could see many agreed with me; they said so, some then, more later. But Duke Bohemond said, "You offer wise counsel, Baron MacEuan, but bold surprise may be well worth the lives of the men we might or might not lose, men who only then become saints by their sacrifice. And we know that here God Himself fights for us. Besides, we will learn all the answers to your questions by this attack, and may win the city besides."

Most of the nobles who had never taken a city or castle, and certainly never seen the defenses of this one, sided with the duke then, not wanting to seem timid or unenthusiastic. So the decision went against my advice, and the attack was ordered for the morrow.

✠✠✠

At dawn on the fifteenth, our first attempt to take Nicaea began at long last. It began with our archers who, at a horn blast, loosed flights of arrows at the towers before them, raining death on the defending archers, hopefully forcing them to cover. At the same horn blast, our men-at-arms, pairs of them carrying long ladders, ran across two hundred yards of open ground to scale the walls. Too late did they discover that the two concentric dry ditches outside the walls had been flooded from the lake, which turned the bottoms into watery quagmires.

The bravest men tried to use their ladders as bridges to crawl across these mud-traps in order to reach the walls. But they made easy targets for the Seljuq archers, and our suppressing volleys of arrows did nothing to force their archers to cover. Instead, our ladder-men died all too easily and much too stupidly, to my outrage and disgust.

So during the day, we mourned hundreds of new saints, and behind our lines dug graves for others who succumbed to arrow wounds.

**The initial ladder attacks on Nicaea.**

I did not endear myself to our leaders that night, for I told them far too forthrightly how wrong it was to kill brave men so stupidly. I suppose it was not my place to do so — that they already knew what I could not hold back. In retrospect, I did not really have to rub their noses, like puppies, in their own dung.

But I could not help it. It took no great military experience on my part, or theirs, to foresee that possibility and outcome. Indeed, I *had* foreseen it and warned them myself. A scouting patrol to the walls during the night would have discovered the trap, and spared us all those unnecessary deaths. We certainly would not win this siege by employing idiocy, killing brave men long before we even reached Jerusalem. Princes can be as stupid as the least-trained squire or groom among us, but we expect that they are not, at least until they prove us wrong in this way.

All this I thought. All this I said.

It was not just a sense of pique at being right and ignored anyway that made me speak so bluntly, although I do admit to indignation. More important to me was that the princes needed to know that I regarded it as my duty to warn them before they committed such egregious errors, for the sake of the men whose lives we held in our hands. I knew that if I foresaw a flaw in their plans, so too would the enemy. So I vowed to speak up, whatever it might cost me — in reputation, popularity, support, whatever. It was my duty as a knight to do so.

✠✠✠

In the self-remorse that followed my tirade, however, I realized one significant fact, one good thing that came from the People's Crusade the previous fall: we hadn't been attacked by either the garrison of Nicaea, nor by the armies of Sultan Kilij Arslan. He might have done so at any time, for there was little doubt that the amassing of huge Frankish armies in Constantinople had not been noticed and reported to him by his spies. And had he caught us on the march, or fallen on us while we gathered around his capital, he might have defeated us, or at least taken a heavy toll on our men. But he did not. Nicaea's garrison remained inside their massive defenses, perhaps hoping we might just go away.

I could only think that because the sultan had had so little difficulty defeating the huge numbers who came against him in October, he now had no fear of us or the new threat we posed.

We did not know where Arslan was. According to my old friend Demetrius, who accompanied us, the emperor's spies had reported that Arslan had taken an army a month or so earlier to confront his rival, King Danishmend, who was then besieging Arslan's city of Melitine, one hundred sixty leagues to the southeast. But whether he was still there or somewhere else, we had no intelligence.

Of one thing I was sure. Once we appeared outside the walls, the garrison commander was sure to have sent messengers out by boat to ride around us and report our presence to the sultan. And unless he was a complete fool, Arslan would be on his way right now, with his entire army behind him and all riding fast, to destroy us and save his capital.

But his time was short. When Count Raymond and Bishop Ademar arrived in a few more days, we would complete wrapping our belt of death around Nicaea. And once we did, his palace, wives, children, slaves, luxuries, and treasure would be trapped inside.

✠✠✠

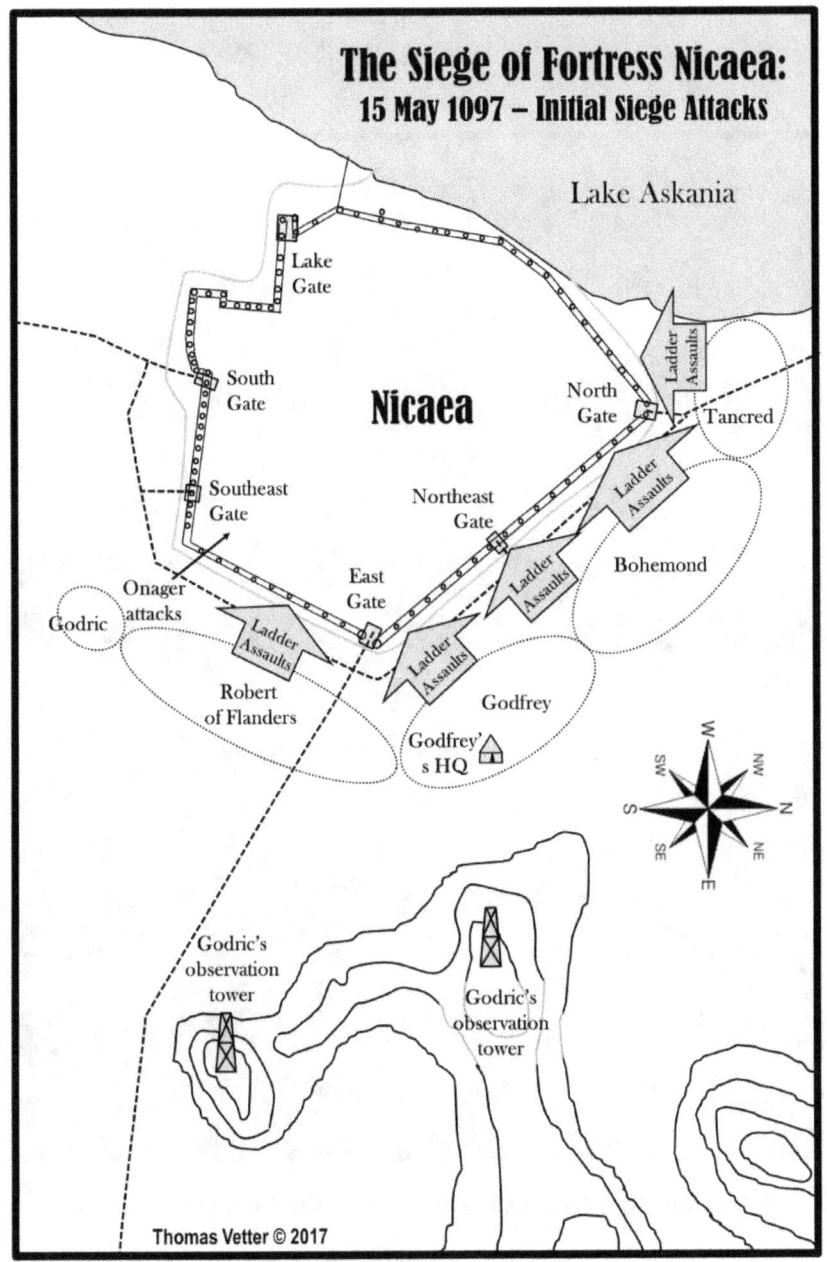

**15 May 1097: The initial ladder attacks.**

Duke Godfrey meets the survivors of the People's Crusade.

# SEVEN

✠✠✠

Early the morning of the sixteenth, after attending the Requiem Mass at dawn to pray for all the men who had died the previous day, Hamish, Cedric, Colin, and I went into the workyard where my builders were constructing the onagers and ballistae with which we would finally crack this egg. They had the first several of each machine ready to test, and I was keen to see how they would do. Once we had these in operation, we would build the bigger brother of *Bone-Crusher*, my first counterweight tree-bucket. I had small faith that any onager could much damage Nicaea's thick walls and triple gates, but after besieging Jarl OdinsØye's tower, I knew that given time, a tree-bucket could batter a hole in anything.

Nearby, my men had gathered big piles of suitable boulders from dry streambeds, and a team of them were weighing and sorting them by weight. And we were just in the act of loading the first stones when hunting horns sounded calls of alarm from our sentry bastions opposite the southern gates.

At the time, Count Robert's force formed the extreme left flank of the entire army, as well as the end of our siege line. And since I needed room to build my engines at my encampment, I did so, perhaps in retrospect quite foolishly, by camping at the extreme left of Robert's sector. Well, it had seemed a good idea at the time . . .

Now it suddenly meant that I was the exposed left flank of the army, and the logical point of attack for Nicaea's defenders.

161

Siege Machinery  – The Onager

Siege Machinery  – The Ballista

**Siege Machinery: the Onager (catapult) and Ballista.**

We could not quite see what was coming, for we were opposite the southeastern-most corner tower, with the southern gates about a half-mile away, and the ground in between was obscured by brush and trees. But from my past experience with the Seljuq and Jerusalemite Turks, I realized that the garrison was coming out against us in force, and I could expect horse-mounted archers, their favored form of attack. And we had no time to lose, for they would be on us in a couple of minutes.

To my closest sentry, I called, "Repeat the alarm!"

Then, to every man in earshot, I yelled, "Archers to the barricades, *now*! Engine crews, stand fast, ready your machines. Every man to arms! Hamish, take command of the siege line, and send every other man to the rear barricades. I will command this end. Cedric, command the rear defenses. Colin, roust every single man left in camp to the barricades, then find Jean and have him bring us reinforcements. We have to hold here, or they will roll up the entire line. All of you, *move*!"

At the command, my craftsmen, cross-trained as archers, grabbed bows or crossbows and quivers. They rushed to the barricades, chevaux-de-frise roped end-to-end, that encircled my camp. They took cover in, under, or behind wagons or hastily-hoisted wattle mantlets. And they did not have to wait, for the Turks leading the charge were already upon us.

Arrows flew thick and fast as hundreds of mounted Turks galloped past, firing their short bows as they did. And it was good that I wore stout chainmail over an armored jack of plate, for I was struck perhaps a dozen times in just the first few moments. But I ignored them as best I could and concentrated on directing our defense. If Heaven wanted me now, I was ready; if not, I had a knight's work to do.

"Onager teams, load stones! Loose at will, fast as you can!" Baskets of fist-sized stones were poured into the spoons of a half-dozen machines, and scores of stones flew with each shot. These arced over the barricades in great numbers, each stone capable of killing the man or horse it struck.

Beside me, a dozen ballistae and scorpios — large crossbows mounted on pivoting stands — were loaded with bolts like spears and loosed at onrushing horsemen as fast as the crews could cock and reload. The size and power of these gave them great range — more than two hundred yards. At such close range, though, they were brutally effective, a dart capable of piercing a horse lengthwise; indeed, capable of completely passing through one man to hit another man or horse behind him as well.

And it was our fortified bastion of archers and siege engines that took the brunt of the attack and divided it, for as we stood fast behind our defenses, killing all we could, the Turkish charge split at our position, as an island divides a river, and horsemen swept down both sides. Some passed between our front line and the great walls of Nicaea, while the rest rode along the rear, past our encampment and then along or through the rear of Robert's.

The standard tactic for Turkish horse archers is to charge the enemy, firing up to a half-dozen arrows on the way in, circle right and away, still firing, then seize more arrows and circle back in another charge. But what worked well for them, shooting a lot of arrows from swift horses, also worked well for us; we had horsemen charging straight at us, directly into the deadly swaths of our arrows, stones and bolts. In consequence, the carnage was great on both sides.

I do not know how many horsemen Nicaea's garrison commander sortied against us that day — perhaps as many as a thousand. I do know that when the battle ended, he had far fewer.

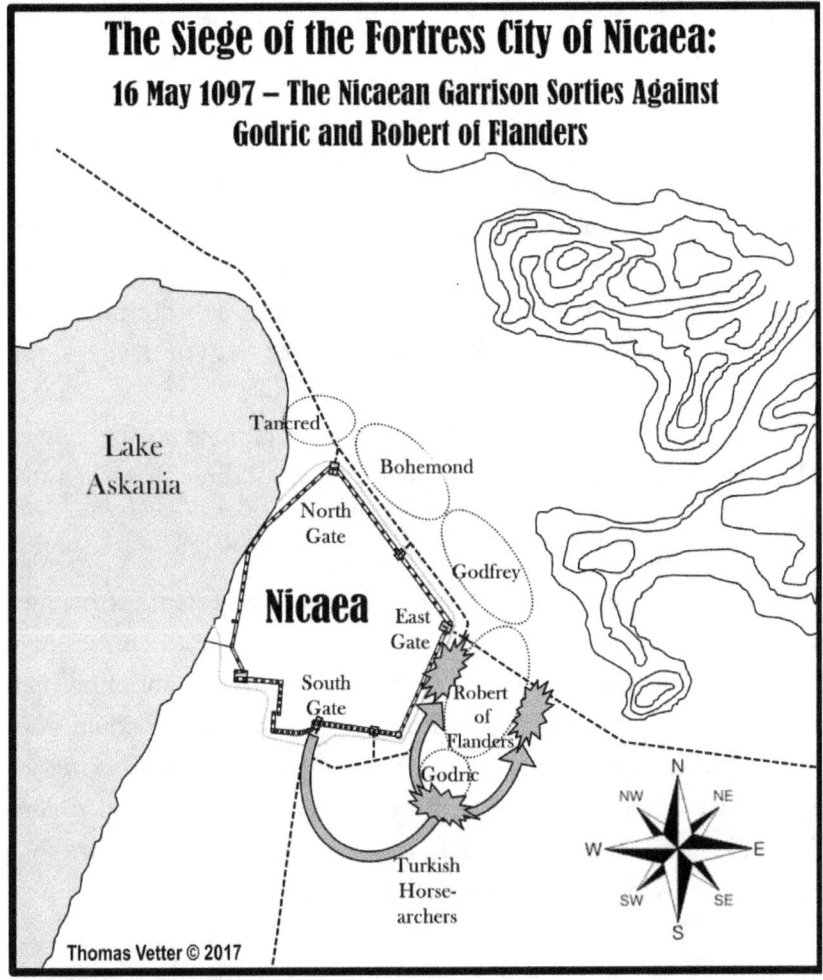

**The Siege of the Fortress City of Nicaea:**
**16 May 1097 – The Nicaean Garrison Sorties Against Godric and Robert of Flanders**

Thomas Vetter © 2017

**The Nicaean garrison sorties against Godric and Count Robert.**

When the first charge swept past, and the Turks realized they could not gallop through our camp as they perhaps had expected or hoped to do, a pair of them — the commanders, I believe — circled at a near-gallop close by to study our defenses. Then they rode back to the rear of their circle, stopped a group of horsemen, and gave new orders. I took bow and quiver from a wounded yeoman and made ready, for something new was coming.

These Turks were no cowards. Whatever the inducements they were offered — whether gold, harems, or Paradise assured — they worked, for they rode straight at the barricades without swerving, their horses close abreast, and crashed into the wall of spear-like sharpened poles that a chevaux is, trying to breach our line. Horses screamed as they were impaled, some of their riders thrown into camp at the impact. But a breach was made, a pile of dying men and horses tangled amid splintered wood. And through the hole came yet more horses and more Turks, certainly not dead or dying — yet.

"Ballistae! Defend the breach!" I cried, and pointed to the danger. The closest machines swung on pivots to shoot directly through the hole.

I called all the men nearby. "To me! To me! Spearmen, form a line, kneel and ground your spears! Archers! Form behind them, shoot at will, kill the horses!" And there we stood our ground, shooting shaft after shaft into targets we could not miss as fast as we could nock arrows, draw, and loose. Horses struck by the deadly darts swerved in terror and pain, crashing into each other, stumbling, and spilling their riders. We had to fall back or dodge the onslaught more than once, but we closed the gap with dead Turks and horses at last.

Meanwhile, as the fight along the southeastern wall continued — with Turks riding, shooting, and circling to attack again and again — the alarms had drawn prompt reaction from the princes to the north. There, knights and mounted men-at-arms, keen to engage their foe at last, ran to their horses. Within minutes of the first alarm, hundreds or thousands of heavily armed men galloped south along both sides of our army to collide with the lightly-armed and armored Turks.

**Defeating the Nicaean garrison.**

And in this there was no contest. A Turkish arrow, loosed close, might, or might not, punch through chainmail. But a Frankish lance, driven by one hundred-stone of horse and man, was unfazed by Turkish mail, and pierced both mail and man so thoroughly that soon no Christian knight still bore his own lance and had to borrow spears or chevaux stakes from crusaders nearby to continue the combat.

A melee ensued then, with Christian knights crashing through the circles of Turks, killing some outright, knocking others from horses to be trampled by the knights behind him, or slashing them open with the deadly blades they swung. And this counter-charge, more than anything, shattered the Turkish attack and drove them into a wild retreat.

The wounded Turks fled first, riding close to their own walls to seek the protective cover of the Turkish archers on the battlements. Some Turks rescued others, and the pairs fled to the gates, which opened briefly to admit them. Had we been ready to exploit this, we might have gained the city this day. Alas, so unexpected was their attack and our victory, that we were not.

Embattled as I was, I did not see all that followed. One moment I was engulfed, and the next, they were gone, with naught but good Christian knights riding hard past us, headed after them. I am told they pursued the Seljuqs back to the very gate from which they had sortied, killing all they overtook.

In the aftermath, we attended our wounded and gathered our dead, and I sent out men-at-arms to dispatch the grievously wounded horses and the downed Turks. Lightly wounded horses we captured and tended, for horses are an asset of war too precious to waste. So too are dead horses, which we pulled into camp, butchered, and ate, or salted or smoked to eat later. Horsemeat is good fare, and our army so large that enough good meat was hard to come by. And I needed horsehides, skinned off and tanned with urine, to fireproof the siege machines that would work close to the walls.

Meanwhile, I remembered the great piles of screaming skulls and scattered bones of the Christian pilgrims slaughtered at Helenopolis and Xerigordon, and it reminded me of a grim duty that my vow to avenge them demanded. So I had every dead Turk's head taken and piled behind camp. For these, I had special plans.

Of the Seljuqs who attacked, we killed in all about two hundred men — I know this because I had the heads we gathered counted — and perhaps three hundred horses, many of each all around my exposed camp. We wounded as many more, I'm sure, but if they lived or died I will never know, for they made it back inside the walls to recover or succumb there.

✠✠✠

The battle occurred in the morning and it took much of the day to cope with the aftermath. I suffered twelve men killed and twice that many wounded, most with wounds from arrows. These kept Anselm and Edward busy, he first with Last Rites for the dying, and then the two of them removing arrows and treating wounds. I counted us fortunate, though, for without the chevaux barricades, all of us would have died in the first wave.

Compared with what would come, this was but a skirmish, a short hard fight involving only a portion of the larger forces on each side. But for the Seljuqs in Nicaea, this was their best effort — wasted. They had sortied all the men — and horses — able to fight, holding back only enough to defend the walls and gates against our overwhelming numbers. And now, except for those great walls, which fought for them as a hundredfold, they were doomed.

And my machines had proven themselves ready. We call the bowl at the end of an onager's throwing arm the "spoon" because, after all, that's what it most resembles. Hurling spoonfuls of fist-sized stones at onrushing cavalry proved a devastating tactic, with a single throw downing both men and horses. I had tried this once before, against Jarl OdinsØye's shipboard Northmen[19], not cavalry. But thanks to study of Vegetius's *De Re Militari* and long discussions of tactics with Demetrius, it seemed the best thing I could think up in a most desperate moment, and I thanked God afterward for the inspiration.

Now the machines were ready, and I was keen to put them into use. So I hunted for Anselm, who had met and studied with the Islamite wise men in Jerusalem a decade earlier. I found him, his brown robe now soaked with blood, at a crude table under an awning where he tended to our wounded. His mood was foul, for he was sore worried for the men he tended, sick of the horrors they had suffered, and angry at the hellish violence that brought it all about. And when I told him what I wanted while he worked to draw an arrow from the thigh of a terrified lad, he neither respected my rank nor spared my feelings.

"No! Go back to Hell, you devil! What you seek is an outrage! I will not help you! Damnation! Hold him still, you dolts!" he shouted, the latter at the four yeomen clumsily trying to control the thrashing boy.

"Father Anselm, I do not want you to help. Just write what I ask, and I will do what I must. If it works as I hope, perhaps we can prevent the killing of many on both sides of these damned walls."

The boy howled then as the arrow came free, and Anselm quickly

---

[19] See "*The Siege Master's Song*" for this story.

stuffed the wound with spider-silk and herbs, and wrapped it tightly with linen bindings to cover the injury and slow the bleeding until it clotted. I would have slapped red-hot iron on it to cauterize it, but he was the physician, and I a blacksmith.

He scowled at me, but dipped a finger in a pool of the boy's blood on the tabletop, and wrote strange marks on a strip of linen. "Copy this, the Arabic phrase you seek. Now get out — I still have too many like him to tend."

His scrawl looked like this: الشيء لك

I thanked him, took the cloth, and left him to his work. But from all over camp I could hear him, alternately praying for another poor soul in Latin, and cursing everyone else in French.

I had my engineers move the onagers up into the front line, facing Nicaea's walls. We loaded a pair of cobbles and launched them at the city. When they failed to clear the second wall, we raised the front of the frame, increased the torsion on the skein and tried again. The stones disappeared over both walls and the distant crash told me the arc was right.

Meanwhile, I had my craftsmen make many strips like Anselm's, copying his markings in horse blood. Then we tied a strip around the brow of each severed head, loaded two of them into the spoon, and loosed them to arc high through the air into the city.

Very soon there arose a new noise: the sound of women wailing in terror and weeping in grief at the discovery of the head of someone they knew. Men's cries soon joined them — these were surely curses and imprecations — and then men rushed onto Nicaea's battlements to launch arrow after arrow at us in rage and despair, all falling futilely short.

All through the afternoon we repeated this, sending head after head back whence it came earlier in the day, each bearing this message in the language of the Islamites: "Same to you!"

Now, should you think my act barbaric, I accept that judgment; it was. But I beheaded only dead men after they came forth to kill me and my men in battle. These very Turks had built their skull-piles by beheading living men, women, and children, all of whom were already defenseless prisoners. So I require that you judge them by the same yardstick, and then tell me whose act was more horrific, and which men the more barbaric.

A short while later, Count Robert came, with Baron Jean in his wake. I could see that my tactic did not meet with the count's approval, for distaste was written on his face as he watched us load and launch heads. With a hard look and frown, he said, "Why do this, Baron?"

I gave him an equally hard stare and I did not break it before he did. Then I grimly said, "I do it for them," pointing to the row of my dead. "And for them," pointing to my wounded, laid out under awnings, where Edward gave them water and checked their bindings. "And for all the Christian dead at Helenopolis and Xerigordon, beheaded without mercy in the tens of thousands by these same men. Now the Seljuqs reap what they themselves sowed. I merely deliver the crop. And though these few may fight us the harder now, all who see or hear of this will now fear us more, and so sue for peace rather than incur our full wrath."

Robert blinked as the idea sank in, and then he nodded thoughtfully. "It is a grisly business that you do, one that makes my gorge rise. I am glad you have the stomach for it. And if it saves lives, out here, inside that city, or elsewhere, it will be worth it. I will explain your reasons and defend your action before the other princes, should any object."

In truth I did not care what he, or any other, thought of my actions or me, but I appreciated his willingness to defend me. But this was not the reason he came.

He continued, "I came to thank you because you saved my army today, perhaps our whole army. Had the Turks succeeded in overrunning you, they would have swept through my camp as well, and the ones beyond. But you blunted their attack and split their strength, buying time for us to rally defenses and then counterattack. We were not prepared today, but you were. I thank God for that, and I thank you!"

Now it was my turn to blink, and my defiance melted with the admission and the praise. I found it hard to speak.

"Sire, I have never had the advantage of numbers, and where I come from, a treacherous attack on a camp is all too common. Defending mine with chevaux and caltrops have become second nature to me." I thought of Mowbray's surprise attack at Alnwick once again.

Robert nodded and said, "Then your misfortunes are my blessing, God's way of preparing you to save us today. Show me all you do; I must now do the same."

So I did.

As it happened, few of the nobles, knights, and men had any qualms with my horrid projectiles, especially all who had also seen the piles of grinning skulls, the only remnant of the People's Crusade. Prince Bohemond sent to me a cartload of ale in gratitude for our victory. I had Hamish share it out among my men and those of Jean, for they were ones who had really earned it.

✠✠✠

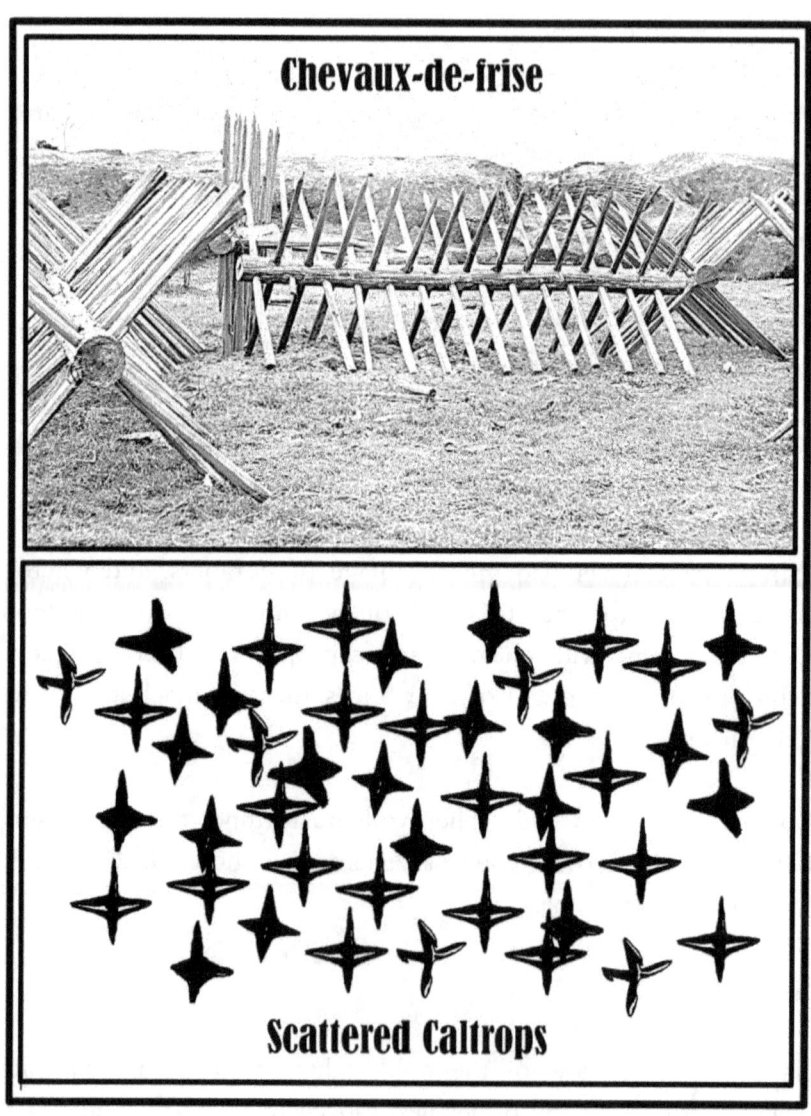

Godric's defenses: chevaux-de-frise and caltrops.

The following day and the several that followed, I and my men were kept quite busy, for we had much to do. At the council's request, we moved pairs of my onagers, with crews of operators to work them, into positions to bombard the northern, northeastern, and eastern gates, with hopes we could batter a way through at least one of them. My ballistae and scorpios were deployed also, set up to kill the crews of the foe's machines, set as they were atop the crucial defensive towers.

All these machines went to work right away, but as I had feared from my study of the city a decade before, they did little damage.

Since our first ladder attack had failed, I knew we now truly had to besiege Nicaea. And that meant we would need to work close to the walls to breach them. So we now needed men skilled with crossbows protecting our sappers as they worked by killing the enemy's archers. So I put Hamish in charge, training many yeomen, offered up from the several armies, to become crossbowmen.

The crossbow is a fearful weapon, deadly accurate in the hands of a man trained to use it, but it does not require the lifelong practice and built-up strength an archer must build to use a war-bow because the crossbow, not a man's muscles, powers the bolt. Once cocked, a crossbow remains ready to loose, and can be rapidly aimed to hit a target of opportunity, such as an archer popping up to shoot his arrow.

We trained crossbowmen to operate in pairs from behind a mantlet, taking turns, one man to cock and load one of two bows while the other man shot the second bow. It took two men at a minimum to move the mantlets, which screened them from enemy arrows, up into effective range before sunup and back at dusk. And while they were employed, their first targets were enemy crossbowmen — who could put a bolt through the arrow-slit in the mantlet to wound or kill a man behind it — as well as the crews of their ballistae, whose darts could pierce even the strongest mantlets to kill the men behind it. After disabling these, they shot every Seljuq archer in range.

It took us a week to ready the first crossbow and sapper teams, and build them mantlets and siege sheds — the long, narrow, tunnel-like shelters of wood, fireproofed with hides. These last we would set end-to-end to form a protected route to the wall or tower we planned to pierce or undermine.

Before we could put these to work, however, other events intruded.

Demetrius used to say, with a shrug and a grin, "Sometimes in life you get shit on your shoes. War drops you in an overflowing sewer. So learn to swim — and, above all — to do it with your mouth shut."

✠✠✠

The Crusaders hurl Turkish heads into the city of Nicaea.

# EIGHT

✠✠✠

It was on the afternoon of the nineteenth of May that a rumor shot along our front line like a bee for its hive. When it reached me by means of my panting squire, Colin, who had run a considerable way to find me, I grabbed the nearest horse and rode hard for Godfrey's headquarters tent near the eastern gate.

It seemed a Seljuq messenger had ridden unawares into a party of Godfrey's Lotharingians cutting wood and brush for mantlets along the eastern road, and promptly been captured. And it was the news he carried that I sought to learn.

The captain commanding the woodcutters had already put a true fear of God in the messenger during the ride to camp, and the man had arrived bleeding only a little, but already terrified a great deal from this initial ordeal. It seems that the captain's pantomime of what was about to happen to the messenger in the short remainder of his present life, and throughout eternity, put him in such a frame of mind.

His name was Ahmed, I believe, and he was about 18 years of age. When I arrived headquarters, Godfrey's lieutenants already had Ahmed convinced of his imminent death, stuffed with pork and lashed along a spitted pig as it roasted, that made him suddenly reconsider all his allegiances, religion, and recent choices in life.

Now Ahmed spoke no language I or my noble Frankish brothers-in-arms understood, but the captain of woodcutters had with him a short, wrinkled, tanned, and most odoriferous Greek scout who was interpreting between Ahmed and his captors. To my great surprise, I discovered it was Demetrius in his old scout's disguise, garlic and all.

But Demetrius had recognized me first, and with a subtle look and a small sign, be begged me not to give him away. So I ignored him and joined the group, all of us focused on poor Ahmed.

Then Demetrius said, "My lords, the captives asks if, before he dies, he might convert and become a Christian, so as to avoid the eternal perils of fire and torture you have said await him in Hell."

Godfrey was there, of course, and it was he who said, "Tell him there will be no conversion and no baptism unless he reveals the message he carries to Nicaea. He and his fellow pig . . ." he indicated the one roasting over the firepit, filling the air with a wonderful aroma, ". . . will roast together, first here, and then forevermore in Hell, as a damned and defiled Islamite heathen."

And to underscore the point, Godfrey sliced a slab of pork from the pig, bit off a chunk, and proffered the rest to Ahmed, who shuddered, gibbered in Arabic, and struggled to avoid contact as Godfrey then smeared the meat against his cheeks.

Godfrey went on, "Tell him that if he tells us the message, one we find to be the truth, we will spare him, baptize him, reward him well, and feed him the finest baptismal dinner this camp can provide, starting with this fine pig and the best wine I have. After all, neither of these does God deny His faithful. Only Islamites are so enjoined."

**Godfrey of Bouillon, Duke of Lorraine, prince of the First Crusade.**

Demetrius duly translated, and Ahmed listened carefully. He knew he was in deep trouble, with certain torture and death before him, and no hope of rescue as a possibility. He sank deep in thought a moment and then nodded his assent. Demetrius did not need to translate that.

The nobles and knights around me instantly beamed with triumph and pleasure, but not Godfrey, who was just as grim as before. "Tell us then, and we will first see if we believe you."

The smiles faded from the Christian faces at that.

As Demetrius translated, Ahmed nodded, and in undoubtedly his most earnest manner, he told Demetrius a tale that the little Greek then reported to us.

"He says he was to make his way to Nicaea by the fastest means, even at the risk of killing the horse. He was to tell the garrison commander that the greatest sultan of all the Seljuqs, Kilij Arslan, had received his warning of the coming of the great Infidel army to engulf the sultan's capital, and that he, himself, the Great Sultan Kilij Arslan, was riding night and day at the head of a great army to rescue the capital from the unbelievers the morning after tomorrow. They will attack from the east with one force along the road to the eastern gate. And when they have the enemy engaged, a second force will enter the city by the southern gates, pass through and sortie by the eastern gate to attack the enemy's rear by surprise.

"He also says that the greatest sultan of all the Seljuqs, Kilij Arslan, will send ahead his fastest reinforcements to arrive about sunrise tomorrow and strike the army of unbelievers by surprise, before reinforcing the garrison. He requires the commander of the garrison to sortie all his able-bodied horse-archers to join the battle. For if these Christians are as cowardly and inept as the Christian army they destroyed last October, the Seljuqs will surely prevail to destroy them all, with thanks to Allah the Most Merciful."

Ahmed gibbered in Arabic again and Demetrius in turn added this:

"He says: 'This is the message I was given to carry, and I swear upon my father's soul and hope for Christian paradise that it is true. If the attack does not come as I say, you may kill me as a liar in any way you choose. But if it comes as I say, I beg you to spare me, baptize me, and treat me thereafter as you would any good Christian.'"

Ahmed's eyes were fervent with truth and the hope we believed him.

At that, Godfrey nodded and said to his lieutenants, "Take the boy away. Do not mistreat him. Keep him tied and guarded against escape, but feed him well whatever he will eat and drink. We must confer upon this news."

They nodded, and took Ahmed away.

Godfrey turned the to face us, his council, for the rumor had spread to all and brought into the tent nearly every commander at Nicaea, including Duke Bohemond. "Well, do we believe him?" he asked us.

Beside me, Count Robert spoke up. "If we are wise, we must. False warning of a surprise attack like this cannot be a ruse, for it only puts us on our guard, which is too foolish if a real attack is planned, and no harm if it does not. Kilij Arslan is not a fool. So I believe this is a gift from God, and that we must prepare and expect attack to come as the messenger has said."

Duke Bohemond said, "The count's words are wise. I agree with him."

Godfrey said, "As do I. We must expect an attack from the east, by way of those roads and from the eastern valleys, and we must prepare for another sortie by every gate of Nicaea, but especially from the unguarded southern ones." Then he turned to me. "Baron Godric, you command our southern flank, and after the surprise attack the other day, I would not have any another commander there. What say you?"

"My lords, God protected us all that day, for by happy chance my defenses were in place and my engines ready to shoot. But my engines and many of my men have since been deployed to bombard the gates and destroy the enemy's siege machines. I also suffered one-fifth of my force killed or wounded in that attack, and few of the latter have yet recovered. And Arslan's scouts are sure to see from the nearest ridge that I am unanchored by any natural defense, and open to attack from three sides, so I will be the point of concentration for both his army and a garrison attack. I fear we are not now strong enough to repeat a successful defense against a much larger combined attack."

Count Robert nodded and said with a frown, "Can we not extend the line? Where are Count Raymond and the Bishop of Puy? We heard they have marched to join us. Why are they not here to complete the encirclement? Can we speed them to arrive in time? With them in place, they counter the garrison attack at the gates and extend our line from Godric to the lake. With them in place, Arslan cannot turn our flank."

Godfrey nodded in agreement at that, and then Bohemond said, "My wagoners tell me Raymond and Bishop Ademar are now a day away, perhaps two. If we urge them to march through the night, perhaps we can have them in place to complete the siege line by dawn."

"Aye!" said many voices among us then, relief evident in their tone.

But Robert said, "Send the messenger by all means, but do not count on them, for it will take even a fast ride most of the night to reach them and they still have to march to reach us after that. We must plan to repel this attack without them."

All saw the wisdom in his words, and grim resolve replaced the relief.

Godfrey said, "I will immediately send them a message to come on with all speed and take their places along the southern wall. And thank God for this messenger — I will spare his life tonight and make a Christian of him tomorrow. But for today, ready your men, erect barricades at the rear of your camps as good Baron MacEuan did, and have your squires and mounted men–at-arms ready armor and horses to ride into Arslan's flanks and rear. *Deus lo vult!*"

"*Deus lo vult!* God wills it!" roared a score of noble knights.

✠✠✠

We all worked hard, then, all that day, and late into the night, strengthening our defenses and readying our weapons and armor for the attack to come. We scavenged Christian and Seljuq spears and arrows from the battlefield, and took all the Seljuq bows as well, for their arrows were too short to shoot from any Frankish bow. I had my cooks prepare a hearty stew of horse and barley in plenty for the evening meal, and broke out the ale as well, for on this meal we would fight all day in our greatest battle yet. And I prayed to see Raymond and Ademar in place beside us when the sun rose.

But dawn came all too soon, and Raymond and Ademar didn't. As the light grew, there was no sign of them anywhere — in line next to me along the near-mile to the lake, or coming around Godfrey and Count Robert, in the battle line north of me along the southeast wall — they were nowhere in sight. I had not counted on them, but I had hoped to see them. Now I was in deep trouble.

But Jean arrived with his knights and mine, and every one of his men-at-arms and yeomen who were able to walk. Today their place was with us.

So I called my men and his to gather around, and this is what I told them: "Four days ago, without warning or support, you did what no lord here believed possible. You fought — and defeated — an attack by mounted Seljuqs who outnumbered us ten to one. You won against those great odds because God was with us, fighting at your sides, strengthening your arms and guiding your arrows to hit the damned heathens who had come to kill you, His faithful. And in this great army gathered here today, no men are better regarded as true fighting men of God than you are. I am proud of every one of you."

I paused and looked around that circle of brothers in arms, and watched them blink with surprise and pride. Then I said. "Today we face another test, one even greater than before. Today they will come again with even greater numbers. They will encircle us on three sides as before, attempt to get through our barriers, and try to cut us all down with arrow, lance, and sword. Today there may be twenty of them for each one of you."

Uneasiness replaced their pride for a moment, and then stubborn courage showed in its place. I could not have asked for more.

"We await the arrival of Count Raymond and Bishop Ademar, who have the greatest army of all. They march through the night to join the line south and west of us completing our siege line around this fortress city . . ." and inwardly I prayed what I had just said was true, for I had no way of knowing if it was. "Soon they will arrive to attack our foes, striking their flanks and rear, doing to them what the Seljuqs plan to do to us. We know it, but the Islamites do not. And then the surprise, the jest, will be on them!"

The men looked at each other with grins and nods of reassurance, and their confidence rose again.

"I tell you all this because you deserve to know what will come, and I know you will fight all the better for it. What we must do is what we have already done — what *you* already did. Stand and fight, here in this, our place. There is nowhere to run, and no reason to. Just stand and kill them, until there are no more. Defend your brothers, for they defend you. And God will again fight for us, for we are His army. *Deus lo vult!*"

"*Deus lo vult! Deus lo vult! Deus lo vult!*" they all cried as one man.

"Now kneel and pray with Father Anselm and me as we ask Almighty God to give us another victory to His glory. Father?"

Then Anselm led us in prayer, said the prayers of general absolution, and distributed the Eucharist to each man. We were all holy then, saved by the Blood of Christ, and as worthy and strong as angels to face the godless foes of Heaven.

✠✠✠

As we awaited the Turks, I reviewed my preparations and thanked God that, out of sympathy for what I faced, the other commanders had sent back my engines and my engineers the previous evening. Indeed, they had sent their own machine and crews to me as well, so that now I commanded three times as many engines as I had four days earlier. With them I knew we would make a good fight of it, but I prayed it would be enough.

All along the rear of our camps, which would now be our front line for this attack, we — Bohemond, Godfrey, Robert, and I — erected barricades, strengthened our chevaux-de-frise with spears and staves, and reinforced them by adding gabions of earth and rock, all to prevent the Seljuqs from again breaching the line as they earlier had mine. I stockpiled cobbles, baskets of stones, sheaves of arrows, and piles of darts everywhere. And an hour before the Seljuqs appeared, Count Robert reinforced me with a full company of his best archers. Every wattle mantlet from all along the front line, it seemed, had been delivered to my camp during the night. Now these all lay flat in place around my perimeter; there was no point in letting the Seljuqs know we awaited them — that might change their plans, and it was certainly better to fight two smaller armies over two days than one big combined army all at once.

We had done all we could. Now all we could still do was wait and pray. And then fight like angels.

Or demons.

✠✠✠

We did not have to wait long.

Ahmed had spoken true, it seemed, for shortly after my speech and our joint appeal to Heaven, the Seljuqs did indeed appear, and not just on the road across the plains from the south-southeast. Indeed they ranged onto the flanking hillsides as well, where the morning sunlight silhouetted them and glinted from helmets, spears, and mail, in numbers far greater than our first foes. If this was merely the "advance party," I dreaded to think of the size of the Seljuq army behind them, for all of them appeared headed directly at me.

As we waited, the Seljuq army halted. They began to maneuver, gathering themselves into units or squadrons, each one a cluster of dismounted men and standing horses. Breakfast, then. I am sure the respite was welcome, for they had traveled hard and fast to reach us. As I watched, a small party, no doubt their commanders, rode up to the crest of the nearest hill to the east, in order to view our lines and plan their attack.

I had no idea how many there were of them, but there seemed to be easily five times as many as made the garrison attack, perhaps five thousand horsemen, and maybe more. I had less than one-in-twenty to stop them.

The sun had just reached two hands above the horizon to mark the start of the third hour when I saw them mount. And as I had the alarm sounded — by word, horns, and flags — their horns sounded also, and they began a slow trot into attack formation, the squadrons spreading into a vast line.

Now, the first mile of road outside the eastern gate — the final mile of their approach — angles east-southeast, flanking a ridge that overlooks Nicaea before the road turns east. And as the Seljuqs came, their leaders, identified the cluster of banners and flags in their midst, moved to my left as they followed the road to the eastern gate. This told me that they meant to force their way through our lines and gain entry into the city by way of the eastern gate.

To Gavin, the young yeoman messenger who lived at my elbow in battle, I said, "Quick, lad, mount and ride, by the Nicaean side of our line, first to Count Robert and then to Duke Godfrey. Tell them the attack centers on the eastern gate." In truth, Robert and Godfrey might have already seen what I did, but assumption is the key to defeat, and if they had not or could not see as I could, my message would provide a timely warning.

"Aye, sire! The attack centers on the eastern gate!"

Then he was gone.

Now it takes mounted men but moments to cover a mile at a trot, and when they struck, it would be at a much faster speed, perhaps a gallop. So we had little time to react, as little as it took to read this.

By now, about a mile out, their squadrons had spread wide, forming a half-mile-long line of cavalry parallel to our siege-line, from the eastern ridge to opposite me. Duke Godfrey, at the gate, would face their right flank, Count Robert their center, and I their left flank.

Why they did not just ride around me to enter the southern gates unopposed, I could not understand, unless they could not see beyond me. Perhaps they did not know we had not fully encircled Nicaea.

And then I realized that they did not care, for they did not fear us. Six months ago, they had destroyed one Christian army of sixty thousand with no effort at all, another sixteen thousand by bottling them up in a fort without water for nine days. Based on these easy victories, they expected us to flee before them, and then to crush us between their irresistible onslaught and a rain of deadly arrows from the walls of Nicaea.

Overconfidence in battle is a terrible thing, when it is based on a false assumption. They assumed our army was like those of earlier when nothing could be further from the truth. And they were about to pay a terrible price to learn that.

From my prior experience fighting Pecheneg and Seljuq horse-archers, I knew they that since they held the bow in the left hand to draw it with the right, they would shoot ahead coming in, wheel their horses to the right in order to shoot to their left, and circle away as they took another handful of arrows to repeat the charge, always circling right. That meant the attackers on their extreme left flank — the rightmost as I looked out at them — would attack us and then break left across our line toward the center as they circled away. And I could take advantage of that.

With that, my own battle plans changed. Hamish commanded our archers and crossbowmen, and I ran to him then. "Hamish! Have your archers shoot at the rightmost incoming horsemen and the crossbows at the closest horsemen as they pass to your left. Make the shots count. Kill the horse first, then the man." A horse-archer afoot was already a dead man, being too lightly armed and unable to flee.

"Aye!" Hamish understood and set about it, calling in his captains.

Then I ran to the siege engines. "Onagers! Load your spoons with stones. Aim as I point you! While they are in range, shoot at will, as fast as you can, and keep shooting while you have targets!"

"Aye! Stones at will, fast as we can!" the captains repeated.

But I was not done. Starting from the right, I had the aim of each machine swung increasingly left, until the last were throwing at a sharp angle across our battle line to our left, to hit the Seljuqs as they circled past and away.

Finally I ordered my captains of ballistae and scorpios — those ever-so-deadly giant crossbows — to kill all the Seljuq officers, watching their banner-bearers to find and shoot the richly attired, better-armored Islamite knights they followed. One shot, one kill, one fewer lord to direct the attack.

Now it took a few minutes to do all this, but I started as their lines began to form and kept at it, ignoring them as their horns sounded and they began their charge — first at a trot, increasing to a canter when halfway in, and staying in that canter as they closed straight in to attack and sweep left along our line. Indeed, I was just finishing as their first horsemen reached fifty yards from our barricades . . .

. . . and hit the belt of caltrops I had thickly sown out there.

Instantly, all the horses who trod on those evil iron spikes were lamed, screaming and rearing in pain and fright, only to be collided with by the charging horses behind them, nailed by bolts and arrows, and battered down by cruel stones hurled at an arrow's speed. Seljuq archers were thrown, trampled or crushed by the maddened horses, then shot with a bolt as they struggled to rise. The horsemen behind them were tossed into complete confusion when their well-practiced battle maneuver dissolved into chaos, and as they reined and hesitated to decide what to do, volleys of arrows and stones hammered them down as well.

"Mantlets up!" I ordered, and the wood-and-wattle shields popped up, turning our vulnerable camp into a small fortress.

A small number broke to the right then, trying to reform their circular charge. But I shifted aim with them and killed them as they tried, forced as they were to stay back under my fall of stones and arrows by the deadly caltrops.

The bulk of my attackers instead were forced by our barrage to my left, where they crowded into the horsemen trying to attack Robert, and throwing them into confusion as well. That rippled further, shoving Duke Godfrey's attackers left.

And now the whole Seljuq attack was off-target, and off-balance. Instead of riding through us, butchering us like sheep as we fled their horsemen, the Seljuq advance force was milling in chaos, and dying as Christian arrows reached out, almost twice as far as their own could to plunge into their midst.

And they appeared about to break and run in-masse, when our horns sounded again and our Frankish knights — heavily armored, riding huge destriers, and bearing heavy lance and shield — burst from hiding behind us along the siege line, to charge out around my right and through a gap in Godfrey's line in a two-pronged envelopment.

The Seljuq commanders on their promontory saw this much too late, and their horsemen never did. Our knights charged at the gallop into the Seljuq flanks and rear, and then right through the massed Turkish horsemen. A vast melee ensued, and Christian lances and swords brought death to many more Turks, who were too lightly armed and armored to defeat a Frank. Instead, those that could fled helter-skelter, east into the hills. Most never made it.

✠✠✠

The battle the morning of the twentieth did not last even an hour. We took relatively few casualties, while the Seljuq advance force was cut completely to pieces. Afterward, we made no effort to save their wounded or take prisoners — after all, they had not done so with our people, so they had no claim on Christian charity.

They fought in hopes of gaining their prophet's paradise. In turn, we accommodated them, and sent them all to wherever he was. Neck-deep in unquenchable fire at the very bottom of Hell seemed right to me.

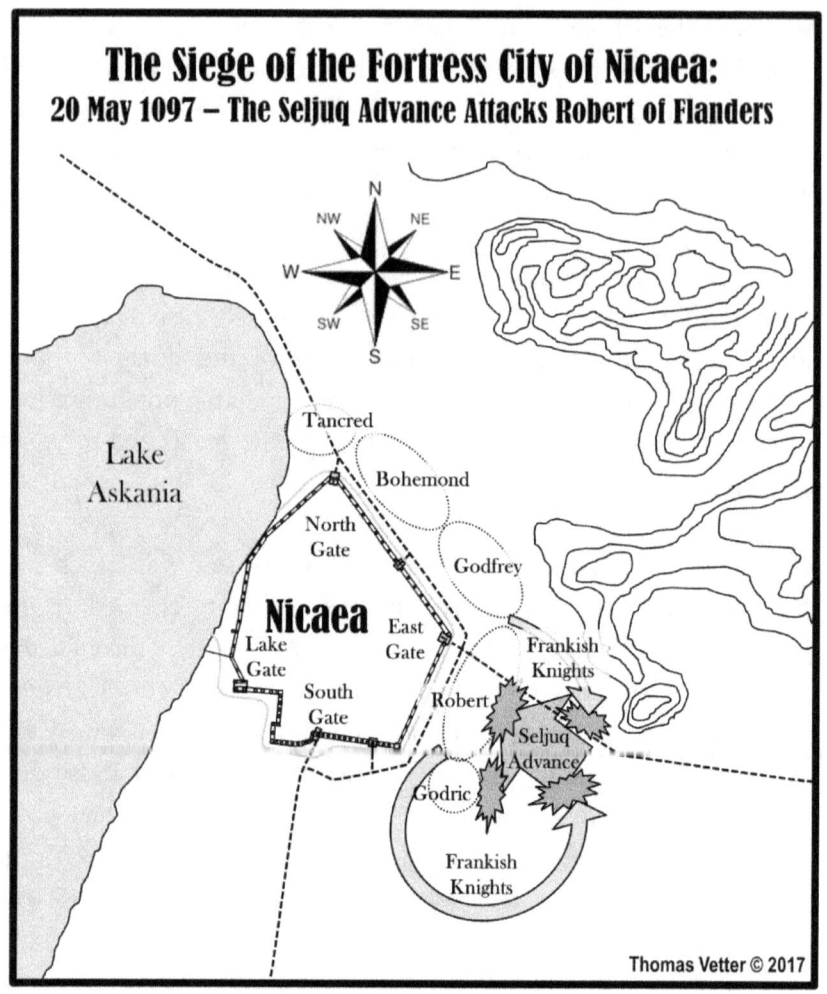

20 May 1097: The Seljuq advance attacks Robert of Flanders.

✠✠✠

# NINE

✠✠✠

Successful as we were in that battle on the twentieth, our troubles were not over, for the force we had defeated was not the main Seljuq army, just their swiftest vanguard. We still had to face Sultan Arslan's full army when it arrived to attack us again, at the third hour on the morrow.

But that was no reason for gloom. God had just given us a great victory. He was indeed fighting with and for us. So we dispatched the enemy wounded, cleared away the corpses, and dragged in the dead horses — the new supply of fresh horsemeat meant we would fight well-fed. We recovered arrows, stones, Seljuq weapons and armor; then we sharpened and repaired our own. After all, we needed them all again tomorrow. And we cleared the battlefield, partially to make the Seljuqs wonder about the success their vanguard had had, and partially to protect our own destriers from stumbling over corpses in the fight to come. This time, it was not just I that piled Turkish heads; every commander of note had his own pile, too.

Ironically, I suffered far fewer killed and wounded in this fight than on the sixteenth — probably because we were better prepared and better protected, and because my tactic to force the Seljuqs toward their center minimized the attack on my — or any — position.

About noon, Jean found me conferring with Count Robert in his headquarters tent. "My lords, when we scouted the hills to the east

195

a fortnight ago, I saw something important there that may prove key to victory in tomorrow's fight. Godric, please send for Edward, and then together draw a map of what I describe."

So Edith — disguised as Edward — and I laid out a large fresh parchment. As Jean related his recollections, we drew first a map of our positions around the city and then of the ground to the east.

Pointing, Jean said, "As you know, the ground to the east consists of hills and low mountains. They are forested with good timber and well-watered by small streams. Two miles north of us — here — is a valley that leads east a league, well into the mountains, ending at a place where a stream ponds in a low spot — here. There, another draw begins, running along here, southwest a mile, and another mile south, to here, where it opens onto the plain, across which runs the road the Seljuqs used yesterday. The draw is rugged, but rideable by mounted knights, and would let us bring a force around behind Arslan's army by a well-hidden route.

"I believe if we sent a large force of mounted men-at-arms to that pond today, they could come through the draw to counterattack the Seljuqs from the rear as they attack us tomorrow morning. We saw how well our knights destroyed their attack today. While our siege line holds them in place, we can hit them with mounted knights from the north — here along Bohemond's and Godfrey's sectors; in their rear by this eastern route I describe; and from the south with another contingent of mounted knights from the south — yours, mine, and Count Raymond's, if they are here. The entire Seljuq army will be surrounded, and their horse-archers will have no place to hide and no room for their hit-and-run attacks."

Robert and I were in awe. It was a brilliant stratagem, and just what we needed. Robert said, "A outstanding plan, Baron! Come! Let us take it to Godfrey."

Not a half-hour later, Godfrey and Bohemond had not only agreed to and praised Jean's plan, but put out a call for volunteers, knights, and men-at-arms ready and willing to spend a night by the pond. Jean was given command, and I could tell he was proud and elated by the honor. The response was so enthusiastic that Jean had to turn some away, men who promptly volunteered for one of the two other cavalry wings. They left at the ninth hour, and made a cold camp at the pond, with no fires to alert any Seljuq scouts, before darkness fell.

I dearly wished to go, but I had my own critical role to play. Many of those Turks who had fallen this morning were downed by my stones, or thrown when their horses were struck. Tomorrow I had an even bigger task, this time against fifty thousand Turks, perhaps more.

✠✠✠

Around mid-afternoon, my old friend Demetrius came to my camp, still in his old disguise as a scout, and stinking again of the garlic he hid in his clothes.

"I came to thank you for not revealing my identity the other day, and to praise the splendid performance of you, your engines, and your men this morning. The student has surpassed his mentor, and I could not be more pleased."

"Thank you, old friend. I see you are up to your old tricks. Are you here among us as Alexios's spy?" I said with a grin.

"You know him well — and me," he replied, with a smile of his own. "But my real reason is one I hesitate to confess, to any but the closest of friends . . ."

"Well, you can be assured of my friendship. What is this secret?"

"I've been a scout and siege engineer all my life — since I grew from boyhood and joined the army . . ." he paused, ". . . but I've never actually been at a real siege — we haven't besieged any place in all that time, though others have besieged us. My expertise is all theory and training, and no actual experience. But I hear you have six successes to your credit." *That must have been Anselm,* I thought. 'No one has ever taken this city by force, so I came to watch and help you be the first."

I was thunderstruck, and realized then that I had never actually asked him about his sieges — it never occurred to me to do so. Apparently, curiosity isn't really a strength of mine.

So I grinned, and punched his shoulder. "Well, Demetrius, I'll keep that secret, too. Many now think me a genius for wheedling all I know out of you. It will do me no good to undermine you. So stay close, and together we'll figure out how to take Nicaea."

✠✠✠

Late afternoon we learned that, after riding all night, our messenger had found Raymond and Ademar at Helenopolis. Their armies were buying food for the days ahead at the last real source, still a full day's march from Nicaea. Understanding instantly the danger facing us all when he learned our message, Raymond immediately called in his commanders, ordered them to march an hour hence and push their contingents hard, all day and through the night, to reach Nicaea by dawn. Then to us he sent his fastest courier to carry his vow to arrive by dawn on the twenty-first, no matter the cost.

This news spread fast, and lifted spirits in all the Christian camps.

So I spent the evening among my troops, moving from fire to fire, greeting, jesting, praising, and emboldening the men. Music and song rose from the encampments all along our siege line, the hearty, savory smell of roasting horsemeat everywhere.

I found Colin and Edward sitting together — they did that often lately, I noted, and I wondered if there was more than comradely feelings between them, given the secret they shared. But they always maintained a proper manner, consistent with preserving Edith's disguise, so I left their friendship alone as their business. I did note that Colin and Anselm were never far from her, and each took their own pains to ensure Edith's safety, especially in battle.

I was up late seeing to all, and at two hours past sunset conferred with Robert to report readiness, get new orders and any fresh news. Raymond's latest messenger had just arrived: Of the ten leagues Raymond had to cover, they had, by their mid-afternoon brief halt for supper, reached the shore of Lake Ascanius, about halfway. And Raymond and Ademar renewed the vow to be in position by dawn.

I retired then for a few hours of rest; I had to be up by first light — an hour before dawn — to ensure we were up, fed, and ready to fight by dawn, start of the first hour. The sultan might or might not attack us at the third hour, but when he did, he would find us ready.

✠✠✠

Barely was I up when I heard the weary tramp of men and horses. A wide column of them marched along our eastern front line, a small group of monks on horses in front singing the prayers of Lauds, the pre-dawn vigil service, so that all would know them as Christians and not mistakenly attack them as the sultan's Islamites, come in the dark.

I gave a fervent prayer of thanks, then, for Raymond and Ademar had come. And with Colin, I mounted and went out to meet those worthy lords, who rode together just behind their vanguard.

"My lords! I am Baron Godric MacEuan, and until now I have commanded the army's southernmost flank. We have not much time. I am to brief you on our plans for this day's battle, and what you may expect of the enemy. I am to help you ready your armies."

"Thank you, Baron, for your kind greetings and news," said Bishop Ademar. "What we expect of the enemy today is that they die!"

I realized, then, that Ademar was more cleric than warrior, although this was by no means always so. He might be Pope Urban's official commander of this crusade, but I did not believe he really knew anything of military campaigns.

But not so Count Raymond, who said, "God willing, of course, Your Excellency. But we have come far, and our men are footsore and weary. In a matter of hours we must be ready to fight as never before. We need to hear what the baron has to say, and no time to waste. Baron, you were saying . . ."

"My lords, from my position here, you are to range yourselves west, along the southern walls. This is my squire, Colin, who will show you the city's southern gates and help you position your armies between my lines and the lake. Count Robert's men and mine cooked up food through the night so your men might eat after your long march and before the hard fight we face. We will fetch it to you immediately. Colin, sound the horn."

Colin blew a call that notified the cooks to load the cauldrons in the wagons and send them along. Then he and the count's squire rode off to the van to position the new contingents, and I took

Raymond, Ademar, and their aides to my tent to eat as I briefed
them on our positions and plans, and answered their many urgent
questions.

✠✠✠

Ahmed was vindicated. As the sun rose, out on the plain to the east
we could see them come, in numbers easily five or ten times those
of yesterday. Sultan Kilij Arslan had arrived as he promised, to save
his capital.

Back with me again, Colin and I watched them, then, far out on the
eastern plain. By the glint of sun on armor, I saw them begin to
spread wide and divide into two great columns, the northern one
heading along the road to the eastern gate as the Turks had done
yesterday. Duke Godfrey's men would bear the brunt of their
attack.

But the other column moved wide to the south. That made no
military sense, until I remembered that Ahmed had said the sultan
expected to enter Nicaea unopposed through the southern gates,
pass through the city, and attack Godfrey in the rear from the
eastern gate. And that meant they expected to split our army in the
center, then use each of the two columns to destroy a wing of ours.

I explained that to Colin, then I said, "Ride now to Raymond. Urge
him on the signal to send his knights and mounted men-at-arms out
along the lakeshore and then east to hit that column in the flank
and rear. If they do, the Turks will be pressed toward me, where my
engines will take down many of them. And the squadron of knights
that go out between my position and his will hit them again from
the other flank."

Colin understood, and ran to his horse. And with that, I had done
all I could. Now it was all up to the fighting spirit of good Christian

men, and in the hands of God.

✠✠✠

Two hours after sunrise their horns sounded, and on they came. And that began the longest, and hardest, day of my life until then.

The two separate hordes of Seljuq horse archers came at us like two great waves. The enormous eastern column spread wide, forming a great north-south storm of men and horses, which crashed against the barricades of Godfrey, Robert, and myself, then ebbed away in great swirls of circling riders gathering another fistful of arrows, and sweeping back in to strike again. Their arrows flew thick and fast, and soon every stationary surface facing them — the mantlets, gabions, and even the uprights of my engines — all wore protruding arrows.

The smaller second horde rode past me well to the south, then turned toward Nicaea up the road to the central southern gate. That they were not expecting what confronted them quickly became clear, for they rode, not as in the charge we faced, but as a bunched column of riders expecting a clear path and open gates. So when Count Raymond had his men suddenly rise up from seated and prone positions in the brush and pour arrows into that column from the front and both flanks, the Seljuq consternation was complete. The Turkish van, riding hard down the road to the gate, first suddenly slammed into a belt of caltrops. Up rose a phalanx of men with grounded spears, and in flew a thick cloud of arrows and bolts, throwing the column into chaos. Horses reared and fell, to trip up the beasts following them, building a huge pile of fallen men and animals across the roads. The riders further back were suddenly forced to veer wildly to either side. But as they did, arrows and bolts were shot into them, all aimed for their horses. Then, well-armored yeomen darted out and quickly slew the dazed riders with poniards before scurrying back into our lines.

For my part, the first wave of Turks crashed into my belt of caltrops and floundered, and as they went down, we loosed stones in thick clouds into the oncoming horsemen behind them, one great simultaneous opening volley followed by three rapid flights of arrows from bow and crossbow. Not a Turk got within twenty yards of our barricade. After that it was individual fire by archer and engine, quick as they could, but all aimed shots designed to kill men, individually or wherever they briefly clustered.

Then our horns sounded, and four great squadrons of mounted knights and men-at-arms rode out: those of Bohemond and Tancred swept along the northeastern siege line to the cheers of the Christians there, and slammed straight through the sultan's right flank. Another squadron, Godfrey's horsemen, rode through a gap the duke briefly opened and hit the sultan's horsemen head-on with great surprise. Between me at the southeast corner and Count Raymond along the southern wall, sallied Count Robert's knights. Half of them went left and struck the sultan's left flank, and the other half tore into the disorganized Seljuq horse-archers milling in confusion before Count Raymond's men. And Raymond's knights swept in from the lakeshore to hit the same horde on their left flank and in their rear.

Finally from the east, we heard Jean's distant horns sound the charge, and his mounted men slammed a deadly line of lances into the Seljuq rear, hitting them just where they thought themselves most safe. Jean's men tore through them as an arrow rips through parchment, and left a great many dead on the first pass alone.

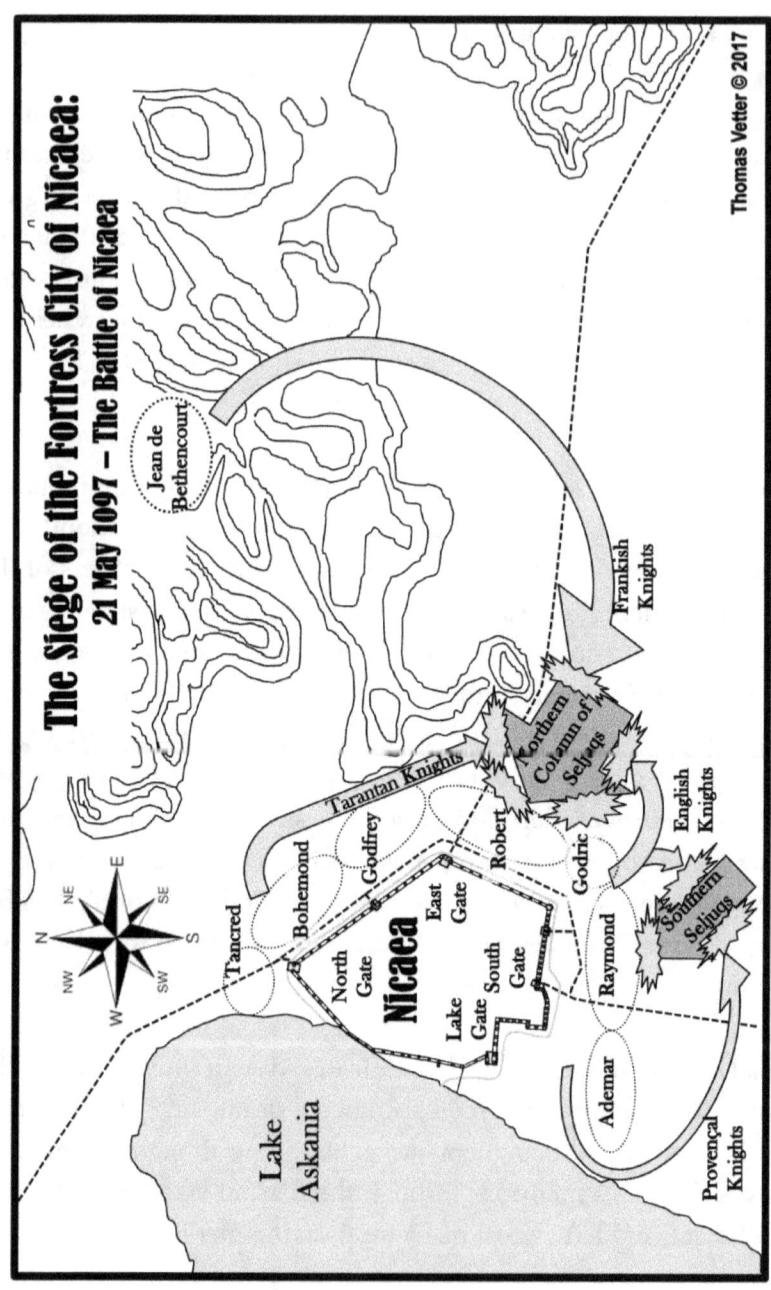

The Siege of the Fortress City of Nicaea:
21 May 1097 – The Battle of Nicaea

Thomas Vetter © 2017

Jean de Bethencourt

Frankish Knights

Northern Column of Seljeqs

English Knights

Tarantan Knights

Southern Seljuqs

Bohemond

Godfrey

Robert

Godric

Raymond

Tancred

East Gate

North Gate

**Nicaea**

Lake Gate

South Gate

Ademar

N NE
NW E
W SE
SW S
S

Lake Askania

Provençal Knights

**21 May 1097: The Battle of Nicaea.**

With that, the entire Seljuq attack was destroyed, and the fight turned, not into the massacre the Turks expected, but a great melee instead, with Christians and Islamites contending in a vast battle of man-on-man. Our mounted knights, armed with stout lance and shield, rode through the swarm and speared mounted Turk after Turk, while squires riding as men-at-arms cut down unhorsed Seljuqs with swords or maces. In desperation, the mounted Turks whirled their mounts and shot arrows at a knight's horse instead of its rider, for our armor withstood their arrows except at point-blank range. Many a knight lost a good destrier there that day.

Once the Turkish charge was shattered and the two armies mingled in desperate battle, I had my engines cease bombardment, for the risk they posed to Christians was just as great as to Islamite. The archers, too, ceased; Turkish arrows might not pierce Christian armor, but Christian arrows had been doing so for a century.

Instead, I gave Hamish command, ordering him to maintain the siege line against a possible attack by the garrison and protect our camp from the Turks. But I took Colin and half our fighting men out through the barricades and we joined the fight afoot. After all, the Turks were mostly on foot as and there was no point getting a great horse like LaochDubh killed unnecessarily.

For my part, I prefer fighting with a bow. I became a skilled archer in boyhood, and learned to use the Turkish bow here in this land on pilgrimage a decade before. Now, Turkish bows and arrows were everywhere, dropped by fallen men. So with my shield slung across my back, I went forth and shot Turks with their own arrows as fast as I could nock them, seizing another full quiver whenever I ran low. With them, I could kill both close and at a distance, put down a mounted Turk or his horse, and pick off their knights as I spotted them. Whenever I did, the men following him were left leaderless, lost heart and tried to flee — futilely, for there was no place to go.

Arrows flew thick at me, too, make no mistake. But I had made my own chainmail using interlinked solid and riveted rings, and there was no stronger mail to be had. I wore it over my jack of plates, with Martun's Damascus steel plates sewn inside, a second layer of armor under my mail. Together, Turkish arrows could not get through, so I collected fresh bruises instead, these atop the ones of yesterday and five days hence.

It was my speed as an archer, though, that most often saved myself and Colin. Time seems to pass slower in battle, enabling me to more easily outdraw or outshoot the Turk swinging a bow toward me. I think that was God fighting for me, then, by giving me greater speed and sureness of aim when I needed it most.

At my side, young Colin fought hard, using a poleaxe to great effect, and then spear and sword-and-shield when its long shaft finally broke. Often it was he who put to rest the men my arrows struck.

Elsewhere all along the line, other Christian fighting men did as I did — I am not special in that — and eagerly came out to fight the Turks man-to-man. Such battle is routinely practiced in our lands, and it is vicious, brutal and nasty work. But to the Seljuqs, it is not so. They win or lose atop a horse. Atop, they win; but off, they die.

The battle went on, then, all through the day. Nicaea was the sultan's capital, and unless he won, with the city he lost his seat of power, his home, his wives and children, his slaves, and all the wealth he had amassed. Kilij Arslan was not about to yield to us.

For some among us, Nicaea was a vast treasure-house, and truthfully they fought chiefly for a chance to seize a share of the riches it held, money that could buy a man land and a manor at home.

But most of us fought to secure this end of the road to Jerusalem. We needed to hold this citadel in order to control our supply line behind us as we went south.

Then, too, we grimly wanted to punish these murderous heathens, men who had murdered some seventy thousand Christian pilgrims, on top of the many tens of thousands of other peaceful Christian pilgrims and inhabitants they had killed, enslaved, raped by fornication and unholy wedlock, and made their serfs throughout this land. And vengeance is a powerful motivator.

As our Christian fighting men were wounded, broke or lost their weapons, or weakened from thirst and fatigue, they were able to retire into our lines for water, a mouthful of food, or another weapon, only to return to the fight, or enable a fresh man to go forth. No one wanted to stay within the lines, it seemed, for to do so was unmanly and unworthy of the red crosses we all wore. But the Turks had nowhere to go, except to a city they could not reach. And so throughout the day, they got weaker, while we did not.

It was darkness, then, that finally ended the battle. We fought until we could not tell who opposed us, and then cautiously withdrew, using our battle cry, *"Deus lo vult,"* as our watchword to get back inside our lines. In the dark, we could hear the wails, whimpers, and cries of the wounded on both sides who could not leave the field.

And the pitiful cries continued all night, growing fewer and feebler as dawn approached.

✠✠✠

When the sun rose, we went out to succor our own men and dispatch the enemy still living. But night, blood loss and thirst had claimed many before we ever reached them.

I mounted then and rode slowly over that great battlefield, surveying what had happened. I knew we had won, for there was no sign of the sultan's army to renew the fight.

Godfrey and Bohemond sent out patrols to search out the enemy. But all they could find was a great trail of foot-and hoofprints, spattered with blood, and headed to the east, to mark the sultan's line of retreat.

Bohemond had his men take the heads from a thousand Turks, load them in carts, and send that grisly treasure off to Emperor Alexios in Pelecanum.

Kilij Arslan, realizing that he could no longer save his city, chose to save the remainder of his army instead, and withdrew, leaving Nicaea to its fate. The city was as yet unconquered, but there would be no one else to rescue it now. In time — and we now had all the time we needed — the great fortress would inevitably fall to us.

I would see to that.

Despite the success of our tactics in destroying the Seljuq attack at the start of the fight, it was a costly battle. Both we and the Seljuqs lost thousands of men killed or wounded. And most of the wounded soon died: of battle fever; weakness brought by exposure and poor sanitation; or the sickness that came with the millions of flies that quickly bloated the dead just beyond our lines. Indeed, we spent a fortnight burying all the men we could, and eating, smoking or salting meat from the thousands of horses littering the battlefield. But we could not beat the flies, and they brought sickness that did far more to kill our army than the Turks could.

In the end, the ground outside our encampments became a vast graveyard of Christians and a stinking, writhing, and festering bed of rotting Turks and horses. I will never get that stench — one that lasted and only got worse over the next five weeks — out of my head.

✠✠✠

In the meantime, Godfrey had kept his word, freed Ahmed, had him baptized by Bishop Ademar and rewarded him with fine clothes and silver. And with that Ahmed became a popular figure everywhere — our newest Christian brother, whose timely warning had spared so many Christian lives and cost many more Islamites theirs. That his warning and salvation came only under dire threat, we forgave.

✠✠✠

In the euphoria that follows great dangers survived and victory won, all in our camp were upbeat, cheerful, and confident. Yet at midday Anselm came to me, greatly upset. He had tended the wounded all yesterday and through the night, lying down to rest finally an hour before dawn, when all had been tended or given Last Rites. And he had slept well into the day in consequence.

In a low but anxious tone, he said, "Godric, I cannot find Edith. She assisted me all of yesterday and through the night, caring for the hurt. But she is not with them now, nor in the tent asleep, nor has anyone seen her today. I greatly fear for her safety."

Alarm filled me. If someone should discover her woman-hood, it might put her virtue at risk. But if they learned of her royalty, the danger of kidnap for ransom was enormous.

"Thank you, Father. I'll find her," and immediately set off to do so.

"Colin! Colin! Damnation, squire, where are you?" I shouted, seeking him throughout the camp. But he did not answer, and no one had seen him either, anywhere in the not-terribly-large camp of mine.

I went looking for Hamish. "Did you send Colin on an errand?"

My concern was evident, for Hamish said, "Nay, I did not. What's amiss?"

"Colin's missing, as is Edward. Anselm came to me just now, most anxious that Edward cannot be found in camp. And while Colin can take care of himself, Edward is in serious trouble."

Hamish looked puzzled, and I realized then that we had never made him party to Edith's secret. So I did so, and then apologized. "For her safety, the fewer who knew it, the better — and those three knew long before I learned of it last month."

With a wry smile Hamish said, "Well, that explains a lot! I always thought Edward clever and odd, but never a woman — certainly not that little girl we took to Romsey. Grown up, she has!" Then he frowned, and his face took on a look that must have matched mine. "I'm going to find Big Tom and his mates. If they are gone, we'll know who took them. If not, those rogues will know who did." And off he went.

I fumed while he was gone, but he was back soon enough.

"Those bastards are gone as well. They passed through our lines just about dawn — I found the man who had sentry duty and let them through. Said there was five of 'em, and that they wanted to go out to take the coins off the dead and dying. They promised him a share for letting them pass. He knew Tom's voice, but couldn't recognize the others. One seemed reluctant to go, while the sixth came a bit behind the five, sayin' he was with 'em." Hamish's disgust was obvious.

I said, "Dear God Almighty! They left at dawn and it's now noon. They have a six-hour start, and if they found horses out there, they could be five or six leagues from us. But which way?"

Hamish frowned. "It's all desert and Islamites to the east, and even more of each to the south. If it's ransom they want, they need to go home. Only Scots will pay for a Scottish royal. You would, but they know you'd never let 'em live to spend a penny once they freed her, and they'll die even quicker if you learn they harmed her. So they'll head north to Constantinople or west to the seacoast to try to find a ship to Bari."

He paused and then said, "I'll organize two rescue parties to search for them, one along each route. Who will lead them?"

"I don't know — I need to speak with Count Robert. Choose ten willing and trustworthy men for each party while I do. I'll propose that Cedric lead one party while I take the other. I'm leaving you in command here. Jean will surely aid you, should you need it." He nodded, and I ran to a horse and rode directly to Robert.

✠✠✠

As I entered his headquarters tent, Robert greeted me with a smile; but it faded as he saw my face. "What's wrong, Godric?"

"Sire, I have just learned that a band of rogues from Duke Robert's army, who snuck among ours as we left Bari, has kidnapped my squire Colin and my clerk Edward and fled with them at dawn, hoping to use them to extort ransom from me."

I did not reveal Edward's secrets because there was no need to do it, though I knew Robert would certainly have kept them. A secret is only safe if untold, and revealed only to the trustworthy with a true need-to-know.

But what I did say was enough, and Robert was both concerned and sympathetic. "How may I help?"

"Though I regret need to abandon you for a time, my people's need is both immediate and greater. I intend to take out a rescue party now, find and rescue my people, and hang the malefactors. My deputy, Hamish, will command my contingent as ably as ever. Sir Cedric will lead a second party to search the alternate route, for he did so often for me while I was sheriff in Alba. We will be gone no more than a fortnight. In that time we will either succeed, or all opportunity for rescue will pass beyond our power to do it."

"Why not pay what they ask?"

"Because they left me no demand, nor way to pay one. And because once payment is sent, the rogues are more likely to cut my men's throats and flee with the money than to set them free."

He nodded and said, "Then of course you must go; I'd trust no other to save my people, either. Godspeed to you, and may He give you success."

✠✠✠

Hamish had Sir Cedric and our men ready to ride when I reached camp, and I delayed yet only long enough to make a plan that all understood. Colin and Edward would live only as long as Big Tom and his men felt safe and able to profit from them, and inwardly I feared they had already cut Colin's throat, for alive he was a threat as well as another burden.

"Cedric, take your men and follow the northern shore of the lake to the west, then to the coast and along it back to Helenopolis. That way should be free of Seljuqs, and your force enough to deal with any likely enemy. Search for their trail — five or six on foot, or a mix of that many afoot and ahorse. I am guessing that if they caught loose horses, they put Edward on one and Colin on another, trussed and tied to their saddles. Big Tom will demand a horse as their leader, and then the others will ride only as there are enough additional horses to go 'round. But it's hard to catch horses in the dark after they've been terrified by battle and blood, so they'll only catch those wounded, lamed, or with snagged reins, and that will slow them to a walking pace, while we ride fresh mounts.

"So go at trot and canter alternated, with short walks to keep your beasts from foundering. Unless these rogues hide, you may ride up on them. Ask all you pass after them — you know what they look like. At the coast, check the ports for signs of them and ask shipmasters if they have seen or spoken with them. If not, leave word I will pay a pound of gold . . ." At this, there were gasps and whistles all around, for that would buy land and a manor at home, ". . . to those who rescue my people alive, but nothing to those who get them killed — and a pound of silver for the four rogues — dead or alive, makes no matter.

"Don't get Edward and Colin killed, though. Let the rogues exchange them alive in order to live. Getting our people back alive is more important than punishing those bastards. God will do it in His own way, even if we cannot.

"Go all the way to Helenopolis, and if you have no success, return here. If you get reports of them, follow as best you can, but send a rider to Hamish with word of all you learned and where you go, so we may assist or follow you. Avoid trouble, if you can, and return within a fortnight, succeed or fail, as soon as you know which.

"I and my party will follow the road to Helenopolis, the only route they know, in hopes they are foolish enough to use it. If I have news of them, I may follow them by land on to Nicomedia, or use the ferry to Pelecanum to overtake them. But I, too, will return within a fortnight.

"Cedric, Any questions? Hamish gave you money for expenses?"

Cedric said, "Aye, sire, more than enough; and no, no questions. And thank you for the commission; I've been in need of a ride like this." Then he added, "Do not fear for Colin; it is they who should worry. And we all like Edward, who has treated us and our friends well. We will do all we can to bring him back safe." And I could see that the men all mirrored that sentiment.

"Godspeed to all of us, then. Let's ride!"

✠✠✠

I led both parties out a route that avoided the caltrops and, as soon as we cleared the cluttered battlefield, turned north. Initially we rode together and quickly, for the sun was high, and a party of six not hard to spot. I was keen to make up the distance behind them, so we rode at a trot, cantering when we could. Each league we could make up made rescue more possible. It was four leagues to the point the two routes diverged, and we reached it before the eighth hour. From there, the roads ran nine leagues north through the mountains to Helenopolis, or eight leagues west along the lake to the coast. At a walking pace, I guessed they were now either two leagues west of the road to Helenopolis, or two leagues north of us along it.

I waved farewell to Cedric and we parted ways. He headed west while I went north. I pushed hard up the road — if we kept up this pace, we might overtake them in another hour or two. I truly hoped we could catch them before dark, for my concern for Edith had only grown.

A half-hour later, mid-way between the eighth and nine hours, my hopes were answered when we met one of Bohemond's daily supply trains — a long line of carts, laden with provisions and headed for Nicaea. The knight in command looked hard at me and said, "Be you the Baron Godric MacEuan? If so, I have news for you."

I halted us alongside him. "I am. What news?"

"I am Reynard, knight of the Duke of Apulia's retinue. Half an hour ago, about a half-league back, we passed three well-armed yeomen on foot, a lad on a lame horse led by a squinty rascal named Big Tom on a horse limping from a wound. Half a mile behind them was another, a squire on a good horse — young, tough, and armed to the teeth with lance, sword and crossbow. He gave his name as Colin. Said others who might follow were seeking him and Tom, and then he described you: big, well-armored, tough, scarred cheeks, blue eyes, and red-blonde beard. He said you would pay well to learn of them and that they head for Helenopolis at a walk."

I thanked him warmly with words and silver, and we then pressed on hard. Tom's scoundrels were now just a league ahead,[20] moving

---

[20] If, after they met, Reynard walked south a half-hour, and Big Tom north a half-hour, each going at a one-league/hour pace, how far apart would they be when Reynard met Godric? One league. But I have no idea when the trains from Chicago and New York would pass.

at a walking pace along a route I knew better than they did — after all, I had built this road myself not a month before.

We were already pressing the horses as hard as I dared, traveling about eight miles every hour. I knew we could cover forty miles a day at this rate without harming them, so we only needed to keep up this pace.

A short while later, at the marker for the twentieth mile, we overtook Colin.

As I had hoped against all odds, and rejoiced when I realized what Reynard's report meant, Colin was the sixth man — not the captive I had feared, but their first pursuer, trailing Tom and his men as he tried to figure out how to rescue Edith. I was proud of him then, but I have to say, I never saw a man look so relieved.

"Sire! Am I ever so glad to see you and all these good men! Tom and his band are up ahead, just around that bend," he said, pointing northeast, up the valley through which the road wound.

We slowed to his pace then, walking our horses, both to rest them and remain out of sight of Big Tom for the moment.

"I am glad to find you on their trail and not their captive, Colin. I feared I would find you dead along this trail by now. But why did you rush off after them instead of coming to report they took Edward?"

"Sire, I've been trying to answer that question myself, and kicking myself, as you should now do to me. I was bringing a bit of breakfast to Edward, intending to relieve him from his caregiving for a time, but could not find him. Then I saw Tom an' his rogues going through the lines, and realized they had Edward with them. I could tell they were friendly with the sentry so I dared not trust him. I wanted to sound an alarm, but feared they might then kill Edward, and hide among all the others out there to fetch in our wounded and plunder dead Turks before any could be roused to pursuit. All I could think of was to follow them and try a rescue when the opportunity seemed right. As it was, I sent messages back to you with three parties, the last of them Duke Bohemond's supply train."

I nodded. "We met them a short while ago and got your report, thank you. What matters now is not what you did wrong, but what you did right. You know where they are, where they go, and you sent me news that found me wherever I might have been along this route. Well done." Colin looked relieved at that.

Then I frowned. "Now, how do we take them without getting Edward killed or harmed?"

Colin said, "I've been thinking about that. If we could put a party ahead of them to ambush them, with another behind to herd them into it, they'd hurry to escape the pursuing party and ride into the trap unawares. We might get them all in one quick go."

"That is a good idea!" I said, as I dug my codex out of my clothes. "Let me see — I think I noted something useful about this route. Ahh, here it is! Two miles ahead, this road makes a hard turn right, east two miles through a valley before gradually turning north again. But there is another route, midway between markers 21 and 22, through a parallel valley that rejoins this road at marker 25 near the little village of Hürriyet. That route was both shorter and easier, but at one point there was an unbridged ravine and stream, impassable by wagons, so I chose this route instead. But now, if we used it as you suggest, to put half our party ahead and half behind, we could ambush them at Hürriyet. Well done, Colin!"

In war, we say that good enough now is always better than perfect too late. Here, we might have no better chance, and we had no time to lose. So I gave Colin half my squadron for the pursuit party, while I would take the mounted archers and crossbowmen over the other route and lay an ambush.

For a time we followed Tom's little band at a distance together. When we reached the alternate route, we separated to put our plan into action.

Once on the southern trail through the parallel valley, we rode at a canter to cover the distance and get ahead of Tom while we were out of his sight. The ground was open and flat, easy to travel — except for that fordless ravine just south of Hürriyet. Horsemen could scramble the sides and swim the stream, but wagons could not cross there.

At a walk, it would take Tom an hour to reach Hürriyet; it took us a third of that, tired though our horses were. They could rest while we awaited Tom.

I chose a spot where the road bent left to pass between a grove on the north and buildings on the south. Marker 25 was there, where we could shelter out of sight and watch Tom come on. For his part, Colin would kick his horses to a trot as the hamlet came into sight, coming up fast and hopefully forcing Tom to rush into hiding in the settlement ahead.

We dismounted there, and I posted half my men beside a building, and the other half across the road in a grove. I took a crossbow, readied it, and then watched them come.

As I hoped, they heard cantering horses, saw Colin's horsemen coming up fast, and panicked, running to reach our location. But weary as they were after walking so far, they could not outrun even weary horses to reach hiding in the place we waited.

"Damnation! Quick, men — mount up!" We climbed into our saddles and rode out to intercept Tom's bunch, reaching them as Colin came up behind.

As we closed in, they recognized me and then Colin. There was a moment's hesitation, and then Tom's compatriots turned to flee, running off the road. Unbidden, six grim horsemen cut them off and knocked them flat.

Tom yanked Edward's horse alongside his, pulled his seax, and put its tip to Edward's throat. "Let us go, or I'll kill her — I mean it!"

My crossbow was centered on his face. Without shifting my gaze, I spoke. "The three on the ground — kill them!" Strangled screams told me it was done. Tom's eyes widened at that, but he did not move. I would have preferred to spare them, but I needed Tom to know I was deadly serious if I was to save Edward.

"Harm her and you die, too — horribly, and not quickly. I'll cut all the skin off you myself, an inch at a time, and rub salt into each wound. It'll take me weeks to kill you that way." My voice was flat and grim; I meant every word, and he knew it.

Fear flickered in his eyes. "And if I let her go?"

"Not if, when. We'll chat awhile. Then I'll give you the pound of gold I pledged to the man who saved her, and release you into a place of safety."

"Your oath of honor as a knight on it?" He nudged the blade against her jaw, and a drop of blood trailed its way down her neck.

"I give you my solemn oath as a knight and baron."

"I cannot hope for better," said Tom, dropping his blade. In truth, he hadn't much choice.

My men surrounded him then.

✠✠✠

We were in the eleventh hour by then — late afternoon. The sunlight would last another four hours, but we wouldn't reach camp tonight and the horses needed water, fodder, and rest after the pace we pushed them. So I elected to stay here the night and return to camp tomorrow.

Hürriyet was a Christian village, one that had been much oppressed by the Seljuqs into providing a hefty annual tribute in the form of crops and beasts for meat. Its folk were generally happy to be back in a Christian realm, especially since the passing Christian supply trains meant commerce with Crusaders needing meals. They were only too happy to tend to our needs, and we ate well of local fare that night. I remember their melons were good.

We camped in a grove beside the town — something we were all too used to. I had Tom searched for hidden blades and then bound in a sitting position to a tree. Two men at a time kept watch on him, through all the night watches. I would take no chances with him. When we ate, I had Colin feed him — I wasn't about to untie Tom to do it for himself.

While he did, I went to Edith and took her away from the others so we could speak in private. I could see the ordeal had taken a heavy toll on her; she had been bound to her horse all day, under a constant threat of death and worse all that time. She looked worn, and for the first time, I could see the woman she truly was. "Are you all right? Did they harm you?"

She gave me a small smile, tinged with something else — affection, perhaps. "No, they did not — they jested and threatened me all day about what would come tonight, but today they had no time to carry out their threats."

She shook her head as if to clear those thoughts, and then said, "Thank you, and God bless you! All this long day I wasn't sure if you even knew I had been taken. And then suddenly you appear from nowhere and rescue me."

I gave her a smile. "Now, not long ago, when I needed saving, you did all you could — even shedding your clothes and dignity to do so. I could not do less." Then I patted her hand. "Edith, I am truly glad we got you back safely."

Then Colin came up and tended to her with great compassion. He knew without asking that I wanted him to see to her needs and that I could fend for myself while he did.

When we were set for the night, I went to question Tom, sending his guards to eat. "You aren't really of Duke Robert's men, are you, Tom? In fact, I'm guessing *Big Tom* is only a *nom-de-guerre*[21], isn't it?"

"It is." Tom's commoner's accent had fallen away, and the squint had vanished. He looked almost normal. "My name is Thomas d'Avranches of Tutbury. I am a natural son of Hugh d'Avranches, the Earl of Chester, knight in the court of King William II of England."

---

[21] *nom-de-guerre:* French for *"name of war;"* an alias or pseudonym.

Then he paused. "You do not remember me, but I remember you well, when you came to Gloucester with King Malcolm four years back in 1093. I was among the lords and knights in the pavilion that day — when you were the last Scot to leave, and insulted my king and us with your *gesture* as you did. I vowed then to repay you for that insult."

The notion was incredible. An English knight had marched a thousand leagues into a distant war just to answer an insult. "You followed me all the long way to Nicaea just to avenge that?"

Tom smirked that ugly little smile of his. "No, I was well paid to come here. King William remembers your insult also, and he was never one to forgive anything like that. Other reasons brought me."

"And what would those be? Why kidnap my clerk?"

"We both know she is not your clerk. I know who she really is — Edith, eldest daughter of King Malcolm III. I first saw her in Gloucester in 1093 when Malcolm had her fetched home. I found her again at the convent in Durham, but she slipped away in the night. I trailed her to Dunfermline, only to learn she went to Cenachedne to become your clerk. But I couldn't get close enough to kidnap her then, nor for long after." Tom grinned. "Honestly, I cannot believe that you were such an idiot! Fooled by her disguise into accepting her as Edward and then making her your clerk. But I thank you for doing it because, after you did, keeping track of her was child's play. I had only to follow you."

I bridled at that, but said, "And yet, here *you* are — trussed like a chicken to a spit. What was the point of all this sneaking pursuit?"

"Isn't it obvious?"

"Not in the least! You seek to take revenge on me through my dead king's daughter? You could have confronted me anywhere, and I would have happily given you the chance to die for your honor."

"My God, you are a thick one! No! You were not my target — she was! King William covets all Scotland, not just the lowlands. And now, having eliminated Malcolm, he has killed, corrupted, and co-opted Malcolm's sons, eliminating the heirs to the crown and improving his own chances to gain Scotland's throne. But Edith can perpetuate Malcolm's line and his heirs, so she needs to be removed as an obstacle, too."

I was stunned at Rufus's treachery. I knew he was a greedy man and an evil king, but the extent of his perfidy was beyond my capacity for comprehension. "So why kidnap her? Why didn't you just kill her today?"

"And then do what — take her head back? No! I needed her alive — for now. I needed to be able to prove that it was done and that I did it, not just claim I killed her in a far-off land. I'd never get my lands and titles that way."

"What? Lands and titles? Rufus promised you lands and titles for killing an Alban princess? Where, for God's sake? Swamps in Essex?"

Tom was triumphant at that. "No, he promised me the Earldom of Fife, and with it, all of your lands!"

"Rufus would do that to punish me for that gesture? I am flattered to know it offended him. I now see he deserves so much more!"

"Yes and no. You did him a huge service in destroying Mowbray. But you, more than any other, thwarted his plans in Cumberland

and Northumberland. You get along with his brother, Duke Robert, whom he hates. And you insulted him publicly during a truce, when he could not have you attacked. He really can carry a grudge, you see. He wants you dead."

I snorted. "He deserved it then, and worse now, the sneaking murderer, for killing *my* king during a truce. Had he the ballocks, I'd have fought him, or you, or anyone else he chose to name, to settle the matter in trial by combat. Why didn't you just challenge me openly?"

"I've seen you fight. I was at Alnwick — on the other side — and we have fought together here in three battles already. I have no illusions about being able to kill you face to face."

"But you have tried to kill me? When?"

Tom frowned. "I have tried, when it should have been easy. You managed to survive my archer in Italy — I don't know how — that bodkin point should have had no trouble piercing your chainmail. But when he didn't come back and you did, I knew it hadn't worked. My mushrooms came close, though. I was sure I had you then, cold and helpless in that big tent of yours. But that fool of a priest saved you — God knows how."

Again, I was stunned. First, the archer's attack, and then poison mushrooms. Thomas of Tutbury had tried hard to kill me. And I still could not understand why.

He shook his head. "After you called us over that night, I knew you were onto us, and we were running out of opportunities. But thanks to that old bastard, Hamish, I couldn't get close again. I decided my chances of success were poor and getting worse. And I have no intention of getting killed on this foolish adventure to Jerusalem —

three close-fought battles in one week are three too many. As it was, I shot you three times with arrows in those fights, but that damned armor of yours saved you, and I couldn't get close enough for another weapon. You owe Hamish much, if you didn't know it."

"Why do you tell me all this?" Now I was truly curious. I would have kept such things to myself.

"I only tell you now because I have you bound by your given word, with an oath I know you are honor-bound to keep. And because it pleases me to show you what a fool you have been. Others will no doubt yet do what I could not. But I head home on the morrow with a profit for my trouble. Your gold is revenge enough."

He smirked then, but I read anxiety beneath the superciliousness.

I had had enough by then of Sir Thomas. He might be a knight, but his code of honor was same one my dearly departed half-brother Andrew had professed: Knighthood as a tool for personal gain and self-aggrandizement, not the service of God, king, and countrymen.

I rose and said, "Enjoy the fine evening. You return with me to Nicaea on the morrow."

"Why go to all that trouble? Turn me loose now."

"You want your pound of gold, don't you?"

"Aye, I do want that. You won't forget your oath along the way?"

"Oh, no, Sir Thomas of Tutbury, my oath you have — and it, I shall not forget."

✠✠✠

I could not sleep easily that night, despite my weariness from the recent battles and a long hard ride. For I had learned a petty act of spite on my part four years earlier, a foolish gesture to return the insults heaped upon my king, had earned me King Rufus's enmity, entangled me in his schemes to gain the throne of Alba, and nearly got me killed on five occasions. I *was* an idiot.

But that epiphany revealed something more: I had become principal protector of the Alban monarchy, both in war and peace, just as my father had been before me. Once again, I protected the heirs of Malcolm and Margaret: here and now at Nicaea just as I had at Alnwick and Edinburgh. Edith could produce Alba's future kings as readily as could her brothers, which is why Rufus wanted her either under his control or dead. And I might be half a world away from Alba, yet I still did just as my father had before me. My action at Gloucester had only sent me along a path God had destined for me.

Guardian then, as well as idiot. I could live with that; indeed, I already had. And with that, peace came, and I slept soundly.

✠✠✠

The following morn — the twenty-third of May — we rode back to my encampment. I had traded the wounded and the lame horses to a stableman in Hürriyet for two animals of dubious quality but sound limbs, knowing he got the better of the bargain — he would heal and sell them to other knights for a good profit — but we needed sound horses under us now.

Before we rode, I gathered my men and addressed them. "First, let me thank you for your fine work yesterday. We saved a person dear to me only because you were brave, tough, and unrelenting. Each of you deserves a share in the reward I promised, and you shall get it when we reach camp."

Big smiles lit up the circle of faces around me, and smoothed the way for my next topic.

"There is another matter here I must address. By now, you all know that Edward is not as he purported to be: a man serving as my clerk. Edward is, in fact, a woman who disguised herself among us by dressing and working as a man. In truth, Edward is really my mistress, Matilda. And I ask all of you to keep this secret with me for reasons that should now be obvious: her safety. The men we pursued here yesterday kidnapped her to extort a ransom. Some carelessness exposed her to that threat, and I am determined she will not be so threatened again. Do I have your word to remain silent on this, and to continue to regard her and address her as Edward?"

The men looked at each other and back at me, and one of them said, "Aye, my lord — we will, if you wish it. But you should know that most all the men in camp already know Edward's a wench, and knew it almost as soon as she joined us in Scotland. We all figured you was just takin' a bit o' sweetbread, so to speak, on campaign with you, same as them other nobles is — meanin' no disrespect, o' course. An' we thought you knew we knew. As for us, we're just glad to have someone like 'er who tends our sick an' wounded like she does — she's right tender-like. So we'll keep yer secret, and 'erself safe." He closed with a nod of emphasis, and the rest all said, "Aye!" in unison.

At that, I was dumbfounded. They all had known about Edith since Scotland, and I hadn't? Big Tom was right: I *was* an idiot.

Yet I realized then I had still done something useful. In declaring Edith my mistress Matilda, I supplied a reason for protecting her and her identity based on a supposed fact that was readily believed and already widely accepted, largely thanks to base behavior among

227

my fellow nobles — an ironic word in this context. And in so doing, I managed to keep Edith's royalty still a secret among just a few. And if my reputation for marital fidelity suffered in order to keep that secret — well, I would bear that humiliation for the sake of Edith, my godparents, my country, and my sense of personal honor for doing a knight's duty. That, and hope Aleine forgave me once she knew the truth.

✠✠✠

As we mounted up, I sent one well-trusted man-at-arms north to Helenopolis, and from there west, to find and fetch back Sir Cedric and his men. They had had a long ride with no result, but one of us had been certain to have that, and it might have been me.

On the ride back, I spoke privately with Edith, and in low tones told her of my conversation with the men. She was most amused by it, particularly the fact that only we two had been fooled all this time: I by her, and she by everyone else in camp. She did have one question: "Matilda? Why Matilda?"

"The first name that came to me. I did not wish to give them your true name."

She nodded. "I suppose that was wise. More importantly, I like that name: Matilda . . . Matilda! I may well use it in future."

And as it happened, she did.

✠✠✠

It was midafternoon when we arrived at my encampment. For once there was no fight going on. Sultan Kilij Arslan had given up his capital as a lost cause, preferring to save the remnants of his army for a better opportunity rather than make further futile attempts to rescue the city. And with his departure, I knew, despair ruled Nicaea.

Before I did anything else, I kept my word to Tom. I gave Colin a set of instructions, and then went to my tent and took from a strongbox there a purse containing a pound's weight of thick gold coins.

Then I returned to Tom, helped him from his horse — for his hands were still bound — and led him to my front line, which faced Nicaea.

"Thomas, I gave you my oath to give you these coins — a pound of gold. Here they are. And I gave my oath to release you into a place of safety. Nicaea is the only safe place hereabouts for a man like you, especially as wealthy as you now are." Then I turned to Colin. "Help him, will you?" Tom hefted the coins and grinned at him.

At Colin's nod, two of my engineers picked Tom up, seated him on the onager's spoon nearby, and quickly tied his bound wrists to his ankles.

As outrage replaced the look of shock and disbelief on his face, I said, "I gave you my oath, Thomas Tutbury, to release you. I do it now. Enjoy your flight to safety." Then I pulled the release lever.

Big Tom arced through the sky then, with a scream that alarmed both battle lines. Despite being about a hundredweight — the very heaviest weight a fully torqued onager could throw at that distance — he sailed over the outer wall. I do not think he cleared the inner one, which is twice as high. Whether he lived or died, I neither knew or cared. If he survived, he would certainly never walk again.

In his terror, Tom dropped his bag of gold to clutch desperately at the onager spoon, and after he departed, Colin picked it up.

"Too bad he forgot that," I said. "Ahh, well! Share it out fairly among the men of both rescue parties and this onager crew for their services. You and Sir Cedric are due a fair share, as well."

Colin grinned and nodded, and the onager crew murmured their amazed thanks, as word of what had just happened buzzed away throughout the Christian ranks.

For my part, I was glad to have Edith safe in camp, my secret assassin discovered and punished, and order restored. That was well worth the gold it cost.

✠✠✠

The Battle of Nicaea.

# TEN

✠✠✠

My satisfaction was short-lived, though. Soon after, as I washed fifty miles of dust from my throat with the first ale I'd had in days, Hamish appeared, much exercised. "I am just back from Count Raymond's camp, with news you'll not like," he said.

I handed him a cup and poured him ale as well, and he downed it in one go.

"You know the great timbers you bought in Constantinople and we worked so hard to haul here to build your tree-bucket . . ." he paused, and an icy chill flooded me, as I anticipated what he was about to say.

". . . Count Raymond's men spotted them when they came through, what — two days ago? Aye, then. And yesterday eve without asking his men commandeered them, and hauled them to his camp. Going to build a siege tower from them, I heard."

I nodded and said, "I'll go speak to him now. He'll return them to me when he knows what I have planned. I only wish to God we had not wasted this entire week in battle and whatnot. She would have been built by now, and already punching a gap through those walls big enough to let through his tower."

✠✠✠

Count Raymond greeted me with civility and good humor, and though I was loathe to do what I was about to, for the sake of our future relations, I had it to do if we were to fight together as we went forward, rather than fighting each other.

"Welcome, Baron! Good to see you again. Have you come to allow me to reciprocate your early-morning hospitality of two days hence?"

"I wish it were so, my lord, but no. I am here on grim business, about a matter of serious wrong between us, and I cannot pretend anything else until we settle it."

He frowned. "I am sorry to hear it. What is there that so disturbs our friendship?"

"It is this: At considerable personal cost and great trouble, I brought here great timbers from which to build a siege machine, one like no other, one of my own design, certain to breach this city. But I just learned that while I was away on an important matter, your men took them from my camp to construct your tower."

His frown deepened. "Ahh, yes, I did hear you had to go — where was it? Oh, yes! — rescue your clerk, I believe. I hope you were successful. Damn strange business, kidnapping a clerk. Someone said he's a she, and she's your mistress, but that can't be right. If it is, I must say, I thought better of you." My frown stopped him there, but he was in truth as honest as he was right.

He sighed then. "I am sorry. I did instruct my men to collect timber to build a tower we use in France, but I expected them to cut trees in the hills, not steal wood. They should not have commandeered yours. Let us go stop their work now so you can recover your timber."

But it was too late. When we reached his building site we found, to my horror, that each of my greatest timbers had already been cut, each sawn several times lengthwise into long beams to serve as the tower's corner uprights, and now far beyond saving. Indeed, his men were still cutting the last of the posts when we got there.

Hell and damnation! Shock, dismay and outrage all competed inside me to see which might own me. I was furious, of course, but dismay won out, for there was nothing I could now do about it.

Not so Count Raymond. He, too, was furious and embarrassed by the heedless actions of his men, but at that moment, I was his major concern.

He punched a fist into his hand. "By God, I will punish them, the thoughtless fools! No doubt they took your wood because it was close by, and easier to take than to cut and haul trees from the forests around us." Then a thought struck him and he clapped my shoulder. "But! You will rejoice to know that your wood will frame my — no, our — tower. And I will repay your costs and see you credited for your contribution when we succeed."

I shook my head. "Count Raymond, I thank you for both offers, but I do not seek the punishment of your men nor credit for your tower. Those timbers were specially chosen for their size and wood-type to build my engine. Without wood like it, I cannot accomplish my task as siege master to Count Robert and Duke Godfrey."

"Well, I am sorry for the injury and inconvenience we have caused you, Baron. Can you not go and cut more trees? Indeed, we could cut them for you. We owe you that!"

"Nay, my lord, it would do me no good. I bought and hauled in those timbers because I knew no such wood can be found here. Your tower could have been built from anything growing here, but I cannot use these local trees, for they have neither the size nor the strength to serve my needs. And I am certain your tower cannot succeed, or I would have cut wood and built a tower instead."

My discouragement was evident and it distressed him. He shook his head. "I understand and am sore sorry, Baron. I *will* recompense you and rebuke the lazy thieves. But tell me, why do you say a siege tower will fail to take this city? They have never failed me before."

"Because Nicaea has double ditches outside the walls, which must be filled in and compacted at the site of attack, and that we must do while under attack from the walls and flanking towers. Many of us will die doing it. Then, inside the ditches are two concentric walls, the second one higher, with other walls perpendicular between them to form killing boxes inside them. Your tower will get men into those boxes, but it cannot get them over the second wall. And so, unable to advance and unable to retreat, our men have but one outcome: Dying in those traps."

I saw that my words troubled, but did not convince him. I was not through, though. "My tree-bucket is unique. With it I can batter a vast hole, first in the outer wall and then the inner, within a fortnight. I intended to punch a gap through both walls to create a way through that cannot be closed or mended, for my machine will batter through every repair as easily as the wall itself. The rubble from the outer wall will fill in the ditches as it came down. And I could clear or destroy the flanking towers with siege engines as well. We do not have to sacrifice men to do what hurled stones can do for us instead."

I could see him deflate at this, but he shook his head. "I fear you may be right, but I must hope you are not. My siege-men tell me we can succeed, and now we certainly must try, for your timbers are gone and the future of our campaign now depends on my tower."

There was nothing more to say. So I wished him well and returned to my tent, where I poured out my exasperation to Hamish and Anselm. Hamish shook his shaggy head and sighed. "I let you down. You entrusted me with command and I've failed you in a most damnable way." And never have I seen him, or any man, look so filled with sadness and self-loathing. Despair tempted me to agree and turn my outrage on him, but I knew better, and regard for Hamish won through. Dejectedly, I said, "Nay, Hamish, the fault is Raymond's, not yours. In truth, it is not even Raymond's."

Now, sometimes despair has a strange effect on me, and triggers in me a weird reaction. I suddenly recalled what Demetrius often said at such times. I realized then that it had just happened to me — right up to my chin. So I quoted him then.

"Demetrius used to say, 'Sometimes in life you get shit on your shoes. War drops you in an overflowing sewer. So learn to swim — and, above all — to do it with your mouth shut.'" Then I added with a wry grin, "Demetrius was right."

I cannot say it comforted Hamish, but as it happened, it helped me.

My timber was gone and there was naught I could do about it. But Anselm handed me a skin of spirit and said, "For some things, this is the best medicine I have. Drink and pray."

So I took his advice, for his counsel was invariably good. And as tired and dejected as I was, it took little of either spirit or prayer to put me to sleep.

✠✠✠

The following morn I suffered in payment for my sins of anger and gluttony the previous night, but I did so in silence, knowing that I deserved it. And that ordeal had a hidden blessing, for in my sleep Saint George appeared to me and said strange things, not all of which I recalled when I awoke. But I did remember these:

*"Persistere vincere," "Pluribus unum,"* and *"Cum ferrum se fidi."*

*Persist to win. From many, one. With iron, bind them.*

I had no idea what Saint George meant, but the vision was memorable enough to keep me pondering both his apparition and his mottoes.

And somewhere in the midst of my pain and bemusement, my mind found a useful thread. I began to think about how I could use wood I could get, rather than the wood I no longer had, to build the machine I knew we had to have. I had no faith in Raymond's tower — though I confess when finished it was a splendid machine — simply because it could not conquer both walls. And other than my tree-bucket, no other engine or tactic would work any better. So I puzzled over these three strange phrases even as I returned to the grim business of war.

✠✠✠

Raymond's tower was now our best hope for any success at the moment, and my craftsmen now had no better employment, so I lent them to the count to speed the completion of the tower. It was better than having the men fuming with idleness.

Meanwhile, I went to report my return to Count Robert, as well as the success of my rescue and the loss of my timber, and to gather news of our latest siege plans and progress.

"I am glad you were able to rescue your er, clerk," he replied, and I became sure the rumors of "Matilda" had already reached him as I noted a new undertone of disapproval in his manner. Robert would never be one to have a camp mistress, of that I was certain, and his disappointment at discovering I did made me badly want to confess the truth. But I could not do so without renewing risk to Edith. So I remained silent and accepted his unstated and undeserved rebuke.

"I could not do otherwise," I said. "I apologize, but I needed to do it."

"No, of course not!" he acknowledged. She was a woman, after all, and he a knight. "Men who do things like that must not be allowed to escape punishment, and no one failed to notice the punishment you applied. What did he do, to deserve one that harsh?"

"Apart from kidnapping Edward, he took payment to murder me for punishing the men who killed my king, made five attempts to kill me, and very nearly succeeded more than once. It was necessary to promise to release him in order to save Edward's life. So that is what I did — I released him."

Robert nodded, then, and said, "I agree, then; he deserved it and more. As for the loss of the timber, that *is* unfortunate. I'm not certain I understand how any machine can do as you say yours does without miracles or sorcery, but Duke Robert has attested to the truth of your claims and I will not call him liar, nor you. Besides, we need every advantage here — the enemy presently holds all of them, even though we've won the battles and hold the field."

Then he thought a moment, and said, "But we already have a siege in place and need to make every effort to take the city. If you cannot build your machine without timber, figure a way to get more or use what is here. Meanwhile, do your best to aid the efforts of others: repair the engines that break, and build more to clear the towers. And thank you for keeping the peace with Raymond. Not many men who had their plans wrecked by another would then aid him. I commend you for that. Now go one step further and study the city afresh to find a weakness — there *must* be one we can exploit with Raymond's tower. Figure out where best to attack with it, and I will see to it that the council heeds your advice. Maybe we can make a success of this dog's breakfast yet."

I admit I was discouraged, and it must have been evident, for he punched my shoulder and said, "Take heart, Godric. It's a setback, not a fatal blow. You're the best I have, and you will find a way. So go do it — we are counting on you!"

So I did. After all, his counsel was wise, and what else could I do?

✠✠✠

While Raymond worked to build his tower, I stayed busy in other ways. After all, there was much to do.

Just east of my camp atop the closest ridge overlooking the city, I had an observation tower built of lashed trunks and wooden poles. From it I studied the city daily, looking for weaknesses and assessing the success of our onager bombardment. Demetrius frequently joined me there. And it was from there that we began to focus on the southeast tower.

Built to strongly defend the point where the eastern walls met the southern walls, it was twice the diameter of the towers that studded the southern walls at twenty-yard intervals, and the eastern walls every thirty yards. And because of its size and position, it filled the entire space between the inner and outer walls, creating, in effect, a bridge across both. A street ran from the tower, through orchards and gardens, directly toward Nicaea's center.

I pointed it out to Demetrius. "Look there! If we could use Raymond's tower to capture that tower, it would get us over both walls and down inside the city. See, the gardens grow right to the walls there, so the Seljuqs cannot use their horse archers to charge our flanks, and there is no way to get behind us — all counter-attacks have to come from the front. We'd have a defensible perimeter in front of us and walls behind us. If we clear the flanking towers too, we can pour men over the walls where they would be hardest-pressed to stop us."

Demetrius agreed, and added, "I wonder if that tower is filled solid with rubble, or built with internal chambers. If the latter, we might be able to undermine the tower from the base of Raymond's tower. It's a good alternative — a second way to achieve our goal."

I nodded and said, "Let's get Count Robert and Count Raymond up here as soon as we can to see if they agree."

✠✠✠

Like many other commanders that week, I sent my men out onto the battlefield of the twentieth and the twenty-first to gather and bury our dead, drag away the corpses of Seljuqs and horses to dump and bury in a nearby ravine, and glean the field of still-useful items: armor; mail; helmets; saddles and harnesses; weapons, both whole and broken — we could repair or re-forge broken weapons as arrowheads and engine fittings — and arrows, especially the arrows. We used thousands of arrows every day, and so could never have too many. Of the many thousands shot at us, we gathered all we safely could. We put the women and children with us to work as fletchers, their nimble fingers repairing the goose-feather fletches that steadied an arrow's flight. And then we sent those arrows back again to kill the men who had first shot them at us.

And it was one afternoon when I was idly watching a small cluster of these fletchers at work that I saw a sight that prodded my memory and popped an idea into my head. A small boy was standing beside his mother, clutching a half-dozen arrows for her to fletch, when Saint George once again whispered in my head, *Pluribus unum. From many, one.* With that, I suddenly realized what he meant. I lacked big timbers, but had no shortage of smaller ones. If I could make many of them into one by bundling them, I could build my engine. But how? And it was then that his second phrase came back to me: *"Cum ferrum se fidi — with iron, bind them."* I could make a bundle of smaller timbers into a bigger one by shaping them to nestle together and then wrapping the bundle with straps of iron.

And with that, I had my answer. In my excitement and gratitude, I snatched up the little lad and kissed his forehead — an act that quite startled him into tears and alarmed his mother into outrage, but I quickly mollified her with a silver penny. Then I dashed off to find Hamish and put him to work.

✠✠✠

From my tower-top, I had no difficulty convincing Count Robert that the Gonatas Tower (its name in Arabic, meaning *gardens*) was the flaw in the defenses he had urged me to find. He promptly brought up Count Raymond to my vantage point, and we jointly put our case to him.

Now Raymond was the richest of the princes, and had brought here the largest army. It was he that Bishop Ademar, the Papal Legate and Pope Urban's direct representative, accompanied. For these reasons, Raymond believed himself God's chosen commander of our army — although he alone thought this. But thought it he did, so we had to appear to cater to his notion of command and call his attention to the Gonatas Tower in a way that made it the one *he* chose. We were sure that if we *told* him Gonatas was the obvious site, we would trigger Raymond's opposition to it, one potentially fatal to our entire enterprise.

So with the greatest care as Raymond listened, Robert and I went through a process of exploration, Robert asking about each potential attack site, and I pointing out the advantages and disadvantages we incurred at each. Only Gonatas offered many more advantages than disadvantages, but Robert made a pretense of favoring the eastern gate, while I haggled for the southern gate. Soon Raymond wearied of the debate.

"Stop! You two make my head hurt. It's obvious that the southeast corner tower is the best site — Gonatas, did you call it, Baron? That's the spot! Roll up the tower, clear the defenses nearby, and pour in a solid stream of men. We can bring up others under the protection of my tower's fighting top, and send them up and over with ladders. Call yourselves siege masters, do you? Hah! Guess it takes an old warhorse to crack this walnut!"

The decision was made. Robert gave me a wink of congratulations even as we praised the wisdom of Raymond's analysis and applauded his choice.

✠✠✠

At my urging, Hamish promptly took parties of men into the forests east of us and soon had a stream of thirty-foot trunks, lopped smooth of limbs, enroute to camp. Better yet, Raymond's tower was framed and far enough along for me to allow me to recall my craftsmen. I promptly put them to work building a tree-bucket half-again as big as *Bone-Crusher* had been.

Over the next two weeks, we worked hard. My timber-smiths first stripped and then shaped the many trunks with adzes into timbers. For the frame, we built a large square base of timber, reinforced by other timbers along the two diagonals. One diagonal I selected as the central axis of the engine, and along this we built in parallel two great triangular uprights with a four-foot central gap between them. These supported the throwing arm with an iron axle spanning between the apexes. The two uprights were laterally braced by timbers from the apexes down to the ends of the orthogonal corners of the base. This made the whole structure very strong and fairly rigid — qualities I had discovered to be most critical during my experiments in creating the machine five years earlier at home in Cenachedne — for every bit of that strength would be needed to control the violent actions that occurred when the throwing arm was released.

As this was done, my best craftsmen built the main throwing arm, which required the most skilled work. For it, we cut six flat [hexagonal] sides around a single central trunk. Then we fitted six more timbers around it, cutting three matching flat surfaces on each so that all seven timbers nested in a tight bundle. While we fitted them, we held these seven together with broad straps of leather, woven from scavenged Seljuq reins. And when they nested snugly, we replaced the leather straps with orange-hot iron bands, placed every two feet along the entire length, spiked closed into a ring and quenched so that they bit into the wood.

Meanwhile, my blacksmiths melted down scavenged iron into bars and began making spikes, straps, brackets, and fittings. I was kept busy overseeing their work, at one point stripping off to my breeks and leading the team forging the throwing arm's axle and support brackets when they could not get it right on their own.

The last item we built was a great box-shaped wooden bucket, strapped and reinforced with iron, that hung by iron straps from an iron axle set in the lower end of the throwing arm. This box we would lastly fill with round river rocks and sand to create the counterweight that powered the machine, giving it a great strength to hurl boulders with great speed, power and accuracy.

Along with these main components, we built the other fittings: a windlass to pull down the mighty arm; a woven leather pouch set between two thirty-foot braided tail ropes to form a sling, one end of which would be fastened to the free end of the throwing arm, the other fitted with an iron ring that hooked on a tail-pin on the same end of the arm. During a throw, as the sling was whipped forward and swung past the tail-pin, the ring slid free, and the sling opened, releasing its projectile to fly in a great curve up and forward toward the target.

I pushed my men hard, working them from dawn to dark, and incentivizing them with silver and ale, so that we could get this engine into use. Raymond might take the city before we finished, but if he failed, it would be up to this machine and me rather than him to, as he put it, "crack the walnut" called Nicaea.

✠✠✠

For all the importance I placed on my engine, though, others no less determined than me put all their energies into their own solutions. Count Robert and Duke Godfrey asked me to assess their efforts, learn from them — both what worked and what did not — and offer advice where I could. So each day, I gave Hamish a list of instructions on what needed to be done. At his elbow, "Edward" earned her keep by copying down my instructions and then helping Hamish see them carried out. Meanwhile, I rode off to assess progress on all the siege projects going on around the city, taking Colin with me, of course.

One of these was a "fox," as they called it — a "testudo" or "tortoise" in Vegetius's terminology — that was being built at the considerable personal expense of two Swabian lords, survivors of the massacre of the People's Crusade at Helenopolis, who had come with Peter the Hermit and joined Godfrey's retinue. These two, Count Hartmann of Dillingen[22] and Henry of Esch, had great hopes that they would be among the first into Nicaea, to quickly recoup their expense with loot from its fabled riches. They hoped, they told me, to be able to push their machine, a high-gabled triangular shed, up to a tower they had selected near the east gate, and from its protected interior, mine through the wall to access its tunnel into the city. But when I inspected their "fox," I had my doubts.

It was strongly built, I admit. They had spiked solid tree-trunks side by side to cross-braces to create the two panels of the roof, covered the top joint with another solid log, and spiked the bottoms to beams, to spread the two panels in a triangle. The space inside had room for twenty men, and the entire structure was set on axles and rollers. On these, Hartmann and Henry planned to roll to their target.

---

[22] Hartmann is one of the author's 26th great-grandfathers. The "fox" cost him much of what wealth he brought, debasing him to the point of having to sell his weapons and armor, live off Godfrey's charity, and fight riding a donkey with Seljuq weapons. But while he never earned fame or fortune from his crusading adventures—rather the opposite—he is among the few named nobles who fought, a rare thing. And he survived to finish the First Crusade, recover Jerusalem, and return home, to father three generations of Crusaders and many more after that.

Count Hartmann was my age, very enthusiastic about his project, and most hopeful for its success. When he learned who I was, he urged me to express my opinion — no doubt hoping for praise of their enterprise and ingenuity. "What do you think of it, Baron? A splendid idea, I thought, when our builder here put it to me," He pointed to a sly-looking fellow busily directing the workmen. "But do you agree?"

I was cautious in my answer, for I did not wish to give him offense. I regret now I was not more blunt.

"My lord, you have built strongly — that roof should withstand firebrands, dropped rocks, arrows, and spears, protecting the men inside well enough. It needs to be fireproofed with soaked hides, for fire arrows bearing burning pitch or tar would otherwise be able to set it afire. And I think it is much too heavy. Those rollers work well enough on hard ground. But when you reach the ditches, you are stopped short. How will you get across? Twenty men cannot lift it, and they cannot push it if the wheels sink in soft fill. You will have to fill and tightly pack the ground in the ditch ahead of you in order to cross it. I fear that cannot be done well enough, and your machine and men will be trapped out there, unable to attack and unable to withdraw."

My words checked his enthusiasm hard, and the notion of getting stuck was a topic that he and his builder had clearly never discussed. His lips compressed as the idea hit home. Then he said, "A problem we must solve, I agree. By your return, we will have an answer."

I hoped it was a good one.

✠✠✠

At other points, the onagers I and others had built were hard at work, trying to batter a way into Nicaea. Many were being used stupidly, each pounding rock after rock at a point in the wall, slowly chipping a hole in the stout brick and tile. But they were much too slow, for an onager does not have the power to hurl a stone, even one as hard as granite, with enough force to do much damage on each throw. In six months one might succeed. The trouble was, none of us wanted to be here that long.

Each day men died, and many more were wounded on both sides of the siege. The Islamites, of course, we did not mourn; indeed, each one dead or wounded was one fewer enemy to resist us. But we lost many men each day too, to arrows and sling stones in stupid attacks on walls we could not climb and at gates we could not batter down and could not burn. Far too many foolish Christian knights and lords thought nothing of throwing their men against the defenses only to have them repulsed, bleeding and dying for naught. Were this Jerusalem, it might be worth the horrific waste. But this was Nicaea, and though the basileus and some of the princes wanted it, it was not our goal. Jerusalem was!

So we could not stay and waste both our substance and men here, for both were irreplaceable in the long run. We needed to take this city quickly, move south, and conquer Jerusalem while we still had the means to do it.

✠✠✠

Another effort I was sent to assess was a mine that Raymond and Ademar had underway. They had built a relatively lightweight sow — their name for Vegetius's *testudo* — a mobile shed with a tough, well-reinforced frame, wattle-and-hide walls, and a pitched roof of planks covered with soaked hides. A crew of men inside had carried it to the base of a tower at a place where the road spanned the ditches near the southern gate, and placed it so that it protected the miners inside while they dug and pried out the tower's brickwork.

They also had built had an ingenious smaller version of the sow, a sort of three-walled roofed mantlet, that the relief teams used to cross the open ground — the relieving men sheltered in it as they carried it to the sow, and the men they relieved did the same as they returned to our lines. This they called the piglet.

Colin and I accompanied a team out to the sow one morning, to see their work and help where I could. They were close to breaking through, but did not do so, for that would only give the enemy a way to shoot arrows into them in the sow. Instead, they worked hard around the edges, enlarging the size of the opening so that once they broke through, men could actually enter the tower, not merely peer in.

But it was going too slow. Each day there increased the risk that the hot sun would dry the protective hides sufficiently to enable the Seljuqs to finally set the sow afire.

"We need a way to break up the brick, sire, something faster than chipping it out," complained the team leader, a scarred Provençal man-at-arms named Henri. "Have you any ideas? And could you do something about the bastards above us as well?"

Rocks thrown from the tower ramparts above crashed down on the roof, shaking the entire structure before bouncing clear. The din was tremendous, and terrifying, and cracks evident in the roof-planks.

I thought a moment. "Have you tried coals and vinegar? Pack hot coals in the hole to heat the brick, then rake out the coals, and dash the brick with splashed vinegar. It should shatter that fire-baked brick and weaken the mortar to make it easier to break free."

Henri nodded. "We haven't, but it's worth trying. Thank you!"

I said, "I'll see the count sends you a brazier, charcoal, and vinegar right away. And I'll clear the tower top for you." He nodded and resumed work while I and a few men returned to our lines by way of the piglet. I sent Colin back to camp to fetch a scorpio, and then I went to see the count.

✠✠✠

Count Raymond quickly agreed and sent Henri the items I suggested. A short time later, Colin brought my scorpio loaded on a packhorse. This pedestal-mounted siege crossbow is highly portable, operable by one man, and deadly accurate out to a range of four hundred yards. He and I set it up behind a mantlet just out of Turkish bowshot, and I sat on a stool and went to work.

How I loved that machine! I could cock it, load a bolt and then sit and wait, aiming at the tower parapet, waiting for a Seljuq to hoist a rock. A trigger press, a *SNAP*, and the bolt would fly, just a blur in a shallow arc that ended in the man's face, throat, or chest. Often, the rock he struggled to lift finished what the bolt started, braining him as it fell.

An hour later, I could see wisps of smoke float up from the sow. A brazier inside burned charcoal furiously, and periodically a burst of steam arose with a loud sizzle as they splashed vinegar on hot brick. Henri waved at me from the sow to signal both success and gratitude. By then I had sent a half-dozen Turks off to roast in eternal fire, and the rocks fell no more, for no one willing to throw them was left.

An hour later, the count had three squads of crossbowmen in place to keep the target tower and the ones flanking it clear of archers and peltasts.

Before I left, I used fire-bolts to set ablaze the hoarding[23] on the adjacent towers and walls, and thereafter Raymond's archers kept the Seljuqs too busy fighting fires to attack the sow.

✠✠✠

Good progress was made each day on my tree-bucket, but since my machine was both big and complicated, it wasn't as quick to build as I had hoped — and certainly slower than it would have been if I had had my original timbers. And since breaking parts of the machine was, in my experience, too common a problem, I had to fashion nearly enough replacement parts for two machines in order to keep the one operating. And this took time, altogether too much time.

✠✠✠

For his part, Count Raymond's efforts to build his siege tower were no less determined, but I began to realize that, because of its size, getting it right up to the Gonatas Tower was a problem, for the flooded double ditches outside the tower would have to be filled with a solid base of rubble and earth so the tower could cross them. And when I pointed that out at the nightly war council one evening, it struck all discussion dead.

"How do you plan to get such an enormous amount of fill across deadly ground to do that?" Duke Godfrey demanded of Raymond, but he had no answer.

---

[23] Roofed wooden protective structures atop castle battlements, towers, and walls to protect the defenders from arrows.

Now I had already obsessed about this problem futilely until I saw the count's sow and piglets. The logical answer was to build more siege-sheds like them, and I said so, praising them for their simplicity and effectiveness. And that gave Raymond what he needed — a solution that he himself had created, and a plan to keep moving forward.

So for a time he halted work on the tower, and built instead another sow, an entire litter of ten piglets to ferry rubble to the sow at the work-front, and big, two-wheeled push-carts to transport the fill from within the cover of a piglet.

✠✠✠

In the wee hours of the night on the thirty-first of May, I made another trip out to the sow mining through the tower at the southern gate. In just two days, Henri's men had made substantial progress, and had dug a hole six feet in diameter through six feet of solid masonry. Now they were finally ready for the breach. For this, we had built a battering ram: a heavy beam that had until recently rested along a wall of the sow now hung from the sow's frame, tipped with an iron beak whose forging I had personally overseen.

The breach would be made in the pre-dawn hours, and a torrent of men were already up, preparing themselves to pour through that hole with the dawn.

Count Raymond was there with me, of course. A good leader needs to go before his men to give them heart, and Raymond was a warrior of renown. Moreover, this event was of such importance that if we succeeded, Raymond would surely become the heralded head of our entire army.

As first light broke, Raymond said, "Let's begin!"

"Heave!" Henri called, and every man in the sow pulled hard on lines attached to the ram, pulling it back until its suspension lines were nearly horizontal. "Ready, *loose!*"

We released the ram, which swung forward and down through an arc that drove its beak deep into the remaining brick with a ground-shaking *thunk*. Chips flew from the hole, and brick-dust filled the air. Peering into the breach, Henri said, "Again! Heave . . . loose!"

*Thunk!* Our world shrank to those few sounds as the ram did its work again and again.

On about the twentieth blow, the sound of impact changed. *Thunk* was replaced by *crunch*, and we knew we had broken through. Ten more blows and Henri gave the order: "Pull back and tie off." We were through.

With a torch for light and a round Turkish shield for protection from arrows, Henri scrambled into the breach. Raymond and I, similarly equipped, followed. Henri pushed his torch through the hole to light the void beyond, but something was wrong. "*Merde!*" was all he said. For the damned Turks had entirely filled the tower with stone rubble.

We tried clearing it until sudden slip of stones nearly crushed us. We realized that the Turks had pulled up rounded paving stones, which could easily slip and pour through our breach to kill us all. We would make no entrance here today . . . or ever.

The disappointment was crushing, especially for the men who had labored in that sow day and night for so long. I, too, felt it bite hard. But Raymond was philosophical — another mark of a good leader.

"Well, men, it was worth the try. Were they less cunning and less desperate, we'd be inside cutting their throats right now. But you just proved they can't keep us out forever. We'll wade through their blood and gold yet, and soon."

And despite dismay and exhaustion, all his men grinned at that idea.

✠✠✠

A siege tower like Raymond's, and archers shielded by pavises.

# ELEVEN

✠✠✠

May had passed, and June was upon us. We had been camped around Nicaea for more than three weeks with little to show for our efforts, and I fumed more every day, because Nicaea was not our goal; Jerusalem was, and this was not getting us any closer to that goal. In essence, we were merely here to do Emperor Alexios a favor by recovering one of his cities that he could not. But in doing so we were jeopardizing our means and very likelihood of then still being able to recover Jerusalem. It was maddening to think on it for very long. So I did not; instead, I worked.

But the arrival of June brought with it reinforcements. First came the long-promised contribution of Alexios: a force of two thousand peltasts[24] under the combined command of his generals Manuel Boutoumites, Tzitas, and my old friend Tatikios. As their siege-line position, they asked for and were given the southwestern corner of the city, where the walls indented to the north along the lakeshore. It was an unlikely point to make a breach, and troops as ill-equipped for assaulting a fortress as they were completely lacked the means to achieve one, so I confess we gave them little thought, and counted on their support not at all.

But close behind them came Duke Robert of Normandy and Count Stephen of Blois, our companions on the march from France to

---

[24] A force of light infantry, traditionally equipped with helmets, shields, and javelins. Not really more than a token contribution by Alexios, in this case.

Bari. We had not seen them since we left Bari, and I had often wondered if they had not simply given up and turned back for home. But now they were here and keen to make the difference.

The first question was where to post the newcomers, and it arose in the military council that very day. The southern wall was encircled last and most thinly, that entire sector presently covered by Count Raymond and Bishop Ademar, while Count Robert held the southernmost half of the eastern wall south of the Eastern Gate. Here was the place most in need of reinforcement with the newly-arrived additional numbers.

So the first suggestion was to move Robert north, and Raymond and Ademar west, so that Duke Robert and Count Stephen could slip in, with Duke Robert adjoining Count Robert, and Stephen adjacent to Raymond. The trouble was, I was part of Count Robert's contingent and together with Baron Jean de Bethencourt held the southeast corner. And it was there that Count Raymond and I had our siege machine construction yards, which we could not now move.

As the debate swirled for a time around them, I saw the two Roberts confer quietly, consult with Count Raymond and reach an agreement with him. Then they called for quiet.

"My lords! My lords!" said Duke Robert, "My good friends, Counts Robert and Raymond, and I offer this idea. It would be best to leave Baron Godric and Baron Jean emplaced where they are to continue their good work while we take positions to either side. Baron Jean and Sir Hamish will command their siege line while Baron Godric focuses on siege efforts to breach the city walls. And as part of that, Count Raymond agrees that Godric should oversee construction of the count's siege tower. Around them, Count Robert proposes to move north, and I will move into line between

Godric and him. And Count Raymond and Bishop Ademar will move west, so that Count Stephen can take position between Raymond and Godric. In this way we leave our best chance for success of a breach undisturbed, and reinforce the siege with minimal disruption of what is already in place."

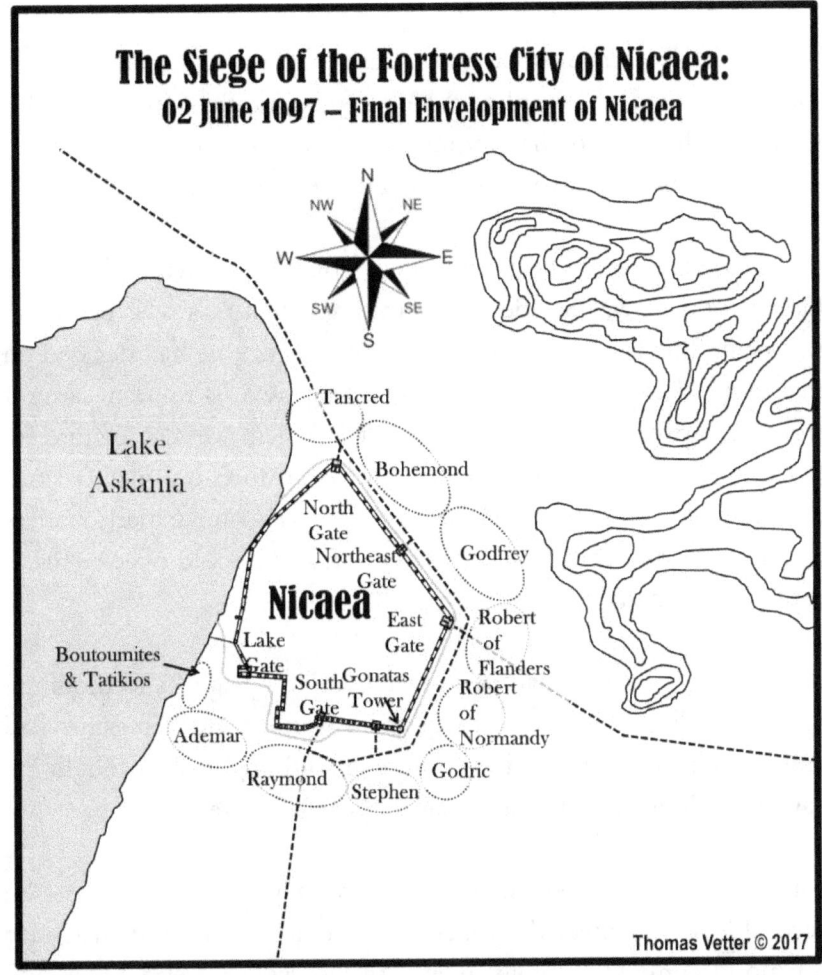

**02 June 1097: Final envelopment of Nicaea.**

I could tell that the words were the duke's, but the wisdom chiefly Count Robert's. In any case, it settled the debate like oil on water.

It took several more hours that evening to work out all the plans, and most of the following day to accomplish them, but by nightfall on the second, all of us were in place. Now, only the side of Nicaea on the lakeshore was still unblockaded.

✠✠✠

With my new responsibility to Count Raymond, I found myself suddenly tasked to complete the construction and outfitting of his tower for him. And that meant I urgently needed to understand what he planned to do and how he intended to use it.

Now, Count Robert and I had already convinced Raymond that the Gonatas tower was an ideal objective, and that was why his tower was being built in a yard adjacent to mine. Once he had decided on that target, he moved his timber to a spot next to mine because it was just opposite his target — after all, a siege tower can be moved, but not very easily or terribly far. And from then on, we built our machines side-by-side, which proved optimal — my expert builders could now work both projects as needed, and I could oversee his as readily as my own.

By now he — we — had his tower framed, upright, and mounted on great rollers. Double walls of thick wattle were being installed and the horsehides that Kilij Arslan had so thoughtfully brought his cavalry to donate, soaked and nailed over the entire structure.

With Demetrius, I sketched a plan for a windlass drive on the second level to power the rollers, and then I requested that Count Raymond come at his convenience to discuss what else we should build.

Now Raymond had his own builder, a Lombard named Luigi of Torino, to whom Raymond had already promised fifteen pounds of silver to build his tower. Initially there was some friction between Luigi and myself about how we should proceed, until I realized that the silver mattered more to him than the actual project.

In the teeth of his latest tirade, I smiled at him. "Master Luigi, if you agree to help me complete this tower as Count Raymond wishes, I will ensure you get your promised silver. You do not have to, of course; you can depart right now without it. But if you hinder me in completing it, I will make sure you are the very first man onto or into Gonatas Tower."

He shut up and stared at me, while I just smiled back at him. When he noticed that my smile did not reach my eyes, which said something else, his manner changed and he smiled in the same way. "My lord, it would be my pleasure to be of assistance."

I did not believe a word of it, but he certainly believed me, and that was all I cared about. In the event, his resistance stopped, and we got on well enough in time.

☩☩☩

When Count Raymond met with me to discuss the tower, it was soon clear we had different notions about how to use it, and that he was of two minds all on his own. So I set out to settle the things on which we agreed, and they proved to be these:

- Our fifty-foot tower would have four levels connected by internal ladders;
- The highest level would be a fighting platform, equipped with scorpios we would use to clear the top of the Gonatas tower and its neighbors;
- The third level would have a drawbridge, set at a height and of sufficient length to cross to the top of Gonatas;
- The second level would (and already did) house the windlass

engine to drive the tower;

- Finally, the lowest level would house . . . something (and there we stuck).

It was the lowest level about which Count Raymond was undecided, and where our conversation focused. If the tower failed to enable us to cross over and take the Gonatas tower, what was our alternate plan? Should we install a ram and batter a way in? Or should we undermine the tower foundation?

We could not come to an immediate agreement, so we opted instead to press on with the settled details, think about the secondary plan for two days, and meet again with Demetrius, Luigi, and Henri.

✠✠✠

Meanwhile, the new sow and piglets were ready, and the time had come to fill the ditches so that we could soon roll the siege tower to the Gonatas Tower. On the third of June, Count Raymond organized a small army — many hundreds of men — lined up side by side to pass forward rocks and baskets of gravel others dug from a dry streambed, while another line of women and children passed the emptied baskets back to the dig site. Raymond had all this fill piled close to the front line where the piglets could collect it for the dangerous work that would follow.

Meanwhile, in the safety of our lines, each pushcart was filled, and within the cover of a piglet, it made the two hundred-yard journey to the sow, the front of which had been pushed over edge of the ditch so that the cart contents could be dumped from within its cover. And as each empty piglet departed, another laden one arrived, bearing loads of rock alternated with gravel. The rocks went in to build a solid base that could bear the weight of the tower, while the gravel filled the voids and locked the rocks in place. And as the sow inched forward, the heavy cartloads compacted the fill already in place.

And I noticed a strange thing. As they worked, the several crews — for the sow and all the piglets — all sang *The Siege Master's Song.* Yet I could not make out the words, for it was sung in other tongues.

Within a week, we would have both ditches filled and compacted, creating a path wide enough to get the tower to the Gonatas Tower. And unless already inside Nicaea by then, we planned to attack it on June eighth.

✠✠✠

Count Raymond and I again met on the fourth to decide on the lowest stage of the siege tower. This time I introduced Demetrius — with the latter's permission — as Alexio's "Megas Anticensor," or siege master (which in actuality he was) and my mentor. This surprised the count as much as it had originally surprised me, but Raymond quickly welcomed the counsel of a siege expert who also knew this city well.

The question we now considered was this: If we do not succeed in taking the tower from the top, should we again attack the wall, as we had with the earlier sow, by digging through the brick? Or do we instead undermine the foundation?

The former meant we ought to put in a battering ram or a long lever for prying out rock; the latter meant we would dig a tunnel from inside our tower down, out, and under the foundation of Gonatas, shoring up the structure until our tunnel was complete, and then burning the out the shoring to collapse the tower.

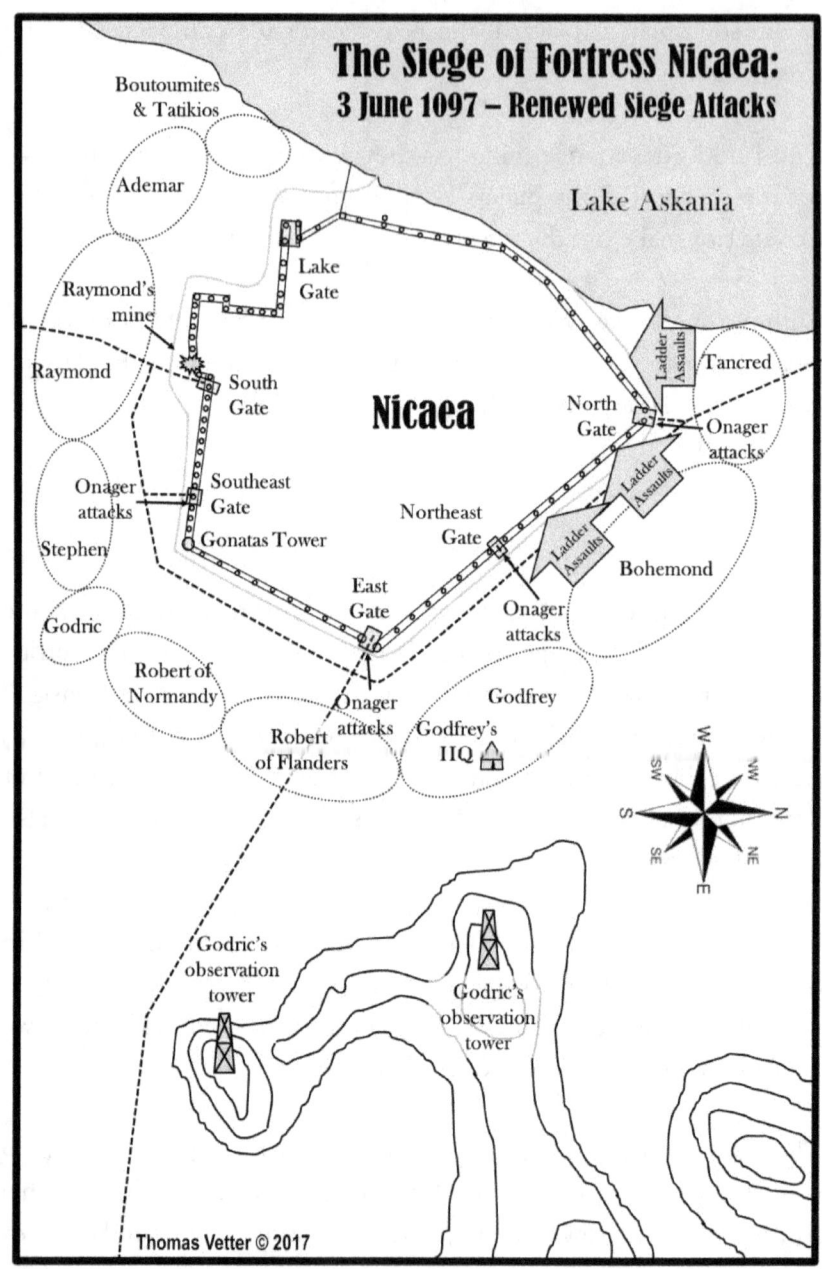

**The Siege of Fortress Nicaea:**
**3 June 1097 – Renewed Siege Attacks**

**03 June 1097: Siege attacks are renewed.**

When the question was so framed, the answer became easy to find, and it was Demetrius who helped us see the solution to the dilemma. "My lords, you worked hard to dig through six feet of masonry. But as you worked, an equally determined enemy filled that tower with rock ripped from nearby streets to foil your efforts. So if you now attack Gonatas in the same way, you must expect they will defend in the same way. You must do something different, something that they cannot counter."

As ever, Demetrius's advice was sound, indeed, unassailable. And it made the decision easy. Doing something different meant tunneling to undermine the foundation and topple Gonatas. For that, we would need a trap door, shoring, candles for light, tools, and lots of sacks to haul out dirt. The piglets could ferry supplies in and dirt out. But we needed no ram and no lever.

And this was only our alternate plan. We would still try to go over the top first, and we counted on that plan's success.

So our tower was nearly ready and this decision gave us all we needed to finish. With those matters settled, Luigi and I went back to work, he to complete construction, and I to get all in readiness to use it.

✠✠✠

I was still engaged daily in sorties from camp to observe and aid the many siege efforts around the eastern and southern sides of the city. I had heard that Hartmann of Dillingen and Henry of Esch were close to employing their fox, so later on the fourth I went to see it.

The fox was as heavy as ever, but they had taken my earlier advice and installed larger rollers, which raised it higher to clear uneven ground, and they had added more rollers, spreading the weight to cope with softer ground. It was as good as it could be.

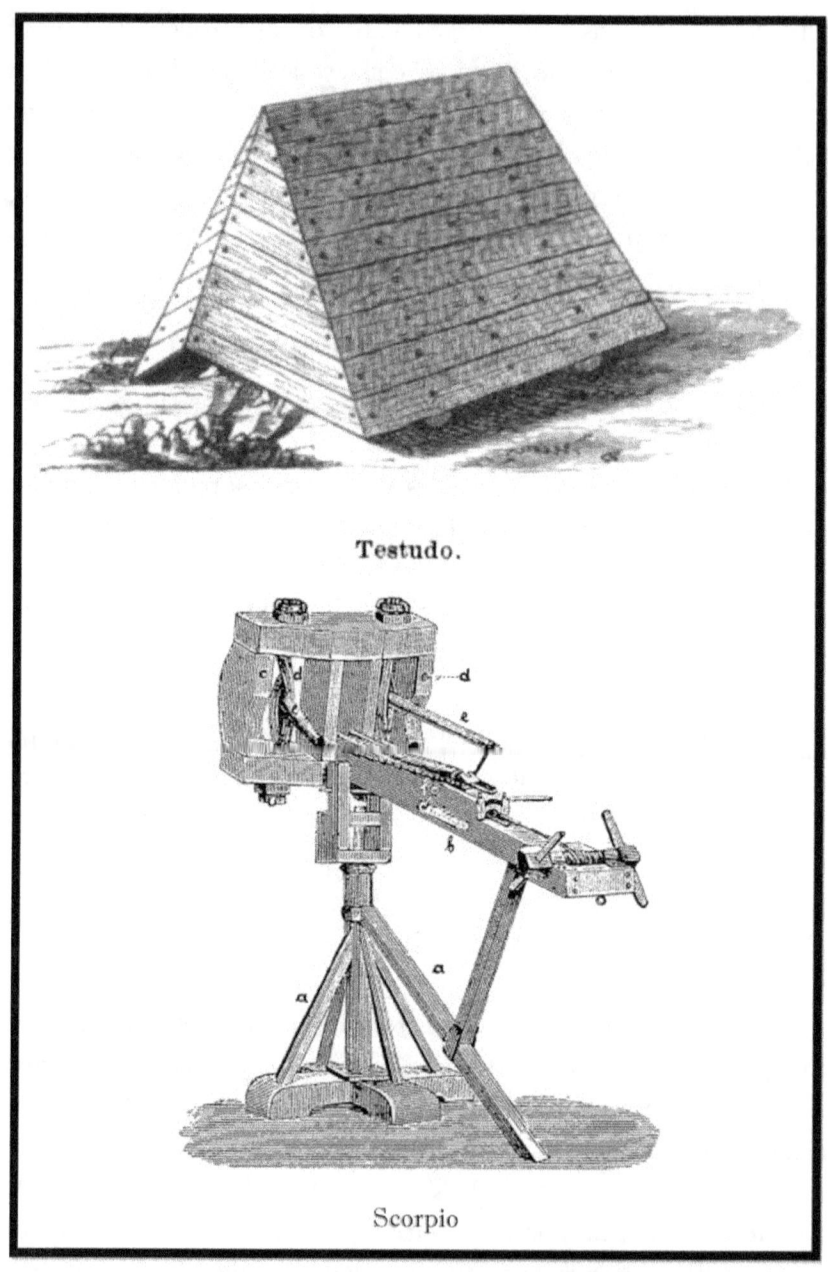

Testudo.

Scorpio

**A testudo like Hartmann's fox; and scorpio, a long-range crossbow.**

Still, there were the ditches, and they couldn't cross them with this as it was. So I went to Count Hartmann. "My lord, how do you now plan to cross the ditch?"

"Ahh, Baron, good to see you again! We won't. We're going to attack the eastern gates. We've been practicing, you see. We can move and maneuver the fox well on the hard-packed road, and if we use the roadway we don't need to cross ditches. We install a ram today — Count Raymond gave us the one you made — and then we are ready to go."

"You know there are three separate gates, set one beyond another, to bar the eastern entrance?"

"Yes, thanks to you; we got that information from Count Robert, but he said you did the original scouting. The onagers have damaged the outermost gate, but cannot get at the other two, so we plan to go through the first to attack the second, and then the third. We'll hack off the metal covering the wood with axes. Then we'll burn the wooden doors with skins of oil, and when they are weak, we'll batter them until the wood or hinges fail. We can withdraw as readily as we can enter over the roadway, so we can make repeated sorties until we get through all three. What do you think?"

It was a bold plan, one that would win everlasting renown for the men who executed it if it succeeded. It was prey to countless perils as well. But this was war, those were only to be expected, and the prize — Nicaea — was worth all that risk.

"May God give you and your men success, sire." I said.

✠✠✠

My tree-bucket was close to completion now. We were making

good progress even while also working to complete the tower, forge the ram beak, and repair the many siege machines — onagers, ballistae, scorpios, and others — as they broke under heavy use. Barring another catastrophe or a siege breakthrough that made it unnecessary, my treebucket would finally be ready to hammer Nicaea into submission in just a few more days, on or about the seventh, I judged.

✠✠✠

But at dawn on the fifth, I was up and present opposite the eastern gate to witness Count Hartmann take his fox against the enemy. He and nineteen chosen men — knights, men-at-arms, and skilled siege men — would be her first crew.

Not one to miss such an opportunity, Peter the Hermit, who had led the Peoples' Army — with Hartmann and Henry in its ranks — to disaster at this very city, now appeared to bless the fox and its crew as it mounted its first attack. I confess I was more interested by the final preparation than in the hermit's words, especially since Peter was as weak a preacher as he was a military leader. So I am afraid I lost all interest in what he said and cannot recall his words. Nor does it matter.

But a short while later, the now-hallowed twenty warriors entered the fox and closed its wattle-and-hide rear door. Then with the ear-splitting scream of wooden rollers turning on wooden bearings, the fox began its slow trundle up the road toward the outermost eastern gate.

The noise it made could not fail to alert the Seljuqs; and the fox was only halfway to its target when the archers on Nicaea's tower-tops began shooting flaming arrows and fire-bolts into it, trying to set it alight. But the wetted hides refused to burn, so it soon it looked like a rustic altar to the Mother of God, aglow with supplicants' candles. As it reached the gate, Nicaea's defenders changed their mode of attack, and began bombarding it with dropped stones and flaming torches. But the fox's steeply sloped sides deflected these missiles with no perceptible effect.

Now, the outermost gate had already been battered for days by our onagers, hammered with stones as heavy as a hundred-weight, and the doors were now more splinters than planks, their metal covering shredded by the impacts to the point of falling away. But the gate still stood and barred our way — the Turks had no doubt propped heavy timbers against the other side to help withstand our bombardment.

In place at the gate, the men in the fox wasted no time. I could not see all that they did, but Hartmann himself told me of it later. First, he and his men ripped away the protective metal to expose the wooden inner core. Then they began pounding the hinges with the battering ram, my iron beak biting deep with each blow, splintering away the wood that held the hinge-spikes firm. Soon, the doors began to sag.

Within an hour, the top hinges were destroyed. After two hours, the middle hinges were irreparably weakened. The crew again adjusted the ram slings to strike at the lowest hinges. The fox itself was still intact, although it had absorbed an equal number of hours of brutal attack by stone and flame.

At the end of the third hour, I could see that the gates were essentially freestanding panels, held up only by the props, not the hinges. So the men in the fox changed tactics again for the next phase of assault: first they hammered staples into the bottoms of the doors, anchoring a heavy chain to each; then they doused each panel with Danish pine tar, a portion of which I supplied from my own siege stores. This done, they backed the fox away, paying out chain as they did, and with fire-bolts of their own, they set the wrecked gates afire.

Slowly and noisily, the fox backed toward our lines, the gate-doors now burning furiously. When they reached the full length of the chain, they attached the chains to the battering ram and swung it hard, using its momentum in reverse to jerk the bottoms of the doors outward and tear them away from the props. After a half-dozen jerks, the doors finally tore free, falling backwards with a crash and a huge cloud of smoke and sparks. Its job done, the fox trundled back to our lines even more slowly, as it dragged the still burning doors behind it.

With the fox safe again in our lines, Hartmann's waiting siege-men scraped away or smothered the flaming debris embedded in the fox's roof and opened its rear door. Twenty brave, coughing, and completely exhausted men emerged amid our hearty cheers. Behind them, one of the three barriers into Nicaea now burned in the road, and the gaping maw of the eastern gateway showed that the way to the second gate was now largely clear.

The day had been a triumph for the ingenuity of Hartmann's engine and the courage of his men. I took satisfaction in the effectiveness of my suggested improvements and the strength of my ram beak. As I watched, the siege-men stripped off damaged hides to replace them with fresh ones, repaired the damage, and replenished the tools and supplies. Tomorrow, the fox would tackle the second gate.

✠✠✠

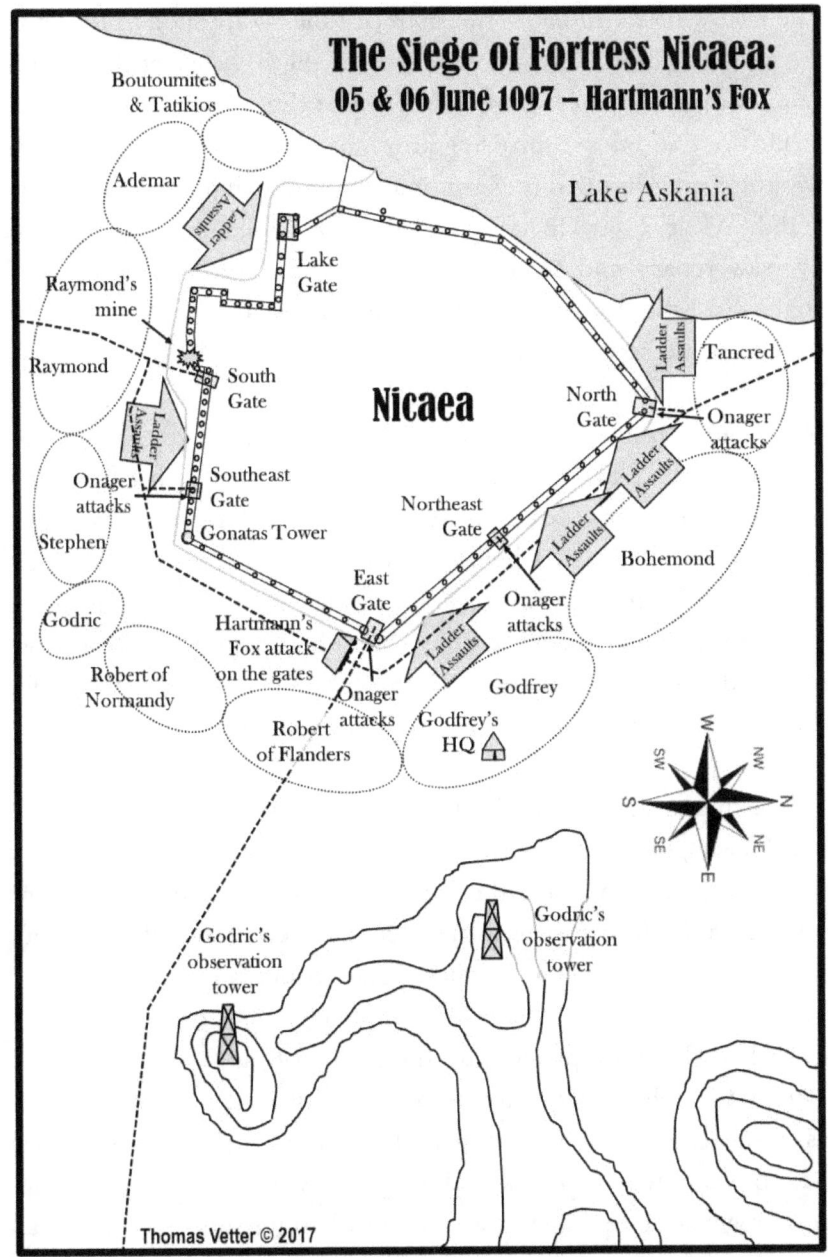

**The Siege of Fortress Nicaea:**
**05 & 06 June 1097 – Hartmann's Fox**

05 & 06 June 1097: Hartmann attacks the Eastern Gate with his fox.

The following morning — the sixth of June — I hoped to return to the eastern gate for the second sortie of the fox against the middle gate, but other matters intruded. A leg of the tripod we were using to lift the tree-bucket throwing arm into place snapped at a hidden weakness and dropped the arm onto the frame, injuring two men as it did. While I saw them attended to, assessed the damage, and oversaw repairs and corrective measures, the fox made its second attack. So I did not see what happened, but I questioned those who did and relate here now what they said ensued.

Now, late in the previous sortie, Count Hartmann broke fingers on his left hand trying to clear a tangle in the chains just as others heaved on the ram. Learning this, I had sent Anselm to treat him that afternoon, which I believe is why his fingers were ultimately saved. But for the second sortie he was useless as a member of the fox's crew, so he reluctantly allowed another go in his place instead. It would have been Henry of Esch, but he had been down ill for three days with the soldier's most common ailment, loose bowels.

So Hartmann's lieutenant the previous day, a knight named Liudolf von Geislingen, led the sortie. As before, a select crew of twenty of the count's men manned the fox and trundled off to tear out the middle gate. Having successfully proven their tactics the previous day, they were confident the middle gate would fall today.

They had difficulty penetrating the gate-road as far as the middle gate — the Seljuqs had thrown rocks and timbers into the roadway as obstacles to block their rollers, but the crew pushed these clear with poles they plied through the gap below the frame — and they soon reached the middle gate. And they had just begun their assault on the gate-doors when the Turks attacked with a new countermeasure.

After seeing what the fox could do, the Turks had, during the night, prepared for it an evil surprise. In the darkness they lowered a small party from the ramparts into the gate road, dug a shallow channel out through the middle gate, and scraped a shallow basin in the packed earth where the fox would sit as its crew worked to destroy the gate.

Now, as the fox crew stripped the metal from the middle gate, a sudden gush of flammable oil flowed down the channel into the depression under the fox. A trail of fire promptly followed, and in an instant, the Christian onlookers could see flames erupt through the gap between the road and the frame of the fox.

Apparently the depression was small enough and the fox wide enough so that most were not standing in oil when it caught fire, for the crew instantly abandoned all thoughts but self-preservation, and pushed mightily to heave their machine away from the gate and off the pool of flames.

They were quickly clear of the fire, and had the fox moving at a remarkable speed — for it — when the Turks dropped a beam across its path. And as the fox's rearmost rollers struck it, the shock of the impact — magnified by momentum, the force of twenty men pushing hard, and all the battle damage sustained in hours of heavy bombardment — all proved too much. The fox crashed to a sudden stop, and the entire structure collapsed, crushing the twenty men inside. Any not killed outright died in the wreckage as it burned.

Great cheers arose then from the Nicaean ramparts — their war cry, "*Allah-u-Akbar*," and other heathen babble — thinking their god had delivered them. But he had not. God had instead just made saints of twenty bold Christian warriors.

Among us, the previous day's joy turned instantly to an ebullition of rage, and spontaneous flights of arrows rapidly silenced the Seljuqs, forcing them to cover. When I learned of it that afternoon, I climbed to the top of the siege tower and there stayed until dark, killing the Seljuqs on the Gonatas Tower with a scorpio, venting my fury with purpose.

In His wisdom, God decided to spare Count Hartmann and Henry of Esch. For days afterward they grieved, unable to fight or rest until we finally took the city and they buried their men properly. For now, the wreckage of the fox lay inside the eastern gate, barring our entry even more effectively than had its gate.

✠✠✠

By now, many ladder assaults had failed — Duke Bohemond favored these, and stupidly sent one after another against the northern walls, always believing the next would succeed, when all it did was reduce the size of his army. The sow had been foiled by ingenuity and the fox was no more. Our onagers pounded walls and gates, slowly damaging them, but could not create a vital breach. Only Raymond's tower and my treebucket remained. If his tower could not take Gonatas, all would depend on my treebucket. I prayed one of these would succeed.

✠✠✠

Bohemond favored ladder attacks on the walls of Nicaea.

# TWELVE

✠✠✠

The attack by Raymond's Tower — as we now called it — on Nicaea's Gonatas Tower was planned to begin on the eighth, but our attack actually began during the night of the sixth, when other preparations I made were put to use. First among these were my siege platforms.

Now, Gonatas might have been Nicaea's largest tower, anchoring the defenses of the southeast corner, but it was by no means solitary. Indeed, the city had defensive towers every twenty, thirty, or fifty yards along the walls, depending on which side you faced. And Gonatas was flanked by such neighbors, each one topped with siege engines like a ballista or small onager, and scorpios, of course.

It was these towers that posed great threat to Raymond's tower. Not only did they threaten our men on and in it with sudden death, but they also had the power to damage or destroy the tower itself. Onager projectiles could hammer the frame, smash in its wattle walls, and crush machinery, while ballista fire-bolts might punch through the wattle-and-hide to set the interior ablaze. But the wicked little scorpios were the worst, killing our scorpio-men and archers on the tower-top and thereby leave the tower defenseless against further counter-attack.

So before we could attack, we needed to kill the enemy operators serving these flanking engines, and then keep those tower-tops unmanned while we ideally destroyed their machines. And it was for this task that I built my platforms and erected them just beyond effective bowshot.

These platforms were simple, cheap, yet effective: tripod towers of lashed poles twenty-five feet high, with floors and walls of wattle pierced by archer's slits. Inside each, I put two powerful scorpios and three skilled siege-men. Two men shot the scorpios while the third called down shot adjustments for an onager and a ballista operating in support of each platform. The scorpios were there to kill enemy siege men; the onager and ballista, to destroy the enemy's machines.

During the night of the sixth, we erected these platforms in darkness, which might sound difficult, but was not because they were already largely pre-built on the ground. One side was a triangular frame of poles, with horizontal braces lashed every five feet, and a wattle panel hanging near the top. At the apex a third leg was lashed, loosely enough so that as the triangle was raised, the lashings tightened as the bottom of the third leg was maneuvered to form a tripod. Once erect, we lashed horizontal braces on the other two sides, working from the bottom up, and then pulled up the wattle panel to form a floor for the weapons nest, supporting it by horizontal braces and then reinforcing it with more wattle matting, cross-laid. A ladder lashed to the side gave access to the nest, where poles and more wattle mats were added to form protective sides. And on those sides we then hung Turkish shields gleaned from the battlefield, to armor the nest-top.

When the platform was ready, we hauled up two scorpios in sections, set them up, and we were ready to fight. With all the manpower I had at my command, each platform took only about an hour to erect and equip, even in the darkness. We set up the first platform one hundred yards north of Gonatas in Duke Robert's line, and a second one hundred yards west of Gonatas in Count

Stephen's sector.

Each of our scorpio-men was assigned the pair of towers opposite him, and instructed to put a bolt into any man who showed himself. Meanwhile, the "sighter," as we called him, would watch the fall of shot from each onager and ballista, and call down corrections for the next. I took for myself the sighter's job for Gonatas and the three towers to its north, while Sir Cedric, my former squire and most skilled siege-man, sighted for the three towers west of Gonatas.

And so it was that at dawn on the seventh, a duel began, in which we set about killing the Nicaean tower crews as they tried to do the same to us. I had the opening advantage, since the sun at my back brightly lit the Nicaean towers, even as it blinded the sentries there, while they tried to discern what new devilry we had created during the night. And with that advantage, we had an easy time of it for the first half-hour. I smashed the ballista on Gonatas and the next tower north with quick onager hits, and my scorpio-men struck down the scorpio-men on all four towers before the sun was even high enough to enable them to effectively shoot back.

After that, it became much more deadly. Cedric and I soon found it necessary to use the Turkish shields I had reinforced and modified with slits through which we could continue to see as the count of arrows sent at us increased from a drizzle to a highland squall. Most of the arrows shot from the walls fell short, but even so, arrowhead hits soon rang the nest shields like church bells, and my face shield was struck more than a dozen times. A bolt hitting there will knock you on your backside — I know, it happened to me, twice.

But we retained the advantage of our early start, and by the end of the day, not a siege machine on those seven towers was still functioning. We had smashed four, burned three with fire-bolts, and killed or wounded dozens of their siege-men, chiefly scorpio-men. Still, I knew it would start all over again tomorrow, for I knew in the night the Turks would bring new engines and operators from other towers, rearm Gonatas and its neighbors, and ready themselves to kill.

✠✠✠

On the morning of the eighth, with a great groan, Raymond's mighty siege tower began its slow crawl across the arrow-flight of empty ground between our lines and Gonatas Tower. It was an awesome sight — the largest wooden construction I had ever seen, apart from the greatest of churches. But churches merely have to stand where built, not crawl hundreds of yards; for that, I think this tower the greater achievement.

Now, some who were there thought that invisible horses pulled it, or invisible men pushed it. Indeed, many even feared that demons made it move. None of that is the truth. Instead, it was propelled by a crew of men on the second level, pushing long windlass[25] levers to turn a vertical shaft, driving a system of cogs, drums, and hawsers that turned the rear axle, and with it, eight saw-toothed wheels. When I selected my crew of artisans the previous year, I hired a pair of men who built water-driven gristmills and windmills, specifically to gain their knowledge and expertise in building this kind of motive system. I saw a such a drive in Constantinople in 1087 inside one of Demetrius's siege towers, and having surveyed this city then as one of many potential future siege projects, I knew I would need the means to build such self-propelled towers in this campaign. Now that day was here.

---

[25] "Windlass" is the word Godric used, but what he described is today called a capstan. He adapted wooden machinery found in gristmills and in use since Roman times. But "capstan" is both a Spanish name and shipboard invention to hoist anchor of the 14th century, so Godric could not have known it.

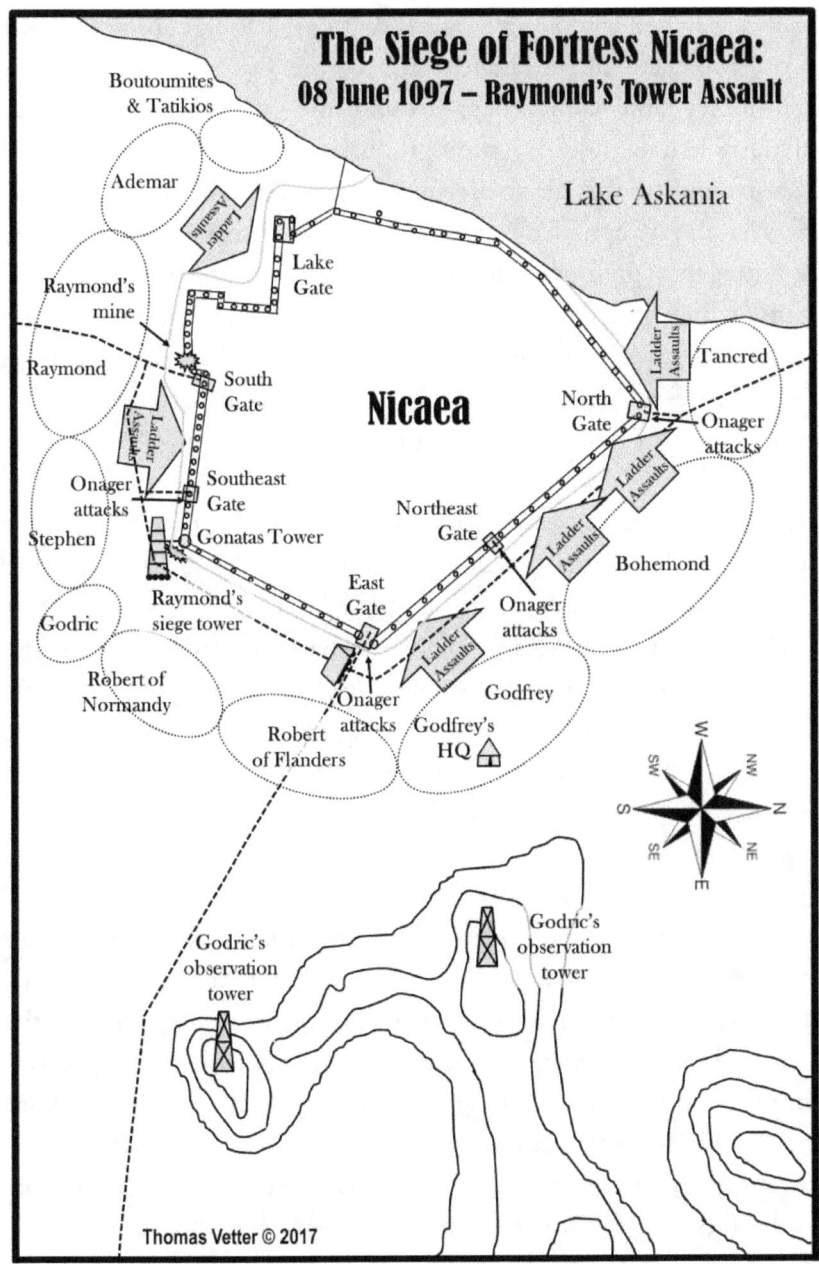

**08 June 1097: Raymond's tower assault.**

So as I watched it moving forward that day, I took enormous pride in our achievement, and hugely enjoyed the awe and amazement of the nobles and commoners around me, who had never seen anything like it. Indeed, I promptly had a flapping flock of excited bishops and priests, all vociferously demanding the opportunity to exorcise the demons from it, until I explained that angels propelled it. When they then clamored to know how we secured angelic aid without their intercession, I gave the credit to Father Anselm and his miraculous spirits (the truth — for Luigi and I had decided on the drive design while sharing a cup). So they left mollified but still mystified, and I returned to my deadly work.

The tower advanced even slower than an old monk walked, while our "piglets" scurried around it, moving aside rocks and other obstacles from its path. From my platforms the scorpios did their deadly work, and my onagers and ballistae bombarded the enemy's towers, forcing enemy engine crews to choose between attacking Raymond's tower and fighting back against my platforms. During the night, I had erected another two platforms to increase pressure on their defenses, and countering their replacement engines with more of our own.

Around my camp the clamor grew, as both Duke Robert and Count Stephen readied companies of knights and men-at-arms keen to be in the fight at last, and eager to make the final charge across the field and up the tower into Nicaea. It was a dash of danger two hundred yards long . . . long moments sheltering under mantlets and shields from the deadly rain of arrows, the slow climb up the tower's steep ladders, the final dash over the drawbridge, and the hard bloody fight down through Gonatas into Nicaea's streets. Many carried other ladders, for once Gonatas was ours, we could clear the adjacent ramparts to bring more men into the fight directly over the walls.

Raymond had chosen to lead the attack from inside the tower, with Luigi commanding its operation, so I returned to my platform, where I could best survey the battle and act in support or rescue, depending on what transpired. We had worked out a detailed plan of attack, and through a system of signal flags we could communicate to adjust it, but the essence was pretty simple: Get the tower to Gonatas, signal for the troops to charge, drop the drawbridge and take the damned city at last.

I was surprised when Count Robert and Jean showed up at my elbow without warning, having made the perilous climb to my nest through a fitful storm of arrows, but thanks to God's protection, both made it unhurt. The three of us — well, the two of them, for I was busy killing Seljuq engines and men with my engines most of the time — watched the tower roll forward, a strange trail of toothed and smooth tracks in its wake.

It took about two hours for Raymond's tower to reach the causeway built across the ditches. In that time, the Turks had shot hundreds of flaming arrows into its face and flanks, but the hides — freshly wetted during the night — extinguished the flames outright or kept them from burning more than their shafts. I was glad we had added a perforated trough around the fighting-top to re-wet the hides with buckets of water. As it was, the machine resembled the supplicants' candelabra in Dunfermline Abbey just after Queen Margaret died.

Then the tower started its final journey across the causeway. The crossing was slower, for the path had been built under increasingly intense attack the closer it got to Gonatas. I prayed, then, it was good enough and wished I had thought to erect my platforms sooner.

The tower succeeded in crossing the first ditch and kept going, starting over the second. And then it stopped. I had a signal sent to the tower: Had they reached Gonatas?

Yes! The base was close to Gonatas, and they were almost ready to signal the charge when I saw the tower shudder, and begin to lean back, farther and farther. The fill had failed, shifting and spreading. The tower now leaned perilously, and could no longer be moved.

Over the course of another hour, we exchanged a flurry of signals. The base was right against Gonatas, but because of the backward lean, the drawbridge tipped back so far it was impossible to lower. They could keep the fighting top manned to defend the structure but filling the tower with men threatened to topple it, destroying the machine and killing those inside.

When I reported that news, Robert and Jean said as one, "*Merde!*"

I mentally translated to the Saxon equivalent, and that brought back Demetrius's maxim: *Sometimes in life you get shit on your shoes. War drops you in an overflowing sewer. So learn to swim — and, above all — to do it with your mouth shut.*

So instead, I grinned and said, "Well, at least the beast is in the right place. Good thing we have a backup plan. Let's make that one work!"

✠✠✠

I hurried to the line, found a piglet, and had its two-man team ferry me to Raymond's tower. There, I conferred with Count Raymond and Luigi.

We crawled down through the trap in the lowest floor and inspected the base as well as we could. It was beyond remedy. Not only had the tower settled into the causeway fill, but it had snapped the axles like twigs as it sank in. The tower would stay where it was.

From the drawbridge level and then the fighting top, we cautiously surveyed the drawbridge. We had built it to span twenty feet, in case we could not get close enough to Gonatas, but now that extra length worked against us, for the tower tilt made the bridge too heavy to push back through vertical so we could lower it. And without the bridge we could not reach the Gonatas ramparts.

Our main plan was in shambles, but we were not ready to quit. We had formulated a secondary strategy against this possibility, and we were in an ideal spot to make that work. We would dig.

And it was then that Luigi said, "But let us not dig as you did at the southern tower — through hard brick and stone. This ground is firm but loose, and easier to dig away. We should dig under the foundation, and shore up the tower with timbers. We make a big hole that way, and fill it with brush and tinder. Then we set it afire, burn out the shoring, and whoomp! Down comes Gonatas, making a big hole in the wall. Then we use the tower to go over the rubble and we are in! What do you think?"

I said, "Luigi, it is a good plan. If the Turks think we are doing as we did and fill Gonatas up with stone, it will only speed the collapse. We should assign men to pound on Gonatas's walls, so they think we are mining through the brick, while we dig underneath instead. The piglets can bring in fresh diggers, shoring and brush and haul away the soil we dig out. It will mask our actions and may fool the Turks. Do you agree, Count Raymond?"

Now Raymond had been greatly discouraged since the machine tilted, shredding his internal dreams of victory and glory. But this plan buoyed him up, for we might yet salvage victory from the setback. And he was never one to admit defeat. So he nodded, thoughtfully at first, and then with determination.

"Yes . . . yes, I do! I like it, and you shall have whatever is needed to make it succeed."

✠✠✠

So all the rest of the eighth, the sow and piglets scuttled back and forth, exchanging men and ferrying mining supplies to Raymond's tower. Now we did not need men to storm the ramparts; we needed diggers and miners. We needed shovels, shoring, and soil-bags, not arrows and poleaxes. And the failure of the tower to put us over the top began a new contest: to get into Gonatas, or topple it, before the Turks could fill it with stone.

Hence the frenzied shuttles. Digging is brutally hard work, and wears men down quickly. In this race, speed counted, and we had men in plenty, so rather than press ahead with tired men, we replaced them hourly, and the soil came out in torrents.

The digging this time was not through ten feet of stone; it was down — from the trapdoor in the bottom of the tower we dug, going just deep enough to stay well below the surface and then toward the tower. When we hit Gonatas's foundation, we would dig down along the wall of rock, hoping to find dig-able soil under the great stones, not bedrock.

Luigi stayed to direct the operations while Raymond and I returned to our lines. He set off to find all the miners and diggers he could, and I sent men out to cut trees for shoring and bundles of dry brush. These we would send out as we could, and stockpile them in the tower until they were needed.

Now, the fight still raged throughout this time: Raymond's tower-top and my platforms dueling the closest Nicaean towers and ramparts. The Turks were determined to burn our siege tower, and we were even more determined they should not. So the piglets stayed busy ferrying out arrows, bolts, and skins of water when they were not conveying miners and their supplies.

Yet, all this activity only occupied part of my energies and part of my head. As much as I wanted this attack to succeed, another part of me had already concluded that only my tree-bucket was going to get us into Nicaea. And once I reached that conclusion, I delegated the tasks in support of Raymond and Luigi to others, and set out to put it to use.

✠✠✠

My tree–bucket was ready. All that remained was to select a target on which to employ it, erecting it, filling the counterweight (bucket) with stones, and moving up the weighed and sorted projectiles. So on the morn of the ninth, I sent word to Demetrius asking him to join me at the ridge-top platform, and went up there myself.

I was looking for another kind of target — a place where my heavy bombardment could hammer a hole that the Seljuqs could not repair, plug, or backfill. I had studied this city and its walls daily for weeks, without success in finding that spot. But we were running out of options. So I said a prayer to Saint Michael and Saint George, God's mightiest warriors, asking their help to defeat God's enemies.

And they heard me and assented that day.

It was Demetrius who first saw it. From the platform top where we stood, he pointed at a place on the southeastern wall. It might have been a trick of the light, but the wall there seemed to look different from the rest of the structure. "What about there?"

We stared at it until our eyes watered before we understood what we saw. The walls there weren't two — they were one, and there was one tower missing, like one tooth in a smile, creating a sixty-yard hole in the normal thirty-yard spacing.

"It's a good place for a breach. Too bad the wall there is so thick," he said. Indeed, it looked as if the entire space between the walls had been built solid.

"What if it's not?" I asked.

He stared at me, then frowned. "Not what?"

"Filled. What if it's hollow and roofed over, like a building?"

"What kind of building?" he asked, but I could see he realized it was possible.

"I don't know. A cistern maybe. Or a granary, barn, or stable."

He nodded. "It's possible. But what good will breaching it do? As soon as we begin to bombard it, they'll fill it with earth and rock."

"Not if they don't have time. The tree-bucket could punch through the roof and both walls within hours, with us right behind. And the tree-bucket will do its work in dark as well as daylight. If we hit it all through the night, we could create a breach by dawn. And once we're through the roof and near wall, anyone inside trying to fill that void will be pulverized by the projectiles aimed for the rear wall."

He nodded slowly then, seeing it in his mind. "That could work."

"I'll go inform Count Robert," I said. "That's in his sector. I can have *Malleus Dei* in place to start tomorrow."

"What's *Malleus Dei?*"

"My tree-bucket. *Malleus Dei* is Latin for *God's Hammer*, and you taught me a weapon like that has to have a proper name. You'll agree when you see it at work." And I grinned at the thought, remembering what I did to OdinsØye's tower with *Bone-Crusher*.

But Demetrius said, "No, let's keep this news to ourselves for now, and see if we can't learn whether we are right first."

"How can we do that?" I asked.

To my great surprise, he said, "I'll ask my spies inside."

✠✠✠

"How does it go?" was my first question for Count Raymond when I returned. The old man looked worn, but confident. The demands of command brings reports and requests for decisions at all hours and leaves little time for rest, so campaigning takes a particularly heavy toll on the older commanders. But those reports must have brought news of progress, for Raymond seemed ebullient.

"The diggers have reached the bottom of the Gonatas foundation. They did not find soil, but what is there is almost as good, and perhaps better — sandstone. Not as easy to dig as sand or soil, but much easier than rock or brick. And there is little seepage of water from the lake or the ditches, so it won't flood out and drown the fires. They think they can dig a mine under the whole east side in a week."

I absorbed that news and thought out loud. "A week. That means the mine will be ready on the sixteenth. It will take another day to fill the mine with brush so we can set it afire and burn out the shoring — the seventeenth. The fire will need to burn for a half-day or a day before it collapses — on about the eighteenth. Does that seem right?"

Raymond nodded. "That sounds right to me, assuming things go as the diggers say. But it counts on one huge condition: that our siege tower survives. The damned Seljuqs are doing everything they can to burn it. They had it afire twice since yesterday, but we managed to put out the flames both times. I fear they will succeed and leave us without a way to complete the mine."

"Maybe we can both hamper their efforts against the tower and cause them a greater worry to draw their attention elsewhere . . ."

"And that is . . .?"

"My machine is ready. I've been looking for a good target on which to use it. If I destroy the tower-tops adjacent to Gonatas, rather than just the engines on them, they won't be able to remount engines there every night, and that will leave only Gonatas, which you can keep clear from the tower. It might gain us enough time to finish the mine . . . you know we'll have to burn the tower, as well as the mine, in order to get through a breach of Gonatas."

He frowned, and then nodded. "You're right. Well, so be it! We can pull anything of value out of it this week before we do, and we weren't going to take it to Jerusalem anyway." That last thought made us both smile.

"Then we have a plan. I will place *Malleus Dei* to strike the towers to the north today, and they'll have a hard time putting anything up there afterward. Then we'll crush the western ones."

Raymond said, "You will be busy, so I'll inform the council of our plans this evening. They haven't had any success elsewhere since the fox was destroyed, and even our failures are going better, so they will raise no objections. And when your machine succeeds, they will offer us every encouragement and suggest many other places to use it."

He paused then. *"Malleus Dei* — Hammer of God. What a wonderful name! Can it live up to it?"

I nodded and said, "Come and see!"

✠✠✠

Near my weapons platforms Duke Robert quickly cleared an area, and by late afternoon, *Malleus Dei* was assembled and ready to throw. As I did previously with *Bone-Crusher*, I built it to readily assemble, disassemble, and move, and we had it set for just such a use. My wagonloads of stones arrived to fill the huge bucket as we set it up, and the projectiles followed. And by the tenth hour, long before the sun was too low to interfere with my sighting from the platform, we hurled our first stone.

Now, I had no experience with a machine this big, nor had we the chance to test the engine before this, so the first throws were quite wild. Initially, they fell well short of the city, as we made the initial adjustments of sling length and release pin, and those poor throws drew hoots of derision from onlookers in our lines and taunts from the wary Turks — indeed, one throw went straight up and nearly annihilated the machine. But I had endured a good deal of practice with *Bone-Crusher*, and the tenth throw crossed Nicaea's wall. That raised cheers in our ranks and silenced the Nicaean ramparts.

After that, each throw got better. We were still throwing too long, but that didn't bother me; in fact, the crash of hundred-weight stones caving in roofs in Nicaea made me quite cheerful. And as screams and cries of anguish reached us from Nicaea, spirits among us soared.

Demetrius had already heard what I was up to, of course, and quickly appeared. Delighted with an invitation to join me on the platform to watch, he was ecstatic, bouncing with excitement at each throw. Count Raymond came as well, and with effort, climbed to my perch.

We hit the first tower north of Gonatas well before the sun was so low that its glare made it hard to see well. The stone struck hard, shattering the brick rampart, and bounced into the city. I ordered another of the same weight and no other changes — as ever, I kept notes with charred stick on parchment — and we hit the tower-top again. Brick and dust flew, and the men up there fled their post. And as the sun set, we could see fires burning inside Nicaea where roofs and upper floors had collapsed into the kitchen fires.

In the final hour before dark, we hammered the tower a dozen more times. Little remained of its protective rampart, which looked like broken teeth rather than a wall, and the structure was now useless in fight, for it afforded no protection from our arrows and bolts.

We christened the engine *Malleus Dei*, the 'Hammer of God' then, using some of Anselm's best spirit, and went off to supper in my camp in elated for the first time in weeks. And as a reward, I left the remainder of spirit for the tree-bucket's crew to share. They were singing *The Siege Master's Song* — what else? — as I left.

✠✠✠

At the nightly military council on the eleventh, though, a new question arose. We knew the Nicaeans were not completely cut off, and never had been, because they had boats to cross the great lake, operating through the water gates on the western side of the city, while we had none. And Tancred, who held the northwestern side of Nicaea, reported that the Seljuqs continued to bring foodstuffs and forage into the city by means of those boats.

"That won't do," said Duke Godfrey. "If we can take the city no other way, we need to be able to starve them into submission. And we can't do that if they can replenish stores by means of the lake."

"It's worse than that," Tancred replied. "My watchers think there may be Seljuq troops in those boats as well."

A murmur went around the headquarters tent. An unending stream of fresh food and healthy troops meant we might never force Nicaea to capitulate. Bohemond said then what many others were thinking: "If they can bring in food and men, they can also take out the sultan's family — and his treasury!"

Now, I had not come to Nicaea for loot, and the treasure of Kilij Arslan held no lure for me. But I knew I was unusual in that. All of us were here at our own expense, or the expense of a great lord as his retainer. Most of the knights and nobles here were second sons and younger, and lacked the inherited wealth that went to their eldest brothers. For that reason, many had come as much in quest of earthly as spiritual treasure. And if all the earthly wealth was smuggled out of the city before we could take it, their spiritual reward might be great, but it could not fill an empty belly.

"We need to stop those boats. Is there a way?" I think it was Count Stephen who asked that. "Couldn't we put men at all the landings?"

Count Robert shook his head. "That would take too many men away from the siege — it's a big lake. And those men would be vulnerable to Seljuq horsemen; we know the sultan left horsemen to watch us — I see them daily on the hills overlooking us. They may not be able to take on the army, but small squads they would gladly slaughter."

Stephen asked, "Can we sink or burn their boats?"

Count Raymond said, "Baron Godric could sink a boat with a single stone from his astonishing new engine — have you seen it? Throws a stone heavy as a man two hundred, even three hundred yards. And it hits in the same spot again and again! Truly, it is a wonder! But it would be a great waste to sink boats with it rather than punch a mighty hole in this damned fortress and be done with it. If we do not topple Gonatas within the week, I think we will need Godric and his Hammer to open us a door." He smiled at me with approval, and I nodded my thanks.

"So what do we do?" asked Duke Robert.

Count Robert replied, "We need boats. With boats we can intercept their boats — seize them, use or burn them, and blockade the city from the lake itself."

Godfrey frowned. "But there are no boats — we've looked. They are all inside Nicaea or on the bottom of the lake. And we have neither the means or the time to build our own."

Count Robert replied, "There is one man we know who has boats in plenty — and it's time he actually helped us: Emperor Alexios."

Bohemond shook his head. "Yes, he has boat and ships. But they float on the sea, not on this lake. What good will those do us?"

Again, Count Robert had an answer. "We ask Alexios to bring them to Gemlik — the closest seaport west of the lake. Baron de Bethencourt knows that area — I had him scout it last week. Baron?"

Jean said, "Count Robert is correct. There is a level route of ten miles direct from Gemlik to the western end of the lake. If we were to get large boats or small ships from the emperor, we could haul them on rollers over that route. We certainly have the men to do it."

Raymond chuckled, "And it would serve that bastard Arslan right. All of you saw the countless number of ropes his army brought with them on the twentieth to take us as slaves. Let's use them to pull those ships here instead and finally hem in Nicaea completely!"

Approval of the notion sounded around the great tent, and Godfrey said, "I'll send a messenger to the emperor straightaway and request suitable ships. With luck we could have them in days. Any dissent?"

There was none, of course, and with that decision, Nicaea's neck was finally put in the noose.

✠✠✠

The Ultimate Weapon of its Age:
The Counterweight Trebuchet

Malleus Dei, the counterweight trebuchet.

# THIRTEEN

✠✠✠

Over the next three days — the eleventh through the thirteenth —
*Malleus Dei* demolished the fighting platforms atop the towers
flanking Gonatas. First we battered the three towers to the north.
Then I moved the engine to another position in Count Stephen's
lines, and from there we hammered the three towers west of
Gonatas into rubble. The transport between sites took almost a day,
but I realized that if I could add removable heavy axles and wheels
to the counterweight, we could move it like a cart. So I had my
craftsmen build these, and that saved us much effort later on.

Once we had the range correct in terms of stone weight and sling
length, we only needed to keep the machine aligned with the target
— I use a pair of sighting sticks set in the frame in line with the
center of stone fall — and keep throwing. Sir Cedric and I had
experience at this from our use of *Bone-Crusher*, but my engine
crewmen soon became so adept that once I placed the machine and
worked out the adjustments for correct range, they would hammer
that target again and again without further help. Leaving Cedric in
command, I was free to see to my other duties.

The spectacle of *Malleus Dei* at work quickly drew lords, knights,
and commoners to watch, especially after the praise Raymond had
showered upon it in the council. Duke Robert's lieutenants kept
them well back, let most watch for a throw or two, and then sent
them off. The nobles and knights were allowed to remain as they
wished, in a safe spot with a good vantage point, and for several

days the princes and commanders sent their squires and pages to find me, asking me to come explain its operation. Within a day, Godfrey, both Roberts, Stephen, Tancred, and Bohemond came to see the tree-bucket in action. It elicited great praise and admiration for its power and accuracy, from great men and common soldiers alike, and for its creation I was, for a time, the most popular man at Nicaea. Again and again I explained how it operated, to the point that after Cedric had heard it many times, I let him attend to that, and share in the glory.

Only two men who came to see it were not effusive at the sight. One of these was Manuel Boutoumites; the other was Tatikios. I did not know why, but I would soon learn.

Boutoumites commanded the cohort of peltasts that Alexios had sent us, while Tatikios was the emperor's liaison with our military council. Because of that both of them had a different mission than we did. We were there to capture the city. They were there to see that after capture, it was returned to the control of the emperor. I know because Tatikios — who was forever indebted to me for saving his life a decade before — told me as much.

So when they saw *Malleus Dei* blast big chunks of stone from the city's ramparts, they did not see it as the key to regaining the city; they saw it in terms of the damage that would have to be repaired after we took it, gave it back to the emperor, and departed south on our continued march to Jerusalem. And that made them glum, even a bit hostile.

I realized then that, in retaking Nicaea in return for Alexios's support, we were really only performing a favor, doing something for him he could not accomplish on his own, but it really had nothing to do whatsoever with recovering Jerusalem for Christ and Christendom.

✠✠✠

I did not know then that I had just changed the nature of war forever. I saw *Malleus Dei* merely as a marked improvement over *Bone-Crusher* — bigger and more powerful. And when I built them, I thought of both as but a better form of onager. In that I was wrong, for although I knew my new creations were mighty, I had only begun to discover how to use them to their full potential.

But I did learn, and quickly, and in time came to realize they were indeed different. The power of their blows was greater than any weapon that yet existed, like harnessed lighting or earthquake. But what was truly better was their accuracy. Getting an onager to hit the same spot more than once required real genius, but *Malleus Dei* had shown that a counterweight tree-bucket — or *trebuchet*, as my Frankish colleagues, incapable as they were of ever mastering our language, came to call it — could do it over and over. And that was its true value: being able to hit the same spot repeatedly to pound holes through the stone defenses.

Onagers had not completely lost their worth. Dropping firepots and severed heads into a fortress could destroy the will to fight among the besieged, and induce a surrender. But hammering holes through gates and walls brought undoubted victory.

You may ask why we did not use *Malleus Dei* on the gates. It was a good idea, and a question Duke Godfrey asked: "Baron, if you can hammer towers and walls with your splendid machine, why not just pound in the gates?"

"I would, my lord, but the arc of throw is wrong. Towers and walls have no overhead protection, but the gates do. And I cannot throw with a flat enough trajectory to clear the gatehouses to hit the gates themselves. Worse, Nicaea has triple gates in succession, so that even if I can destroy the first one or two, we are still barred from entry."

With that he saw the truth of it, and reluctantly agreed.

And you may wonder why we did not simply follow our initial success with a massed ladder attack in that sector. In truth, I still wonder if that might not have succeeded. But although the towers were useless, the walls between them were intact, and their ramparts still deadly. The space between the walls remained a deathtrap, and the ditches still imposed a fatal delay to men crossing open ground at the point they were most vulnerable to archers. We needed to make a real breach through both walls to create a path into the city, and I was already working on a plan to do just that.

Meanwhile in the mine under Gonatas, Luigi continued to make good progress. The sappers had excavated a large hollow under the eastern side of Gonatas, and shored it with timbers as they dug, to prevent a premature — and incomplete — collapse, as they continued to dig to the north, south and west. Luigi was confident our estimate of setting the mine-works ablaze on the seventeenth was holding.

✠✠✠

While we awaited word from the emperor regarding the boats we had requested, we all pressed on with our respective projects. And after seeing what the tree-bucket was able to accomplish in its initial outing, I had a new an idea to put to the military council — the night of the thirteenth, I think it was.

"My lords, I want to use my onagers to hurl firepots into the city and start fires. I seek your approval to do so," I began. Instead, I ignited a firestorm in the headquarters tent.

Now fire in a besieged city is a fearsome thing. It burns storehouses and dwellings, destroying provisions the inhabitants hope to use to outlast their attackers. It steals away precious water, which must be poured out to fight its spread. It terrifies the inhabitants, for there is no place to flee from it, and nowhere afterward to stay. It destroys the very stuff that enables the garrison to fight, weakening their numbers and their will to hold out. But it leaves intact the things most of us hoped to get from the city — gold, silver, and other precious goods.

So most of the lords were immediately and enthusiastically in favor of my suggestion. The men most vehemently opposed to it were, as you might have guessed, Boutoumites and Tatikios.

"No, no, no!" cried Boutoumites. "You must not burn the city! We hope to reclaim it for the basileus, not deliver him its ashes! Do not adopt this plan. You cannot control fire, and do not know what damage it will do. Find other ways!"

The argument went on for quite a while, and by the end of it, many of us there were convinced that Tatikios and Boutoumites cared little, if anything, in what was necessary to retake Nicaea, as long as when all the hard work, bleeding and dying was done, Nicaea ended up intact in the hands of the emperor. But in the meantime, I lost interest in the squabble I had started and departed, tasking Colin to send word to Demetrius enquiring if he had any news for me.

✠✠✠

Demetrius found me in my camp on the morn of the fourteenth, studying the carefully rendered map of Nicaea that Edith and Anselm had made for me from all my sketches, pondering where next we ought to employ *Malleus Dei*. He brought good news.

Now, in my tent I had no secrets from my closest associates, but from his reluctance to tell me outright, it was clear that he did. So I said, "Let's take a walk."

When we were away from others, he said, "I enquired of my spies inside the city — do not ask who or how, I beg you — and they have sent me word. Your guess is correct. The spot in the wall we saw is indeed a storehouse. The Seljuqs used it to store siege machines and arrows, many thousands of them, and other military stores: saddles, bridles, and the like. But they say it is now nearly empty, for the stores it held have been used up in the defense of the city."

I studied him hard then, and saw only sincerity in his face. "Do you trust that these agents are telling you the truth?"

"They are Christians and relatives of mine. They want the sultan's foul foot off their neck, and his religion out of their lives. They know what is at stake and they can be trusted. In turn, I promised your help in protecting them when the city falls."

I frowned. "In return for that information, I pledge gladly to do all I can for them. But in all honesty, I do not know if it is in my power."

He nodded and said, "Your assurance will do, because I know you will act for them if you can. But none of us have any control over what will be."

"So, do you now agree that I make the case to Count Robert to employ *Malleus Dei* there and pound us a new entrance into Nicaea?"

"I do. And I will enjoy watching it done," he said with a grin.

"Good. Tell your people this: I will ask the council to ensure that any inside the city who display a Christian cross, however crudely made, and can say a *Pater-Noster* in any tongue but Arabic, will be spared during the sack of the city. I think that's the best I can do at the moment."

"I will. And I know they are grateful for your effort on their behalf."

I smiled. "We did not come here to abuse fellow Christians. There are plenty of Seljuqs in Nicaea who are far more deserving."

✠✠✠

Demetrius's news was hugely valuable, a true treasure, because it meant we had the right tool in *Malleus Dei* and the perfect place to use it to finally breach Nicaea. So I wasted no time and hurried to Count Robert with my news. But he was not in his tent or his camp, nor did his lieutenants know precisely where he was. So I waited a half-hour for his return or news of where to find him, fuming all the while. And in the end, I got neither. I left word with his second that I had urgent news for his ears alone, and left to attend other matters.

On reaching my own camp, I learned that one of Count Raymond's pages awaited me. "Sire, the count has sent me to inform you that his men have completed their work, and he awaits your inspection and advice on the next stage of the project." As was our custom, the lad had been given a message to recite verbatim, not entrusted with the actual details, which protected him as well as the secret nature of the mine, for he could not tell what he did not know.

Nonetheless, I understood: the mine had been successfully dug, and Gonatas shored up in the process. Raymond wanted my opinion on its adequacy before we started to fill it with brush. I needed to go out to view the mine and concur that we were ready to do that.

So I thanked the boy with a coin and a smile, and went to tell my own lieutenants where I was going. After all, when Count Robert returned and sent me a messenger, he would need to know where to find me.

✠✠✠

The mine was as frightening and grim a place as I have ever been. Dug to only about three feet of headspace, and lit only with a few fat lamps, it was more burrow than mine, or even a crypt tomb. And it was filled about every two feet in every direction with fat wooden posts, wedged in at bottom and top to support the great weight of the tower.

I crawled in from the tunnel to assess its size, careful not to disturb any of the posts as I did. Deep inside, I found Luigi and his two lead diggers, Tomas and Antonio, all absolutely filthy with sand and soot, the whites of eyes and teeth set off by sooty black faces, shiny with sweat. But they grinned hugely with pride in their achievement.

I looked both sappers in the eye, looked around, and then nodded my appreciation. "How did you do this?" I asked. The question was not just to satisfy my professional curiosity — I could have figured it out; it was to give two masters of a difficult profession the chance to display their mastery and take credit for a job well done.

Tomas spoke first. "Sire, we dig only a little way under a stone before we insert a post and wedge it tight. Then we dig around it. Every time we make the gap wide enough to crawl through, we add another post. And when there is room for another digger, one joins us, but digs in an opposite direction, adding posts as he goes. The sand and rock we dig out is scooped into wooden shoes, as we call them, slid out through the tunnel, hoisted out and dumped into bags in the tower. Then the piglets take them away."

Antonio finished their report. "We followed the line of stones above along the outer edge of the foundation until we knew its shape, and then we dug back the middle, always shoring with two or three posts under any single small stone, adding more the bigger it is. Now, the entire eastern half of the tower stands on our posts, and the mine is ready to fill with fascines[26] of brush and kindling."

Luigi had one more element to add. "Just outside the foundation we dug upwards, to just below the surface. Once we light the fire, we will break the ground there, so that the fire will have both a draft and a chimney, like a furnace does. This will help it burn faster and more thoroughly." I knew from direct experience as a blacksmith making crucible steel that what he said was correct.

I noticed it was hard to breathe, and said so. They grinned at that and Luigi said, "Only a few men can work in here or the place becomes *mala* — sick, and the men must leave for a time, or become sick also. But if the candles can burn, we can work, so we watch them, and only add men if the little flames stay well."

"Why does the air become sick?" I asked, for I had never heard this.

"No one knows, sire, but we know it is true. As it is, we are all used to it. We dig until we feel poorly, and then go up into the tower. Soon we feel better, and while we are gone, our lamps recover, too."

---

[26] Bound bundles of cut branches and sticks. In Britain, these are *'faggots'*, but Luigi was from Italy, and Raymond from France, so they use the Roman term.

I nodded, and noted to myself that I must remember that. It might be a mystery why it happened, but it was an important thing to know.

"You men have done well, and I will tell Count Raymond you have earned everything he promised you." The three grinned at that, and I knew I left three very dirty men very happy.

✠✠✠

Raymond accepted my report with satisfaction and pleasure. I knew he might have gone by himself, and did not really need me to judge if the mine was ready. But I was a witness now to the work they had done, and if it did not succeed, I could truthfully attest that it was not the result of an inadequate effort, or poor expertise.

He smiled and said, "We'll begin filling the mine with fascines right away. Thank you for your help — especially in destroying the flanking towers. Once we set fire to the mine, nothing can save Gonatas; when she falls, so does Nicaea."

✠✠✠

Soon after my return to camp, a message from Count Robert arrived, telling me the count had returned and awaited me in his great tent. I rode there straightaway. It was late afternoon on the fourteenth by then.

"I'm sorry I missed your earlier visit," Robert said. "Duke Godfrey and I were called to Duke Bohemond's camp in secrecy. He said he wanted our views on his new weapon, which proved to be a great battering ram on wheels. He says he'll set it ablaze, ram it into the northern gate and wedge it there, to burn his way through. He has two more built, to burn the gates beyond the first, but he hasn't figured out how to get past the ruins."

Then he sighed. "But that wasn't the real reason for his summons. He's come to realize that whatever happens here, he won't end up the king or duke of Nicaea. He came to get a better principality than Apulia is, and since it won't be Nicaea, now he wants to be ruler of Antioch. So he is trying to secure our support. And in doing that he also eliminates us as potential rivals." Robert shook his head. "It's madness everywhere. I hope your urgent news is good — we truly need some."

What Robert told me was a shock, but it was not really unexpected. I knew many, perhaps even most, of the knights and nobles came with us in hope of winning wealth and power here, ideally in the form of lands of their own. But most kept it to themselves, more as a dream than a goal. The shock was that, in Bohemond's case, his ambition was naked and his goal foremost, so brazen that before we won, indeed, before we even began, he was demanding the greatest prize be his. And what, besides showing up to demand it, had he done? Get a lot of men killed for nothing. Raymond, Hartmann, and I had done more, and most of our men survived the attempts. It was disheartening, even infuriating.

Then I shook it off. I did not care. I came to recover Jerusalem, and what Bohemond said or did was inconsequential. It was what I did that mattered to me.

So I said, "I do have news, and it is all good. Count Raymond's mine is complete, and he is preparing it now to burn out the shoring. That will topple Gonatas, I believe, and give us an entrance. But it will take time to burn both the tower and the mine. Meanwhile, Demetrius and I found a spot in the wall, opposite your lines, where a breach by *Malleus Dei* is practical. There is an empty storehouse there, built between the walls. We can breach the outer wall and roof, and the door in the inner wall will complete the way in. I want to move my tree-bucket to the site and begin bombarding it straightaway."

Robert looked hard at me, then said, "That it is as you say, I believe. How you know this — that the storehouse is empty — I have difficulty understanding. But that does not matter. I tire of all the wearisome politics we engage in here, when war is our business. Dear God, the damned Greeks are worse than Bohemond! At least he fights to win the city, not whine about sparing it." He shook his head.

Then he looked me in the eye and grinned. "By all means, bring here your splendid engine, and hammer us a door. I will take great pleasure in watching it happen, and I promise Boutoumites and Tatikios will not interfere with you, even if I have to bind and gag them to do it."

We grinned as I thanked him, and was about to leave when a messenger arrived with news and summons to a council in Godfrey's tent. The emperor had sent us boats, and they would reach Gemlik tomorrow.

✠✠✠

The fifteenth was a hectic day. The previous evening the military council quickly agreed to take half our force — mostly the camp followers, women, and least vital fighting men — to make an eleven-league walk to the town of Gemlik and drag the emperor's boats from the sea to Lake Ascanius. The rest would remain to keep the city bottled up by land and prevent the success of a potential mass sortie by Nicaea's garrison in attacking our most vital works: Raymond's tower and *Malleus Dei*.

To prevent Nicaea's garrison from knowing what we were up to, the boat retrieval army, as it was termed, was rousted an hour before first light, fed well, and marched in strict silence out of our lines and south, taking the shorter route to Gemlik over the little road that runs along the southern shore of the lake. It was more cart track than road, but most of our folk were afoot, moving in small bands, so it was enough.

I dearly wanted to remain behind to focus on moving *Malleus Dei* and readying her for the breach, but the council — particularly Godfrey and both Roberts — insisted that I would be needed, perhaps vitally, in figuring out how to get such large vessels across ten miles of ground. And I have to admit that they were right.

The line commanders, including Baron Jean and Hamish, would stay behind to defeat any attempt by the garrison at a breakout or raid on our works. And since I could not stay, I assigned Sir Cedric and Colin the task of overseeing the disassembly and transport of *Malleus Dei* to Count Robert's lines. Demetrius agreed to remain and help them locate the site opposite the storehouse. But I instructed them not to reassemble the engine; to do so might potentially warn the Seljuqs prematurely of our intentions. It would not take us long to do, but it might be days before we could do it, given the huge intervening chore we were embarked upon. And I did not want to find that storehouse packed full with earth and rock when I finally broke through the wall.

✠✠✠

Edith came with me, riding Colin's horse at his invitation, for our horses did not get enough exercise during the siege, and this was good for the horse as well as the woman. Now that everyone in camp knew "Mathilda" was a woman and thought her my mistress, we had dropped the pretense of her masculinity. She wore female garb when it suited her — after all, skirts do afford women some privacy during calls of nature. But she had grown to like wearing male attire, especially for occasions like this. And now none thought it strange when she donned breeks to straddle a horse.

We had not seen much of each other in recent days — her rescue was but three weeks earlier, and yet that seemed an age ago now. War keeps you busy, I'll say that, and she was as busy as ever, clerking for me and tending the sick and wounded. Still of an evening, we might get a few moments to chat, and it seemed to me that she was actually enjoying herself when events were not grim. For a prince, war was serious business, and campaigning a regular part of life. But for a princess, campaigning is highly unusual, so this great pilgrimage was for her the adventure of a lifetime.

The kidnapping, disclosure of her femininity, and revelation of our supposed affair, did allow me to make one change. I had an apartment added within my tent for her, so she no longer had to live as a man among men. It was consistent with our newly disclosed relationship, and gave her added privacy and protection. She might still serve as my clerk, but I could never forget she was my godsister and a royal princess.

✠✠✠

The trek to Gemlik took us the full day, for it was half-again as far as we typically journeyed on a regular day's march. We stopped to rest five minutes every hour, and at midday for a meal of bread and cold meat. So it was past the twelfth hour and nearing sunset when we finally reached the little fishing village of Gemlik.

The night was fine, however, and the folk with us were used to living outdoors. So the men brought in firewood as the women set about turning the cartloads of stores we brought into a supper. And soon all along the shore, fires warmed food and people as they sat in clusters to eat, talk, and rest.

Tired as most were, the common folk quickly ate and lay down to a well-deserved sleep. Only the sentries and lords were still awake, for I and my brother nobles still had work to do. After seeing to our folk, we turned to the project we came to undertake.

Hauled up on the beach were two dozen vessels: bigger than boats, certainly, but not cumbersome as the ships I knew, being more sleek. The rigging had been struck, but in any case was unneeded, for these vessels were propelled with oars, many pairs of them, not unlike the great Danish longships I knew from home. Here, they employed a design the Byzantines inherited from the Romans and Greeks, ships they called galleys.

It made my task easier, for these vessels had a thick and strong keel, a relatively light hull, very little superstructure, and no castles — as the above-deck structures were commonly called. In Alba, such ships are commonly moved by sliding them over logs laid across the line of travel, intended not to roll along but rather to serve as a slick rounded surface over which the hull could more easily slide. And from my experiences with the boats I used to besiege OdinsØye's tower, I knew we could move these fairly well in the same way.

So in a final council well past dark, when Godfrey asked me what I thought we ought to do, I described that technique, and made my recommendations based upon it. The council liked the idea and plans were quickly made. Then we all turned in for a few hours' rest before the time came to begin again.

✠✠✠

The sixteenth began for me at first light once again. There was a quick breakfast before parties of woodcutters set off into the nearby woods accompanied by teamsters leading horses. In no time, the first logs started coming in, cut by others into man-high lengths and laid across our line of march at six-foot intervals.

Now all the ropes that Kilij Arslan brought with him came to be used against him. One end of each was tied to a galley oar-port and handed to a pair of pullers, many of them hauling together to slide the hull up the bank and along the line of "rollers." The women would wet each roller with water, and the water, weight, and friction soon stripped away the bark, leaving a slick, round surface of green wood on which the keel slid, moving much more freely and easily than across the rough ground.

Fortunately, the route before us was relatively flat and level, and once we had the galleys up on the rollers they were fairly easy to move with a team of about a hundred pullers assigned to each boat, a knight or noble in command of each team.

I directed the laying of the rollers, choosing the route where the line of rollers ought to go. I sent ahead some of Jean's scouts to plant spears with cloth-strip pennants at hundred-foot intervals to mark the way.

Once we had all the galleys out of the water, our supply carts became handy, for rather than cut more trees, teams of folk simply loaded them by picking up the rollers behind us to be carted up to the front, where they were re-laid and wetted to serve the first ship once again.

Thus we proceeded, making about a half-mile to a mile an hour. We had a harrowing incident or two, where the route descended a small incline and the pullers suddenly found they had to brake the descent as the ships began to slide down the gentle slope. After nearly wrecking a ship, and spending a frustrating hour levering it back onto the rollers to resume our march, I had Count Robert remain at the spot to brief the next team of pullers to hang back and ease the vessel down the slope. Two hulls later, he had enough experience that the rest gave us no difficulty.

In the end, the first ship reached the lake by late afternoon, and one after the other, we slid them into the water. We found Boutoumites there, after he led their crews overland to the lake to re-man the ships and row them to Nicaea. Alexios had given him command of the fleet, so Tatikios and Tzitas commanded their land force back at Nicaea.

With that, the near impossible had been done: a fleet of Byzantine galleys with experienced crews now rowed the waters of Lake Ascanius, and there was nowhere they could not go. There was now no place ship-borne Nicaeans could go, either. Our encirclement of Nicaea was now complete, and sooner or later the city would have to surrender, or die.

Our folk settled down to an evening meal, a night's well-earned rest, and a daylong walk back to Nicaea. Not me. I had a fortress to take. So as soon as things were well in hand, I, Count Robert, Edith, and a small band of knights and nobles made a night ride back the way we had come. It was midnight when I fell into bed, and I slept like one dead until the usual camp noises woke me at dawn.

✠✠✠

The seventeenth began with a rare mid-morning military council. Most of the nobles who commanded contingents had returned via night or early-morning rides, and with the galleys underway across the lake to blockade the city, we needed a new plan.

Duke Godfrey began it. "My lords, I believe our victory here is finally at hand. Yesterday, by our people's hard work and the blessings of God, we succeeded in encircling Nicaea at last. They have no hope of rescue now, and they know it. And I believe we are now all in accord for an all-or-nothing push to take Nicaea at last."

Our roar of approval made clear that he had surmised correctly.

"So how will we do it? What are we ready to do?"

Count Raymond spoke up then, and said, "My lords, the undermine of Gonatas Tower that my brothers, the Bishop of Puy and Baron MacEuan, and I have dug is complete and ready to ignite. I require naught but the consent of the council to light the fires. Once lit, nothing can save Gonatas from toppling within a day — two at most."

Another approving roar went up, with cheers of "*Deus lo vult!*"

Then Count Robert waved for quiet, and said, "With no disrespect meant whatsoever to Count Raymond and his wonderful mine, we have an additional plan I intend to implement. Our ever-resourceful siege master, the good Baron MacEuan, has found a spot in the walls most vulnerable to his tree-bucket, the amazing *Malleus Dei*. And I propose that while the mine burns, he hammer us a hole into the city as a guarantee that, God willing, tomorrow or the following day, no matter what, we will all finally enter Nicaea by one entrance or both!"

At that, "*Deus lo vult!*" rang out over and over. Count Raymond had the council's unanimous consent, and I a new target to bombard.

✠✠✠

A short ride later, I found Sir Cedric and Demetrius awaiting me at the chosen spot. Cedric was curious. "What was the council shouting about, sire?"

I grinned at him and said, "The council applauds our enterprise, and heartily endorses what we are about to do. I see you got her here. Any difficulties?"

"None we couldn't manage. The counterweight is always the biggest challenge but the new wheels make that relatively easy. She is ready to erect, and we have projectiles sorted, weighed, painted and in plenty."

"Outstanding, Sir Knight! You couldn't have done better. It's almost as if I trained you myself." I'm afraid that the prospects of what we were about to do had me in such overflowing good spirits that I was a bit giddy. But I could not help it — I do love putting a tree-bucket to work.

He looked at me hard, then, reading my mood to see what inspired it, and said with a smile, "Then you're not going to bite my arse again?"

Demetrius looked at the two of us. "Again?"

I ignored the little Greek and said, "Only if you continue to dither here asking irksome questions instead of assembling our tree-bucket so we can properly deflower this maiden fortress at last."

"Aye, my lord! At once, my lord! Just as you wish, my lord!" Cedric was grinning now, both of us blazing with tree-bucket fever.

Demetrius persisted. "Godric! What did he mean by *again*?" But we ignored him — torturing Demetrius was one of life's true pleasures.

I said, "Ahh, that's better! Very well, Sir Cedric — proceed! I'll be back in two hours to set the sling length and stone weight. But in the meantime, I'm off to find some pots . . ." And as I climbed back into the saddle, I added, ". . . and don't tell that story to Demetrius, or they will have heard it in Jerusalem by sunset."

Cedric laughed outright, Demetrius cried, "What *story?*" and I nudged my horse in the flanks.

Oh, yes, giddy indeed.

✠✠✠

The Crusaders' war machinery.

# FOURTEEN

✠✠✠

About noon of the seventeenth, I sent word to the council that *Malleus Dei* was ready. In short order, both Duke Godfrey and Count Robert appeared to witness the spectacle. I had a large semicircle of other onlookers around us, and had to employ several knights to keep them back — sometimes the great stone went backwards when things went wrong, and I wanted no more good Christian souls on my conscience.

I had already calculated and tested the range, with a small dimple in the wall now marking the point I wanted the breach. So I offered the two princes the honors of the first throw. The count demurred in favor of the duke.

Godfrey stepped up, took the release lanyard from me, solemnly said, "*Deus lo vult!*" and tugged hard.

With a snap, the holding strap released the long arm. In a blur, it whipped up and forward as the great counterweight fell, and the sling whipped in an arc that made the hundred pound rock fly like a pebble. Instantly, a ground-shaking *CRACK* resounded, and two hundred yards away, my dimple suddenly had a mate beside it.

"Lord God Almighty!" said Godfrey, in awe.

✠✠✠

Now our work began in earnest. Every few minutes, another stone flew. Every few moments, a great stone struck that wall with a sound like a sharp thunderclap, and brick and mortar exploded as sharp chips. The two dimples were joined by a host of others. After a couple of hours, they had merged into one big dimple, which got bigger and bigger with every passing hour.

Before darkness fell, I made several other casts for which I did not ask permission. These were fire-pots — clay vessels filled with Danish tar, and set afire just before launch. I had brought up an onager for just this purpose, since they use a spoon rather than a sling — much better for burning projectiles, and able to throw several pots together.

Now there was a very good reason for throwing these, and a better reason for not asking permission. I wanted to create a circle of fires in the area beyond the intended breach, so that the Seljuqs would have to expend their efforts through the night fighting them, rather than on working to fill the storehouse solid with earth and rock.

My father had once told me, "Never ask a question whose answer you do not wish to hear." This was the time to employ that advice. From my earlier request to use fire I learned that Boutoumites would violently oppose it, thereby stupidly putting the whole project at risk by giving the Seljuqs time to counter it. So asking the council for permission would only entangle them in my actions crossing Boutoumites. But once the fires burned, all Boutoumites could do was to turn his rage on me, and no Greek existed in all Byzantium who could best me in a fight. I knew, for I had spent months here training the best knights they had.

So I acted on my own volition, never giving it a second thought. Soon my target was backlit by a number of small fires that grew larger and brighter as the darkness grew. Several hundred yards south, the flames burning Raymond's tower grew as well, a huge pillar of flame growing ever-higher, and lighting that entire area nearly bright as day.

That done, we went back to work. I figured I had twenty feet of wall to break through. I estimated we were getting between a half-foot and a foot of penetration per hour over the entire area of the breach, so stopping for the night meant losing six to twelve feet of progress. I wanted the first breach to be mine; stopping only gave the damned Turks more time to stop me, and Raymond's mine more time to take down Gonatas instead.

So I had food brought in, fires and torches lit to give us light to work, and a fresh crew to relieve the original. And nobody got much sleep that night. Inside Nicaea's walls, the terror of the consequences that followed our impending victory grew, while outside, the whump of the tree-bucket's launch, and the thunderclap of stone on brick, created a rhythm many could not bear. But halfway through the night, when Cedric returned to relieve me, I lay down nearby and had no trouble sleeping. To me, the music of the tree-bucket is the sweetest lullaby.

✠✠✠

At dawn, the fight for the city renewed everywhere in deadly earnest. Count Robert came to see what progress we made, and found us still hard at work. "How does it go, Baron?" he asked.

"Sire, I believe we are nearly halfway through. Because these walls are so thick, as we go deeper, we must continually widen the circle of the breach, and the added area takes time to hammer. I think we will break through tonight, tomorrow at the latest."

"Good news! We cannot be sure when Gonatas will fall. If it

topples today, Stephen, Raymond, and Ademar will storm the breach immediately. If it does not, Godfrey and I will plan to go through your breach tomorrow. Can you keep the Turks from plugging it again?"

"Yes, I believe I have a way to make it too great a hazard to block up again once I breach. I've not tried it before, but it should work."

"I saw fires in the city last night inside the breach-site. Boutoumites is outraged, of course. Was that your doing?"

"It was. The Turks filled the first tower Raymond attacked with rock and rubble before we could break through. I didn't want them filling this storehouse with rock and earth last night, or today. You may tell General Boutoumites that I fight for Christendom and the emperor, not his aggrandizement. Alexios will never rule this city until we force it to surrender first. My sword is ready to answer for my actions, if the mighty Boutoumites has the courage to face me. If not, he can . . ." and there, I confess, I described something only a Pecheneg would do.

Robert chuckled. "Never fear. Boutoumites will rant, but I doubt he has ever used the sword he wears — the prissy bastard prefers tricks and bribes to battle. Thank you for making our consent unnecessary, but the entire council endorses your actions, be assured of it."

"Thank you. Please tell the council I am grateful for their support, and Boutoumites that he has nothing I want. Did Raymond set the mine afire, as well as the tower, last night?"

"No, the Nicaeans finally managed to set Raymond's tower afire. I think they believe it is still crucial to our plans, and were unaware that we planned to burn it ourselves. Raymond said they succeeded just as Luigi's diggers laid a fuse of tar-soaked rope through the mine to fire it and completed opening a second airshaft. The two barely escaped — the fire reached the leftover fascines in the tower and the whole interior went up in a great blaze. Fortunately, a bold crew in a piglet stayed despite the flames, and all escaped safely."

"Thank God for that! They are brave men, those miners, and most deserving of their fee."

"Amen!" said Robert, who bade me well and took his leave.

✠✠✠

Raymond's tower had burned through the night, collapsing shortly after I went to sleep, but the wreckage continued to burn in a great heap. And after the tower's flames had finally died, the smoke that continued to rise from Gonatas's base told us the mine fire was still hard at work.

For my part, I focused on the breach, repeatedly recalculating and readjusting the sling length and stone weight to put the impacts where we needed them. I found we could count on slight variations in each throw to move the impacts around a center, and rarely did the projectiles go too wide or too high once we had that right.

Hour by hour, I drilled deeper and deeper into that wall. Ten feet . . . twelve . . . thirteen. My men brought in cartloads of river boulders from dry streambeds to the east and south, and still I sent them out for more. Those we threw started to accumulate in the ditches just outside the breach-site.

Elsewhere, I am told, Bohemond and Tancred mounted another useless ladder attack, and all around the city, arrows flew in flights as attackers tried to get to and over the walls and the defenders tried to keep us back. The onagers in our lines threw spoons of stones at the defenders, braining many in an effort to clear wall and tower-tops. But nowhere was a breach achieved all day.

✠✠✠

By late afternoon, the progress I was making with *Malleus Dei* grew faster — I think it was because the rear side of the wall was failing, cracking outward under the repeated heavy impacts — and that made the rock and brick at the point of impact more prone to break. We were getting better than a foot of penetration an hour now, and the area of the breach big enough to ride a horse through.

I was changing crews at four-hour intervals, to keep up the pace. The engine was showing serious signs of fatigue as well, for the forces needed to throw those great stones took their toll on it, too. *Hold together just a little longer, my darling,* I prayed. *A little longer, and we'll be in.*

Dusk came. I had fires lit and torches placed, and we hammered on. I ate bread and cold chicken from one hand as I checked alignment with the aiming sticks for the many-hundredth time with the other.

It was getting hard to see the results of our work, so I had Cedric use the onager to throw firepots into the breach — the burning tar and oil adhered to the sides and burned on, lighting the hole. About every fifth throw by *Malleus Dei*, Cedric threw another pot.

It was about three hours after dark, the fourth hour of the night, when Cedric threw a firepot, and we watched it arc into the hole and disappear rather than burst, as had all its predecessors. But an instant later, a brilliant glow arose, and illuminated the breach — from the other side! And as the flames there grew, it revealed a hole in the wall the size of a Turkish shield.

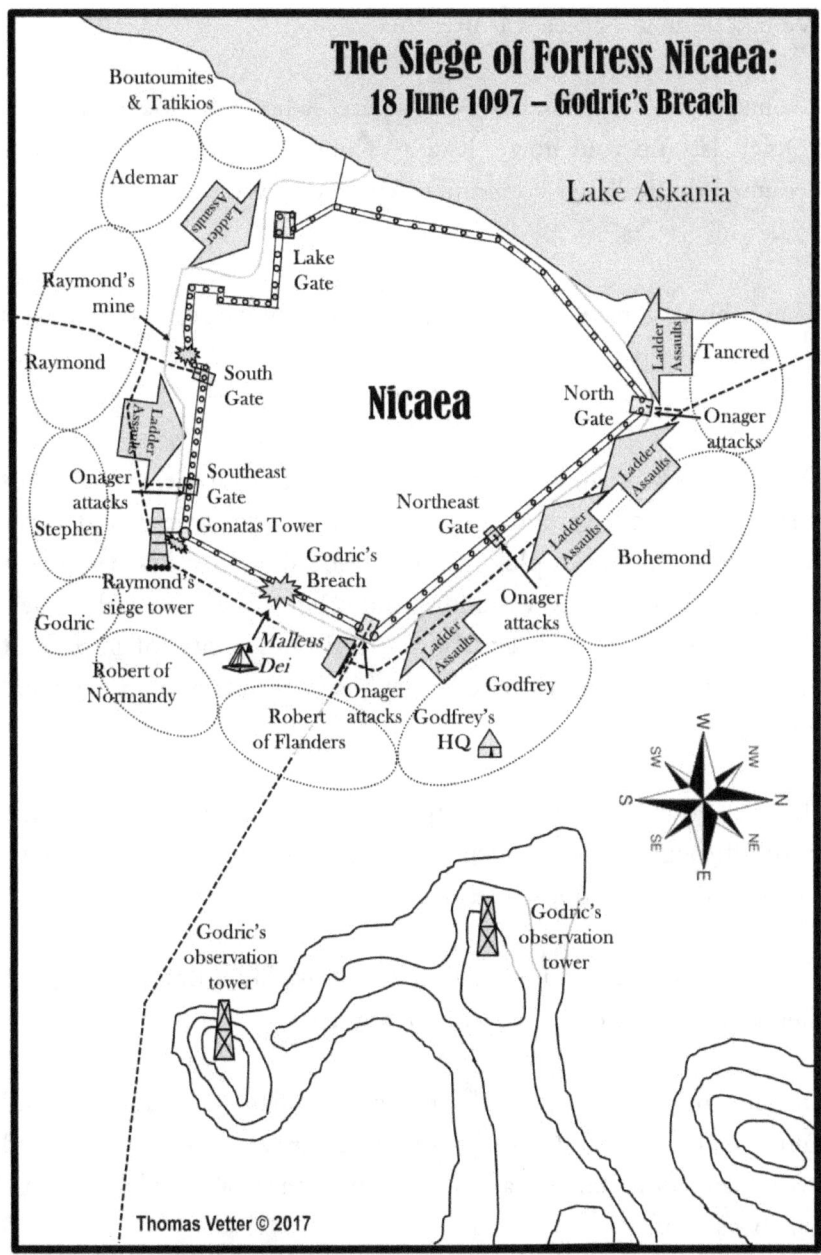

**18 June 1097: Godric breaches Nicaea's walls.**

We had done it! Nicaea was breached!

"Colin! Colin!" I called to my squire, who was dozing nearby. "Quick, lad, on your horse. Ride to Count Robert. Tell him I have breached the wall and continue to enlarge it. We will have entrance by dawn!"

Colin shook himself awake, repeated my message, and ran to a horse.

✠✠✠

On we worked, and the breach grew. Now some stones shot through the hole without contact, and I knew that would deter anyone from trying to plug the hole; indeed, after it killed the first to attempt it, no others would try. But other stones struck the sides, bounced and tore stone and brick from both points of impact. A mound of rubble had gathered at its base, creating a ramp we could run up.

Hour by hour, the hole grew larger, and soon we it was big enough to run through — at a crouch, I admit, but big enough. The Seljuqs would have to face our blades at last.

Suddenly, from the south there came a noise like a thunderclap, and then a great ground-shaking thump and roar. Gonatas had fallen!

Despite the hour, suddenly every Christian was awake. And hundreds of thousands of us took up the great battle cry, over and over again, until there was no one in Nicaea who did not know what was coming:

*"DEUS LO VULT! . . . DEUS LO VULT! . . . DEUS LO VULT!"*

It was too dark to attack. There was every chance that in the dark, in the confused midst of a melee in the breach, we would attack and kill our friends as well as our foes. We had to wait until dawn to launch our attack.

But at dawn we *would* come, scores of thousands of us through two breaches, both of which I had helped make.

Nothing in Nicaea could save it now.

✠✠✠

In our lines, no one went back to sleep; indeed, now no one could. Men-at-arms sharpened blades, filled quivers, donned armor, and prayed to live through what followed. Women and children built cooking fires and fixed breakfasts a man could fight all day on, for no one knew how long or tough a fight it would be. And after the fight came the looting, with everyone eager for that. All knew that Nicaea was a rich city — the splendor of its great walls spoke to the money that it cost to build them and *that* spoke to the great wealth they guarded. And to the hordes of common-folk who had marched, and worked, and sweated, and starved, and struggled to get here to take this city, a share of that wealth, gathered on a first-come basis, was their just temporal reward. It might not be right, but it had ever been so. To the victors go the spoils.

And all around the great city, near and far, I could hear voices in song, the words not always intelligible, but the tune unmistakable. The whole Christian army was singing variants of *The Siege Master's Song.*[27]

Its verses were these:

---

[27]If you would like to see and hear *The Siege Master's Song*, a video can be found here: https://www.goodreads.com/author/show/7170207.Tom_Vetter and here: https://youtu.be/aKypcrA_qos.

*We've brought up the army.*
*We camp at your door.*
*Our peace terms you refuse,*
*So now you'll get war.*

*Come out now and fight us,*
*We'll entertain you.*
*And many will die here*
*before we are through.*

*Climb over, dig under,*
*Or pound a way through.*
*We'll use every weapon*
*To bring death to you.*

*Your towers will tremble,*
*Your garrison fall.*
*Your ramparts will tumble,*
*Starvation for all.*

*We'll cave in your rooftops*
*With boulders we cast.*
*With fire we burn all*
*So nothing will last.*

*Your loot we will plunder*
*And your daughters too.*
*We'll give them fat bellies*
*So as to spite you.*

And between each stanza came the refrain:

*Your castle can't save you.*
*We'll never withdraw.*
*Until you surrender*
*We stay at your wall.*

To us Christians, it was a vow of determination, a declaration of the
extent to which we would go for victory. To the Islamites, it was their

funeral dirge. As we prepared to conquer, the Turks prayed for salvation.

✠✠✠

The entire army gathered itself, prepared. Portions of the siege line on the north and on the south thinned, as those most eager to enter the city swelled around us, their huge grins and eager expressions betraying the reason for their sudden appearance. I'm sure if any signal had hinted at it, many would have risked the long run over the open ground to be among the first in. But I kept them back in the same way I ensured that the breach remained open, by throwing great stones and firepots through the hole.

First light came and the anticipation grew. Duke Godfrey, Count Robert and their handpicked men-at-arms arrived, pushing back the hordes, and preparing to head the initial assault.

"By God, Baron, you do good work!" said Duke Godfrey when the gray light grew enough to show us the breach. "With you among us, we cannot fail to retake Jerusalem!" It was the finest compliment I had ever received.

Then dawn broke. I thought the city unusually quiet for one on its last day as the Seljuq capital, but put it down to a terrified garrison with nothing to hope for.

Then, as sunlight lit up the battlements at dawn on the nineteenth of June, defenders hung battle flags from the walls. But the men were Greeks, not Turks; and their flags were the banners of Manuel Boutoumites. Nicaea had surrendered in the night to him.

✠✠✠

The Nicaeans pray for salvation from the Crusaders.

# FIFTEEN

✠✠✠

It was over. Nicaea had fallen. After sixteen years under the boot of the Seljuq sultans, the great city had been returned to the Byzantine Empire. And at that moment, hundreds of thousands of Christian warriors, in a dozen tongues, collectively cried, "Shit!"

For seven weeks we had toiled, fought, sweat, bled, and many among us had died to recover this city. Now it was done, yet all of us stood outside and gaped, as Greeks who had done nothing to make it happen rejoiced on the ramparts.

I stood with Duke Godfrey and Count Robert as the banners were unfurled, and remember their reaction exactly: Stunned shock, as in one pole-axed; realization of a truly terrible occurrence; and then complete outrage at the undeserved unfairness of it all. Godfrey said then what we all thought: "May God damn that treacherous little prick! Robert, let's summon the council."

✠✠✠

As the army was ordered to stand down — after all, suddenly there was nothing more to fear as well as nothing more to fight for — the council gathered in Godfrey's great tent, and for once all the princes and almost all the great nobles were in attendance. Many knights came as well —knight is the lowest rank of nobility, and they were usually welcome — but today the great tent was full, so the knights were asked to gather outside, with apologies for the lack of space.

We expected then to see Boutoumites, but out of fear to confront our outrage, I believe, he did not elect to appear, sending instead a fat, fussy, and very pompous little Greek envoy, who addressed us thusly: "My lords, I am envoy to General Manuel Boutoumites, who sends apologies at his inability to attend your council this day. The demands of restoring order and mitigating the terrible damage done to his city are great and urgent, and keep the Victor of Nicaea quite busy . . ."

At that obscene title, a great growl, punctuated with hoots of derision, erupted from us, and drowned him out entirely until Duke Godfrey, banging sword on shield, managed to restore order.

". . . *quite* busy. Henceforth he will be unable to attend these sessions, but he urges you to send your enquiries and petitions to him . . ."

*Enquiries and petitions* set us off again, and Godfrey had difficulty regaining quiet.

". . . via myself and his counterpart, General Tatikios. In gratitude for this victory, Emperor Alexios I, Basileus of the Eastern Roman Empire, has appointed General Boutoumites Dux of Nicaea, and in that role, in the name of the emperor, he thanks you for your service in this campaign, acknowledges your substantial assistance in recovering the city, and requests that all hostilities to the city and its inhabitants cease. Under the terms by which the city was surrendered following his successful assault last night, all Turkish combatants are now prisoners of war under his protection, and all of Nicaea's citizens will be accorded the emperor's protection of their persons and property. The city is off-limits to all in this army except those to whom the dux gives passes. These will allow not more than a total of ten of you and your men inside the city at any time . . ."

At that, bedlam fueled by outrage reigned again. Godfrey had to climb on a table and bash dents in his shield to shut us up.

"Finally, the dux pledges this: In gratitude for your aid in the recovery of the city, the emperor has pledged to shower with gifts of money, fine horses, finery, supplies and alms for your people, all those counts and nobles who have given him their oath, and those who did not but will now do so. And the emperor forbids your departure until all the great nobles among you who have not given him their oath come to Pelecanum and do so."

The mellifluous sounds of the words *gifts, money, fine horses, finery, supplies,* and *alms* suddenly had a much-pacifying effect on the crowd in the great tent. But the phrase *forbids your departure* just as quickly disquieted us again.

Worried that we might lose all control and do the envoy violence, Duke Godfrey tried to thank him for his message and hustle him out of the tent. But as he endeavored, with difficulty, to get the little man safely out through a mob of outraged nobles, the envoy insisted on remaining, protesting, "Wait . . . wait . . . I have not finished. The Dux also demands that the man who defied his ban against firing the city be handed over for punishment . . ."

And I knew that meant me.

But Godfrey was one of us, after all, just as outraged as the rest of us. He did not know that I overheard as he spun the envoy around, grabbed the neck of his robe in a hard fist and snarled into his face.

"Tell the 'Victor of Nicaea' this, exactly as I say it: In obedience to our oaths, we will abide with the emperor's terms. But I know that last demand came not from the emperor. The man you would punish is the man who won your victory. He will *not* be punished for that. And unless the dux recants, I will bring every last man in this great army, armed for battle, into Nicaea to see that he does. Do you understand me?"

The envoy's eyes were wide, for he had never been handled or treated so. His many chins wobbled as he nodded vigorously. "I understand," he managed, at last.

Godfrey dropped him, gave him a glacial smile, and smoothed his tunic. "Good! Leave us now. Thank you for your service."

The envoy gathered up the shreds of his dignity and scuttled off to so inform the so-called Victor of Nicaea. Godfrey watched him go, then turned to me with a grin.

"Well, Baron, it's true you do break up the crockery from time to time. But without you, we'd still be sitting here when Christ returns. This isn't the last door we need you to kick open. Think no more on it."

Then he clapped me on the shoulder, and called for quiet once again.

✠✠✠

Over the course of the next week, many things happened. These are the ones I recall now.

Foremost was the insistence of the now much-cursed Dux of Nicaea, Manuel Boutoumites, that all the nobles among us who ranked as counts or higher and who had not yet given their oath of fealty to the emperor, now return to Pelecanum and do so, before Alexios would allow us to march on. In truth, he had not the physical means to stop us. But because most of the princes were bound by oaths they had taken in Constantinople months before, they were now morally bound to obey Alexios and his agent. So here we sat.

Meanwhile, Alexios added a sweetener, distributing many handsome presents among the nobles who had given their oaths, promising the same to those who would do so, opening his vast coffers to distribute funds among the multitudes, and then sending us a huge market so that we could replenish our stores and supplies before we marched on. As we did, Alexios used a promise of further rewards to prompt Duke Bohemond to pressure the remaining count to comply with the emperor's demand.

Ironically, it was Bohemond's own nephew, Tancred, who resisted, headstrong as ever. Tancred had previously disguised himself as a common footsoldier to sneak across the Bosporus. Now we all sat here because he refused to give his oath to Alexios, stating to all who confronted him that he had given his pledge of fealty to Bohemond, and followed his orders alone. Bohemond alternately pleaded and raged, trying to move him, to no effect. So at last he demanded that Tancred accompany him to Pelecanum.

Now, from personal experience I knew how persuasive Alexios could be, and had experienced firsthand his almost hypnotic charisma. So I was truly impressed to learn that Alexios had no power over Tancred. Instead, the encounter went thus:

Tancred said, "Sire, I have given my fealty to my uncle, and obey his command. I follow his orders and he follows yours. That should be sufficient, should it not?"

Alexios said, "In most cases, Lord Tancred, it should. Yet should your uncle die on this campaign, what then — who commands you?"

335

"Then I command, as I do in most respects."

**Emperor Alexios Komnenos I.**

Alexios nodded. "And that is why I require your direct oath, Lord Tancred."

"My Lord Basileus, you have promised many gifts to the nobles who make this oath. I thank you for your generosity, but I need none of them. I will give you my oath, though, if you will give me but one gift: This tent above us. Give me that, and my oath is yours."

At that, all those present gasped, and Duke Bohemond gaped, with astonishment, for there was no other tent as great in the entire world. First of all, it was enormous — all the buildings in Alba were smaller, except Dunfermline Abbey Cathedral alone. It had many rooms, and its cloth turrets rose more than thirty feet. The tent's throne room looked as if it would allow more than five hundred people.

Secondly, it was monstrously cumbersome. Demetrius told me that it took an entire caravan of camels to transport all the cloth, poles, guys and stakes, rugs, curtains and furnishings, and a small army of men to erect and strike it. On this campaign, it was completely impractical for everyone but an emperor.

So why did Tancred demand it? I cannot say with certainty, but I believe he wanted Alexios to refuse, and thereby give him excuse to avoid the oath. Tancred was as ambitious as his uncle, I knew, and he had come to carve out a kingdom of his own; a goal that an oath of fealty to the man who was his rival in that goal would stymie. So avoiding fealty would have been important to the man I knew.

However, if the emperor did give him the great tent, Tancred could then lord it over all of the other princes, who had settled for much less, the huge edifice constantly reminding them of that fact wherever we went. That would have soothed the vanity of the man

I knew.

What might Alexios have done then, and how would Tancred have responded? Alas, we will never know, for other events forestalled them, when Palaeologus, aide and kinsman of the emperor, was overcome with umbrage at Tancred's arrogance.

Outraged, Palaeologus confronted Tancred. "How dare you, you Danish pirate upstart!" And he gave Tancred a shove that knocked him on his arse. Tancred jumped up and drew his sword, to the shock and horror of all at the impropriety, and Palaeologus did the same. A great disaster was imminent, but Alexios was quicker than the rest, and jumped up from his throne to stand between the adversaries. Bohemond rushed forward, too, and restrained Tancred, saying, "Tancred! No! Stop! You bring shame upon yourself to attack the emperor's kinsman!"

At that, Tancred came to his senses, and with effort, regained control of himself. He then sheathed his sword, and said, "Great Basileus, Lord Palaeologus. Forgive me. I am a better knight than this." And with that, he knelt, and said, "I give you my oath now unreservedly."

Alexios accepted it and rewarded him as handsomely as he had the rest. But the tent he kept.

✠✠✠

One big question plagued all of us Franks. We knew Boutoumites had played a duplicitous game, pretending to support the siege while he secretly negotiated the Seljuq surrender, only at the last minute to betray us and snatch for himself the prize that our blood, sweat, and toil had won. And we despised and hated him for it — the whole army, to the very last man.

But had Alexios and Tatikios also conspired in this? Did they support and aid him in his efforts, or did he act alone? That we did not know. And because we did not know, we knew we could no longer trust either of them. Indeed, that betrayal planted in us such a deep distrust of their now naked double-dealing that none of the princes would ever trust either of them again.

Though I had no interest in loot from Nicaea, I felt the betrayal as deeply as the rest, for I had worked harder than most to capture the city, and felt robbed of my victory at the last moment. I still believe to this day that Nicaea would have never fallen, never surrendered, never been returned to Christian rule, without my efforts, and in particular, without *Malleus Dei*. They could have surrendered to the Byzantines at any point before we breached the walls, yet did not. They only did so after I had created two irreparable ways in, in the final moments before we invaded.

I could not let it rest, either. I found Tatikios in his tent and privately confronted him. Since I had saved his life in battle at Philippopolis, he had been in my debt, and that had created a special relationship between us. Now that was imperiled.

"Lord Tatikios! Did you know what Boutoumites was up to? Were you a part of his conspiracy? Did you work to deceive us Franks into doing all the bleeding and dying while you secretly helped negotiate this surrender?" And when he denied it vociferously but would not meet my stern gaze, I had my answer.

"You treacherous bastard! You weren't worth the saving, were you — then or now!" I shook my head, furious with him, and somehow with myself as well.

Tatikios took umbrage at that, not that I cared, and said, "I serve my empire and my emperor first, whatever it costs me: my nose, my life, my friends. Nicaea is our city and it must remain that way. We never set out to merely exchange a Seljuq ruler for a Frank. Surely you can understand that — you, of all people. We discussed it often enough."

He shook his head. "Did you not come to help us recover these lands to Christian governance? Were any of you going to stay on here and defend us from the Turks, who will surely return to retake it? Or were you going to march south as soon as the city was secured, leaving us to repair the walls and towers you shattered, to rearm and re-garrison the city, and to defend it anew against Kilij Arslan's army?

He was pleading with me now. "Know this. It is one thing for a great Frankish lord to want a kingdom, and quite another thing to keep it. Your army is mighty and can do what we cannot. But unless you stay, the task of defending this land reverts to us as soon as you leave. And it does not serve that interest to allow the savages in your ranks to rape and rob and murder the populace of a city already unfortunate enough to have been first raped and looted and *then* enslaved for years by the Turks. We only sought to spare them that, so that they celebrate their liberation, not mourn all the fresh outrages you would perpetrate upon them."

Now it was my turn to take umbrage. "It is *your* mistake to betray the very men you begged come rescue you — men who came at their own great expense; men who struggled, bled, and died trying to accomplish the task you just acknowledged only we could do. Yes, some among us want lands and kingdoms. And why not? If you want us to stay and fight for you, do we not need lands and livings to make that possible? It was you who lost this land once already to the greed and barbarism of the Islamites because you are not strong enough to hold it. How will you hold it without us?"

My fury with him and Alexios grew, even as I gave it voice, just as fire does when bellows feed it air. "Yet how can we now trust you — you who backstabbed us in the very moment we gave you victory. You need us, yet you fear us so much that you refuse to trust us. You demand our fealty, knowing that our honor will bind us to keep our oaths. But you do not act honestly with us in return, which the act of oath-giving compels on your part. And in breaking your half of the compact, you have freed us from keeping ours. I never thought the great Emperor Alexios to be so desperate as to be that stupid."

I turned on him and with steely glare, I stared into his soul. "Yes, there are greedy, savage men among us. Yes, we might have looted the city for three days, as the custom of war allows. Yes, we might have left the women of Nicaea with bellies full of huge Frankish babies — not that you scrawny little Greeks couldn't use some real men to fight for you in the future. But because you are ruled by fear rather than honor, you did not make an honest case of it and ask us to spare the city. You could have offered us a market for resupply and shared out some of the sultan's ill-gotten treasury to reward the men who sacrificed so much to get you all the rest. Yet you did not.

"We are Christian men of honor, who deserved respect and honest dealing for having come to fight and die for you. Yet you have been dishonest with us from the beginning, and dishonest with us even now. So if we do not trust you ever again, if we now carve out kingdoms and loot every city we take, if we turn on you and fulfill your every fear, ask yourself this: Why don't you deserve it?"
I could see my truth hit home, sparking across his face a sudden look of horror that acknowledged their idiotic conduct. And he slumped into a chair, diminished in that moral defeat.

With that, my rage subsided. So I asked one more question before I left him. "Tell me the truth — was Demetrius a part of your plot?"

He shook his head, absently, and I believed him.

✠✠✠

For the next few days, I put my men to work, dismantling my engines and repacking the critical parts against a certain future need to build them anew. We dismantled and burned our platforms and defenses, too, so that Kilij Arslan could not simply move in and use them to retake the city. We gleaned many hundreds of thousands of arrows from the killing field between our lines and the city's walls — after all, we were certain to need arrows as we fought our way into Jerusalem.

The Byzantines did host us a huge market then. Nicaea was unable to do so, diminished as it was by the siege. But Alexios used his navy to transport goods and provisions to us, both by way of Nicomedia and Gemlik, the little navy we had created on Lake Ascanius carrying half of it the final leg. Whether my rant at Tatikios had anything to do with it, or it was pure serendipity, I cannot say. So we re-provisioned then, each as best as he could, for the long hot march ahead of us across Anatolia.

Alexios kept his pledge of gifts to us finally, and from the princes I received a huge chest of silver and gold as a mark of their gratitude, monies I knew I would need to keep my retinue fed and watered. Our horses were in good shape, for there was sufficient forage and water for them in abundance around Nicaea. But against the dryness of the deserts ahead I took precautions, filling barrels and skins with water that we loaded in our carts.

One thing I did then that proved wise with prescience: the timbers for *Malleus Dei* and my other great engines I did not burn. Rather, these we bundled and lashed atop great wheeled axles. Then I had Sir Cedric command a party of men and horses to haul them to

Gemlik, where they were consigned to Master Lamphros of the trading ship *Saint George*. With him I had earlier made arrangements to collect these, store them in his warehouse on Kalymnos, and deliver them to me when and where I sent him word.

✠✠✠

Under the terms of the surrender, the emperor allowed the Seljuq garrison to leave Nicaea with what they could carry, accompanied by a Byzantine escort that got them through our ranks unmolested. Alexios had the sultan's family and the Seljuq generals escorted to Constantinople where he treated them well — even though those same generals tried and failed to overpower their escort on the way. And eventually Alexios released to Kilij Arslan his family and harem without demanding the ransom we would have sought.

✠✠✠

Altogether, we spent fifty-two days at Nicaea. On the evening of the twenty-fifth of June, the night before we marched on, my comrades and I gathered for the first time in a long while in my tent: Jean, Edith, Hamish, Cedric, Colin, Henri, and Father Anselm. We were there to try Anselm's latest spirit. It wasn't too bad, I thought — potent, though it tasted like melons cooked in piss.

Edith set hers aside. "Father Anselm, what is in this? It's ghastly!"

"He's been experimenting with horse urine again, I'll wager," said Cedric, who knew all my Anselm stories too well.

Anselm shrugged. "It was the only thing I could get during the siege that would ferment — spoiled melons. It tastes poorly, but its spirit is strong all the same — just like us."

"It is certainly not anything I would choose to drink, were I home," said Jean. "But then, we are not at home, or my lovely wife would have opened a proper barrel for us in celebration." He shrugged and drank.

"And what reason, exactly, do we have worth celebrating?" I asked. My mood was sour, I admit. For more than seven weeks we'd been here, encamped at Nicaea, trying to take the second-toughest fortification I knew of in all the world, only to hand it over to an unworthy set of bastards without even setting foot in it. In that time, I thought, we could have walked to Jerusalem. In truth, I was morose, even sullen, still trapped in anger and frustration and brooding over Boutoumites and Tatikios.

Any of the others might have answered, but they left it to Jean who, as my knight, still held an authority with me the others lacked.

"Well now, let's see. Are we dead? No, certainly not — all of us live! Maimed or ill? No! How about stuck in the desert outside this damned stone fortress? No, not any longer! Thanks to you and *Malleus Dei*, that great wooden wonder, we are on our way again, bound for Jerusalem, the City of God. Death may yet lie in wait for us all, but it will not happen here, taking an unneeded city for an ungrateful empire, instead of the one city God wants for Himself. So let's celebrate that!"

I had to admit, Jean had a good point, as he usually did. What *had* I to mope about? We — indeed, I, more than any other — had just taken a city so far beyond the experience of any Frankish siege lord that every prince in the army had gladly given me a portion of their treasure from Alexios in gratitude. We were free at last of this obstacle, and we left it secure again in Christian hands. We were now free to march on toward our true goal, which had always been Jerusalem. And all of us had, by God's grace, survived the perils of the deadliest siege I had yet known, unharmed.

At that — whether it was that epiphany, Anselm's astonishing juice, the heart-lifting prospect of marching on, or realization that victory here put us closer to recovering Jerusalem — I felt much better.

"Well, here's to that, then!" I said with a smile. "But my cup is empty. Somebody give me Matilda's. I'll drink it."

"Not so fast!" she said, snatching it up. "It might taste like pears and pee, but I won't get anything better soon. Sorry, Father." And she patted his hand.

Anselm gave her a wink. "Maybe not. I traded some of this with his greatness, Duke Bohemond the Worldly, for some real fruit. There will be better things to come yet, my dear."

"Let's have a song!" cried Cedric, reaching for his flute. "Who's for a round of *The Siege Master's Song*?" And I groaned aloud.

But sing we did. And, our spirits raised, we drank all there was.

✠✠✠

Alexios rewards the Crusader princes for the recovery of Nicaea.

# AFTERWORD

## The New, True Story of the "Manuscript"

### ✠✠✠

As I have previously acknowledged at the end of *Call to Crusade*, my opening tale of discovering and translating Godric's long-lost manuscript was a tool of fiction, one I employed to intrigue and draw you, my Treasured Reader, into the story. I hoped that in thinking it *might* be true, it became more meaningful and interesting for you to read and me to write. And I hope you will forgive the artifice as writer's license.

Yet since then real events have since transpired to suddenly reveal a truth even more strange and more thrilling: **Two years after starting this project, I have discovered that there is indeed a real manuscript of sorts, one I cannot fully comprehend, yet swear is both real and true.** One of the most remarkable and inexplicable experiences I've ever had occurred when, while writing this book, fifty-plus years of genealogy suddenly enmeshed me with my story. Let me explain.

I first became interested in history and its interconnections with my family as a lad of twelve. In 1962, during a stay with my paternal grandmother in New Ulm, Minnesota, I witnessed the centennial of the 1862 Sioux Uprising — now termed "The U.S.- Dakotah War." There was a parade, historical exhibits all over town, lectures and presentations, and ceremonial dances by Dakotah descendants in a re-erected teepee village near town.

As we experienced the events of the week-long remembrance of that sudden, violent, and tragic conflict, it occurred to me to ask my grandmother whether "we" — that is, our family — had been caught up in it.

My grandmother had been born and raised in New Ulm, and always had a remarkable memory for people and relationships there. But she could not answer the question, for her family arrived there two decades afterward, and her husband's family never spoke of it. Instead, what she could do and did was to patiently and accurately answer my unending stream of questions over the next four years, supplying five generations of genealogical information about our family. From that start, I spent the next fifty years researching my family history, and that avocation built in me skills I now employ to write these books.

Now, in the five decades I spent digging up dead family members — figuratively speaking, of course — I never found anyone other than Swabian commoners and Lutheran-reformed Vikings. No presidents, nobles, or celebrities. No horse thieves or renegades of note either. No one you might find in the Encyclopedia Britannica, or Wikipedia, for that matter.

But in September 2014, a long-stymied lineage unlocked, and a time vortex pulled me in. The discovery was so thrilling it took me away from writing **March to Nicaea** for three solid weeks.

I fretted as I followed new clues back in time, knowing I ought to be writing instead of pursuing this new lead. But the intrigue kept growing; the new records I found kept reaching back in time, and whispering as they led me on that just a little further lay the answers to the preposterous puzzles in my DNA — oh, yes, I've had that analyzed, too. But those molecular teases of royal links and strange ethnicities were wholly at odds with my long and well-documented record of Swabian peasantry.

Back I went through the centuries: 1600s . . . 1500s . . . 1400s . . . 1300s! Suddenly, the surname prefix "Von" appeared, the one that denotes Germanic nobility. It led me to Swiss barons whose castles are visible with Google Earth. And these were followed by counts all over Switzerland, Austria, and Germany. Very cool!

And when I reached the eleventh century, I got a surge of euphoria. I hoped I might yet find a real Crusader of my own, an ancestor I could write into the *Siege Master* series as I have done here with my wife's ancestor, Baron Jean de Bethencourt, a real First Crusader.

But that didn't happen. Instead the plot twisted again, in a direction I couldn't anticipate and, indeed, still cannot fully comprehend — offering me a truth even stranger and so much better. For the one maternal line I started with had become several, and then many. And as I followed those new great-grandparents back, I suddenly found that my ancestors had ruled Swabia . . . and Saxony . . . and Germany.

And then there he was! Charles Martel, "The Hammer," Duke and Prince of the Franks, Mayor of the Palace of Austrasia, and de-facto King of the Franks! He was my thirty-fifth great-grandfather! From him and my 33rd G-GF Charlemagne, the first Holy Roman Emperor, I descend.

Charles Martel! The savior of Europe, who at the Battle of Tours in 732 AD so badly thrashed the Islamic army of invaders led by Abdul Rahman Al Ghafiqi, Governor-General of Al-Andalus, that he drove them completely out of France, back over the Pyrenees into Spain. His was the first repulse of Islam over Christendom since the followers of Mohammad had begun, a century before, to try to bring the entire world into submission to Islamic hegemony by means of the sword, using a campaign of conquest, terror, violence, murder, rape, slavery, extortion, and forcible conversion. Does any of that sound familiar?

I thought then that I could not have been given a better heritage, and I still do. But in one sense I was wrong, for it was not over.

Charles's lineage descends in a complex and tangled sequence of early kings and tribal rulers from the rulers of the Roman Empire itself. But his ancestor and mine, King Merovech, is said to have sired all of Europe's royal houses. I am, like no doubt many others, an unrecognized and undistinguished heir to that lineage, so I do not say this to boast; rather to wonder. But let me finish this tale before I do.

As I said, from Merovech came all of Europe's royalty; and from him another ancestor, my thirty-second great-grandfather, Alfred the Great, King of Wessex. And that changed everything.

You see, in writing **Call to Crusade**, I had already researched the lineage of Alfred and knew that many of my historic characters had blood ties to him: Queen Margaret of Scotland is a fifth great-granddaughter, and her children are sixth-great. King William the Conqueror's children married their Anglo-Saxon rivals to legitimize their rule of England, and these unions produced descendants who intermarried with other royal and noble houses. Eventually their stew of DNA ended up in my cells.

Big deal, you say — so what? Show us your crowns and castles. Sorry, I have none — the Black Death took care of those in the 1350s. And that's not why I write all this . . .

. . . for something else, or Someone, is at work here.

It was *two years earlier,* in October of 2012, when I dreamed up Godric MacEuan as a Scottish boy and decided to write a history of the First Crusade through his recollections as a military engineer and siege master. The demands of a plot that could make that work required substantial research and no little effort to weave a plausible fictional thread through the important facts of the real history. And I found that only one man could get my Scottish lad to the one place in the world he could learn cutting-edge siege warfare in an age when all the castles in Europe were wooden, while those in the Holy Land were stone: Count Robert I the Frisian of Flanders, who made his pilgrimage to Jerusalem via Constantinople a decade before the First Crusade's start, and set its train of events in motion.

Then two years later, I discovered that **Count Robert the Frisian is my first cousin, twenty-eight times removed.**

I decided Godric needed to be a knight and a noble to become the siege master the story required, and that required a well-placed family patron. He could have been English, French, or Flemish, but I had already decided Godric was Scottish, so the only suitable patrons were King Malcolm Canmore III and his queen, Saint Margaret Atheling of Scotland, whom I made his godparents.

**The same Saint Margaret, Queen of Scotland, who is my fifth cousin, twenty-seven times removed.**

I gave Godric a privileged start amid Margaret's royal children to give him a rare education and page's training before I wrenched it away and replaced it with one that taught him iron and woodwork so he could design and build novel siege engines. That also instilled a little egalitarian leavening to placate my Swabian peasant ancestors. I am, after all, American, because my father's ancestors became so tired of the leadership flaws in my mother's ancestors that they gave up and left Europe in disgust to come to America, where merit ruled, and started afresh, re-leveling the playing field in the process.

And all these royal children — the Edward and Edith of this book, and their siblings who went on to rule Scotland and England — **are my sixth cousins, twenty-six times removed.**

Well enough, you say — interesting, but coincidence. Perhaps, but there is more.

When I made all these genealogical discoveries in September 2014, I was already two-thirds through drafting **March to Nicaea.** As you now know, it stars the princes who led the Crusading armies:

- **Count Robert II of Flanders, my second cousin, twenty-seven times removed.**
- **Duke Robert Curthose of Normandy, my second cousin, twenty seven times removed.**
- **Count Stephen of Blois, husband of my second cousin, twenty-seven times removed.**
- **And Duke Godfrey of Bouillon, stepson of my third cousin, twenty-nine times removed.**
- **Even our villain in this tale, King William II Rufus of England, is my second cousin, twenty-seven times removed.**

And there is a final twist. My genealogy continued, and the records led me back another fourteen hundred years. Seventy generations before me along this same lineage, **my great-grandfathers were kings of the Galatians** — Celts who in 281-277 BC left the Toulouse region of France to invade and settle in the central Anatolian highlands around Ankara, just fifty leagues from Nicaea. There they intermarried with royalty from all over western Anatolia.

The Romans highly regarded my seventy-first great-grandfather, Deiotarus, King of Galatia, as an ally, and he was friends with Pompey, Cicero, Marc Anthony, and Julius Caesar. **Their descendants were the same Galatians that Saint Paul converted and wrote of in his epistles; the same Christians Islam overran centuries later, seeking to kill, enslave, or forcibly convert; the same Christians Emperor Alexios pleaded Count Robert the Frisian and Pope Urban to help save; and the same Christians the Crusaders came to rescue.**

Want proof? Here's the lineage:

**Deiotarix of Galatia, Chief Tetrarch of the Tolistobogii, King of Galatia** (105 BCE - 42 CE)
>  my 71st great grandfather, a contemporary of Julius Caesar

**Adobogiona of Galatia, Princess of the Tectosages (80 BCE - )**
>  daughter of Deiotarix of Galatia

Amyntas of Galatia, Tetrarch of the Trocmii, King of Galatia (60 BCE -)
>  son of Adobogiona of Galatia

Artemidoros of the Trocmii, King of Galatia & the Trocmii ( - 50 CE)
>  son of Amyntas of Galatia

Caius Julius Severus ( - 98 CE)
>  son of Artemidoros

Caius Julius Bassus (45CE - 101)
>  son of Caius Julius Severus

Caius Julius Bassus (70 - 117)
>  son of Caius Julius Bassus

Julia Quadratilla Bassa (100 - 141)
>  daughter of Caius Julius Bassus

Aulus Julius Proculus, Nobleman of Ephesus (120 - 156)
>  son of Julia Quadratilla Bassa

Julia Quadratilla (140 - 202)
>  daughter of Aulus Julius Proculus

Gaius Asinius Quadratus Protimus, Proconsul of Achaea (165 - 235)
>  son of Julia Quadratilla

Caius Asinius Nichomachus Julianus, Proconsul of Asia (185 - 230)

son of Gaius Asinius Quadratus Protimus
Quintus Anicius Faustus Paulinus, Imperial governor of Moesia Inferior (180 - 230)
son of Caius Asinius Nichomachus Julianus
Quintus Anicius II Faustus Paulinus Toxandrie (210 - 260)
son of Quintus Anicius Faustus Paulinus
Marcomir de Toxandrie (220 - 281)
son of Quintus Anicius II Faustus Paulinus Toxandrie
Gonobaud I de Toxandrie (245 - 289)
son of Marcomir de Toxandrie
Merogais Ragaise de Toxandrie (270 - 307)
son of Gonobaud I de Toxandrie
Malaric I of Toxandrie, First King of the Franks (295 - 360)
son of Merogais Ragaise de Toxandrie
Mellobaude de Toxandria von Worms, King of Worms (320 - 376)
son of Malaric I of Toxandrie
Flavius Richomeres (Richomer) of the Franks, Comes Domesticorum of Emperor Gratian (350 - 393)
son of Mellobaude de Toxandria
Theudemeres (Theudemer) of the Franks, King of Franks
son of Flavius Richomeres (Richomer)
Clodius VI "The Long Haired", King of the West Franks (395 - 447)
son of Theudemeres (Theudemer)
**Merovech, Merovingian King of the Salic Franks (412 - 458)**
**son of Clodius VI "The Long Haired"**

**Merovech is said to be the earliest true monarch of Europe, and ancestor of every royal house in Europe. In *The Da Vinci Code*, Dan Brown claimed Merovech was a descendent of Jesus Christ and Mary Magdalene. Were that true, I too would be a "holy grail".** ☺

Childeric I, Merovingian King of the Salian Franks (437 - 481)
son of Merovech
Clovis I 'The Great', Merovingian King of the Salian Franks, 1st King of all Franks, Consul of the Roman Empire (466 - 511)
son of Childeric I
Clothaire I "the old", Merovingian King of the Franks, King of Soissons,

Orleans, Rheims and Paris (497 - 561)
> son of Clovis I

Sigebert I, "The Lame", Merovingian King of Franks and Austrasia (445 - 509)
> son of Clothaire I "the old"

Chloderic I, The Parricide, Merovingian King of Cologne (475 - 509)
> son of Sigebert I, "The Lame"

Munderic Lord Vintry-en-Perthois, Merovingian Prince of Cologne (505 - 575)
> son of Chloderic I The Parricide

Saint Gondolfus de Aquitaine, Merovingian Bishop of Tongres (545 - 607)
> son of Munderic Lord Vintry-en-Perthois

Bishop Bodegisel, Merovingian Governor and Duke of d'Aquitaine (562 - 610)
> son of Saint Gondolfus de Aquitaine

**Saint Arnulf de Heristal, Bishop of Metz & Patron Saint of brewers (582 - 640)**
> son of Bishop Bodegisel

**Perhaps ancestral memory turned Saint Arnulf into my "Father Anselm, Forefather of Distillers," perhaps not. But I ask you, how cool is it for a son of Celts and Germans to descend directly from the Patron Saint of Beer!**

Ansegisel von Metz Dux (military duke) (602 - 679)
> son of Saint Arnulf / Arnoul de Heristal

Pepin II of Heristal Mayor of the Palace of Austrasia (635 - 714)
> son of Ansegisel von Metz

**Charles "The Hammer" Martel, Duke of France (676 - 741)**
> son of Pepin II of Heristal.

**Martel led the Franks to victory at the battle of Tours (732 AD), and with a brilliant campaign, drove the Islamites from France.**

Pepin III "the Short", King of the Franks (714 - 768)
> son of Charles "The Hammer" Martel

**"Charlemagne", Emperor of the Holy Roman Empire (742 - 814)**
> son of Pepin III "the Short"

Louis I "The Pious", co-Emperor with Charlemagne (778 - 840)
> son of Charles I "Charlemagne"

Gisela de Aquitaine, "Princess Of The Holy Roman Empire" (821 - 874)
> daughter of Louis I "The Pious"

Hedwige/Helwise di Friuli (836 - 903)
> daughter of Gisela de Aquitaine

Hucbald I Von Dillingen, Graf (Count) of Dillingen (874 - 909)
> son of Hedwige-Helwise di Friuli.


**The "Count Hartmann (II) von Dillingen" of this story is Hucbald's 4th great-grandson and my 26th great grandfather along a different intermediate lineage.**


Luitgard Von Dillingen (895 - 970)
> daughter of Hucbald I Von Dillingen

Manegold Von Sulmetingen (960 - 1057)
> son of Luitgard Von Dillingen

Beate Von Sulmetingen (954 - 1032)
> daughter of Manegold Von Sulmetingen

Wolfrad von Alshausen (977 - 1065)
> son of Beate Von Sulmetingen

Wolfrad II von Veringen (1060 - 1122)
> son of Wolfrad von Alshausen

Marquard I von Veringen-Sigmaringen (1102 - 1165)
> son of Wolfrad II von Veringen

Manegold I von Veringen, Pfaltzgraf Sigmaringen (1138 - 1186)
> son of Marquard I von Veringen-Sigmaringen

Willibirg von Veringen (1163 - 1220)
> daughter of Manegold I von Veringen

Walter III Von Vaz Freiherr (Baron) of Vaz (1218 - 1254)
> son of Willibirg von Veringen

Walter IV von Vaz Freiherr (Baron) von Vaz (1210 - 1255)
> son of Walter III Von Vaz

Walter V von Vaz, Freiherr (Baron) von Vaz (1240 - 1284)
> son of Walter IV von Vaz Freiherr von Vaz

Margarethe von Vaz (1265 - 1343)
> daughter of Walter V von Vaz Freiherr von Vaz

Ulrich V von Aspermont (1276 - 1340)
> son of Margarethe von Vaz

Ulrich VI von Aspermont-Rawenberg (1329 - 1381)
> son of Ulrich V von Aspermont

**Here in 1350, the Black Plague intervened, changing the family fortunes by wiping out the economic base on which a feudal system depends: people!**

Ulrich Rawenberg (1352 - 1420)
> son of Ulrich VI von Aspermont-Rawenberg

Heinrich Ronberg (1385 - 1450)
> son of Ulrich Rawenberg

Jacob Ronberg (1410 - 1470)
> son of Heinrich Ronberg

Johann (Hans) Rhomberg (1442 - 1517)
> son of Jacob Ronberg

Bartholomäus Rhomberg (1480 - 1529)
> son of Johann (Hans) Rhomberg

Thomas Rhomberg (1509 - 1570)
> son of Bartholomäus Rhomberg

Ulrich Rhomberg (1560 - 1605)
> son of Thomas Rhomberg

Thomas Rhomberg (1580 - 1647)
> son of Ulrich Rhomberg

Ulrich Rhomberg (1608 - 1670)
> son of Thomas Rhomberg

Felix Rhomberg (1653 - 1710)
> son of Ulrich Rhomberg

Jakob Rhomberg (1677 - 1731)
> son of Felix Rhomberg

Franz Josef Rhomberg (1719 - 1778)
> son of Jakob Rhomberg

Josef Franz Peter Rhomberg (1745 - 1810)
> son of Franz Josef Rhomberg

Maria Katharina Rhomberg (1789 - 1852)
>    daughter of Josef Franz Peter Rhomberg

Franz Martin Mohr (1821 - 1894)
>    son of Maria Katharina Rhomberg

Sophia Mohr (1860 - 1952)
>    daughter of Franz Martin Mohr

Emily Cecelia Forstner (1889 - 1975)
>    daughter of Sophia Mohr

[my mother]
>    and finally, your author

Tom Vetter

**To quote my English cousins, I am gobsmacked.**

I set out to retell an important and thrilling chapter of world history through fiction. **Without any foreknowledge or even suspicion, I crafted a tale about the real deeds of the historic people who did them . . . all of whom turn out to be members of my family:** the cousins, who are the protagonist's godparents and friends; my cousin, whose pilgrimage triggered the First Crusade; my cousins who led the First Crusade to recapture Jerusalem for nearly a century; and my distant cousins, the very Christian people the First Crusade was launched to free from Islam's cruel rule.

When I published *Call To Crusade*, I gave it a motto: **"The book is fiction, but the story is true."** By that I meant that the core of the story, and many of its people and events are real, actual history. My author's notes make clear what is fiction and what is history.

Now I discover that the motto is quite literally true.

**HOW THE HELL CAN THAT HAPPEN?** I don't know. But now I really, really, really want to find out!

All this makes me wonder what larger forces are at work here. I do not believe in reincarnation, and do not expect to find that I am Count Robert or Hartmann reborn. But now, when I see a battlefield in my mind's eye — before, during, and after battle — I have to wonder: Am I really writing all this from pure imagination, or is there some kind of ancestral memory upon which I draw?

I don't know. Perhaps in time I'll find out. I do know this. Whether this series earns me my own personal fatwa or not, I have to keep going. **The Family is counting on me to finish.**

✠✠✠

**P.S.:** And yes, it turns out they were! Fully half of my then-living ancestors, on both my mother's and father's sides, were entangled in the 1862 U.S.-Dakota War as victims, survivors, and combatants. But that's another story! ☺

✠✠✠

# AUTHOR'S NOTES

✠✠✠

The foreword notwithstanding, this is a work of historical fiction. Baron Godric MacEuan of Cenachedne is a fictional person, and his "manuscript" is my invention, intended to draw your interest to a period of history that has since been both overly romanticized and entirely demonized. Present scholars and commentators tend to condemn the Crusades out of some supercilious sense of moral superiority, attributing all the worst of motives to Pope Urban II, and denigrating the Crusaders as cruel aggressors descending on peaceful Muslims to seize Jerusalem and the Holy Land, when the reverse was at least as accurate. I hope in this work to present a rebalanced version of the First Crusade, with Godric as both witness and narrator to the most significant events.

Godric MacEuan is a fictional man, but he stands in for the real man or men who devised, built, and fought with the most devastating weapons yet created to that point in history, the siege engines used in the Crusades. Having realized that no one has yet undertaken to tell their story beyond the unvarnished historical facts, and those being precious few, I decided to do so. It is, I believe, a fascinating and a worthy tale, so I created Godric and gave him the task and title of Siege Master, prototypic medieval military engineer in order to tell it.

✠✠✠

Until the harnessing of exothermic reactions, starting with

gunpowder, nothing was more awesome in battle than the siege machines, and their penultimate, the trebuchet. Even today, siege engines inspire excitement, whether they hurl pumpkins a half-mile across farm fields in Delaware or boulders at real castle walls. If you doubt this, rent *Kingdom of Heaven* and watch Balian of Ibelin and Saladin use their trebuchets and siege engines in the fight for Jerusalem. I do not think anyone with a pulse could fail to enjoy the sight of a flaming piano being hurled hundreds of yards to splintery destruction, except perhaps the sons of Steinway.

In many ways, writing historical fiction is a much bigger challenge than writing pure fiction, inasmuch as one must find a way to interweave a fictional narrative through the most significant and exciting scenes in a series of larger historical events. The need to research actual events, historical details, and geographic settings is continual. For this the invention of the Internet and several key websites remain invaluable, particularly Wikipedia and Google Earth. To these, my gratitude is everlasting.

Indeed, writing a knight's story in the late eleventh century is problematic. Classic medieval tales feature castles, monasteries, and armored knights, but this tale takes place at the dawn of the High Middle Ages. The castles that existed were few — motte-and-bailey structures built from wood. Most of the monastic houses were at least a decade in the future, and knights only wore chainmail or gambeson coats; plate armor was centuries away. So writing the truth, or at least realistic verisimilitude, required that I abandon all the usual conventions.

Other authors I admire have done wonders to bring dusty history from other eras to life, in some cases to the point of filling the air of imaginary surroundings with the stink of battle, of gunsmoke, blood and shit. Notably, Bernard Cornwell has done this with the Napoleonic War, Poitiers, and Agincourt, while Patrick O'Brian did so with the Royal Navy during the selfsame Napoleonic War. None but historians have yet written of the First Crusade, and certainly not in fiction. I hope you think my muse and I have done it justice.

✠✠✠

This novel is essentially real history, rewritten with a fictional thread that weaves through the most interesting elements, and with Godric as narrator. History does not permit the embellishment, speculation, dialogue, and subplots that make events come to life in the way a story does, so historical fiction that remains true to history while delivering a tale readers can live vicariously does a service to both, I think. And that is how I have written this series.

That said, the major events you read here — the dates, the events, personages, routes, places, battles and outcomes — are real history, not fiction. Elsewhere in these notes I identify the fictional persons and elements I created, so you can discern my handiwork from the actual events. But the core of this story — indeed of the entire series — is historically as correct as I can make it.

If you have joined the *Siege Master* series with this book, you will no doubt have noticed and wondered about the references made to other people and places and to earlier events, all of which took place in the two earlier novels. In that sense, you should know that the five books in this series comprise one big novel, served in five segments so you don't need to lug a 2,000-page book around. But to follow plot elements that began one or two book earlier, you may wish to read the earlier books before going on.

✠✠✠

Though Godric is fiction, many of the other characters in this novel are real, and I have tried to keep them true to their historical nature.

King Malcolm III ("Canmore") and Queen Margaret are historical figures, and Margaret was not only a queen, but also a saint. Her husband has been described elsewhere more harshly than I have done, but that could be more the result of English propaganda than reality. In fact, Malcolm reigned thirty-six years at a time and place where keeping one's crown three years was a true achievement.

Princes Edward, Edgar, Edmund, and Princess Edith are historical figures, as are Counts Robert I and Robert II, Duke Robert, King William Rufus, Arkil Morel, Robert de Mowbray, and Emperor Alexios. Tatikios was real, though Demetrius is regrettably not. Fathers Thomas and Anselm, Hamish, Cormac, Carrick, Cedric, Colin, Aleine and Isabeau are fictional; but Jean de Bethencourt, Sir Lethold, and Sir Engilbert de Tournai are fictionalized real persons. And of course, Godfrey of Bouillon, Bohemond, Tancred, Ademar, Raymond de St-Gilles, Stephen of Blois, Kilij Arslan, and Manuel Boutoumites are all historic personages

✠✠✠

The letter from Basileus Alexios to Count Robert the Frisian is historic if controversial. Although there are references to the letter in other surviving contemporary accounts that indicate it existed, no actual copy survives to this day, and some historians doubt it did. Whether it, alone or with others, induced Pope Urban II to call for Christians to go to the aid of Alexios is moot. An appeal was made and the appeal was answered overwhelmingly. No one maintains that the First Crusade was spontaneous.

✠✠✠

Historical records say that my wife's early ancestor, Sir Jean de Bethencourt, joined Duke Robert Curthose of Normandy and Count Robert II of Flanders in the First Crusade. Little else is known of his life, but the Bethencourt coat-of-arms ("<u>argent, a lion rampant sable, armed and langued gules</u>") are identical to those of Count Robert II — except for a background field of silver vice Robert's gold — suggesting a relationship. Those arms are also identical at core to those of Orchies in Flanders. For those reasons, I gave him a key role in Godric's saga as a companion of Robert II and Godric.

✠✠✠

*De Re Militari* ("Concerning Military Matters") is a Latin work by Publius Flavius Vegetius Renatus written around the year 450 AD on Roman military matters. In four volumes he discusses military recruiting and training (Book 1); the organization of the army (Book 2); campaign operations and tactics (Book 3); and siege machines and techniques and naval warfare (Book 4). A copy of this book exists today in the British Library from the collection of Robert Bruce Cotton and dates from the eleventh, possibly late tenth century. It was widely read from the fifth century until well after the introduction of gunpowder, and considered the most authoritative treatise on warfare known in Medieval Europe. It would have been a vital training manual for a siege master during the Crusades, or so I believe. For this reason, I put a set of the books into the hands of Godric to inspire and authentically shape his natural engineering talents.

✠✠✠

The term "league" has been used to describe a measure of distance since Roman times, and throughout European history, although the distance it defined varied. My working definition is the distance a person or horse generally walks in an hour, which seems to be the underlying basis of most of the definitions. I chose the general English value of three miles to a league, which generally worked since the many French versions varied around that. I wasn't terribly slavish about the calculation, as this is fiction, not rocket science. I hope it suffices.

✠✠✠

Properly speaking, I should not have used the term "Byzantine" in this work. The empire called Byzantine today did not call itself that; this is a modern convention. The Byzantines thought themselves the continuation of the Roman Empire and therefore called themselves "Roman," although they spoke Greek and followed Greek Orthodoxy. But at the same time, we have a city of Rome filled with (medieval) Romans and a Holy Roman Empire occupied and governed by Germanic peoples that contained no Romans at all. I decided it would be much kinder to my readers to use the less-confusing term "Byzantine" to refer to the empire of Alexios, and let the historians take umbrage with me alone.

So, too, do we have a similar problem with the words "Crusade" and "Crusaders." These terms were not used during the First Crusade, and only came to be much later. At the time, the participants thought of themselves on an "armed pilgrimage" to rescue the Eastern Roman Empire, and the holy sites in and around Jerusalem, in service to Christ. In consequence, I have used the term most sparingly and generally have not called the people who went "Crusaders," as these terms in the narrative as anachronous. I use them only in the preface, these notes, and of course, the subtitle so that you, Dear Reader, could readily tell the historic period and theme of the work. And since the many engravings I have included were originally created to illustrate histories of the Crusades, I have retained those references.

A Little About Medieval Hours Of The Day:
Long before clocks came to exist, ancient peoples still measured time in hours, determining time the apparent rotation of the sun

around Earth during the day and the moon and stars at night. The first reference to "hours" is found in the Bible, in the book of Daniel. Later in we hear from Jesus Christ Himself, "Are there not twelve hours in the day?" (John 11:9 KJV).

In the Middle ages this system was still in use, and here is how it worked: An "hour" was an increment of time equal to one-twelfth of the daylight part of the day. Thanks to the tilt in the Earth's axis, daylight is extended in summer and shortened in winter, so medieval summer "hours" were longer than winter "hours". The day began with the first hour at sunrise, approximately 6 to 7 am on a present-day clock, as follows:

First hour: 6-7 am                    Seventh hour: 12-1 pm
Second : 7-8 am                       Eighth hour: 1-2 pm
Third hour: 8-9 am                    Ninth hour: 2-3 pm
Fourth hour: 9-10 am                  Tenth hour: 3-4 pm
Fifth hour: 10-11 am                  Eleventh hour: 4-5 pm
Sixth hour: 11 am-12 pm               Twelfth hour: 5-6 pm

There are an equal number of hours, counted the same way through the night. So the first hour of night began at sunset, about 6-7 pm and the last or twelfth hour of night would be during dawn at about 5-6 am.

✠✠✠

The battles I describe on the sixteenth, twentieth, and twenty-first of May are historically true, and happened much as I describe. The location, terrain, placement of units, numbers involved, and tactics used are as close as I could glean from the sparse contemporary accounts of those fights, or surmise through direct study of the battleground via Google Earth. Rebuilding an entire battle from a single sentence requires a lot of insight and supposition. Jean's column through the mountains and Godric's engines are fiction, of course, but they reflect what I would have done, if I had to fight in their shoes.

Kilij Arslan did have tens of thousands of Christians beheaded after the battle outside Helenopolis, including those who were judged unfit as slaves and sex slaves; and another six thousand men at Xerigordon. Those diabolical precedents so incensed the Crusaders that they then set aside the usual medieval rules of war and Christian mercies for certain, but not all, Islamic foes. As we will see, the Crusaders have long been falsely alleged to have massacred every Islamite, as well as all the Christians and Jews, in Jerusalem (these had, in fact, largely been expelled months before by the city's rulers). But this is actually a result of dramatic literary hyperbole by the early chroniclers — who were not present — exacerbated and repeated by Reformation-era anti-Catholic revisionists. Had they actually done so, however, it is understandable why they might have wanted to avenge Kilij Arslan's massacres.

Bohemond did indeed load the heads from a thousand Turks in carts and send them to Emperor Alexios. What Alexios thought of the gift is not recorded. And the Crusaders did indeed catapult Turk heads into Nicaea, an act that so terrified the Turks that they surrendered the city to Boutoumites, their only condition that all Crusaders be kept out.

Either way, the Crusaders earned such a fearsome reputation that even today, a thousand years later, the worst expletive radical Islam can think of to hurl at America's current fighting men is "crusader." Perhaps they should rethink that, for all the many modern warriors I know in the U.S. Armed Forces, and particularly among the Marines, take it as a real compliment and wear it proudly, as the Marines do the WWI German epithet, *Teufelshunde* — "Devil Dogs"

✠✠✠

Sir Thomas d'Avranches of Tutbury, AKA "Big Tom," is fictional, though his purported father, Hugh d'Avranches, the Earl of Chester, is historic, did hold Tutbury Castle, and did sire many bastards by his many mistresses. Would King William Rufus really have tried to have Princess Edith killed? History is silent on the topic, and perhaps I do him an unjust disservice. But he clearly wanted to gain control of Scotland for himself, if not to wear its crown. He did manipulate people and events in Malcolm's succession to gain an outcome in England's favor, so I don't think I strayed far from the truth.

As for Edith, she did disappear for the balance of his reign. Perhaps she truly did need to hide where Rufus could not find her. As it was, his brother, King Henry I, succeeded where Rufus did not: he married Edith, who was promptly crowned Queen Matilda, a much-honored Norman name. In so doing, he strengthened his right to rule England through her descent from both English and Scottish royalty, and built a basis for his descendants to claim the Scottish throne.

And, in an ironic twist that proves that God — or Cosmic Karma, if you prefer — really does have a sense of humor, I learned one really interesting fact, undiscovered until I reached the middle of this book. After entering a marriage of political advantage, Henry and Matilda developed a strong affection for each other despite his infidelities, and among their courtiers, the pair soon earned Saxon nicknames that mocked their rustic ways: these were "Godric" and "Godiva." Out of all the names possible, why Godric? Did Edith murmur it at an unfortunate moment? Oops! We can only guess.

✠✠✠

The sequence of major events throughout the book is correct, and as close to actual dates as I could determine. The major events in the Siege of Nicaea and battle of Dorylaeum occurred as I say. There was an initial sortie of the garrison, handily repulsed by Count Robert. My messenger Ahmed is a fictional person, but a real messenger was captured and did reveal Arslan's battle plans, just as Ahmed did. Later, it is said, the messenger did escape into Nicaea. Kilij Arslan did show up with his army when he learned his capital was under siege. No doubt thinking that time was of the essence and the enemy no stronger than the one butchered just months earlier, his vanguard did ride ahead to engage the Crusaders on the twentieth, to their utter defeat. Then Sultan Arslan attacked again on the twenty-first with his whole army, much as I describe; to his great surprise and horror he was beaten so badly that he did have to abandon his wives, family, treasury, slaves, capital, and garrison to whatever befell them. But Alexios did preserve and return them later, as I related.

✠✠✠

Count Hartmann von Dillingen and Sir Henry of Esch are historic figures, and their fox and its fate is real history. I fictionalized events to better fit the sparse facts — since the ditches formed a real barrier that would have stopped the fox from reaching the wall, attacking the gates just made more sense. Just how and why the fox collapsed is unknown, but the outcome was the same. The tactics the fox and the Seljuq employed are accurate if not actual.

Count Hartmann is my twenty-sixth great-grandfather, and the contemporary chronicles specifically mention him at Nicaea and Antioch. He lived through those perilous events and returned home to father sons and grandsons. Four generations of them participated in later Crusades.

✠✠✠

Count Raymond did build his tower — though not with Godric's fictional timbers. He did dig his way into a southern tower from a sow, only to find it filled with stone. The piglets are my invention, but they are based on actual mobile battlefield shields. I believe the southeast tower is Gonatas — its name comes to us through historical accounts that describe it in that location. Raymond's tower was unable to bridge the gap and capture Gonatas, but just why this was is not reported. Raymond's tower is reported to have been used as I describe, sheltering and defending the sappers working to undermine Gonatas; it was burned, but again, the accounts are confused and vague. I did my best to assemble the facts and then make some realistic sense of it with fiction.

✠✠✠

The expedition to haul boats from the sea to Lake Ascanius is also factual. Some of the chroniclers state — incorrectly, I believe — that they were brought from Civetot/Helenopolis over the mountains and through the woods pulled by oxen, not people; an approach entirely impractical, given that mountainous terrain, and foolish when the path from Gemlik to the lake was unbarred by either mountains or woods. It should be pointed out that the chronicles were written later by men who were not there, and they wrote to glorify their patrons, not record an actual history, so for their purposes the more impossible the task, the better.

✠✠✠

Reports of how Nicaea was finally breached are maddening. Part of this is due to the fact that those accounts were written to highlight the deeds of their patrons, not to report any unflattering truths. There was an unnamed Lombard (played here by Luigi of Torino) who was said to have successfully undermined a wall or tower, but the city surrendered while the fire that caused the breach still burned. There are also references to breaches by siege engines. Paul Chevedden[28] thinks the counterweight trebuchet was first used in combat at Nicaea, and this forms the historic basis for Godric's *Malleus Dei*.

Online I found photos via Google Earth of a great hole in Nicaea's outer wall where I said *Malleus Dei* made its fictional attack, and the images contain shadows that make the storehouse between the walls plausible. It would have been just the kind of site a tree-bucket could exploit. But who blasted that hole, when, and whether with trebuchet or cannon, I cannot truthfully say. I just hope Chevedden is right.

The Google Earth images showing the southeast tower I call here "Gonatas" are relatively poor, but they do appear to show that the tower has been blasted or toppled, leaving a breach. Who did it and when, I cannot say, but I would not rule out Raymond and his mine.

In the final event, who breached Nicaea, and how, did not matter beyond this: at the end of the siege the Seljuqs were so terrified of the Crusaders that they chose to surrender themselves to the mercies of the Byzantines rather than face the terrible wrath of the grim ironclad men about to come over and through the walls. And they were right to do so, for men who could take that city by force were bold, tough, determined, and truly fearsome!

✠✠✠

Lethold de Tournai is a factual and famous knight, and he holds a special place in history. He and brother Engilbert were the first two knights into Jerusalem. As we shall eventually see, their courage will

---

[28] Chevedden, Paul E., "The invention of the Counterweight Trebuchet: a Study in Cultural Diffusion"

impel them to, while under attack, cross a narrow plank to reach the ramparts from Duke Godfrey's siege tower. When Lethold lived, Tournai was a city in Flanders, and both Lethold and Engilbert were members of Count Robert of Flanders's retinue. Certainly historic figures of such great courage must be honored in any fiction that recounts their deeds.

✠✠✠

Tatikios is a historical figure, and history records that he did wear a prosthetic nose made of gold to hide his disfigurement. I treat him more kindly than do the contemporary accounts; for his role in negotiating the secret surrender of Nicaea, the Crusaders forever after regarded him as a treacherous agent of Alexios.

✠✠✠

Demetrius is pure fiction, but the title and office of *anticensor* as a commander of military engineers is historic fact. An anticensor would have known how to build and operate the emperor's siege equipment, for that is what a military engineer did; and Vegetius does describe all but counterweight trebuchets in his *De Re Militari*. According to Anna Komnene, the Byzantine Empire owned and used all the equipment I describe.

✠✠✠

It is Anna Comnena who wrote that her father, Emperor Alexios — a successful general before gaining the throne — personally invented the counterweight trebuchet and sent it to the siege of Nicaea. Trebuchet scholar Paul E Chevedden[29] argues most convincingly that the counterweight trebuchet was, most probably,

---

[29]Chevedden, Paul E., "The invention of the Counterweight Trebuchet: a Study in Cultural Diffusion"

first used at Nicaea, and Alexios is the only recorded claimant to its invention. But Alexios did not want the Crusaders to take and sack that city, and so cut a secret deal for the city's surrender instead. Given that, why would he then give them the only machine capable of breaching its walls? The notion is even more unlikely when we learn how concerned he was that the Crusaders, especially his old enemy Bohemond, might try to seize Constantinople, and with it, the empire? Certainly in those circumstances you wouldn't give your enemies the very tools to could achieve that outcome. So was the idea for the counterweight trebuchet actually his, or did some other now unknown worthy — like Godric — invent the trebuchet elsewhere and first employ it there? We may never know.

✠✠✠

Godric has already endured much, but he is still a young man when Pope Urban's call in 1095 launches the Crusades. The great Christian army has just achieved its first victories, but there are yet many more miles to walk and battles to fight to gain Jerusalem. So Godric, Anselm, Jean, Cedric, Hamish, Colin, and Edith must press on. Why ? Because — Deus lo vult! — God wills it!

✠✠✠

# ACKNOWLEDGMENTS

✠✠✠

This series and its author owe a debt of gratitude to a number of sources and authors. Let me offer thanks and tribute to them here.

First, I owe much to fellow author, teacher, and mentor of distinction, **Ms. Holly Lisle**. Her writing courses and professional counsel first inspired me to play the rough-and-tumble sport that is professional writing and independent publishing; and though I have no idea where all this will lead, I neither fear the journey nor regret beginning it. One of her teaching exercises coaxed my Muse to conjure up Godric as an older man, battle-scarred, sweat-soaked, and coated in the dust of the Holy Land. And while I alone remain responsible for Godric MacEuan, he would never have been born as a creature of ink and imagination without her help.

I owe a very great deal to two wonderful online tools, without which the historical and geographic research necessary to write a work like this is so much harder. To **Wikipedia** I owe thanks for the speed and agility it provides in researching historical facts, biographies and descriptions of places the story involves. And **Google Earth** supplies me with maps and photographs that lent accuracy to my geography and my descriptions. I commend them for their work and offer them my gratitude.

Other authors and works supplied biographic details, facts, narratives and historic context or details. Among the best of these was *The Siege of Jerusalem*, by **Conor Kostick**, whose description of the siege of Nicaea is both the most comprehensive and comprehensible. Also of great value is **Hilaire Belloc's** classic, *The Crusades*. His explanation of the true causes for the Crusades, the reasons for their early successes and ultimate failure are well worth reading. I heartily recommend both books to all who are interested in the Crusades.

Once again, I need to thank my best friends, beta readers, and board of literary advisors, Messrs. **H. John Pagan** and **David Hermann**, for their unflagging interest, continual encouragement and ever-helpful critiques of my books. Their enthusiasm for the books push me on, and what they like about them has made me a better author. They will always have my gratitude.

Finally, I owe everything to my bride of forty years, **Gabriela**. Dementia has stolen much from her and she can no longer appreciate any of my literary works. But her illness, and my commitment to care for her, made my writing both a welcome outlet and a potential hedge against future want. So her gifts and sacrifices in support of my art deserve my gratitude and acknowledgment, and will always have it.

And any anachronisms, historical errors, typographical mistakes, misspellings, formatting screw-ups, and other publishing faux-pas: I claim all of them as mine alone.

✠✠✠

# ILLUSTRATION CREDITS

✠✠✠

**Front Cover:** composite image by Thomas Vetter from images by Sundraw Photography (Stock photo 275227214), Andrey Valerevich Kiselev (Stock photo 176536817), and MichelAubryPhoto (Stock photo 241263826) all used under license from Shutterstock.com:

**"Deus lo vult! God wills it!" Pope Urban calls for the First Crusade.** GodWillethIt! - Alphonse de Neuville [Public domain], via Wikimedia Commons.

**For the Defense of Christ and Christendom.** For the Defense of Christ. Gustave Doré (1832-1883). Public domain in the United States and country of origin (France) (author's life plus 70 years or less).

**Extent of the Christian Roman Empire in AD 335.** Map. Original work by Thomas Vetter © 2017.

**Remains of the Byzantine Roman Empire in AD 1096.** Map. Original work by Thomas Vetter © 2017.

**Extent of Islamic conquest in AD 1096.** Map. Original work by Thomas Vetter © 2017.

**The War Cry of the Crusaders.** Gustave Doré (1832-1883). Public domain in the United States and country of origin (France) (author's life plus 70 years or less).

**The People's Crusade in Hungary.** Walter the Penniless in Hungary. Gustave Doré (1832-1883). Public domain in the United States and country of origin (France) (author's life plus 70 years or less).

**The Departure.** Gustave Doré (1832-1883). Public domain in the United States and country of origin (France) ( author's life plus 70 years or less).

**Count Robert II of Flanders, a prince of the First Crusade.** Robert de flandre croisé. Henri Decaisne (1799-1852) [GFDL (http://www.gnu.org/copyleft/fdl.html) or CC BY SA 4.0-3.0-2.5-2.0-1.0 (https://creativecommons.org/licenses/ by-sa/4.0-3.0- 2.5-2.0-1.0)], via Wikimedia Commons.

**The Soldiers of Christ make the Vow of the Cross.** Priests Exhorting the Crusaders. Gustave Doré (1832-1883). Public domain in the United States and country of origin (France) (author's life plus 70 years or less).

**Godric's route on the First Crusade: Cenachedne to Bari.** Map. Original work by Thomas Vetter © 2017.

**Duke Robert of Normandy, a prince of the First Crusade. Robert** normandie. Henri Decaisne (1799-1852) [Public domain or Public domain], via Wikimedia Commons.

**The Crusaders march through Rome.** Force of Leo IX Departing from Rome. 19th-century illustration. Eon Images. No US copyright applies.

**The First Crusade on the march.** The First Crusade. Bayard and G Burgun. 19th-century illustration. Eon Images. No US copyright applies.

**The Crusaders cross the Adriatic from Bari to Dyrrachium.** Landing of Saint Louis in Egypt. G. Burgun. 19th-century illustration. Eon Images. No US copyright applies.

**Godric's route on the First Crusade: Bari to Constantinople**. Map. Original work by Thomas Vetter © 2017.

**Medieval depiction of Constantinople.** Woodcut from Hartmann Schedel's Weltchronik [Nuremberg Chronicles], published in Nuremberg 1493). Published before 1923 and public domain in the U.S.

**Alexios Komnenos I, Emperor of the Byzantine Roman Empire.** Taken from a Miniature of the Byzantine Emperor Alexios I Komnenos (r. 1081-1118), being blessed by Christ. Unknown. Vatican Library (Rome), 12th c. manuscript. This work is in the public domain in its country of origin and the United States, where the copyright term is the author's life plus 70 years or less.

**The triple walls of Constantinople.** Source photo 115461100 licensed from Shutterstock.com. Recomposition as a pencil sketch by Thomas Vetter.

**Duke Bohemond of Apulia, prince of the First Crusade.** Bohemond I of Antioch. Merry-Joseph Blondel (1781-1853) [Public domain], via Wikimedia Commons. This is a faithful photographic reproduction of a two-dimensional, public domain work of art. The work of art itself is in the public domain for the following reason: The author died in 1853, so this work is in the public domain in its country of origin and other countries and areas where the copyright term is the author's life plus 100 years or less.

**Peter the Hermit preaching the Crusade.** Gustave Doré (1832-1883). Public domain in the United States and country of origin (France) (author's life plus 70 years or less).

**Raymond St-Gilles, Count of Toulouse, prince of the First Crusade.** Raymond IV of Toulouse. Merry-Joseph Blondel [Public domain], via Wikimedia Commons. This is a faithful photographic reproduction of a two-dimensional, public domain work of art. The work of art itself is in the public domain for the following reason: The author died in 1853, so this work is in the public domain in its country of origin and other countries and areas where the copyright term is the author's life plus 100 years or less.

**Four princes of the First Crusade.** Four Leaders of the First Crusade (1095) - Alphonse de Neuville [Public domain], via Wikimedia Commons.

**Godric's route on the First Crusade: Constantinople to Nicaea.** Map. Original work by Thomas Vetter © 2017.

**Tancred of Hauteville, Prince of Galilee.** Merry-Joseph Blondel [Public domain], via Wikimedia Commons. This is a faithful photographic reproduction of a two-dimensional, public domain work of art. The work of art itself is in the public domain for the following reason: The author died in 1853, so this work is in the public domain in its country of origin and other countries and areas where the copyright term is the author's life plus 100 years or less.

**The remains of the People's Crusade.** The Remains of the First Crusaders. Gustave Doré (1832-1883). Public domain in the United States and country of origin (France) (author's life plus 70 years or less).

**07 May 1097: Initial placement of the Crusader armies.** Map. Original work by Thomas Vetter © 2017.

**The initial ladder attacks on Nicaea.** The Siege of Ptolemais. Gustave Doré (1832-1883). Public domain in the United States and country of origin (France) (author's life plus 70 years or less).

**15 May 1097: The initial ladder attacks.** Map. Original work by Thomas Vetter © 2017.

**Duke Godfrey meets the survivors of the People's Crusade.** Godfrey-Meets-the-Remains-of-the-Army-of-Peter-the-Hermit. Gustave Doré (1832-1883). Public domain in the United States and country of origin (France) (author's life plus 70 years or less).

**Siege Machinery: the Onager (catapult) and Ballista.** Onager. This image was first published in the 1st (1876–1899), 2nd (1904–1926) or 3rd (1923–1937) edition of Nordisk familjebok. Published before 1923 and public domain in the

U.S. Ballista. By Pearson Scott Foresman [Public domain], via Wikimedia Commons. Published before 1923 and public domain in the U.S.

**16 May 1097: The Nicaean garrison sorties against Godric and Robert of Flanders.** Map. Original work by Thomas Vetter © 2017.

**Defeating the Nicaean garrison.** Defeat of Turks by Crusaders. A. de Neuville. 19th-century illustration. Eon Images. No US copyright applies.

**Godric's defenses: chevaux-de-frise and caltrops. Chevaux-de-frise.** Petersburg, Va. Sections of chevaux-de-frise before Confederate main works. Created/Published: 1865. Image is available from the United States Library of Congress's Prints and Photographs division under the digital ID cwpb.02598. Rights Advisory: No known restrictions on publication. Published in the U.S. before 1923 and public domain in the U.S. Scattered **Caltrops**. Original work by Thomas Vetter © 2017.

**The Crusaders hurl Turkish heads into the city of Nicaea.** Crusaders-Throwing-Heads-into-Nicaea. Gustave Doré (1832-1883). Public domain in the United States and country of origin (France) (author's life plus 70 years or less).

**Godfrey of Bouillon, Duke of Lorraine, a prince of the First Crusade.** From the Swedish book "Illustrated World History, Third Part", Ernst Wallis, Stockholm 1882. Page 249. Drawing after the Statue of Godfrey of Bouillon in Hofkirche Innsbruck. This work is in the public domain in its country of origin and other countries and areas where the copyright term is the author's life plus 70 years or less.

**20 May 1097: The Seljuq advance attacks Robert of Flanders.** Map. Original work by Thomas Vetter © 2017.

**21 May 1097: The Battle of Nicaea.** Map. Original work by Thomas Vetter © 2017.

**The Battle of Nicaea.** Gustave Doré (1832-1883). Public domain in the United States and country of origin (France) (author's life plus 70 years or less).

**A siege tower like Raymond's, and archers shielded by pavises.** Siege Tower. By Francis Grose [Public domain], via Wikimedia Commons. Published before 1923 and public domain in the U.S.

**02 June 1097: Final envelopment of Nicaea.** Map. Original work by Thomas Vetter © 2017.

**03 June 1097: Siege attacks are renewed.** Map. Original work by Thomas Vetter © 2017.

**A testudo like Hartmann's fox; and scorpio, a long-range crossbow.**
Testudo and Scorpio. By Martin Fickelscherer [Public domain], via Wikimedia
Commons. Published before 1923 and public domain in the U.S.

**05 & 06 June 1097: Hartmann attacks the Eastern Gate with his fox.** Map.
Original work by Thomas Vetter © 2017.

**Bohemond favored ladder attacks on the walls of Nicaea.** Storming of
Antioch. Gustave Dore. 19th-century illustration. Public domain in the United
States and country of origin (France) (author's life plus 70 years or less).

**08 June 1097: Raymond's tower assault.** Map. Original work by Thomas Vetter
© 2017.

**Malleus Dei, the counterweight trebuchet.** Counterweight Trebuchet. By
Sebastian Sonntag, Ausschnitt eines Wikipedia-Commons-Bild: Bild:
Trebuchet1.png, Public Domain, https://commons.wikimedia.org/w/
index.php?curid=2790866. This work is in the public domain in its country of
origin and other countries and areas where the copyright term is the author's life
plus 70 years or less.

**The Crusaders' war machinery.** Gustave Doré (1832-1883). Public domain in
the United States and country of origin (France) (author's life plus 70 years or
less).

**18 June 1097: Godric breaches Nicaea's walls.** Map. Original work by Thomas
Vetter © 2017.

**The Nicaeans pray for salvation from the Crusaders.** Invocation to
Muhammad. Gustave Doré (1832-1883). Public domain in the United States and
country of origin (France) (author's life plus 70 years or less).

**Emperor Alexios Komnenos I. By** Anonymous - Unknown, Public Domain,
https://commons.wikimedia.org/w/index.php?curid=198070.

**Alexios rewards the Crusader princes for the recovery of Nicaea.**
Astonishment-of-the-Crusaders-at-the-Wealth-of-the-East. Gustave Doré
(1832-1883). Public domain in the United States and country of origin (France)
(author's life plus 70 years or less).

✠✠✠

# TOM VETTER

✠✠✠

**Those who can, do. Those who cannot, teach . . . or better still, write.** Tom Vetter has done both, living it first and writing about it later. As a naval officer, Commander Vetter served more than two decades and sailed 100,000 miles in submarines during the Vietnam and Cold Wars. He piloted submersibles and the Navy bathyscaph *Trieste II* (DSV-1) on dives as deep as three miles to find aircraft, shipwrecks, and pilots lost on the seafloor.

After several lives' worth of adventure at sea, Tom retired from the Navy to work a second career in information technology, operating a successful IT architecture business for more than a decade. When his wife's declining health required another retirement in 2012 to care for her, writing and publishing became his third career.

Since then, Tom started Tom Vetter Books, LLC, a Virginia-based publishing business, wrote *Thirty Thousand Leagues Undersea*, a memoir of true tales about his undersea adventures, and the first three novels in the five-book *Siege Master* historical fiction series, which retells the saga of the First Crusade as the recollections of a noble Scottish siege lord.

Tom lives with his wife in suburban Washington, DC. And as caregiver duties permit, he writes every day.

# Absolutely Free!

## Sign up NOW on
http://www.tomvetterbooks.com

I cherish all My Readers, and I am thrilled to have you as one of them.

As thanks for signing up, I'll send you occasional news and gifts, and special offers and discounts on my novels and e-books for as long as you like.

I hope that's forever!